**"You must capture the serpents.
Only you."**

Tull watched the Spirit Walker for a long moment. Catching the serpents did not seem like such a big job. It would be like catching guppies in an earthenware jar—except that these guppies were ten feet long and had teeth of steel. Still, it seemed that others should be able to help. But one never questioned a Spirit Walker.

"Are you certain we need to make this journey?" Tull asked.

"I journeyed through the ocean, and there are no serpents in the east or south anymore. Deep in the water, the great ones are dying from illness. Only in the north are there any serpents. I traveled to next summer and saw great lizards swim from Hotland—" Chaa's eyes widened as he remembered the monsters. "If you do not bring the serpents the great lizards will swim across the narrow places of the sea. You must bring the serpents—not only to save this town, but to save many towns."

Don't miss these other fine science fiction titles, available wherever Bantam Spectra books are sold:

Serpent Catch

Dave Wolverton

BANTAM BOOKS

NEW YORK · TORONTO · LONDON · SYDNEY · AUCKLAND

SERPENT CATCH

A Bantam Spectra Book / May 1991

SPECTRA *and the portrayal of a boxed "s" are trademarks of Bantam Books, a division of Bantam Doubleday Dell Publishing Group, Inc.*

ISBN 0-553-28983-7

Published simultaneously in the United States and Canada

Bantam Books are published by Bantam Books, a division of Bantam Doubleday Dell Publishing Group, Inc. Its trademark, consisting of the words "Bantam Books" and the portrayal of a rooster, is Registered in U.S. Patent and Trademark Office and in other countries. Marca Registrada. Bantam Books, 666 Fifth Avenue, New York, New York 10103.

PRINTED IN THE UNITED STATES OF AMERICA

OPM   0 9 8 7 6 5 4 3 2 1

I would like to express special thanks to Derek Hegstead for his hard work on the illustrations, to my wife Mary for her support, and to Betsy Mitchell for her insights and suggestions.

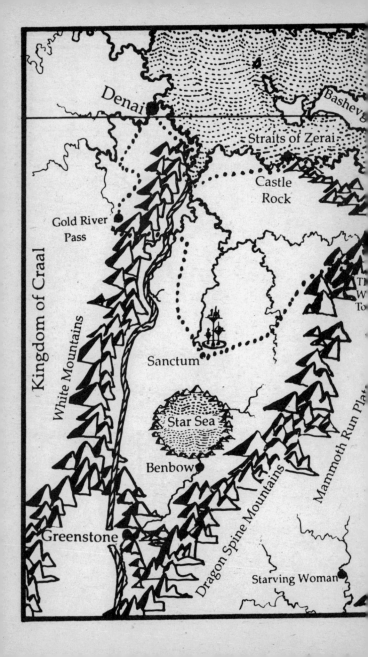

Foreword

In 2866, a group of genetic paleontologists began a great work while orbiting a large moon named Anee, some 1,950 light years from their home world of Earth. Their goal was to build the galaxy's greatest terrestrial zoo by recreating many of the extinct plants and animals from Earth.

The terraformers divided the lands of Anee into three great continents, each to be populated with plants and animals of a distinct period: the Jurassic, the Miocene, and the Pliocene. They collected genetic samples from many places: stinging insects encased in amber supplied tissues necessary to clone many of Earth's larger animals, such as the dinosaurs and the dire wolf; the same amber supplied pollen spores and samples of vegetation to help recreate ancient floras. The paleontologists took tissue specimens from woolly mammoths trapped in Siberian ice and found marrow in the hip joint of a Neanderthal who had died in a peat bog 38,000 years before. Blood samples on an ancient hand ax supplied the genes necessary to recreate *Homo rex*—giant carnivorous ape-men. And when the paleontologists lacked actual tissue specimens, they rebuilt ancient plants and animals protein by protein, gene by gene, basing their work on dyed casts taken from fossilized DNA, bridging the gap between last-known ancestor and last-previous predecessor.

The paleontologists set creatures born in the same era each upon their own continent. To ensure that this separation was retained, the paleontologists created biological walls called eco-barriers. They gave form to great sea serpents that patrolled the oceans, eating any animal that sought to swim from one continent to the next. They filled the skies with genetically engineered dragons that hunted the pterodactyls, which soared long and far over the oceans.

For 212 years the paleontologists worked above Anee in their orbiting space station—until the alien Eridani sent their Red Drones to destroy every Earth vessel that flew among the stars and forced the starfaring paleontologists to descend to their wild planet. Some paleontologists took the native Neanderthals to be their friends, and together they formed an easy alliance in exile.

Other paleontologists took the Neanderthals to be their slaves, hoping to use them to build weapons of war so that they could strike a blow against the Red Drones of the Eridani, and they became known as the Slave Lords. The Slave Lords repeatedly failed in their attempts to escape Anee, and just as a caged lion will turn its thoughts from escape and begin to make itself cozy in its cage, over generations the mighty Slave Lords turned their faces from the stars and consoled themselves with physical gratification, and they turned their military might toward the pursuit of conquest, enslaving both the wild Neanderthals and all their human rivals. The Slave Lords' dominion spread from sea to sea, and their cruel descendants sank into barbarity and decadence.

As the most ancient of the starfaring humans dwindled in numbers and died, the technology that allowed travel between stars was forgotten by all but a few. In a last-ditch effort to maintain the ecological balance of their world, a few remaining paleontologists formed the Creators—a race of sentient wormlike beings designed to synthesize DNA according to plans stored in their crystalline brains—and over the years, as Anee declined into its own Dark Ages, the Creators continued the paleontologists' work, recreating the extinct life forms of the past.

Generations prospered and multiplied, warred and died. On the moon Anee, a portion of mankind was given a second childhood, until on a certain night . . .

Chapter 1
Gravitational Winds

Tull felt a hand gently shake him awake, announcing that it was his turn to take guard duty. *"Tchima-zho, sepala-pi fe.* I finish-gladly and take joy in my coming sleep," Ayuvah said in the soft-nasal language of the Neanderthal, or Pwi as they called themselves.

Tull looked up into the face of the young Neanderthal and blinked to clear his vision. Thor was up, and although the moon was only a quarter full, Tull could see Ayuvah well. The night was warm, and the air around camp was thick with the scent of leatherwood honey. Tree frogs whistled in the darkness beyond the edge of the fort, and out across the plains two male blue-crested hadrosaurs bellowed challenges to one another as they vied for a mate. The dinosaurs had been going at it solid for three days now in the valley below, and Tull was glad that the honey harvest was almost finished. The mating challenges had drawn a tyrannosaur into the valley earlier in the day, and although Ayuvah had killed it with his spear, more were sure to follow. It was time to leave the dinosaur lands and head for the ship to sail back home to Smilodon Bay.

Tull pulled off his robe and stretched. Ayuvah handed him the telescope and a trumpet made from the horn of an ox, then went to pick at the stew beside the fire. *"Adja,* I fear," Ayuvah said quietly. Because he did not say how much he feared, he meant that he was afraid of something unspecific. Seven other Pwi slept quietly around the camp, none of them snoring. The fire was out.

"What do you fear?" Tull asked softly.

"There is a lot of movement down in the valley tonight. The hadrosaurs are mating, and I saw two sailfin carnosaurs come up from the swamp, and many smaller dinosaurs are milling about. I saw something else, I fear," Ayuvah said, thoughtfully. "I believe I saw a lantern shining down by the wide spot in the river. But it was far away—and after a minute it went out. Perhaps it was only a will-o'-the-wisp."

"Egg raiders?" Tull asked. Only humans or Neanderthals would make a fire, and few dared travel in this part of the world. Many young Pwi crossed the ocean at one time or another to steal dinosaur eggs in Hotland, but the egg raiders came only in spring. Back on the continent of Calla, the sailors paid the Pwi well for the eggs and then sold them in distant ports to those who were frivolous enough to hatch the eggs just to see what kind of monster came out. But with autumn coming on, most Pwi would stay away from the dinosaur lands and work on the harvest. Only Scandal the Gourmet, with his love for leatherwood honey, paid them well enough to work in Hotland in this season.

"I do not think they were egg raiders," Ayuvah said. "Egg raiders would not hunt at night. I cannot understand why anyone would be hunting at night in Hotland."

Tull winced to say his next word. "Slavers?"

"Perhaps," Ayuvah said. "Twenty Pwi down from Wellen's Eyes went out on egg raid last spring—and none returned. Slavers could have captured them."

"I've never heard of slavers coming to Hotland," Tull said, but he wondered. A small party of egg raiders would be easy pickings. Over the past several years, the predations of the Craal slavers had increased. Some Pwi even said that it was time to flee the wilderness of Calla and go to Hotland, where the slavers would never dare follow.

Because Ayuvah's words made him nervous, Tull put on his war gear. He pulled a lacquered leather vest made of iguanadon hide over his naked chest, and sheathed his kutow, a double-headed battle ax, at his belt. He took his wooden war shield and a spear, slung the trumpet around his neck, and went to stand guard.

The guard post was a large dead leatherwood tree on a knoll. From the tree, Tull could see the plains below. Although vegetation was trampled and sparse, a herd of two hundred triceratops, each forty feet long, fed on shrubs in the dark grassland. A row of hills to the east marked the leatherwood forests, and on one hill two miles away, a small fire burned in a tree. Tull pulled the telescope from its case and studied the tree. Denni and Tchar, two fourteen-year-old Neanderthals were by the hollow leatherwood, smoking the honeybees into a stupor. In the firelight, Tull could see Denni, with his blond hair, coaxing the fire in the tree while Tchar slept. *Good boy,* Tull thought, *to be so diligent, I'll have to remember to praise him in the morning.* Iguanadons fed on the leaves of trees around the boys, huge and gray in the moonlight. *Good,* Tull thought. *They'll be safe so long as the iguanadons stay near.* Tull looked off to the west, down to the wide spot in the river. It was true that the brush there was thick with movement, and Tull watched the area. If someone had been down at the river carrying a lantern, then as he turned that bend he might have seen the fire burning in the leatherwood tree. If the man were a slaver, he would then douse his lantern and sneak along the brush line in the dark.

Tull wondered, *If forty men crept through the brush by the river in the moonlight, would they scare the dinosaurs into the open?* Tull did not know. A dozen allosaurs on the prowl might scare them. If the men made a lot of noise, they might do the same. Tull turned a full circle, studied the plains carefully. In the moonlight, with his telescope he could see well enough to feel secure. A dozen small oviraptors scurried from the brush near the hills, running for the open. Whatever had frightened them was closing in on Tchar and Denni. Tull hissed through his teeth, fingered the war horn.

Tchar and Denni were young, and if they got into trouble, they might not have the presence of mind to get themselves out. Yet Tull could not blow the war horn without revealing his position. *Should I warn them,* he wondered, *about something that might be nothing.* Anything could have scared the oviraptors.

Below him at the pond, the tree frogs abruptly quit whistling as someone stepped into the water. Tull flinched, looked down. Ayuvah's younger sister, Fava, stood in the moonlight. She was a pretty girl with sandy red hair. Her green eyes, set shallowly beneath her brows, were an uncommon trait that made her look a little more human than most deep-browed Neanderthals. She had large breasts, and decorated her bare legs with many colored ribbons, symbolizing that she was not married. Fava was a sweet girl who seemed genuinely mystified by the world and, therefore, always spoke with a strangely intense inflection, as if trying to convey how strange everything was. She stripped off her tunic to bathe, stepped into the water, and floated on her back, leaving her ribbons on.

For a moment, Tull watched her breasts bob in the water as she floated. "Fava," he whispered at last, "what are you doing?"

"Bathing," she said, sounding genuinely surprised that he spoke. Tull wondered. She must have known that he'd be up on guard duty. In fact, she should have seen him.

"Mmmmm," she sighed, splashing water. "I've been boiling honey down for three days now. All my clothes are sticky and smell like leatherwood flowers. Even my sweat smells-fondly of honey. Tell," she said, speaking Tull's name as well as her Neanderthal lips would allow, "even the hollow between my breasts smells of sweet honey."

Tull blushed and looked away. It was an old game with her. Fava had been chasing him for seven years now, since he was twelve, yet Tull was not sure if she really wanted to catch him. For Neanderthals, all objects, all people, all places hold kwea, the emotional weight that came from past association, and Tull felt strongly drawn to Fava. She'd always been like a little sister to him, and the kwea he felt for her was of a sisterly nature, the kwea of good times spent together. He could not think of her as anything but the little girl she had been, as someone to protect. But lately, the kwea was changing. She teased him more, and he felt a craving for her—the desire to treat her as a lover. Yet he was afraid to make such a move, afraid it would spoil a perfectly good friendship. *Besides, why would she want me, a half-breed?* Tull wondered to himself. Not many women would want a half-human, half-Neanderthal for a husband, and Fava could surely do better. *No, she is just trying to embarrass me.*

Tull breathed slowly and forced himself to watch the grasslands, but he could not concentrate with Fava swimming in the pool, the sinuous waves rippling away from her breasts as they floated in the moonlight. She kept at it for half an hour, then got out and dried herself. Tull kept his eyes averted. Several small dinosaurs gathered down in the valley to eat the carcass of the tyrannosaur Ayuvah had killed earlier in the day.

Once Fava had dressed, she climbed up the tree and stood beside Tull. She was a large girl for a Neanderthal, yet Tull looked down on her. "Tull, will you comb my hair out?" she asked, standing precariously on two branches at once.

"I'm on guard," he said.

"But everyone else is asleep!" Fava insisted.

Tull took the ivory comb she proffered. She turned her back to him and leaned against him while he brushed her long wet hair straight.

"I'll be happy to get back home," Tull said as he combed.

"Why?" Fava asked. "I thought you were happy to come on this trip. You said you were bored with picking fruit and hauling hay."

"I fear," Tull answered, and he told her about Ayuvah seeing a lantern.

"It would be a shame if the slavers come here," she said. "This place is too beautiful." She stood gazing out at the moonlight over the plains. Tull finished combing her hair, then tied it into a ponytail and patted her shoulder. It was still an hour before dawn; a quetzalcoatus with a fifty-foot wingspan soared overhead, hunting for carrion, and began to circle the dead tyrannosaur down in the valley.

"Did I get the honey off?" Fava asked matter-of-factly, playing the part of a little sister again.

Tull smelled her hair. It smelled clean, of mountain spring water. "I think so, Friend."

Fava turned and looked up at him, smiling. Tull could not read her expression: anger, desire, mockery? "Friend," she said, "are you sure? I smelled it here, between my breasts," and she leaned her head back. He breathed the sweet scent of her neck. It had the fruity, flowery scent of leatherwood honey, and somehow it made him dizzy.

Tull glanced up, unsure what to answer, for if he told her the truth, she'd bathe again.

Suddenly he stopped worrying about it: On the hill far away he saw a torch swinging in the darkness. Tull pulled out his telescope and looked at the honey tree: Two miles across the plain, Denni was swinging a brand from the fire. For a moment, Tull noticed nothing else, then he saw a dozen men dressed in black, carrying swords.

"What's happening?" Fava asked.

"Slavers," Tull said. "Pirates from Bashevgo I think—at least they are dressed in black. Denni is holding them back."

"How many?" Fava asked, her voice sounding like a mystified little girl.

Tull counted. "Ten or twelve that I can see."

"Denni can't fight so many. He is swinging the torch only to warn us!" Fava said. She grabbed the trumpet from Tull's neck, pulling it so hard that the leather string broke.

"No," Tull said, "you'll warn the slavers that we are here."

Fava put the trumpet to her lips and blew, letting the deep bellow of the horn add to the mating cries of the blue-crested hadrosaurs on the plain below. Tull felt a thrill of fear and watched through the glass while, as one, the slavers turned their faces toward the sounding war horn.

Fava said, "Now Denni and Tchar know we are coming," the mystified voice of the little girl turned hard, "and the pirates know they have a fight on their hands!"

Tull and Fava jumped from the tree and ran to camp. Ayuvah and the others were already throwing on their war gear.

"Slavers have captured Denni and Tchar," Fava said.

"How many?" Ayuvah asked, pulling on a leather helmet with brass studs.

"I saw only ten or twelve," Tull said. "But there could be more."

Ayuvah faltered, looked at the boys, and Tull stopped and looked at them, too. At nineteen and twenty, Tull and Ayuvah were the oldest in the group. The others were mere boys, none over fifteen, yet they were pulling out their war shields, strapping on leg guards with pale faces. They'd have to fight grown men with years of experience with the sword, and they didn't know how many they would be fighting. They could be walking into a trap. Some of the boys were staring at Tull and Ayuvah with wide, frightened eyes.

Tull wondered, *Is it better to lose all eleven of us, or only two?* Ayuvah was the best fighter and hunter in Smilodon Bay, and the boys would follow him if he chose to fight. But surely if it came to a pitched battle, the boys would lose. *We have no other choice than to fight, even if it means that we are all carried into slavery.*

An hour later, Ayuvah and his party made their way through the dew-soaked fields to the leatherwood forest. They'd been watching for the slavers, but saw no sign of them on the plain. Yet Tull was sure the slavers had seen them make their way across the flat grassland. By now, the slavers knew they would be fighting nine Neanderthals—but would they know that six were only boys, that one in the party was a woman? Fava had come only to help distill the honey, yet she carried a shield and spear as if she were a warrior.

The Neanderthals spread out in a fan formation as they made their way to the honey tree, and in front of them, five tan-and-silver iguanadons slowly crept forward, feeding as they went. They circled downwind of the tree, and as they neared, Ayuvah stopped them with the wave of his hand and sniffed the air, testing the scent.

"The slavers are gone, I think," Ayuvah said, and began stalking through the trees again. A moment later, someone cried out, "Denni! Tchar!"

They found the two Neanderthals tied to the tree in the

morning sunlight, naked, unmoving. Tull could only see
Tchar well, and Tchar's right hand lay on the ground a
dozen feet in front of him. The slavers had beaten Tchar
black-and-blue, and then torn the tree open. The angry bees
had stung him many times, and Tchar's face was so swollen
that his eyes were closed. Tull circled the tree just enough to
see Denni, and then wished that he hadn't. The slavers had
slit Denni's belly open, then inserted a forked stick and
twisted it, unrolling his intestines, pulling them out inch by
inch, and then they had strung them over bushes like ornaments. The amount of blood dripping down Denni's legs
showed that he had been alive and kicking while the slavers
did their dirty work. Tull felt the veins in his neck throb,
and for a moment the world went red as he fought his rage
and grief. Ayuvah went in and cut the boys loose, dragged
them away from the tree and brushed the bees off Tchar.
Rather than anger, his face showed only a forlorn aspect.

"They're dead," Ayuvah said. The others watched the
brush, fearful of an ambush, and the youngest boy began
crying in fear while another made gagging sounds.

Ayuvah searched the camp for a moment, studying footprints. The slavers had worn heavy boots, not the soft moccasins of the Pwi, and their tracks were easy to follow.
"There were only about ten slavers," Ayuvah said after several moments, "They knew we would hunt them if they took
captives, and they did not want to fight us. They must have
thought we were too many."

"We should hunt them like wolves anyway!" Fava
hissed, and Tull could barely restrain himself from leaping
into the trees, following their trail.

Ayuvah studied the faces of the boys. Tull realized that
the slavers would not be hindered by captives. Against experienced swordsmen, the boys would be cut down. Ayuvah
said, *"Tcho-oh-fenna-ai.* It grieves me like death that we can
do nothing."

The Neanderthals carried the bodies of Denni and Tchar
down to the river, and in a brief ceremony they gave them to
the water. The young boys cried bitterly. With these two
dead, it meant that the Neanderthals had lost five men so far

in one summer to the slavers. The others had simply been carted away at night after working in the fields, and the loss was less horrible. Yet it had been a rough summer. When they finished with the funeral, they cautiously returned to the fort, packed their honey, and prepared for the trip home. With slavers about, they could not stay any longer. As a last act, they burned their little wooden fortress on the hill. It had served the Pwi egg raiders for many years, but now that the slavers knew of it, they could never return. The kwea, the pain the boys felt for their loss, would bar them from coming here again. Tull felt sad. Always in the past, Hotland had seemed like a place of escape, a place of freedom, but now the memories of it would be forever tainted with the kwea of death.

Tull was fairly certain that some of the slavers had been Neanderthals, Thralls who had lived so long under the domination of the Slave Lords that they no longer minded doing their dirty work, and because Neanderthals had a stronger sense of smell than humans, the party was afraid that the Thralls might try to track them at night by scent. Because of this, they were forced to travel both day and night, carrying their load of honey, watching for slavers all the way. They reached their ship at dawn, two days later. As they neared the sea, they came to a small hill and looked down at their small sailing ship moored in the channel of a dirty brown river. Little gray pteradons with soft down and spade-shaped tails hunted giant blue dragonflies over the river.

Ayuvah stood for a moment, and a small whirlwind whipped through the grass, collided with him and dispersed. He stood for a long time, just watching the river.

Fava said, "Gladly, I don't think the pteradons would be so carefree if the slavers were hiding down in the brush."

"It's not that," Ayuvah said. "I feel a strange cold . . . so strange." His voice trailed off. "I feel as if Father is here, as if he has come to call us home." Ayuvah closed his eyes for a long moment, breathed slowly. "Yes, he wants us to come home."

"How do you know? Is he on a Spirit Walk?" Tull asked. Ayuvah's father was a powerful man among the Pwi. In his youth, he had served as Spirit Walker, as a guide and counselor for his people. Yet a Spirit Walker could not use his sorcerous powers to explore the paths of the future until he stood at the gate of death, and few Pwi who had the power were courageous enough to use it.

"Yes," Ayuvah said. "There is bad news at home." Ayuvah lifted his chin, as if listening. "It has to do with the serpents, dying serpents." Tull sat and thought for a moment. For a thousand years, the serpents had protected his homeland from the dinosaurs that swam across the ocean from Hotland. They formed a living wall of protection. But over the last three years the number of serpents spotted and the number of hatchlings had been decreasing, until finally last spring there had been no serpent hatch at all. Everyone wanted to believe that it was only a temporary problem, but it sounded like, at last, Chaa had been forced to walk the paths of the future, to use his powers to find a solution to this problem. Ayuvah hesitated for a moment longer. "Yes, I am sure of it—Chaa wants us to come home."

Four days later, the Neanderthals sailed into a long narrow fjord to the port at Smilodon Bay. Two ships were already in the harbor, but the Neanderthals in their smaller vessel sailed past them, right up to the docks. Many of the Neanderthal women and children came to greet them, and Ayuvah told of the deaths of Denni and Tchar. The younger boys carried the news to the family, for it was their duty as friends. One old woman said that Chaa was still on his Spirit Walk, that after five days he was still unconscious, and Fava ran home to see him while Tull and Ayuvah unloaded the boat and each carried two kegs of honey up to Scandal.

It was late afternoon, and a warm gravitational wind sighed down from the mountains, hissing through the red-wood trees. Up on the ridge above town, a tyrant bird, one of the smaller breed of dragons, swerved down the sky toward a redwood. It beat its stiff feathers once, twice, clutched the uppermost limbs in its claws, and swayed in the treetop. Tull watched the tyrant bird a moment, its gaping teeth and blood-red serpentine head with its venomous horn, its cold intelligent eyes. The tyrant bird posed little threat to them. The ancient human Starfarers had genetically programmed it to hunt for different prey. Yet Tull shivered at the sight of it.

Tull and Ayuvah carried kegs of honey from the warehouses at dockside uphill to Moon Dance Inn. Tull eyed the tyrant bird as he walked and flipped his shoulder-length copper hair back to let the wind cool his neck.

Moon Dance Inn was a long, two-story building of gray stone and cedar, with eight columns of hand-carved oak supporting the upper balcony where, later in the evening, half-clad ladies would call down to invite passersby up to their bridal suites. Great thick vines of red roses climbed the oak columns. Two peacocks strutted in front of the inn calling *Ayaah, Ayaah*, as they fanned their tails and warily watched the whores' bastard children run through the streets.

Theron Scandal, the human owner of the inn, shambled out the door, his thick arms covered with sweat and flour from working in the kitchens. He surveyed the street, scratched his beard, noticed Tull and Ayuvah.

Scandal waved impatiently. "Bust a testicle, boys! Get those kegs up here." Ayuvah and Tull hurried into the stifling warmth of the inn, dropped the honey kegs on the counter.

Scandal escorted them to a table, called for plates and mugs. "Only four kegs?" Scandal asked. "I wanted six."

"We got only five," Ayuvah apologized. "We have one more down in the boat. We had trouble—slavers."

"Hunh," Scandal said, preoccupied. He seemed to be gazing inward, and did not ask what kind of trouble they'd had. "Time to settle up then, boys. But first, sit with me a moment." The common room was sizzling hot—the sticky heat of late summer made intolerable by the blistering heat of cooking fires. Green bottle flies buzzed in and out the open doorway, glittering like emeralds when shafts of sunlight struck them. A bowl of hazelnuts sat on the table. Scandal picked up a couple of nuts, cracked them between his thick fingers. At the sound of the nuts cracking, two gray squirrels scurried from the kitchen and climbed into his lap, poked their noses over the table and sniffed. Scandal set the nuts on the table and stroked the squirrels between the ears as they crunched the hazelnuts between their teeth.

A gangly youth brought mugs of dark warm beer, plates of cabbage smothered in pungent white cheese, and sweet sausages that were rolled in grape leaves and flavored with curry and anise. Tull and Ayuvah drank deeply from the beer. Scandal gauged them: Ayuvah was a Neanderthal, strong as an ox, one of the best hunters and guides on the coast. Tull was a young man, almost twenty. He had the broad, round, forward-thrusting face and dark-red hair of a Neanderthal, with thin eyebrows, each hair as distinct as a small copper nail over his deep-set eyes—eyes the yellow-green of dying grass. His hawkish nose was broad and close to the face. His shoulders were wide and muscular. All in all, he looked like a typical Neanderthal, but he had a small chin beneath his thin beard—his only physical manifestation of human ancestry. *Ah, but there's more to Tull than to most Tcho-Pwi,* Scandal reminded himself. *You can see it in his eyes.* Although Tull had the powerful, clumsy hands of a Neanderthal, he struggled to hold his fork in a human grip, between his thumb and forefinger.

It wasn't polite to talk business till after dinner, and Scandal just watched the men for a moment. Tull looked up.

"Don't buzzard over me," Tull said in English, with a deep nasal accent. "I can't eat when you're buzzarding over me."

Enough of politeness, then. Scandal said, "By the Starfarer's hairless blue apricots, I'll come to the point!" He pounded the table with a fist like a sailor ordering dinner. "Next week, I want you men to come with me to Seven Ogre River to catch some sea serpents!" The squirrels jumped from his lap and sped into the kitchen, shouting their warning cry. Scandal kept a large "bird" from Hotland in a cage. The bird had wicked-looking teeth and hung upside down, grasping the bars of its cage with clawed fingers. It twisted its head, and hissed at the men.

Tull shook his head violently, his mouth too full to speak.

Scandal knitted his brows. "Valis, more food!" he called. "Throw a hog in the barbecue pit if you must!" He turned back to Tull and Ayuvah. "Look—I need you! You've probably heard already that we've been down to the hatching grounds and there isn't a serpent left in these waters. Our hatch has been down for three years, but I happen to know that the fall run up at the Seven Ogre was good last year, and I believe that we can go up there and catch some! Why, in Craal, the Slave Lords consider the baby sea serpents to be a delicacy, and they cart them live for hundreds of miles to serve at banquets. So, I got the idea: Why not sneak into Craal and catch us a hundred serpents, then bring them back here and dump them into the sea, restock our waters? We'll handle it just the way Rebamon Strong does his ponds, the way he restocks them with pike every few years!"

Tull and Ayuvah both stared at Scandal as if the human were some madman. "Come now," Scandal said, "it's not a bad idea. Why, after the past couple of years, with the bad fish harvests and men leaving town, it only shows the way we're heading if we don't do something. I know the plan isn't pretty, but several merchants hereabouts even think it's worth trying, and they're financing the expedition. I'm even donating my three-thousand-gallon beer barrel as a container to hold them in, and the masons at White Rock have sold us a wagon and mastodon for the trip. So, how about it? Want to come?"

"To Craal?" Ayuvah asked. "You are crazy! No!"

Scandal smiled and raised a hand to ward off the denial as if it were a blow. In his best bartering voice he said, "Dragging a damned wagon nine hundred miles through mountains infested with saber-tooths, dire wolves, slavers, and giant Mastodon Men—all to catch a barrel of sea serpents—might not sound like your idea of fun, but think of it as an adventure! I've got a handful of humans coming, delightful fellows good for banter, but we're going out into the Rough, where there are only mosquitoes for company. I need you—you and a dozen chinless Pwi with their strong backs to build me a road." Tull kept shaking his head and Scandal kept talking, not pausing to breathe, hoping to say the right thing. "And you, Ayuvah, you can scout our trail. And Tull, you'll be boss of the road crew! Neither of you need to lift a hand the whole trip! Just give the Pwi their orders. You could eat like this—my finest meals! Three times a day! All you have to do is convince some Pwi to come with us—at first I'd thought forty, then thirty—but I'll settle for a dozen, make it twelve!"

Ayuvah spat, "None of the Pwi will go to Craal!"

"Look!" Scandal said, "People are talking. Already they're calling this whole affair 'Scandal's Wondrous Blunder.' Why, when I told the town of my plan and asked for volunteers, men evacuated their seats so fast they left turds on their stools. We haven't even hooked the mastodon to the wagon yet, and already things are falling apart. And when I'm lying cold in my grave, eating dirt and breathing worms, I don't want to lose my eternal sleep worrying that people are still laughing at me. If you won't do it for me, do it for the town. Get it through your thick heads: no fish, no money—and without the serpents to drive the fish in from the sea, we can't catch them! After last spring's failure, the town is doomed! You don't have to piss in the wind to see which way it blows."

"We don't know that the serpent hatch failed," Ayuvah protested. "They could have gone south this year."

"For two hundred years they've followed the currents north!" Scandal answered with a sigh. He'd voiced this same argument a dozen times in the last week, yet no one seemed to want to believe the danger. "I tell you, there are no serpents laying in the hatching grounds at the Haystack Islands. Not one! I went down last week, and I've seen with my own eyes—not only are the young serpents gone, but the old ones that patrol the oceans between here and Hotland are gone. The sea lanes are open."

"Ayaah, I've heard," Tull said. "But you've gotten ahead of yourself. Even if you can bring some serpents back alive, will they do any good? You might put a hundred in the bay and let them grow to eighty feet over the winter, but we don't know why the old ones are dying. What if yours die, too? No. Before you run into the wilderness, you should wait for Chaa to return from his Spirit Walk."

That damned Pwi Shaman again, Scandal thought. "Use a little common sense!" he said. "He started fasting for his Spirit Walk ten days ago. But we've barely got ten weeks to make it to the Seven Ogre River in time for the hatch. We can't wait for him. As for the serpents—I'm sure it's only a local problem. Why, I've talked to a dozen captains, and all of them have seen serpents this spring down in South Port! You figure it—we've had four warm years in a row, and with each warm year, the dinosaurs in Hotland get a little more active, and you know as well as I that a serpent can't always take on a saur and come out alive. Maybe there's been an explosion in the number of sailfins over the last few years and they've cut into the serpents. That would explain why the serpent hatch has been low. But I tell you that this year, here in the east, the serpents are wiped out!"

Ayuvah said, "You have no proof. The great mothers could be laying their eggs elsewhere!"

Scandal smiled, "That's just Pwi talk, not to be taken seriously by real men. We both know the world doesn't work that way. The serpents have been laying their eggs down at the Haystack Islands for hundreds of years."

At another table, a brawny trader with a high voice began swearing loudly, drunkenly. Everyone turned to watch him a moment, and Scandal frowned at the disturbance. The young servant, Valis, brought in some more dishes, meat pies and rolls, blueberries in cream. "Do you really want me to roast a hog?" he asked.

"No," Scandal sighed. "I really want you to get in the kitchen and wash the dishes." The servant left.

Scandal shook his head in wonder, "I have to leave that idiot in charge. He'll burn this place down to a heap of ashes while I'm gone. Here, try these blueberries!" Scandal said with a sigh, urging bowls on Tull and Ayuvah. "I got these fresh this evening from a hermit up on Finger Mountain. He grows them special. They're marvelously piquant, almost tart I'd say—yet still deliciously sweet."

Tull and Ayuvah scooped some berries from the bowls with their wide fingers, and tasted them. "Aaah," Tull said. "They taste as blueberries should only taste in a dream."

"You'd never guess the secret of growing such flavorful berries!" Scandal said. "You'll never guess!" Tull scooped some more berries and chewed them with obvious delight. "It's the soil," Scandal said. "See, the farmer grows them in goat dung. It's what gives them that marvelous piquancy. They're grown in almost pure goat dung!"

Tull put the berries down, "Ayaah," he drawled. "You are what you eat." He smiled and leaned back in his chair and looked at Scandal. "So you want us to take a trip with you out into the Rough, help you drag a wagon nine hundred miles over mountains, fighting off the slavers in Craal with one hand and the dire wolves with the other? All in the hope that we can catch some serpent hatchlings in a beer barrel and somehow keep them alive long enough to put them in the bay?"

Scandal nodded.

Tull pulled at his beard, and the bracelet of red and blue clamshells on his wrist rattled softly. "That sounds to me like Pwi talk, not to be taken seriously by real men. We both know the world doesn't work that way." He added with finality, "None of the Pwi will follow you to Seven Ogre River."

Scandal nodded glumly, gazed at the table. "I know," he said. "But, Tull, you've got that look in your eye. My departed wife once put it succinctly. Even when you were just a child, she said you had 'revolution in your eyes—twin fires of rage and idealism.' Now, if you could just put that idealism to some good use." He stared away. "But I don't blame you. It sounds like a fool's plan. It's all I could come up with. I'm no Spirit Walker . . . I can't see into the future with any degree of certainty, but if we don't do something, well then, we're in trouble. Even if there are still some serpents out there, we can't survive another year without the fish harvest. Men will keep leaving town. And if enough men keep leaving, you don't have to worry about the slavers in Craal. They'll come here."

Tull reached out and grabbed Scandal's arm, startling him. "The men won't leave town, and the slavers won't come."

Scandal eyed him a moment. The word *slave* frightened Tull. Put the boy on the defensive. "Oh, they'll leave town when their families get hungry enough, if only to hunt up in the mountains. Just go out and let your eyes drift—they're already leaving. And as for the slavers, well look, they're already here among us. Every shipping season someone disappears—one or two people—not enough to rouse the town."

Tull said, "You've got fog between your ears! Some merchants who sail these waters have tentacles, and they may snag one or two a year—but you accuse friends of that?"

Ayuvah touched Tull's wrist. "Scandal didn't mean to

offend," Ayuvah warned Tull. He turned to Scandal. "We were attacked by slavers on the trip. Denni and Tchar are dead."

Scandal sat back in his chair, grunted. "I'm sorry," he said. "I had no idea. And here I have been talking about slavers as if they were a joke. Five kegs of honey for two men. It's a bitter trade." Scandal sat a moment, looking off at nothing. "Have a seat here a moment boys, I'll get your pay for the trip," he said softly.

He went to his office, came back out and surveyed the guests quickly, making sure that the customers had plenty of food and drink on their tables. He stopped at a table, told a bawdy tale to a sailor, and winked at one of the whores, signing for her to come sit on the fellow's lap. When he got to Tull and Ayuvah, he held out a bag of coins to Tull, jingled them in his hands.

"Three steel eagles a day, as promised," Scandal said. "I put in a little extra for Denni's and Tchar's families, all right?"

"Ayaah," Tull nodded.

"I made up your receipts," Scandal said. "Put your marks down here." Tull looked at the receipt and frowned, took the quill and signed his name. Ayuvah saw his concern, grabbed his arm, but Tull did not offer to read the human words on the receipt for him.

"I don't mean to push," Scandal said. "But a final word: you can look for work tomorrow and the next day, and with the harvest coming in, I'm sure you'll have work aplenty. But if you come with me, you won't have to look for work. You'll get three steel eagles a day. But it will be a dangerous trip. If you can convince more Pwi to come, just remember it won't be a trip for boys."

Ayuvah spoke up in Pwi. "I have a final word for you: my grandfather sadly-knew a Pwi—Ayanavi the Wise. When Ayanavi was young and happy, the slavers took him to Craal. He tried to escape, so they put him to work in the mines and chained him to the wall. For three years, only the sweet memory of his wife and children kept him alive, and one day he finally chopped off his hand with a sharp stone and escaped his shackles. After hardships that gave him misery in the brain forever after, he found his way home.

But when he got home, his dismay overpowered him, for he found that his wife and children had been captured only five days before, and taken as slaves into Craal. Remember Scandal: that although to you this tale may seem an unfortunate irony, such are the tales of all men who escape Craal. The land is ruled by Adjonai, the God of Terror, and those who enter will find every detail of their lives controlled by him forever after. You speak lightly of making this journey because you do not believe in Adjonai, but he is real. If you go to Craal, he will control you forever after. Even speaking his name, I can feel his hand stretching out from the west. I tell you as a friend—give up your foolish journey."

Scandal looked at Ayuvah. The Neanderthal's face was pale with fear, a strange expression on such a powerful young man. Yet Scandal knew that for the Neanderthals Craal was a place of tremendously evil kwea. For eight hundred years the Slave Lords had been dragging Pwi into that land, and Craal was filled with legendary terrors. Scandal looked into Ayuvah's face, and saw that he could not tempt the Pwi into Craal with three steel eagles a day. The only way he'd get them there would be to drag them in chains. Tull and Ayuvah weren't cowards, but they wouldn't go to Craal.

A powerful cold whirlwind seemed to whip through the room, making Scandal's hair stand on end. It was such a startling change from the sweltering summer heat that Scandal sat back in his chair in surprise thinking the wind would knock the plates from the table. But when he looked, even the feathers on Ayuvah's necklace didn't move.

Scandal reached out with his hand and touched the cold. It stood a few inches in front of him, a wall of cold, and Scandal felt it as plainly as if it were a wall of wood. A green nimbus, roughly shaped like a man, formed in the air beside Tull.

Scandal jutted his chin in surprise, pointing beside Tull. "Spirit Walker," he said.

Tull turned to his left, looked at the green figure.

Scandal spoke quickly, addressing the Spirit Walker, "Chaa, get back to your body! You've been gone for days. For God's sake, the Pwi are getting scared!"

The green nimbus stretched out, touched Tull, and the

young man grabbed his stomach and his eyes opened wide
with terror, and the nimbus faded.

"I can feel him, inside me," Tull said in surprise, holding
his belly.

Scandal watched Tull. "In another five minutes he'll
know more about you than you do," Scandal said. "He'll
know the moment you're destined to die . . . how it will
come . . . whether you'll ever marry." Scandal said it with
awe. The Pwi Spirit Walkers never walked the paths of tomorrow for humans. Scandal had never even heard of a
Spirit Walker who'd walked the future for a half-breed like
Tull. The Pwi had a word for half-breeds: *Tcho-Pwi,* the
unfamily, the no-people. It was not a word used maliciously
as an epithet; it was merely descriptive. Half-breed Neanderthals did not belong—not with humans, not with Pwi. The
biological differences between the descendants of the human
Starfarers and the Neanderthals were too great to be bridged
in a generation, and children born to such a marriage seldom survived through infancy.

Tull held his stomach and Ayuvah said, "This is bad!
This is bad! If my father has resorted to walking the future
for no-people, he must not have seen a good future for the
Pwi."

Scandal considered a moment. *I'll never get them to
come with me to Craal,* he thought. *But I have one chance—
Chaa could send them to Craal. For the Spirit Walker, they'd
ride a scimitar cat into hell.*

Tull and Ayuvah got up and went to the door where circling
flies glittered like emeralds. Tull looked out into the sunlight. Down the street, old Caree Tech stood in her yard,
stirring a stone cooking pot full of lye and lard as she made
a batch of soap. Her eyes were red from the fumes, and the
acrid greasy scent carried on the wind.

"I can feel him in me," Tull said to Ayuvah. "And he
moves from place to place, as if my body were filled with
rooms. He is so cold. There—he has opened a door to my
left lung."

Ayuvah chuckled. "I think he is making Connection

with you. He cannot walk the paths of your future until he *becomes* you."

"He's moving up, toward my head." Tull gasped and staggered a bit as the cold touched his sinuses.

"He is taking his time, learning you," Ayuvah said. "He would not do this for a human, they are too alien."

"There . . . he is moving out now."

"No, he is still within you, still Connected," Ayuvah said. "Feel him, just the slightest cold. He is walking your future."

"How long will he take?"

"It depends," Ayuvah said. "Your future may be short, it may be long. Your path will branch a thousand thousand times. He will travel all of your futures, see all of your potential. He may be with you all night."

Tull felt back with his mind, and he could sense the cold still there. He imagined carrying Chaa inside him for a day, wondered if he would become accustomed to the sensation.

He looked out at the town. The houses were all made of large stones with faded gray planks, bleached by salt spray and sun. The walls of the homes leaned at odd angles, their foundations having sagged over years. Tull was intimately familiar with every stone, every board, every person in this town. A fisherman across the street, Beremon Smit, waved good-bye to his wife and four children and set out south of town, heading toward the mines down at White Rock. *Another man gone,* Tull thought. *One less to protect the town, just as Scandal said.*

A cloud floated overhead, casting a sudden shadow. Caree wiped the sweat from her brow with the back of her leathery hand and looked up. Behind Tull, in the inn, a guest began shouting drunkenly, "You mutant! I'll abort your mutant butt! Where's my knife! I'll abort you!"

Scandal shouted, "Here sir, calm yourself!" but the man responded, "I don't know which is worst in this place—the food, the booze, or the company." It was a line calculated to offend everyone in the room, but most calculated to offend Scandal. Scandal broke a bottle over the counter and shouted, "All right! He's mine! He's mine!"

Tull did not turn to see it. He knew Scandal too well, knew this town too well. He imagined Scandal, big bear of a fat man, pleasant as a pet pig and sometimes just as obnoxious, waving the bottle as he threatened the guest into submission. Scandal was a businessman, and if it came to fighting, he would fight like a businessman, pummeling the other with slow punches calculated to minimize the damage —no profit in killing the customers—as if he were beating dust from a rug.

Tull smiled at the thought. Tull had had many good meals here at Moon Dance Inn, and the accumulated emotions, the kwea, of those good meals left him feeling intoxicated with fulfillment. He felt inside him, felt the icy presence still there. *A Spirit Walker is walking my future,* he thought. *He will know everything about me.* The sense of wonder and fear that came with this knowledge did not mix well with the kwea of satisfaction.

Tull's trick ankle was bothering him, and he began limping home, downhill and across the river to Pwi-town. Ayuvah sensed his need for quiet and said nothing. The wind surged through his hair. After sunset the force of the gravitational winds would combine with the nightly thermal winds that swept down from the mountains. The little town of Smilodon Bay was perched on the east coast of the Rough, a wilderness so large and rugged that the Slave Lords of Craal had never conquered it. Yet on such nights, Tull felt small and powerless, as if the Slave Lords sent the winds, as if his footing were inconsequential and the force of those winds would lift him and blow him out to sea.

On the road north of Moon Dance Inn was the section of town where Tull had been raised. The kwea from that part of town was powerfully evil, and Tull did not go there, for he could feel a shadow looming over it. They walked past a wine shop, and in an alley behind it, Tull had once necked with a young human girl, Wisteria Troutmaster. He could not pass that alley without feeling the kwea of hot arousal from his youth.

Each place they passed held kwea, and as Tull walked through town, he felt like a blind cave spider that spends its entire life in a single web that both defines his world and binds him to it.

Mayor Goodstick's hounds barked from their pens. Outside the mayor's front door, in a small cage, sat the mayor's pet Dryad. She was a small girl with silver hair and skin as white as aspen bark mottled with vertical black and gray blotches. Her natural coloring blended with her native aspen forest. She was a strange, wild creature who never spoke. Three young boys were standing outside the cage, poking at the girl. One of them was Little Chaa, Ayuvah's younger brother.

"Get away from there!" Ayuvah shouted, and he ran and grabbed his brother and shook him by the shoulders. "Touch a Dryad, and she will destroy you!" he said.

Little Chaa laughed. "I could beat her," he said, and he ran off to the woods with the other boys.

"And she can steal your soul," Ayuvah answered, shaking his head at the ignorant youth.

The men reached the redwood bridge over Smilodon River, and the sun shone on both banks. Like the gravitational wind, the steely gray water was just beginning to hiss out to sea as the tides turned. Within hours the river level would drop thirty feet. Now that the fresh water was running, several Pwi women sat washing clothes on the rocks. The riverbank was choked with wild raspberry bushes, and clothing was draped over every bush. Blackberry vines crowded in on the washwomen, and they had tied a brown-and-white goat to a tree so it could eat the bushes down. On the Pwi side of the river, lopsided Neanderthal huts made of driftwood and crooked boards, with weathered hides for doors, sprung up in mockery of the fine houses in the human settlement.

Ayuvah asked, "Friend, I saw you frown when Scandal gave us the papers. You are disturbed. What do the words on the paper mean?"

Tull held out his receipt for their day's labor. "Scandal says he paid us for drudge work. He said we are drudges." Being half-breed, Tull could speak the human word. His accent was nasal, and he pronounced the word as *drege*.

"What does that word mean?" Ayuvah asked.

"It means we are the lowest of the low," Tull answered. "We are like cattle."

Tull flexed his hands, massive hands with strong fingers and knobby joints—the kind of hands made for throwing spears or ripping the hides from animals or digging in the earth. Although he was only half Pwi, Tull's thumbs were tilted so that if he laid his hand flat on the table, his thumb and fingers would all lie flat. Because of this, he could not easily hold objects between his thumb and forefinger—could not touch his little finger at all. Like the Pwi, this lent him a degree of clumsiness unknown among the small, clever-handed humans. Tull felt inside him. The Spirit Walker was still there. Tull wanted to speak privately to Ayuvah, to say something he would not speak in front of others. *But the Spirit Walker knows it all now, anyway,* he thought.

"Remember last year, when I took a job as apprentice to Debon, studying medicine?"

"*Shez,* yes," Ayuvah said.

"I studied his books for months, and when Tchema cut her leg, Debon wanted me to sew it. But when Tchema saw that I was going to sew her leg, she said, 'No! I want a human's clever hands! I'd rather be mauled by a dire wolf than let you do it!'"

"You would have done your best," Ayuvah said.

Tull laughed. "My best is not good enough! Debon talked to me later, and what he said was right. No woman would want me sticking these big hands up her if I have to turn a baby. He was hoping it would work, that I would be accepted among my own people, among the Pwi. But I had to remind him that I am *Tcho-Pwi,* no-people." The kwea of the memory was sharp and painful.

Ayuvah watched Tull's face. "The paper means nothing. Paper is only good for starting fires." He took the receipts from Tull's hands and ripped them in half, threw them off the bridge into the Smilodon River.

"Tomorrow, we can get work picking apples up at Finger Mountain, or we can cut firewood. We can be field hands or loggers. We will not be drudges anymore."

Tull laughed. "You do not see—in Benbow, the humans have reopened the glass factory," he said, speaking of the legendary Benbow glass, a carbon and cesium alloy lain down in a matrix tougher than diamond. "They make drill bits strong enough to drill the rot from a wormy tooth, and in Wellen's Eyes a man is trying to build a machine to speak to humans on other stars. In South Port, they build ships that move by steam. Someday, the humans will live in castles on the stars, while we will live in houses made of mud and sticks and tend their fields. We will always be drudges."

Below them by the riverbank where the Pwi women washed their clothes, a woman shouted and there was an audible gasp from a dozen others. Tull looked down just in time to see the water swirl by the riverbank, and something large whipped away under the water. He could see only a gray shape, forty feet long and sixty feet wide.

At first he thought it must be one of the great sea serpents, but a Pwi woman shouted, "It was a saur! It ate the goat!" And all among the Pwi the cry went up that a dinosaur was in the bay, that it had swum over from Hotland.

The great beast remained in one spot for a moment, then turned and its shadow in the water moved under the bridge and headed downriver. Tull and Ayuvah raced along the street to follow it, heading uphill through the human part of town, up to the lookout point by the inn.

Everywhere, people were running and shouting, pointing at the shadow in the water, for never in all of memory had a dinosaur managed to swim across the ocean from Hotland.

They rushed up through the streets to the lookout point, scattering the peacocks that thought they owned the street, and stood, staring. Smilodon Bay sat between two fingers of mountains, and the bay suddenly widened just past the inn, so that it turned from a narrow river into a three-mile-wide sea lane. The saur swam past the two ships anchored in the harbor, then dived.

The sun glinted off the rolling swells in the bay like beaten copper, greened by age. Tull watched the water for all of five minutes, and then the saur rose and lay in the water, floating at the surface, his great front flippers spread wide, his tapering neck as long as a small boat, sunning himself. A great school of fish had gathered, and the saur sat, head tilted to one side, and waited for a fish to scrape his flippers; then he casually dipped his head underwater and came up with a wriggling silver fish between his teeth. Resting in the water that way, the monster looked much like a giant green sea turtle.

"I'll be damned," a human said beside Tull, "That's a plesiosaur."

Tull was tense, knowing the plesiosaur was out of place,

that a serpent should have devoured the monster while it crossed from Hotland, and he waited for a moment to see the water churn in a maelstrom beneath the plesiosaur, the rush and roar of the serpent's bony gray head and barnacle-encrusted body as it wriggled up to grab the plesiosaur in its scimitar teeth and pull it under. The sailors in town all said that the sight of a serpent making its strike would stop your heart for an hour, stop your breath for a week. Until one saw a serpent strike, one did not know the meanings of the words *awe* or *majesty*.

Yet the plesiosaur kept sunning, and there was no sign of a serpent. "What should we do?" someone shouted, and Tull looked back toward Pwi-town and saw a dozen young Neanderthal men grabbing their spears. They were shouting and laughing, thinking to kill the plesiosaur.

"It must have tasted bad!" a young Pwi boy said, "so the serpents would not eat it! One taste, and they spit it out!"

"We should not let those young men go out in the water in that boat," Ayuvah said. "This isn't like hunting on land!" Tull agreed, but the young men were already in the boat, eager to prove their courage.

A tyrant bird flew out of the redwoods from shore, soared over the water and circled the plesiosaur. Its genetic programming told it to kill the plesiosaur, yet the small dragon could not quite get down into the water to strike a blow with its poisonous horn.

Suddenly, one of the ships in the bay fired two of its cannons, and the tyrant bird dropped, startled, and then caught itself and flapped away. The plesiosaur had been a mere hundred yards from the ship, and it took a ball in the neck and dove. Red water boiled to the surface, and everyone cheered the sailor who'd shown such skill.

The young Pwi men rowed their boat into the harbor, watching the water, spears in hand, but they never found the plesiosaur.

An hour before sunset, Tull went home. He lived in a small stone cottage set on the shelf of a cliff overlooking the ocean a mile past Pwi-town. It was a secluded spot, without a neighbor or roads nearby, and only the tinkling of a small

creek that ran past his doorstep for company. Wisteria grew
at one side of the house, and the scent of the last of the
summer flowers filled the cliffside.

Tull had bought some plums and a small melon at the
market, and he put them in an earthenware jar, then wetted
a cloth in the stream and placed the cooling cloth over the
jar so that he would have the fruit later in the evening.

He looked out at the sea, still watching the water for
sign of a serpent, a sign of the plesiosaur. The gravitational
winds were blowing Tull, as if to lift him, and the hair rose
on the back of his neck. For a thousand years the great
serpents had formed an eco-barrier, a living wall of protection from the beasts in Hotland. But now a plesiosaur had
made it across the ocean, and Tull could feel that wall crumbling. He could almost feel himself being carried like a leaf
in the wind, and he knew his world would never be the
same.

The thought left Tull unsettled, and he felt a need to
open himself to this new idea. *In a while, I need to go see the
Pwi. Fava will be concerned about her father on his Spirit
Walk, and we have two deaths to mourn. But for now. . . .*
He stripped off his bracelets and necklace of colored clamshells, pulled off his long black cotton loincloth with the
emblems of the silver tigers sewn into it, and stood in the
wind. He let the evening sun shine over every inch of his
skin. He thought of Craal, and felt the shadow of Adjonai to
the west, the God of Terror. *Certainly, Adjonai sent the plesiosaur to frighten the Pwi,* Tull thought, and he chuckled,
for it was a strangely Pwi thought. He opened himself to the
fear he'd felt on seeing the plesiosaur. In Hotland, Tull had
seen the gray sixty-foot crocodiles with jaws longer than a
man, sailfin carnosaurs that sunned themselves in the shallows in the early morning, duckbills that traveled in herds of
thousands along the lakesides and trampled everything in
their paths. The plesiosaur was not much, but it was out of
place. It was just the first of these. Tull remembered how
Ayuvah had killed the tyrannosaur only a week before,
throwing his whole weight against the beast and then riding
the spear down to slit it open. He imagined himself with his
spear, fighting such beasts here in Smilodon Bay, and imagined that the fear was blowing through him.

Up in the sky, two great horned dragons soared on the winds, out to sea. They were long-distance hunters and would ride the wind for hours, intercepting any of the larger reptiles that sought to fly from Hotland.

Neanderthal ears are more sensitive than human ears, and far down the dirt road in Pwi-town Tull heard a girl call his name. He pulled on his breech cloth and his bracelets, and walked the trail to the road to see who called him. On the road, a half mile toward Pwi-town, Fava was running, kicking up small puffs of dust with each step.

"Tell," she shouted. "Father has returned from his Spirit Walk! He is calling for you! Something is wrong!"

Chapter 2
Threads of Iron

Tull felt inside himself, and realized that sometime in the last few minutes, when he was not aware, the icy presence of the Spirit Walker had left. He rushed down the road to Fava, and together they ran to Chaa's house. Chaa's large home was made of red stone and much of it was excavated into the back of a hill; deer hides served as summer doors. Tull rushed into the darkness, then stood, letting his eyes adjust. He was familiar with every detail of the house.

Fava pushed him down a tunnellike hallway, guiding him through the cool darkness as if he were a stranger, always touching him, gently and intimately, guiding him with her hands, almost caressing him, in the manner of the Pwi.

Chaa lay on the floor in the back. He was nearly naked, wearing only a black loincloth and a light gray vest painted with daisies and lilacs. His legs poked out like long brown sticks, and his wife, Zhopila, bent over him, trying to spoon broth down his throat. The room was cool and moist, yet Chaa glistened with sweat. His yellow hair was chopped off short, and his yellow eyes glittered deep back under his brows. As soon as Tull saw Chaa, he knew something was wrong. The Pwi call themselves the Smiling People, for they are nearly always happy by nature, but Chaa was not smiling. Indeed, every line on his face was drawn tight with pain and horror.

"Leave us, please. Leave us alone," Chaa said, "Go outside, far away." The women looked at one another. The Pwi did not keep secrets from each other. "Please," Chaa begged, and the women hurried from the house, ran out into the sunlight.

Tull sat cross-legged on the floor, and Chaa stared at him from under his glittering eyes. Chaa was young for a Spirit Walker, only thirty-five, but his magic had aged him. He was also a very kind man, good to his seven children.

Chaa tried to smile, but his face twisted into a painful mimic of a smile. "Help me sit," he said. Tull grabbed Chaa's elbows and pulled him up, leaning him against a pillow.

"Are you ill?" Tull asked.

"I am very weak," Chaa apologized. "My teacher taught me that 'A five-day fast is the beginning of power.' So I starve myself for five days before I take my Spirit Walk, and I drink very little water. It focuses the mind, and brings me close enough to death so I can leave my body, walk the paths of the future. Because of this, people think I am something!" He spat the words as if they were bitter. "But as you shall see, I am nothing! I walk the paths of the future, but the paths branch at every step. I try to guide the Pwi, but how do you guide them when all the paths twist the wrong way? My master always said, 'Once you take a Spirit Walk, you can never go home.' Your perceptions are opened, and you see things in a different way. Never has this been more true than tonight."

Chaa's chest heaved, and he said very slowly, sweat streaming from his face as if the exertion caused him great pain: "In eleven days Scandal the Gourmet will leave to catch his serpents. Go with him. If he is to succeed, you must capture the serpents. Only you. Take Ayuvah and Little Chaa with you to build the road."

Tull watched him for a long moment. Catching the serpents did not seem like such a big job. It would be like catching guppies in an earthenware jar—except that these guppies were ten feet long and had teeth of steel. Still, it seemed that others should be able to help. But one never questioned a Spirit Walker. Their answers, all half-truths and metaphor, tended to displease.

"Scandal leaves in a week," Tull said. "You've been gone longer than you realize."

Chaa waved his hand in dismissal. "He plans to leave in a week. He will not leave for eleven days."

"Are you certain we need to make this journey?" Tull asked.

"I journeyed through the ocean, and there are no serpents in the east or south anymore. Deep in the water, the great ones are dying from illness. Only in the north are there any serpents. I traveled to next summer and saw great lizards swim from Hotland—long-legged running lizards with feet webbed like those of a duck and teeth like those—" he pointed across the room to a small wooden table. A decorative dagger sat on the table, carved from a six-inch carnosaur tooth; evolution had allowed the creature to grow a tooth that was serrated on the inside for cutting flesh. Chaa's eyes widened as he remembered the monsters, but it was not a powerful fear, not the horror etched in his face. "If you do not bring the serpents, the great lizards will swim across the narrow places of the sea. You must bring the serpents—not only to save this town, but to save many towns. You must learn to catch them on your own. If I told you the way, you would try too quickly. The timing is all-important. You would die in the attempt. Yet when the time comes, you must act quickly. And you must act as a Man of the Pwi."

Chaa sat up, leaned forward and touched Tull on the chest, almost a caress, in the manner of the Pwi. "When I entered your body, I felt the pain and hopes of your childhood. I know how you longed for your own death, and the death of your parents. That was a very bad time. But I must tell you, that this day the hope of your childhood has come to pass: Go to the home of your parents! Now! You will find that your father and mother are dead!"

Tull stood up, surprised, and stepped backward, staring

at the shaman. He'd expected Chaa to tell of distant dangers, not deaths in his own family.

Chaa urged him to leave. "It is true! Go and see!"

And Tull ran from the room, heading toward his parents' home in the human part of town, a few houses down from Moon Dance Inn. Fava saw him running, saw the look on his face, and shouted for Tull to stop, but Tull kept running. He did not run fast. His right ankle had been injured when he was a child, and he could not run fast, and Fava ran alongside and she began yelling, *"Tche!"*—help—as she ran, her tone signifying that she was as mystified as ever.

As he ran, Tull was not certain what he felt. All through childhood he'd wished his parents would die, and now Chaa said that they had been mysteriously struck down, and he was not sure if he should hope that it was true, or if he should feel guilty for wishing it would happen. Tull had not lived with his parents for years—had built his own home on the outskirts of town when he was thirteen. Even when his mother had finally given birth to a second child only a few years ago, Tull had not come to visit often. And Tull realized that he was not running to learn if his parents were dead, he was running to learn if his little brother Wayan was dead. Chaa had not said how his parents had been struck down, had not said if Wayan was alive. Tull imagined murderers in the house, and he was glad that Fava was calling the Pwi as they ran. He crossed the bridge over the Smilodon River, and behind him the astonished Pwi shouted, running together like herd animals, the way Pwi always did in a crisis. He rushed up the street past old Caree Tech brewing her soap, past Moon Dance Inn, and from there the road curved inland between two steep knolls.

The sun was setting and the whole quarter of town was in darkness, and Tull's stomach twisted into a knot and he staggered in his steps. Tull's home held many dark memories, and he was loath to enter this section of town, where the kwea of old pain and old fear mingled in powerful, stomach tightening proportions. Although the Pwi said that Adjonai ruled in Craal, Tull could feel the dark god's hand even here. He avoided this part of town altogether except when pressed to enter on business.

His parents' front door was not far—fourth house of

seven among a row of houses built with common walls. Tull
walked toward it, and his breathing came ragged and heavy,
restricted. This home had been a place of captivity for him,
and with each step forward he felt that memory of captivity
growing, the chains and ropes building around him. The
front of the house leaned forward precariously, nearly obscured by broken fish traps, piles of worn furs, barrels of
spoiled salt, scrap metal, and other junk Tull's father sold
for a living. Within the house Wayan, his three-year-old
brother, shrieked in terror. Tull leapt forward and yanked
the door open, thinking to stop the murder.

The house was dim, with only a little light shining
through scraped-hide windows. An orange cat sat on a
crossbeam in the rafters, flicking its tail. Tull's Neanderthal
mother stooped over the dinner table, a blue rag wrapped
around her stringy orange hair. Her face was broad and
fleshy, totally expressionless; her deep-set eyes were empty,
like those of a cow that is nearly dead from giving birth. She
did not smile like a Pwi. She slowly spooned soup from a
large bowl into a cup, using a regular dinner spoon rather
than a ladle. At such a plodding pace it would take her
several minutes to fill the bowl.

"Where is Wayan?" Tull demanded. He heard an answering shriek from the woodshed, through the back door.

"Wayan?" she said, fumbling with her spoon. "He's out
back, playing with Jenks."

A chill shook Tull. *She always does this,* he thought. *She
always calls him* Jenks *instead of* your father *at times like
this.* Tull remembered how his father had "played" when
Tull was young—the petty tortures, the beatings, the bloodied noses. Such things had ended when Tull got old enough
to either run away or fight back. But Tull remembered.

He burst through the back door and into the dim woodshed. Stacks of broken wood encircled the small area. His
father, Jenks, a huge barrel of a human with arms as thick
as trees, was sitting on a chopping block, laughing. He held
the tiny boy Wayan pinned to the ground with one foot, and
the child shrieked, trying to free himself. The family's big
black mastiff stood over the child, greedily licking soup off
the boy's face. Wayan screamed and tried to push the dog
away, but Jenks roared with laughter and shouted, "Come

ahead, eat your dinner, boy!'' and poured more soup onto the child's face. The dog, confused and hungry, ignored Wayan's efforts at escape and lapped the soup.

Wayan looked up and shouted, "Tull, save me!"

Tull rushed forward and kicked at the dog, but it jumped away before the blow landed. Tull snatched Wayan from beneath his father's foot, and Wayan clung to Tull madly, pulling his way up Tull's arms till he reached his neck, where he clung like a frightened monkey.

"Here now," Jenks laughed, "What's this? You're spoiling our fun!"

Tull stopped in surprise. He'd imagined the old man dead on the floor. Only a moment ago he'd felt guilty for wishing it. "Leave him alone!" Tull said evenly, and he could feel the cold anger at the bottom of his soul aching for release. He fought it back, and the effort made his next words come out sounding like a whimper. "Leave him alone!"

"Or what?" his father laughed. "Or you'll cry all over me? Or you'll go home and pout for a week? Great God with your yellow teeth, save me from my whimpering son!"

"Just leave him alone!" Tull said, shaking.

"Ah, we were just having fun!" Jenks smiled. "So the boy's a bit frightened. He'll laugh about it when he's a man."

"He'll never laugh—" Tull said, "Just as I never laugh."

Jenks's face went blank. Tull could see desperation in his father's eyes, could see how his angry words hurt the old man. Jenks had always wanted so much to control his children, to force them to love him. "What . . . what are you saying, boy? Are you mad at me? What do you imagine I've done?"

Give the stupid beast a day and he'll forget what I've said, Tull thought. *That's how it always is. Jenks forgets the ugly words.* Tull looked at Jenks's barrel chest and thick arms. Cruel and empty eyes. Ugliness incarnate.

"By God, boy, if sneers were spears my ass would be dangling from a pole right now," Jenks said. "I'm glad to see you've inherited some of my spine. Speak up! What have I done?"

"What have you done!" Tull shouted and he wished he'd

found his father dead. He wanted to kill him now, and he
wondered if that is what Chaa had meant, that he should
kill his parents. Instead he turned and slammed his huge fist
into the stone wall. Blood spurted from his fingers as the
skin split on his knuckles. Wayan yelped and burrowed his
face into Tull's armpit. For a moment the whole room
swirled in a red haze, and Tull grabbed a stick of wood. His
arms ached with small cramps, the desire to strike out, and
yet he was afraid to strike, so he only shook the stick at
Jenks. Tull spat his next words, trying to strike a blow as
painful as one the stick could deliver: "You want to know
what you've done? You've been the kind of person that even
a starving Thrall whore couldn't love!"

"You ungrateful dog!" Jenks shouted, staggering back in
surprise, as if Tull had never said such words before. His
arms knotted into cords and his eyes glazed. "Don't you
talk to me like that in my own house! What have I done to
deserve such ingratitude? I gave you everything! I'm still
man enough to kick the shit out of you!"

"The way you'll kick the shit out of Wayan?" Tull asked.

Jenks seemed astonished at the accusation. For a moment his anger seemed to collapse in on itself. "Why, uh, I
love the boy! I wouldn't really hurt him. He's my own flesh!
Why, I was just having fun. We were both having fun!"

"Oh, you'd hurt him all right. You'd hurt him. You just
wouldn't kill him. And he wasn't having fun. You and me—
We. Never. Had. Fun!"

Jenks looked around the woodshed at a total loss.

Perhaps I've done it, Tull thought. *Perhaps I've pierced
through that thick skull of his. Maybe he'll go easier on
Wayan than he did on me.* Wayan cringed and began to cry
loudly. *I should go now.*

"Good-bye," he said.

"What? What?" Jenks shouted. "But . . . you can't
leave yet! You . . . you shit! You ungrateful shit. What's
going on here?"

Tull watched Jenks's face redden with rage again. He
sputtered curses, and Tull was unsure if he should turn his
back on the old man, so he backed away, Wayan still clinging to his neck. Jenks shouted, "Don't you close the door on
me!" and began advancing toward the door, kicking logs

from the woodpile. Tull slammed the woodshed door and fled the room. Jenks shouted curses at Tull, while his mother stood at the table, spooning soup into the tiny cup as if nothing were happening. Through all the years, every time Jenks had beaten Tull or Wayan, the woman had stood like that—frightened into doing nothing, like a statue, like a dead thing, Tull realized. His father and mother were both dead inside, dead to the hate and anger that seethed within these walls.

Tull didn't bother to say good-bye to her. He'd stopped caring for her years ago. He stepped out the front door, listened as Jenks kicked open the back door and overturned the kitchen table. A crowd of Neanderthals had gathered, come to see the commotion.

Tull walked down the street toward home, Wayan clinging to his neck. Tull stopped on the corner and found he was shaking with rage. Wayan whimpered, and Tull bounced him on his hip. He leaned his head back and closed his eyes. A drop of blood dripped from his nose. Jenks had broken Tull's nose when he was ten, and now Tull always got a nosebleed when he became angry. Moon Dance Inn was on the corner, not far away, and when Tull turned that corner he always felt a sense of freedom, felt the tightening in his chest diminish. "Don't cry," Tull whispered to Wayan. "Things will be better up here around the bend." He laughed in pain and let the anger wash out of him, then continued around the corner.

Caree Tech was still in her yard, stirring her cooking pot. She crooned, as if speaking an incantation:

Threads of iron, have sewn me to this world.
Threads of iron, have sewn me to this shore.
Threads of iron, have sewn me to this town.
Threads of iron, have sewn me to this street.

It was an old slave chant. Tull glanced at her and jiggled Wayan in his arms, bouncing him as if the child were an infant, even though he was nearly three. And Tull could feel the threads of iron that bound him to this place: the ugly memories, dark and desperate, of his home; the sweet sense of fulfillment he received in passing the inn; the sense of freedom from standing on this very street; the warmth and joy he felt in the presence of Ayuvah. Each was a thread in the tapestry of his life; each bound him to this place, defined his being, even as he struggled to escape such definition.

Wayan's hands were sticky from the soup, and his face was dirty. A small stream washed down through the hills and crossed the street under a culvert next to Caree's house. Tull took Wayan to the stream, dipped the end of his long black breech cloth in the water and began sponging the child's face. Wayan asked, "Tull, will you take me away?"

For a moment, Tull actually considered it. He hugged Wayan to his chest. "No. I'm going on a long trip. It's too dangerous. It's no trip for a child."

"I can't be here!" Wayan shrieked. "I will get hurt from Jenks!"

"He'll hurt you, but worse things can happen in the mountains," Tull said. "There are Mastodon Men in the mountains who would eat you. Besides, Jenks is growing soft in his old age; maybe he won't treat you as bad as he treated me. Just watch out for him when he comes home from hawking his junk, especially after a bad day. If he swaggers when he walks, run and hide from him—far away from the house. Stay away till after dark. Let him work his rage out by beating the dog. And if he catches you when he's in a bad mood, keep away from his feet so he can't kick you. After he beats you he'll want to apologize. He'll want you to hug him so that he'll know the apology is accepted. If you don't hug him, he'll get mad and beat you some more— so give in quick! Understand?"

"Yes," said Wayan.

"Good boy," Tull said, setting Wayan down on a rock. He wiped the soup from Wayan's face with the wetted breech cloth. "You'll get by all right. Now go home. Jenks is feeling sorry for himself now that I'm gone. He'll want to give you something nice so you'll like him. If you're smart, you'll let him." Tull stood up to leave.

"I'm smart," Wayan said, and Tull patted his head. Wayan clung to Tull's legs as if he were just learning to walk. His lower lip trembled and his green eyes were wide with terror at the thought of returning to the house.

Tull considered a moment. He didn't know if Wayan

could understand how Jenks wanted to control them, wanted to force them to love him. The old man had even gone so far as to give them names that a Neanderthal could never pronounce, forever keeping their mother from correctly uttering her sons' names. Jenks was a sick, selfish man, but Tull didn't know if he could describe the illness to a child so young. "And one last thing," Tull said. "Never talk about running away, or Jenks will chain you to your bed!"

Wayan didn't answer, just looked up with eyes wide with guilt, as if he'd done something wrong. Tull reached down and pulled up Wayan's pant legs. The boy had a shackle on his right leg. The same shackle Tull had worn as a child, and if Jenks had been in striking distance, Tull would have killed him. The shackle was thick and heavy, but it was only iron. Tull grabbed it with both hands, and such was his wrath that he pulled it hard enough to snap the hinges. For years as a child he had struggled to break that shackle, and instead he had only bruised and broken his leg against it.

Caree Tech was still crooning "Threads of iron, have sewn me to this house" narrowing in closer and closer, till the lines would end when she reached the part where the threads would have sewn her to her task. Tull knew Caree must have been reminiscing about her sister whom the slavers captured years before. Always the song ended with "Threads of iron, have sewn me to this oar. And threads of iron, bind me evermore."

Tull picked up the broken shackle, headed toward his parents' house. The words to the song hummed through his head, "Threads of iron, have sewn me to this town," and he walked past the bastard children jostling and playing tag by the inn, past the fabric shop and spice shop. "Threads of iron, have sewn me to this street." And he imagined that with each step he was bursting the threads of iron that bound him to this place, snapping the threads that bound him to his father, to his mother. "Threads of iron, have sewn me to this . . ." and he came to his father's house with its crowd of gawking Neanderthals still standing outside the door. Jenks was shrieking and tossing furniture inside. Tull kicked the door open.

Jenks shouted, "What are you doing here?" His face was

red with anger. His nostrils flared and his whole frame shook with rage. He rushed forward. When he was within arm's reach, Tull lashed out with the broken shackle, slamming it into the side of his father's head. Jenks dropped, blood spattering from a gash in his temple.

Tull did not know if he was dead or alive. He did not care. "Threads of iron do not sew me to this family," Tull said. Jenks rolled to his belly and began shaking his head, struggling to regain consciousness. Tull felt a little blood running from his nose, and he wiped it with his sleeve. He threw the shackle to the floor and looked at his mother who quietly stood in a corner, waiting for Jenks's tantrum to subside. Tull said calmly to his mother, "I'm leaving with Scandal the Gourmet. I'll be back in a few weeks. You and Jenks are dead to me now. But if I come back and find this shackle on Wayan's foot again, I'll make sure that you'll both be dead to the rest of the world, too."

Jenks said groggily, "He'sh my son. I own him. I'll do what I want."

Tull spun and headed out the door, trying not to limp, trying not to let them see him limp, and he found Wayan sitting by the stream where he'd left him. *Very obedient boy,* Tull thought.

Wayan grabbed Tull's leg when he got near, and clung to him. Tull ruffled the boy's hair, touching him very softly, and said, "Good-bye."

"I love you. Only," Wayan said, and he let loose of Tull's leg.

You are only a child, Tull thought. *How can you love anyone?* And deep inside himself, Tull felt something was wrong. He could not tell Wayan he loved him back. He was not sure if it were true. If Tull really loved Wayan, wouldn't he have done something before now? In spite of the powerful kwea that seemed to press Tull away from this part of town, wouldn't he have lived at home, been something more than a stranger? *It should not be so hard to love,* Tull thought. *Even ignorant children do it.* Tull felt he should answer Wayan in kind, should tell him he loved him. He did not know what to say to the boy.

Tull pried the child loose. Several of the Pwi were still

watching him, and in the crowd Tull saw Chaa, the old Spirit Walker, being supported by his wife.

Chaa walked forward, put his arms around Tull's neck and whispered in his ear, "When I entered you, I saw your loneliness. You must put loneliness aside. There is no sin greater than loneliness; no vessel can be as empty as a life without love. You cannot any longer be no-people, unfamily. Would you be willing to choose a new family from among the Pwi? Would you become a man of the Pwi?"

"Can this be done?" Tull asked.

Chaa nodded. "There is a ceremony for it, an old ceremony that has not been performed in my lifetime."

That night, 160 Pwi gathered on the banks of the Smilodon River a mile east of town to adopt Tull into the family. Freya, a small moon, was nearly full, and its pale blue light shattered the darkness. In the sky above, one Red Drone—an ancient war machine left by the Eridani to ensure that the inhabitants of Anee never took to the stars—moved in its orbit, a long red tube of light, brighter than a comet. Tull chose Chaa to be his father and Chaa's wife, Zhopila, to be his mother—making Ayuvah his brother. They were his best friends, so the arrangement made sense, and they were a close family. From his childhood, Tull had always dreamed of this—dreamed of being a member of a family like this. The word *Pwi* means both *family* and *person*. As far as the Pwi were concerned, to be one was to be both.

Amid the light from bonfires that reflected in the river, each mother from among the Pwi brought out a favorite piece of leather and told the group why it was her favorite: "I planned to make a coat for my child from this leather," one woman said, "and so I have worked it till it is very soft." "My brother painted a piya bird on this leather," another said, "and so I think it is beautiful." "My son killed the trees-on-head that made this leather, before he left for the House of Dust," a third woman said, and the memory made tears stream down her face. It was only old pain, and her husband comforted her while she remembered the son who had died. Chaa inspected the gifts of leather and agreed that each held kwea—a memory of power, of pain, or of love

—and, therefore, was sacred because it was also a gift from the heart.

The Pwi gathered together and sewed the leather into a great bag. The river was alive with the croaking of frogs, and a cool thermal wind crept down the river channel from the mountains.

When the bag was sewn, Chaa stood before the Pwi in the guttering torchlight and said, "No two men walk the same world. Kwea shapes each man's perceptions. Kwea shapes his loves and fears, and it is often not easy for the Pwi to understand one another.

"Here, we have Tull Genet, a man who has been Tcho-Pwi, and he is hard for us to understand, for he sometimes thinks like a human. Yet I say that he is Pwi, and that it is right for us to adopt him into the family.

"My grandfather taught me that all things are Connected: when a man plants wheat in a field he makes bread from it, and it is easy to see that the man would not exist without the bread, and it is also easy to see that the bread would not exist without the labor of the man. If you are alive to Connections, then certainly you will see that the man and the bread, they are not separate, but are one thing. They are two parts of a greater whole.

"But the bread and the man, they could not exist without the wheat. And the wheat cannot exist without the rain and the oceans and the sun and the soil and the worms within the soil. And both the bread and the man who eats the bread become Connected to all of these things, and they are not separate, but part of a greater whole.

"You are rain and soil and sunlight and wind and oceans. Always there is an ocean throbbing in your veins, and when you exhale, you add force to the winds, and when you work in a field on a hot day, the sweat of your body rains upon the ground, and when you are joyful, you release sunlight in the twinkling of your eyes."

Chaa said, "We are not only Connected to all things, but to all other people. You have known Tull for many years, and each of you feel kwea for him. It is right that he become one of us, that he become Pwi. Who will be the midwife?" Chaa called.

Old Vi, a woman who had served as a midwife many

times, came forward. Chaa gave her his ceremonial dagger with its blade carved from a carnosaur's tooth. Tull stepped into the bag of leather, and all the Pwi set great stones in the bag, sewed it closed, dragged it to the river, and threw the bag in. The bag began sinking, and Tull struggled to tear the bag open before the air escaped. The air in the bag was hot, and smelled of brine and sweat and flesh. Tull manipulated the stones into a pile near his feet, and a bubble of air gathered at the top of the bag. The bag was so large he could not push against the sides to tear it; so he pulled at the seams, struggling to find a weak spot where the leather would tear. He worked at it for several minutes, and the pocket of air slowly seeped from the top of the bag, and, suddenly, enough air escaped so it would no longer float. The bag sank quickly and all air hissed out in a rush. Tull pulled with all his might, ripping his fingernails as he tugged at the leather. He struggled to hold his breath.

And suddenly the bag lifted, pulled from the water by many hands. Tull quit ripping at the bag and gasped for air, but air did not pass through the wet leather. Old Vi sank her knife into the bag near his face, and Tull pushed forward, sucked the air gratefully. Water spilled from the bag, ripping it. Tull crawled out on his belly, panting.

All the Pwi gathered around, holding burning brands of wood from the fire.

"It is a boy child!" Vi said in mock surprise. "Very large —the biggest I have delivered!" The Pwi laughed and cheered.

"A new boy is born into our family," Chaa said, his voice frail and shaken. Everyone quieted to hear the name Chaa would give Tull. The name was very important, a prophecy of the type of person Tull would become. "I have walked the path of his future, and I shall call him *Lashi Chamepar,* Path of the Crushed Heart."

It was not a good name for a Pwi, not the name of an animal or plant—like Chaa, the dark crow of magic and wisest of birds, or Fava, the pear, most generous of trees. The name should describe the qualities of the person named, or the qualities the person would develop. Tull stared hard at Chaa, and the Spirit Walker's face was still drawn in horror, even though he tried to remain smiling like a Pwi.

Then Tull understood: the name described the person Tull would become, a man with a crushed heart.

The Pwi came forward and hugged Tull, welcomed him into the family, all of them talking at once. Fava hugged him. "I have seen you watch Isteria," she said, pronouncing *Wisteria* as best she could, "that human girl. Now that you are Pwi, you will look at girls in your own family," and Tull blushed. By Pwi standards he was obscenely old to be single, as was Fava. Twice, Pwi girls had set their belongings on his doorstep, and he had turned them away. An old man hugged him and reminded, "I have two daughters, and they both need a husband; perhaps one wife would not be enough for you?" And when the marriageable girls in the village hugged him, some hugged him with passion so that their breasts pressed firm against him. He could feel every soft curve on the young women as they advertised their wares.

Some Pwi left early, for they sorely mourned the deaths of Denni and Tchar. But others sang and danced, guzzling beer from a barrel until the air smelled sour and warm and sticky; then they spun madly and jumped into the air until they could no longer stand. When Tull went home to sleep, he went to the home of his new Pwi family.

For a while, he sat up with Ayuvah's little daughter Sava and made her a tiny sailboat from a walnut shell. Ayuvah told his mother about seeing Little Chaa touch the mayor's Dryad, and Zhopila had a fit. "You stay away from that monster!" the old woman shouted in genuine fear. "Or someday she will carry you away from home to be her lover, and make you her slave." She told the boy the story of Tchulpa and the Dryad of the Pines:

Long ago, the Starfarers created many trees and animals —both the mammoth and the redwood and the beasts in Hotland, but their work was not done. So, to finish their work, they gave birth to seven Creators—beasts terrible to look upon: Xicame to rule the fishes of the sea. Mema and Va to rule the birds, lizards, snakes, the three breeds of dragons, and serpents. Dwafordotch to rule the insects. Zheforso to rule the hairy beasts, Hukm, Mastodon Men, and the

Pwi. Theva to rule the deserts and plains. Forethorun to rule the jungles and trees. Each of the Creators gave birth to new plants and animals, filling the world with life and death.

But when he was yet young, a mountain fell upon Forethorun. So, in his place, the six Creators made Dryads to tend the trees.

In those days, Tchulpa, a man of the Pwi with a beautiful wife and six beloved children, went into the forest with his basket to hunt for pine nuts in the month of White, and while he was walking, he heard a woman singing, and he crept toward her and found her singing by a river. Her skin was green, like the leaves of a young pine tree, and softer than the petals of a flower. She was as graceful as a walking deer, and her nipples bobbed like peonies in the wind. Her beauty was above that of any woman.

Her voice was more beautiful than any earthly speech—as if the meadowlark had lent her his song, and she sang of love, so Tchulpa thought that surely this must be the goddess Zhofwa who blows her kisses upon young people so they fall in love. He thought he should hide himself, because he did not want to look upon the goddess.

Tchulpa begged her to leave before the desire he felt for her slew him, for he loved his wife deeply, but the woman pretended not to hear his pleas and she put her lips upon his. And in that moment, he knew she must be the goddess Zhofwa, for the desire he felt for this woman rose up. So great was the lust that it swallowed his desire for all other women. His beautiful wife seemed deformed and twisted in comparison to this goddess. And just as a husk upon an oat stem will sometimes fool us into believing that we have found grain in winter, he thought that surely his beautiful wife was only a husk of a woman after all, and he had somehow been deceived into loving her. His love for his children and the Pwi was swept away, too, in this madness. And when he lay with the woman upon the soft moss of the forest floor, he felt as if he were buoyed upon waves of lust, and he thought that surely he was giving his love to Zhofwa herself.

But when he was done, the beautiful green woman turned her back upon him. He went to stay with her in her home of living trees, but she took no notice of him. During the day she took dung and buried it at the roots of the pines, and she did not give love to him the way that a wife should. She searched among the needles of the pines for grubs and caterpillar nests and then she would squash them, and she barely took time to find food for herself.

At night, she talked of her work among the trees, and of her love for the trees, but she never spoke of her love for Tchulpa. If he left the room to get firewood, she would take no notice and instead talk of her love for her trees.

Tchulpa became sad with the despair-that-leads-to-death, and he realized finally that she had no love in her. Instead, he thought she must be a demon, created by the earth to punish men for how they treat the trees. He remembered his wife, and wished he could see her, but each day he would look upon the Dryad and the kwea of the moment when they first made love would come upon him. He would think back and become her slave all over again, as if he were a Thrall held in chains by a Slave Lord, and he could not leave.

Days melted into months and months melted into years. After three summers, the Dryad bore a daughter with skin as green as pine needles. Tchulpa became angry, for she had not made love to him for three years, so it seemed obvious that she had borne a child from another man.

One day, the Dryad wandered away, and in her devotion to the trees, she stayed away for nights catching moths that were laying their eggs. When Tchulpa found her again, he was furious, for he was sure she had gone off to sleep with another man while he tended her child. In those days, the Pwi did not know that Dryads mate only once and give birth slowly over the years, so he did not know the green daughter was his.

He dragged his wife home by the hair and tried to make love to her, but she fought him away. He screamed and tore his hair out in frustration, but she said, "I love only the pines!" Tchulpa thought that she must have made love to a tree spirit and the tree spirit had fathered the green daughter, and he went crazy. This was in the month of Dragon, and the forest was dry, so Tchulpa picked up a brand from the fire and ran outside and tossed the fire into the pine trees.

The Dryad ran from the hut with her daughter, and she saw the fire raging in all the trees, so she took a knife and stabbed Tchulpa in the shoulder. She screamed, and twisted her face into a mask of rage.

In that moment, Tchulpa looked into her eyes and saw that she was an animal. He ran from her then, but as he looked back into the forest, he saw many green women with doe eyes chasing him. He ran for his life. The Dryads ripped him with their fingernails and bit him with their teeth, but Tchulpa escaped them all. The Dryads' cries followed him through the forest until he reached a band of oaks, and the pine women would not follow him into the oaks.

Tchulpa's heart was torn, for he remembered his love for his wife and children. For a time, he would not eat, but hoped to find comfort in the House of Dust with his ancestors. Yet, he knew he could not let himself die without first telling his wife and children what happened and begging their forgiveness.

When he reached his village, his back and legs were swollen and infected with green pus that ran from him like sap from a tree—the worst kind. He told the Pwi his story, but everyone thought it was fever talking. So they brought him in, lanced his wounds, washed him gently. They thought he must have gone through a terrible ordeal, and his wife was only happy to have her husband alive again, for she thought he had wandered off a cliff and died. That night, as his wife Azha tended him, so happy to have her loved one home again, she put her husband by the fire and fell asleep. She woke to the sound of Tchulpa's cry. A nude woman with skin the color of pine needles stood above Tchulpa, and she ran from the room so quickly and quietly that Azha thought she must be dreaming. Azha rushed to her husband, and he coughed blood into the air. In Tchulpa's chest was a stake, whittled from a branch of blackened pine.

Tchulpa lifted his head and said, "Remember the kwea of the night we became husband and wife? That kwea is upon me. I feel nothing for that animal anymore." Azha nodded and took his hand. With his own blood, Tchulpa drew the joined circles, the symbol of eternal love, upon her hand before he died.

Tull listened and smiled. Years ago, he'd realized that humans always seem to tell stories of conquest, of men who bulldog mammoths into the ground and slaughter each other in battle, but the Pwi always seemed to tell stories about reconciliation. The Pwi told of brothers or lovers or friends who went to war in their youth, and only a great act of love or sacrifice could heal the evil kwea built up over years. Such stories seemed odd—as if the Pwi believed that every fence could be mended, all hate and anger washed away. Tull only had to look at his relationship with Jenks to see how false this notion was. Yet the story of Tchulpa and the Dryad made him happy, for it was backward: Tchulpa did not find happiness until he learned to fall out of love, and that seemed important to Tull. Only the silly ending, with Tchulpa drawing the symbol of eternal love on his wife's hand seemed false. Tull imagined Tchulpa, instead, gasping "Oh shit!" as he died.

Zhopila went to her room to sleep, and the rest of the family lay on the floor in the living room and talked late into the night. Little Chaa, although he was only twelve, made plans to accompany Tull to Seven Ogre River, and finally fell asleep. Ayuvah lay on the floor next to his wife and daughter. Fava, Tull's new sister, lay to Tull's right. Fava's five little brothers and sisters slept on the other side of her. With so many people in the house, the room was very warm.

Tull could not sleep, lying so close to Fava. Her legs were long and bare in her summer dress, and he could feel the ribbons that signified her maidenhood around her legs as she leaned into him. Her hair was scented with vanilla water, and she smelled very clean and desirable. He could not smell beer on her breath, perhaps because it was still so strong on his own. He sat up on one elbow, and his head spun. *It should not be so hard to love,* he thought. *Even ignorant children can do it.* He knew by her breathing that she was still awake, so he wrapped his arm around her to see what she would do, his clamshell bracelet rattling in the dark. She squeezed his hand and placed it on her stomach, drew figure eights on the back of his hand. The figure eight, two circles forever joined, was the Pwi symbol for marriage. Tull did not know if it was better to leave his hand and encourage her or to pull it away and deny his attraction. But among the Pwi, marriage was a sacred thing. When a man and woman married, they married for life, and the kwea became so strong that when one mate died, then, unless they had children, the other mate stopped eating, stopped drinking, and followed his or her beloved to the grave. Only a cruel man encouraged a Pwi to love him unless he were willing to return that love. Tull pulled his hand away.

Fava sat up, very quietly, and straddled his back, her long strong legs hugging his ribs. She massaged his shoulders gently, and bent low so that her hair tickled his back. Her cool lips gently brushed his neck. "Turn over," she whispered. She got off and let Tull roll to his back, then she straddled his stomach and massaged his chest and shoulders. Having Fava on top of him made Tull dizzy with lust. She bent low and whispered into his ear, *"Ah Tell-zhoka-thrall! Ah Tell-zhoka-ta-pwi-randi!* Tull, give me the love that enslaves! Tull, give me the love that makes people crazy!"

Tull pulled her down and kissed her, stroked her face a moment. He stopped and pushed her away, wanting to go no further. When Tull was twelve, he'd heard the word *love,* but he did not believe in it. Having never felt loved by others, he felt none in return. Love was an emotion people pretended to feel, or perhaps a delusion commonly held by the rest of the world. But that summer, Tull's parents had moved to Smilodon Bay, and he met Ayuvah's family—a father who felt pain for his children and cried with them when they hurt; a mother who not only spoke of love but showed it in every small act. For the first time he understood that there really was such a thing as love in the world. Like a tender forest plant that grows in feeble light, he searched inside himself for love, for the ability to love another.

Until tonight, Tull had always envied Ayuvah for his parents. But now, Chaa was his father, and Ayuvah was his brother. *Today, for the first time, I am Pwi,* he thought. *I am a person. I am family. For now, that is enough.* He knew he could take Fava to wife, but for the moment to be part of a real family was enough.

Chaa had stayed late at the party, and Tull awoke at night and became worried, for the old Neanderthal shaman was still weak from his Spirit Walk. Tull got up from the floor and picked his way through the sleeping bodies, went outside.

The air was still. Freya and Woden, the two smallest moons, shone blue and white in the night sky. Tull softly sang an old Pwi song:

> *The sun is finally falling, now the stars shine on the*
> * sand,*
> *And I hear the Darkness conjuring dream images*
> * again,*
> *Darkness brings peace to those who seek it, scatters*
> * wisdom where it can,*
> *For Darkness is lover to the poet, the dreamer, and the*
> * solitary man.*

It was a song of darkness, a song made for lonely men.

From the side of the house, Chaa said, "There is no vessel as empty as a life without love. You should be in the house, making love to Fava." Tull could see him in the moonlight. The old shaman stood with his head tilted to the side. Chaa's face was wet, for he had been crying softly. As he drew closer, Tull could tell by the smell that the old man was drunk on warm beer.

"What is the matter?" Tull asked.

Chaa said bitterly, "If there are gods, I hate them."

"Shhh—speak softly," Tull warned. "They might hear you."

"They know when we will blindly fall into a pit, yet they do not warn us," Chaa said.

"That is why we have a Spirit Walker. That is why we have you," Tull answered. "You are afraid things will go bad for us on this journey. It is drawn on your face. I think you fear for your sons. If you do not want Ayuvah and Little

Chaa to come to Craal to catch the serpents, tell me. But if you want them to come, I will protect them—even from slavers."

Chaa did not speak, and Tull took his hand and led him into the house. *And if there are gods, then I am worse than them,* Chaa thought. *For not only do I not warn my sons of the pit, I send them there to die.*

Chapter 3
Blue Holiday

The morning after the Pwi adopted Tull, Scandal tore out the front wall of his inn and rolled a three-thousand-gallon beer keg into the street. The giant keg, with three taps affixed to the bottom of one end, had been a fixture at the back wall of the inn for thirty years. Yet it was mere decoration, for Scandal never brewed his beer in the giant keg—only filled it several times a year from smaller barrels.

Nearly everyone in town showed up for the event, for it was rumored that the barrel was half-full of beer and Scandal would give it out free!

Yet when a dozen men managed to move the counters, tear down the front wall, and get it into the street, the barrel was only an eighth full—a mere four hundred gallons, barely enough to satisfy the five hundred people who showed up.

They tipped the barrel upright, and Tull stood on top with an ax and beat his way through. The keg was over ten feet tall and twelve feet in diameter and was made of four-inch oak planks, bound with iron rings. When it finally broke, the whole plaza stank of beer.

Scandal said, "Put a few serpents in there, and they'll party! They'll be floating ass-backward within an hour."

"Ayaah," Tull said, and with that, a dozen men tipped the barrel over sideways so Tull had to jump for it, and everyone rushed to steal some beer in their cupped hands.

Scandal's steward, Valis, saw what was happening and shouted, "Stop! Stop!"

"Oh, let them drink!" Scandal said loud enough for everyone to hear. "I can't sell it anyway—not after I let my dog piss in it."

Wisteria Troutmaster came down from her father's home on the hill to see the celebration. Tull stared at her, and she saw no harm in smiling at him. It had been seven years since she'd last talked to him. Seven years since her father had sent her to school in South Bay. Although she'd been in town for weeks, she hadn't spoken to him alone.

"How have you been?" Tull asked. "I know you've been back for a while. I wanted to talk to you, but I was in Hotland most of last month. I've seen you a few times since, but I never got to talk to you. You've changed. You're more beautiful."

"Not beautiful," she said. "Taller, stronger maybe."

"And more lithe, like a dancer," Tull said. She didn't want to hear this, knew that news of this conversation would get back to her father. Tull had grown tall in the past seven years, muscular. When he was young, he'd been like a beast to her, an animal intent on listening to distant music. He stared at her, and she saw that he was still an animal, moving to his own private rhythm.

"I had to study dance in school," Wisteria said.

"A thousand miles is a long way to go to school," Tull said. "What did you learn?"

"At Lady Devarre's School of Merchantry?" she asked. "I learned to shoot a pistol, eat a formal dinner in Craal, balance a ledger, how to screw my competitors yet retain my virginity—all the things a lady needs to know in business." She laughed quaintly, and realized she was trying to seem worldly to him. "I'm sorry," she said.

"Sorry for what?" Tull asked.

"I . . . I just meant, nothing."

"Have things changed much here in town?"

She looked around, "I don't know. I always felt so small and powerless here, invisible, like a leaf blowing in the wind. I was so intimidated by everything here when I was a child. Now the town seems smaller, and all the people I was afraid of have shrunk and grown old." A small gust of wind kicked up, blew her long chestnut hair into her face. She combed it back into place with one hand. She was being perfectly honest with him, more open than she wanted. "You're the only thing around here that has grown."

"Will you be staying?" Tull asked.

"Why, do you want to start where we left off, in the alley?" She realized she was trying to sound worldly again. She'd often thought of Tull, of the afternoon they'd spent together necking, of his warm sweaty hands exploring her breasts. Her attempt at seduction had cost Wisteria her self-respect, her family. Her father learned of it and shipped her off to school the following morning. He had plans for his daughter.

"Yes!" Tull said with such intensity that she stepped back and laughed.

"I think I'd better stay away from you," she teased. "Or my father will have me back in school for another seven years."

Wisteria backed away from the crowd, took Tull's hand. The sun was bright, and the hill above the inn was full of people sitting in the shade of the pine trees. She headed up the hill, looking for shade, and Tull limped along behind.

"Did you hurt yourself when you jumped off the barrel?" she asked, but then remembered how he often limped, how it came and went with the weather. "Oh, I'd forgotten," she said.

From under the shadows of a tree, a thin Pwi woman with leathery skin, ash blond hair turning to silver, rose as if to meet Wisteria. The old woman edged past Wisteria and grabbed Tull's arm.

"Last night, you struck your father!" Tull's mother shrieked in Pwi as if informing him of something he wouldn't remember. Wisteria struggled to catch the words. "You said I was dead to you! I heard you! I held the words in my heart all night! You should not have said such a thing. You killed me with words. How can you be so mad?" She clutched his arm, her fingers digging in and out, in and out, just as a cat will do to someone it loves. Tull tried to pull away, but the old woman clung to him and she was thrown forward a step. Wisteria could tell from the woman's voice that she was sincerely ignorant, that she didn't understand why Tull was mad. Yet Wisteria recalled how Tull had always come out of the house in the morning with cracked lips and a bloody nose, recalled how Feron House had once pulled Jenks off Tull when Jenks tried to drown Tull in a watering trough. Jenks had vehemently denied that he was killing Tull, yet the furor in town had not died down for months. The white scars from the shackles were still on Tull's legs for all to see. Wisteria wondered how the old woman could forget.

"Jenks is evil," Tull said. "He hurt me when I was small; now he hurts Wayan."

Tull's mother bit her lip and watched him from under deep-set brows. She had no chin, and it made her face look like a sheet twisted into a knot. Tull waited for her to deny the accusation, to say something. "You're right," she said. "But I don't know what to do. When you were a baby, I tried to give you to my sister. But Jenks got so mad, I thought he'd beat me, and he kept you." She looked down to the ground in helplessness.

"When did you try to give me away?" Tull asked in amazement.

"When you were small enough so I could carry you in one arm. And Jenks scared me so bad!"

She put her hands up to hide her eyes and wept, but it was only kwea caused by the memory of her fear. Tull touched her shoulder, a Pwi caress. Wisteria could not understand how the woman could weep for herself—not when Tull had taken all the beatings. She was so weak. Wisteria imagined she'd have handled things differently.

"You are not dead to me," Tull told the old woman. "Only Jenks. Jenks is dead to me."

Tull's mother wiped her eyes and looked up into his face. She turned away and walked down the street, shaking like a leaf that trembles in the wind. "Jenks and I are one," she said. "He is my beloved. So we must both be dead to you."

Tull cursed silently under his breath.

Wisteria looked at others on the hill, realized that she was still standing next to Tull, that although she'd hoped for a private conversation, everyone was staring at them, and now her father would surely hear that she'd been with Tull. The humans were watching Tull and his mother in amusement. Here and there people reported the gist of the conversation to those who did not understand Pwi. *Ayaah, they came for a show,* she thought, *and by god's lolling tongue, they got one.*

Downhill, someone shouted, "Phylomon! Phylomon of the Starfarers has come to our town!" Several people were pointing toward the south end of town, and Wisteria looked down toward the bend in the road by the redwood bridge. From the hill above the inn, she could see the warehouse district and Pwi-town across the river. She could not see the blue man, yet the children began running toward Pwi-town.

Everyone in town knew of the blue man—last living child of the refugee Starfarers who had terraformed Anee. Phylomon had wandered the planet for well over a thousand years, outliving his brethren by centuries, kept alive by his ancient technologies, and everyone had heard the legends of how he'd led the attack that decimated the holds of the Pirate Lords at Bashevgo; every saying that sounded as if it had truth or wisdom in it was attributed to him.

Wisteria watched the end of the street. The blue man stepped from the shadows of a pine tree onto the redwood bridge. He was tall, nearly seven feet, and willowy slender, as legend said all men were in the days of the old Starfaring race. His face was eternally young, like that of a twenty-year-old. He wore a knee-length breech cloth made of buckskin, and his naked chest was crisscrossed with heavy leather straps and bangles—a strap for his quiver, a strap for the long narrow sword sheathed on his back, a strap for his packsack. In his right hand he carried a bow of onyx black dragon horn. He wore a necklace with pale silver medallions on it, each made from glowing metal unlike anything native to the metal-poor planet Anee. He had no hair—neither on his head, his chest, nor arms. He could have been a salamander, his skin was so smooth. And every inch of his flesh was a pale, pale blue—the color of the summer sky on the horizon.

Wisteria began running toward him, but the blue man raised his hand to ward them away, and the entire town seemed to stop. The blue man eyed the mayor's pet stegosaur, and everyone in town watched to see what he'd do. The mayor's stegosaur had wandered down from feeding in the hills and walked underneath someone's clothesline. The bony plates running the length of the stegosaur's back had snagged a dark green dress, and it waved in the light breeze like a flag. The stegosaur stood in the roadway scratching its belly by rubbing against the wheel of a wagon, and a cowbird fluttered above the stegosaur's back, angered at being pushed off so comfortable a resting place. The dinosaur was only three years old and, therefore, no heavier than a huge bull. The wagon it scratched against creaked as if it would crumble.

Mayor Goodstick had eight brothers, and people in town had long since learned to look the other way when the mayor's pet monster tore up a wagon or accidentally speared a dog on its tail. "Someday that thing will grow up and trample a child!" all the women in the neighborhood would say. "And then it will have to go!" But, so far, the children had managed to keep from under the monster's feet, and no one dared to demand that the mayor get rid of the dangerous beast.

The mayor's hounds began barking, and the stegosaur quit scratching its belly. Many people opened their windows and doors to see the last Starfarer, for the blue man had not visited this part of the world for fifty years. Yet, strangely, few people spoke.

Phylomon walked softly across the redwood bridge and up the dirt road toward the stegosaur. The beast turned its side toward the blue man, began twitching its spiked tail in warning, and pulled its head beneath the bony plates along its back.

Phylomon reached into his quiver, pulled out an arrow, fitted it to the string of his bow. He studied the stegosaur a moment. Wisteria had often heard men tell of their exploits to Hotland. They all said it was hard to kill a stegosaur. The parietal plate on the stegosaur's skull is very thick, making the walnut-size brain a poor target. Besides, even if the blue man were to hit it, it is the hindbrain on the stegosaur—a thickened portion of the spine—that controls the lashing of its deadly tail, and the hindbrain was hidden beneath heavy hide and armor plating. Phylomon crouched and fired an arrow into the monster's throat, severing the carotid artery.

The stegosaur jerked double and its tail whipped to the side, striking the wagon's front wheel. The wheel splintered and the wagon dropped. The stegosaur's tail lashed back and forth. For a moment it looked as if the spikes would be buried in the planks of the wagon bed, but the planks began to shatter. The tail seemed to be working on its own, striking again and again at the wagon, as if glad to have a target. Blood spurted from the stegosaur's throat, and it kicked its legs as if struggling to outrace death, then it began to roll like an alligator, thrashing with its tail as it rolled. Phylomon went to the wagon, pulled a length of rope from its bed, made a loop, tossed it over the stegosaur's spiked tail, and cinched it tight. The monster thrashed, unaware of Phylomon, and he tied the beast to a tree so it wouldn't knock down the walls of some house in its death throes.

The Pwi came running, shouting to newcomers the tale of the demise of the mayor's beast, and the humans wandered from their houses, curious about this man who appeared so seldom. The Pwi crowded round Phylomon and some of the bolder children even reached out to touch him.

Phylomon straightened his back and his head bobbed above the crowd. People were shouting to one another, and he asked a question so softly that Wisteria couldn't hear him. She'd stood still while he killed the beast, but now she ran toward him again.

No one answered the blue man's question, but several people glanced up toward the mayor's house. Phylomon looked up at the house, and trudged toward it, kicking up dust. People were still talking loudly, and over the din Wisteria heard Caree Tech say quite clearly, "Careful—the mayor has eight brothers!"

Phylomon nodded. A man with so many kin in a small town has great power. Phylomon approached the house, then saw the Dryad sitting in her cage in the beating sun.

Phylomon approached the cage and said with infinite gentleness, "What are you doing here, Aspen Woman?" His voice was very soft and did not carry well—as if his vocal cords had become atrophied after living for years in solitude. He reached through the bars of the cage to stroke her silver hair. The bars were made of mottled aspen—the tree she'd been created to nurture. Her genetic programming would not let her break the bars, even to escape. She was young, just developing her breasts—near the time when her kind were driven into a mating frenzy. "You are a great danger to the people here in town. You should be with your sisters in the mountains, tending your trees."

And for the first time since reaching Smilodon Bay, words flowed the Dryad's mouth. Her voice had a soft musical quality that reverberated like the voice of flute. "The mayor keeps me caged," she said. "He plans to sell me to slavers in Craal."

Several people gasped at the startling beauty of her voice. Phylomon tilted his head, like a robin studying a worm. "So," he said quietly, "first your mayor defies the old laws by bringing a dinosaur to our land, and then he begins selling slaves to boot."

And with that Mayor Goodstick appeared in his doorway, a large man in girth, with more muscle than fat. "I'm not a slaver," Goodstick said. There was only a trace of fear in his voice, and he carried a tone of authority that the blue man's voice could not equal. "The Dryad is in my care. Is something wrong?"

"You mean she's in your *cage.*" Phylomon held the mayor's eye a moment, drew his sword, and sliced at the wooden bars of the Dryad's cage, cutting it as if it were a potato. The Dryad pushed at her bars and began wriggling out.

The mayor blustered, speaking to Phylomon. "But sir! I'm sorry if I've offended you. I mean no harm. Why, I raised that dinosaur from an egg," he said, nodding toward the stegosaur. "The Pwi bring eggs from Hotland every year —and no one ever knows what sort of beast will hatch from them. Why, every boy in town has had such an egg at least once! It's great fun to see what will hatch—but the dinosaurs always die come winter! Only a freak of chance let this beast make it through the winters! And, as for the Dryad, why, she's not human! It's not as if I were selling a human! She cost me a great deal—and I've fed her these past three months hoping to get a decent price for her!"

Phylomon listened to the mayor's blustering words without watching him, then turned a questioning eye. Wisteria looked at the mayor and tried to imagine him as Phylomon must see him. Goodstick was a large man, and strong. Not the kind to be easily bullied. And the lines in the mayor's face were hard and secretive.

"I will gladly buy the Dryad," Phylomon said calmly. He reached down to his belt and pulled out a small bag, loosed the string that bound it, and dumped the bag's contents into his palm. Diamonds, sapphires, and pearls gleamed in his palm. The whole town gasped. "Take whichever stone you think fair."

The mayor eyed the stones and concentrated. Sweat began to break out on his forehead. Obviously he did not want to appear greedy—greed is the father of sin. The girl was not worth even a large sapphire, Wisteria knew. The mayor took a diamond. A medium-large diamond. A diamond that could buy a ship.

Phylomon smiled at the mayor, as if pleased with his choice. "What town is this?"

"Smilodon Bay," the mayor said, suddenly distant, fearful. He thrust the diamond in his pocket.

"And if you went to war tomorrow with Thrall pirates, how many men could you muster?"

Without hesitation, Goodstick answered, "Eighty-six men of war. More, if you want old ones or young."

"Then have a hundred men of war down at the docks at dusk. Have them bring their weapons," Phylomon said, "for I will speak to them."

Most of the town stood within hearing range of Phylomon's words, and the rest of the people seemed to be on their way. Wisteria watched the mayor intently. Lady Devarre had taught her girls to try to read a competitor's thoughts just by the way he held his head, the way the nervous lines crinkled near his eyes, the timbre of his voice. Mayor Goodstick knew there was no threat from pirates and he feared to gather the town. Phylomon could be plotting to turn the townsmen against him. "So be it," the mayor shouted with false enthusiasm.

"I have often heard good report of the inn of Scandal the Gourmet," Phylomon said. "Is this the town where it lies? Could someone tell him that I'd like a room for the night?"

Scandal's bellowing voice cut through the crowd. "You can tell me yourself!" he said, and the townspeople laughed, a false nervous laugh.

"I've heard you have a bed in one of your rooms—a very special bed, guaranteed free from vermin," Phylomon said softly as Scandal shoved the crowd aside, making room for his belly to squeeze through. "Is that room available?"

"Well, a bed is only as free of vermin as the man who's sleeping in it. If you want *that* bed, you'll have to hike up your breech cloth and let me check for fleas, just like every other customer!" Scandal said, playing to the crowd.

Phylomon smiled and pulled up his breech cloth, exposing his legs. Scandal grunted and bent over, making a great show of examining the blue man's legs.

"I hereby declare this man to be totally free of vermin!" Scandal announced, laughing. "And, therefore, worthy of my finest room—free of charge!"

Several people cheered. Now that the introduction was over, the crowd began to thin. Phylomon said, "Then show me to your inn." Phylomon took the Dryad's hand and helped her rise. Together they made their way across the town and up the hill to the inn.

Wisteria searched the crowd for her father. She was unsure what to make of the blue man's visit, and wanted to ask her father about it, but he was not in the crowd. She rushed home to the large house on the north end of town. Her mother quietly prepared lunch in the kitchen. Her father sat in a large upholstered chair in his study, reading *The Sayings,* a book of wise words purportedly spoken by Phylomon over the centuries. Beremon Troutmaster had graying hair and bright blue eyes. He was a learned man, knowledgeable about the arcane mathematics and physical theories that let the Starfarers travel faster than light, a man who'd made a fortune backing shipping ventures in dangerous waters, a man others feared because he himself was a rare genetic throwback to the Starfarers—Beremon Troutmaster was a

Dicton, one of the few humans left on Anee who carried the extra pair of genetically engineered chromosomes that were the Starfarers' greatest legacy. Beremon could calculate nearly any mathematical problem instantly, and from birth he had known every word in the ancient universal trade language of the Starfarers, English. As a Dicton, Beremon was marked from birth to become a man of power, and he lived true to his promise: Because of the extreme gravitational pull of the gas giant Thor, Anee's tides could fluctuate by a hundred feet in hours, and during raging storms, a strong gravitational wind could send a sailing ship a thousand miles from its destination overnight and leave it smashed against a rocky coast. By using his knowledge of mathematics to calculate the shifting tides, the precise moment when the gravitational winds would surge, Beremon reduced the risk to his own ships, and over the years he expanded his hold on the shipping industry until, by age forty, he'd become the most powerful shipping magnate and financier in the Rough.

"Father, Phylomon the Starfarer is in town!" Wisteria said loudly.

"I know," Beremon said, "I heard the shouting."

"What is he doing here?" Wisteria asked.

"He often travels from continent to continent, studying animal and plant populations, doing what he can to keep nature regular. If he had skin the color of any other man's, we'd think him a vagabond. We'd let him stay in town a day or two, watch our clotheslines and gardens to see what he steals, and the mayor would finally sic his dogs on him and send him on his way."

"That's not what I mean," Wisteria said. "I mean, what is he doing here, in this town, now?"

"He doesn't visit towns often," Beremon said. "He tires quickly of us short-lived people who can never attain a mental caliber equal to his. He is a man of great intelligence, and he lives alone, and when men like him live alone, their thoughts begin to travel in strange, circular paths. Who am I to guess what he might be thinking? Perhaps he has heard of Scandal's quest? The innkeep has made no secret of it. Or perhaps his visit is coincidental. I've heard from sailors that he's been in Craal the last few years, and down south in

Benbow two years ago, he caused quite a stir. It seems that he's quite taken aback at the way slavery has become a fad in the last century. He's begun to enforce some of the laws of our ancestors. If you have time, you might persuade a few friends to begin cutting wood for funeral pyres."

Wisteria's stomach tightened. She'd feared as much—he'd come to kill the mayor and the other slavers. She feared to speak her next words even more. "Will he kill you?"

Beremon looked up from his book. He smiled weakly. "You think so little of me?"

"I'm sorry," Wisteria said. Yet she knew he was a slaver: When she was a child, her mother had had a running feud with a neighbor woman named Javan Tech for several months. Javan had accused Wisteria's mother, Elyssa, of stealing some nails, and no matter what Elyssa or Beremon did, Javan kept trying to prejudice others against them. Finally, in desperation, Beremon caught Javan and tied her in their basement for a week until he could persuade the mayor to help stash her in the hold of a departing ship. Wisteria herself had helped feed and water the woman.

"Sorry?" Beremon asked. "Don't be sorry. I made one mistake when I was young. Carting that bitch Javan out of town and selling her to Craal seemed a good idea at the time. A fun idea. We got rid of a problem, and made some pocket change in the bargain. I still think it was a fun idea. But remember, My Apple, it was only once."

"I saw Tull today—we talked," Wisteria said. "I wanted to tell you, before you heard it from others."

"I'm not surprised that he found you. The Pwi are like dogs that way, always sniffing at the source of joy. You will not see him socially, of course," Beremon said. "You are the daughter of a Dicton, and if you are lucky you might give birth to a Dicton. Your body is a great asset, and you should marry only into the finest family. I will arrange a suitable marriage shortly."

"I'm sorry," Wisteria said, backing out of the study, out the door, not sure if she was sorry for seeing Tull or sorry because she would be forced to marry a stranger. Talking to her father like this was always unbearable. The look of disgust he'd had on his face when he learned of her affair with Tull, the guilt she'd felt when she fed Javan, the powerful passionate love she felt for Beremon, her own father, all became so jumbled in her mind that she could not think straight while in his presence.

"Sorry?" Beremon asked. "Sorrow does no one any good. You will, of course, stay away from Tull?"

Wisteria remembered her training at Lady Devarre's School of Merchantry. Her father was offering a good marriage, power. Something Tull could never give her. She straightened her back and nodded. "Of course, Father, I will stay away from Tull. I'm sorry."

She closed the door behind her and stood outside the room a moment, letting her pounding heart calm. "Oh yes," she heard Beremon say, "I know you'll be forever sorry."

A crowd of over a hundred gathered at Moon Dance Inn, all of them eager to hear of the blue man's doings. Phylomon calmly sat and ate, the wild Dryad at his side, and the people were amazed to see such a pair sitting on the weathered oak stools of the inn. Scandal himself bustled back and forth between the common room and his kitchen, offering Phylomon course after course of his finest foods—honey muffins, truffles, lamb ribs barbecued in plum sauce, broccoli spears under a blanket of fine white cheese, a baked pudding made with rice starch and covered with a layer of blackberry tart.

When he could no longer stand it, one townsman asked, "What are you doing here?"

"He's eating pudding!" Scandal said protectively, not wanting the locals to bother his celebrity.

Phylomon looked up from his plate. Even from his stool, he could see out over the crowd. "I was in Wellen's Eyes a few weeks ago and heard that the serpent hatch had failed. I came to investigate," Phylomon said.

"Ayaah, it failed," Scandal said, "and it will fail again next year. There is not a single serpent at the laying grounds at Haystack Rock. I've got me some men, and we're heading for Craal in a week to catch some serpent hatchlings. Bring them back here and put them in the bay."

"Alive?" Phylomon asked.

"They wouldn't be any benefit dead," Scandal answered. "I know it can be done. Why when I was young, I met a chef out of Greenstone. He had a recipe for serpent—young serpent in honey with chestnuts and peppers. The Crawlies catch serpents in the Seven Ogre and transport them by wagon three hundred miles to Greenstone, and send them out by ship all across Craal."

"Yes," Phylomon said, "many fishermen at Seven Ogre go only for the serpent catch." He looked down at the table and his eyes became unfocused, as if remembering those distant lands.

Scandal said, "I figure we can take a few boys over the mountains, fill up my beer keg with serpents, head down to Denai, buy us a small boat, and sail the cargo to Castle Rock. With the serpents nesting, we wouldn't dare try to get the boat through the Straits of Zerai, but we can ship them overland to Bashevgo, along with our boat, and then put the boat back in the water. We'll have a three-man crew at Bashevgo building a barge big enough to house the serpents —since they'll be hitting a growth spurt—and then we can sail the serpents home."

Phylomon considered. "That sounds like a fanciful plan, but the serpents *do* make it to Greenstone. How many serpents do you think you can catch?"

"I figure that if we get there early, we can bring in the little ones—three footers. I could hold a hundred of them in the barrel. By the time we reach Bashevgo ten days later, they'll be six footers, and by the time we get them on a barge and ship them home, they'll be fifteen to twenty feet long."

"A hundred serpents to patrol this coast is not many," Phylomon said. "By spring they'll only be eighty footers. I'd prefer that you brought back a thousand."

"What?" Scandal said. "Ten mastodons? Ten wagons?"

"But even with only one wagon, I'm afraid you will never get into and out of Craal unnoticed," Phylomon said. "You underestimate the Blade Kin." Phylomon became silent for a moment, and no one said a word. The Blade Kin, cruel warriors culled from the darkest prisons in Craal, were skillful fighters, far more highly trained than the pirate slavers of Bashevgo. "They keep a better watch on the Rough than you know. Over the last several years, the number of escaped slaves has increased, and the escaped slaves make constant war upon the mountain fortresses of the Blade Kin. It will be difficult to pass them.

"Still," Phylomon added, "If there are no serpents here in the east, I will come with you."

Scandal clapped his hands for joy.

"But first," Phylomon said, "I have other business here. A new college opens in Benbow soon, and they need a printing press to print books. I understand that you have one here in town?"

"Ayaah," one of the merchants said, "Sort of. A fellow from the south came up here and tried to sell us one a few years back. He was a crazy youngster with grand ideas. The press was made in Craal, and we wouldn't be able to get spare parts. He didn't have the money to ship it elsewhere. No one bought it, so he dumped it into the bay."

"Fools!" Phylomon said, standing and looking at the lot of them as if he were in shock. Those nearest townsmen backed away, out of sword's reach. "Why do you hamper me at every turn? Surely your schoolmasters here realized the import of that press. Could you have not spared one steel eagle for it? How do you ever hope to regain the stars when the highest bit of technology you are willing to master is the use of a gun? Damn the lot of you to hell! Isn't there one among you with foresight?"

A young farmer from Finger Mountain came running into the building, sweat streaming down his face, as if he'd just run the whole three miles to get there. The man had frantic blue eyes that were too wide, like the eyes of a simpleton. "Phylomon, Good Sir! Heal my daughter! She's deadly sick."

Phylomon looked to the back of the room and shook his head sadly. "Who am I to heal your daughter?" he asked.

"I've heard," the young man said, "that if you spread your skin upon a sick person, you can heal her. Heal my daughter, please!" He pushed his way forward through the crowd, fell to his knees in front of Phylomon.

Phylomon shook his head, "Those are children's stories, Friend," he said, lifting the simpleton to his feet. "My blue skin *is* an article of clothing, and in the ancient days all Starfarers wore them just as you wear leather and cotton and wool. It is a symbiote, an animal with a mind and will of its own that drinks my sweat to stay alive. In return it protects me and gives me long life."

"Then maybe you could give it to her," the farmer begged, "for just a while. Maybe it could protect her!"

Phylomon shook his head sadly. "If your daughter had a skin like mine, she too would be immune to disease. But I can no more remove this blue hide than you can remove your own skin. I'm sorry, but my touch won't heal your daughter. I have no magic powers."

"What can I do?" the farmer begged, and he fell to sobbing.

Phylomon lightly touched his shoulder. "Perhaps I can help her. I know something of medicine. Stay for a bit. I'll come to your home as soon as possible and do what I can for the girl. But now, I must prepare for sunset," Phylomon sighed, and the big blue man took the Dryad with him to his room.

At sunset the Pwi threw a party in Phylomon's welcome, as if it were a holiday, and many of them painted themselves blue and danced through the streets with flutes and drums. They tied streamers to every tree and brought their finest lamps down to the docks to hear Phylomon's words. Someone brought a beer keg to dockside and they roasted three pigs in a great bonfire in the middle of the street. Everyone sang, and laughter filled the air. Most people were oblivious to the fact that Phylomon had asked the men to come dressed in war gear, and only a few men brought their shields and war clubs.

Six hundred men and women with screaming babies and tired, ecstatic children were present. The Pwi celebrated, and the smell of beer and cooking pork filled the air. The sounds of music and laughter were so persistent that soon the gaiety spread among the whole crowd. Everyone showed up—even old Byrum Saman, who'd been too sick to move from his pallet all summer, had been carried down to the docks a mile west of town. Only two ships were moored in the harbor.

Woden, a small white moon like a single blind staring eye, was up, and Phylomon's pale skin gleamed dully as he entered the crowd. The Dryad stayed in the room. Phylomon carried his long, thin sword in its scabbard.

Wisteria waited in the crowd, standing next to her father and mother. Tull Genet came and stood behind Wisteria. She couldn't help but be conscious of him behind her, waiting, as if after seven years she would once again fall into his arms.

The blue man seemed tired, and the crowd was disorganized. The men did not march in their war gear and line up in front of him like a real army might. It had been twenty years since they'd mustered, and those few who remembered to dress in battle gear seemed embarrassed to have pulled out old war shields with cracked leather, maces that had never been swung in battle. Among the crowd, only two men had guns—crude single-shot rifles.

Phylomon walked down to the wharf and stood with his back to the water and began to speak. "People of Smilodon Bay," Phylomon said softly, so softly that Wisteria held her breath to hear, "I have asked your men to come in war gear because you are in danger from slavers. Here in Smilodon Bay, you are far from Craal, and perhaps you are not aware of your enemy's power. We here in the Rough number under sixty thousand, yet if you combined the armies of the Seven Lords of Craal, you would find that they have over six million men who bear arms. These are not sometime warriors— these are men who fight with the sword day in and day out. These are men who kill one another for a living. In the past, the great distance between Smilodon Bay and Craal has served to protect you. But the Rough is shrinking. Every year, the borders of Craal move closer and closer. Every year their power grows. If the Seven Lords were not so busy fighting among themselves, they would have swallowed you long ago.

"Soon—perhaps in a year, perhaps twenty—the slavers will come here and swallow you anyway. I've known them long enough that I can tell you what will happen. They see no difference between owning people like you and owning orchards." He pointed at two of the younger boys, both humans. "You and you, the slavers will castrate you before your mothers' eyes, and you will be made house servants. The slavers think it no more indecent to castrate you than to castrate a bull." He pointed to Wisteria and two other young women, "You will be branded and turned into whores. You Pwi will be shackled and put to work in the mines and fields, and you," he said, pointing out several grandmothers, along with Byrum Saman on his sickbed, "They'll smother you with no more thought than they would slaughter a milk cow that has outlived its usefulness.

"I have spent my entire life fighting the slavers, but some of you seem to be ignorant of their crimes. Seven years ago, in Craal, I collected testimonies from slaves detailing the accounts of their capture. Some of them were captured by your townsmen." A woman shrieked in disbelief. Others stiffened and looked around, studying the eyes of neighbors. Some muttered, and the sound of shifting feet threatened to drown out Phylomon's voice, so he shouted, "Those slaves shall be vindicated this night!"

Phylomon held three slips of paper. He stroked the middle of his seven medallions, and it began to gleam like a firefly. A Pwi woman gasped at this sign of magic. He read, "Six years ago, I, Molliron Hart, was taken slave in Smilodon Bay. I was walking down the road just after dark when Jassic Goodstick and Denneli Goodstick caught me and raped me. They carried me to the hold of a merchant ship and sent me here."

The crowd roared in anger. Denneli Goodstick tried to make a run for it. A woman stepped in front of him, and he slapped her in the head with a mace, cracking her skull. Several men grabbed the Goodstick brothers from all sides, disarmed them, and dragged them shrieking and kicking toward Phylomon. The injured woman bled profusely and sat on the ground, stunned, while a dozen people tried to help her.

"Here's the ones that did it!" someone shouted. Wisteria stared with her mouth open. *It's started,* she thought. *It has started.* She was not surprised to find that these men were slavers. From her childhood she recalled that Jassic and Denneli were two of the meanest men in town.

Phylomon stepped in front of Denneli Goodstick, a tall thin man with a haggard face. Denneli stared at the ground, and he shook as if with a chill. "What have you to say for yourself?" Phylomon asked.

"Does it matter?" Denneli asked. "You caught us. I'm a dead man."

"Dead you are," Phylomon said. He turned to the townspeople and said just loud enough to be heard by all: "When the first Starfarers fell from the skies, there were three hundred and twelve men and women. You are descended from them. In the past thousand years your bloodlines have crossed and recrossed countless times. You look at the person standing next to you, and though he may be a stranger, you share so many genes that he is as much a brother as if you were born of the same mother. I myself have fathered five children in the last eight hundred years. Most of you could not cite your genealogy without finding that I am one of your forebears. When you sell one another into slavery, you sell your brothers and sisters. The people I kill this night, are *my own* children!" And with that he spun and jabbed with his sword. Denneli staggered back, a ragged hole in his throat; blood spurted as if from a broken pipe. He began coughing blood.

Denneli's children shrieked and his wife fainted. Phylomon turned to the crowd: "Does Molliron Hart have any brothers or sisters, any relatives at all?"

One woman shouted, "Me!"

"Then in the morning, you will go to the homes of these men, and take possession. Their homes and everything within are yours. The families of slavers will not profit from these condemned men's crimes."

Phylomon stepped up to Jassic, a heavy, robust man with a thick beard. He could not have been more than twenty when he raped and sold Molliron Hart. Jassic was watching six directions at once, looking for a place to run; three townsmen held him from behind, and one man put a noose around Jassic's neck. He fought the noose, and white spittle foamed from his mouth.

"Anything to say for yourself?" Phylomon asked.

Jassic's lips trembled. He blurted, "Wait a minute! You can't do this to me! Wait! Grab him, boys!"

Wisteria searched the crowd. Although several men shifted their feet, none of the "boys" came to Jassic's rescue. Both his wife and his mistress covered their faces with their hands. Phylomon watched Jassic's eyes, trying to see who

Jassic called to, then rammed his sword up under Jassic's chin and into his brain.

Phylomon read his second letter: "I, Javan Tech—"

Wisteria heard a shriek rise from her own throat, condemning her. Her father shouted beside her and swung a knife. They had stood near the back of the crowd so Beremon could make a hasty retreat if need be, yet Beremon tripped in his hurry to run. Tull Genet grabbed Beremon by the shoulder, to steady him, but then Tull must have realized he'd caught a slaver, for he swung Beremon in a great arc, threw him back into the crowd and followed after, still blindly clutching Beremon's doeskin jacket. Beremon's hands suddenly emptied as he dropped his knife on the road. Wisteria's mother, Elyssa, fainted, and Wisteria caught her as she fell.

Several young men dragged Beremon forward, and Tull clutched Beremon's jacket in confusion, still surprised at having captured a slaver.

Phylomon continued, "Four years ago in Smilodon Bay, while I was walking up the hill at night, Beremon Troutmaster caught me. He and his wife, Elyssa, kept me in their basement, and sold me slave a week later."

Several people gasped in surprise. Two men took Elyssa from Wisteria's arms and looked up at Phylomon. "Not the woman!" someone shouted, but Phylomon nodded.

The young men forced Beremon to his knees, forced him to kneel in the blood of two dead men. Tull stared at Wisteria in dismay, his face drained white, and she knew that Tull had heard her scream. He knew of her guilt. With a word to Phylomon Tull could condemn her to death.

Wisteria felt as if she'd taken a physical blow. Every muscle in her chest seemed to spasm in pain, forcing the air from her lungs in tight, ragged breaths. She was afraid for her parents and blamed herself. She should have known Beremon would stumble into Tull.

Phylomon waited a moment until Elyssa regained consciousness, and several men held her lightly.

"Do you have anything to say for yourself?" Phylomon asked. Beremon began weeping and shaking his head, then his back straightened and he seemed to regain his dignity. "I only did it once. My wife is not to blame."

"Damn you! May God screw you for what you did to my daughter!" a woman shouted at Beremon and Elyssa.

Beremon stiffened at the curse and said bitterly, "I think he just has."

Phylomon looked into Elyssa's eyes. "Did you help take Javan Tech slave? Did you keep her in your house?"

He did not need an answer. Her face was drained pale with guilt. "Yes," she said.

Phylomon put the sword to Beremon's throat and asked, "Madam, please turn your head."

Elyssa turned her head to the side, shaking badly, and began to weep. Her gray hair looked almost golden in the torchlight. She watched Phylomon's blade from the corner of her eye.

"Please," Phylomon said, "This is hard enough for me. I don't want you to see it."

Elyssa nodded her head slightly, trembled, and closed her eyes. Phylomon jerked his sword up away from Beremon and jabbed Elyssa under the throat, nearly severing her head in one quick thrust, and the audience groaned as one to see the woman die.

"Thank you," Beremon said. Wisteria realized that he thanked the blue man for executing Elyssa quickly. Phylomon struck with his sword, piercing Beremon's right lung, then kicked Beremon off the dock. Beremon floundered a moment in the deep waters of the bay.

Wisteria cried out. Her mother lay sprawled on her back, her head held to her body by only a flap of skin, staring at the sky. Wisteria could hear her father splashing in the water, flapping his hands feebly as he tried to stay afloat. Her legs felt weak and she dropped to her knees and listened to the splashing, a single cough. "God!" she said, "God! He's drowning! Stop this!" Yet no one moved to help him. She staggered forward to save him, and someone caught her from behind, wrapping strong arms around her, and lifted her into the air. She kicked him in the shins and twisted around.

It was Mayor Goodstick. "Say nothing! Don't step into this mess. Not here! Not now! Later!" he whispered, and she realized what might happen if she tried to save her father. Beremon suddenly quit splashing as he sank beneath the waves. She held her breath, waited for the sound of him surfacing, gasping for breath. But she heard only the lapping of waves against the docks. The water in the bay became placid.

Elyssa lay staring up at the moon. Wisteria sank to the ground and began gasping for air, trying to scream.

Phylomon read from the last slip of paper and came up with five names, and three more people died—another Goodstick brother, an old woman, and one of the scraggly seamen Jassic had called to for help. One perpetrator of the crime had died of a fall seven years earlier, and another had long since sailed away.

When he was finished, Phylomon stepped away, neck and shoulders hunched as if exhausted to the bone. He said softly, "It never becomes easier."

The merriment and celebration among the Pwi had long since died. Phylomon made his way through the crowd and everyone stepped back, mothers clutching their children, all of them staring hard at the blue man.

Wisteria felt empty, desolate. As a child, she'd feared that people would find out that she had carried food for Javan Tech, that retribution would come. And finally it had.

Seven townsmen were dead. Some people in the crowd wept with relief at finding that lost friends and family members had been alive only recently. Others wept in bitterness because fathers and friends, husbands and brothers had been slaughtered before their eyes. Yet no one spoke against what had happened; no one said it was unjust. That hurt Wisteria most of all.

A hundred yards down the road, Phylomon turned to the crowd, and for the first time his soft voice carried an edge. "Many of you children will grow up hating and fearing me—fearing that I will come back again. I will rob you slavers of your sleep. *And that fear of discovery, fear of justice, is what this world needs.*"

That night, Wisteria Troutmaster lost her home to the Tech family. All thirty-seven of them scoured the house, pulling out the beds and furniture, the jewelry and money, the food and family books. Wisteria was weeping uncontrollably. By lantern light Javan's older sister Devina Tech came and reached out to Wisteria. For a moment Wisteria thought Devina was seeking to comfort her, but instead she grabbed Wisteria's platinum necklace and savagely tore it from her neck.

"I'll take that, and the earrings," Devina said, grabbing at Wisteria's ears. Wisteria wrenched away and slapped Devina in the nose. The older woman looked at Wisteria and her face twisted in rage. "It's small enough payment for my sister," Devina said. She reached out as if she would pull Wisteria's hair, and Wisteria knocked her hand away.

Wisteria took off the earrings, handed them to Devina. "Here," she said. "You've now been amply paid for your sister. I'm sure it eases your loss."

Devina seemed to catch herself, regain a semblance of dignity. "You can keep the clothes on your back," Devina said, as if bestowing a gift, and she hurried back to the house. Several younger family members fought over booty. They were worse than junkyard dogs. Worse than pigs. After so many years away from town, Wisteria didn't really know these people anymore. Yet their actions revealed their nature. For years Wisteria had felt guilty for what her family had done to Javan, had found it hard to look others in the face. *Tonight, the guilt dies,* she thought.

Within an hour old grandmother Tech stood back in the street and cackled, "That's my house! I'll live in the finest house on this coast!"

Wisteria wandered through town, crying softly. She had not eaten lunch after the blue man came to town, had forgone dinner in her worry. Her stomach began to cramp from hunger. She wandered the streets and found that down by the docks the partygoers had left the carcasses of the pigs still cooking. Many lanterns still burned, and she could make out the streamers hanging from trees. She gagged down a bite of the burned meat, drank a single swallow from the barrel of beer.

Wisteria heard a twig snap behind a house. She looked into the shadows and glimpsed the mayor's Dryad stealing clothes from a line, her hair and skin silvered in the moonlight. The Dryad wore a long knife on her hip. When she saw Wisteria, the Dryad moved off without a word, heading into the woods outside town. Wisteria wished that she, too, could run from this town.

Wisteria took a step, and something crunched under foot. She reached down and picked it up: a panpipe dropped by a Pwi—all that was left of the blue holiday.

Chapter 4
A Fun Idea

That night Phylomon returned very late and bone weary from treating the farmer's daughter for a parasitic worm infection. He unlocked the door to his room and found Theron Scandal sleeping on his bed, a single yellow candle burned down to a stump. Phylomon woke the innkeeper with a kick.

"Oh, oh," Scandal said groggily. "It's late."

"I agree," Phylomon said. "I'd heard that this room didn't have vermin. I fancied that meant that for once I would sleep alone in a bed. What can I do for you?"

"I'm worried about this trip," Scandal said. "I told you that we had three humans coming with us, but I'm afraid that after tonight they won't be coming anymore."

"They backed out?" Phylomon asked.

"You killed them," Scandal corrected. "Denneli and Coormon Goodstick, along with Amondi Rinn."

"Three slavers were going with you? Makes you wonder how much a human innkeeper is worth on the slave blocks in Craal, doesn't it? I'm sure you would fetch a fine price as a house servant."

Scandal's eyes widened. "They wouldn't!"

"They planned to," Phylomon said, "yet they were going to a lot of trouble just to get you . . ." The blue man bent his head in thought. "With the fishery down, I suppose some in the town have moved elsewhere. Have you lost many fighting men?"

"Ayaah," Scandal said. "They've been leaving all summer, looking for work down south. I've been worried: we've got three cannons pointed at the bay, but they wouldn't do much good if pirates came overland. They could sail a ship up Muskrat Creek during high tide, and walk over the hills in an hour. Sixty men of war, at night, could do a lot of damage."

"The slavers wanted your quest to fail," Phylomon said.

"Perhaps," Scandal said. "I've never liked Denneli Goodstick—you could tell me he rapes babies, and I'd likely believe it. But not the others. Coorman—not him. He was a wild kid, but he'd changed. He didn't know about it."

Phylomon looked out the window, Freya had joined Woden in the night sky, and it was getting lighter. "I killed three men named Goodstick tonight. They were your mayor's brothers?"

"Ayaah," Scandal said.

"I believe they were in it together," Phylomon said. "Jassic wanted his 'boys' to kill me. He may have been the ringleader. Still, leave an open invitation for others to join us on the trip to Seven Ogre River. Perhaps our enemies will introduce themselves. I'll kill the next man who tries to join the quest. But what of the Pwi who are coming? Can they be trusted?"

"The Pwi didn't choose to come," Scandal said. "We've got a Spirit Walker in town. He ordered them to go."

"I've known many a Spirit Walker who couldn't look five days into the future. Is this one any good?" Phylomon asked, then he realized that he could find that out himself, and he excused himself from the room. He stepped out into the darkness, looked around. If the Spirit Walker had seen the future, it didn't make any difference which way Phylomon went, the shaman should be waiting ahead. Phylomon walked up the hill above the inn, through the brush, where the pines hid everything in shadows. A single large redwood stood atop the hill.

When Phylomon reached the redwood, the voice of the Neanderthal came to him from the shadows. "I am here," Chaa said softly. "I have been waiting for you."

Phylomon saw the Neanderthal then, sitting in the moonlight. He bowed to the shaman in respect.

"Sit," Chaa said. "The night is lovely. It is good to enjoy the darkness while we still can."

Phylomon sat at Chaa's feet and waited for the Spirit Walker to speak. He knew the man would say only what he desired to say, and Phylomon had seen the vast psychic powers of the pure-blooded Pwi too often to deny the man's right to speak.

"You fear to take the serpent journey, for you fear that your enemies will have power over you," Chaa said. "I tell you this: Your enemies *will* have power over you. You must walk the path of the crushed heart. If you go on this journey, perhaps it can succeed. Yet succeed or not, within three years you will die for your efforts. Your death will not be easy."

Phylomon answered, "I suspect that if we took a poll of the dead, none of them would say that their deaths were easy."

Chaa nodded. "You have long been a protector of the Pwi . . ."

"Not just of the Pwi," Phylomon said. "My people are a danger to themselves. Always they have sought the easy path back to the stars, but their road leads them only down. Long ago, when some of our Starfarers proposed taking the Pwi as slaves to build their war machines, I warned them against this path. Now, the slavers in Craal have fallen so far . . ."

"That the time has come when you can protect us no longer," Chaa said. "The armies of Craal swell to six million. All your efforts to stop them will be vain. But Tull Genet can destroy the armies of Craal."

Phylomon drew a deep breath in surprise. "I've battled the Slave Lords for eight hundred years, and in all those years I have lost that war one slow bit at a time! Their warriors outnumber us a hundred to one. Tell me that you do not speak in half-truths! Tell me plainly that my death will mean something!"

Chaa considered. "The paths of the future branch a thousand thousand directions in a man's lifetime. Because of this, it is impossible to walk all of a man's future. Even the best Spirit Walker can only see a few years down the road, and even then he may be mistaken. But I did not have to walk far into Tull's future. I tell you that within two years Tull can crush their necks. The armies of Craal can fall. But only if Tull first makes the serpent catch."

"Then I will go with him, no matter what the price!" Phylomon said.

Chaa said, "I tell you now, the day will come when you will regret this decision. Do not be afraid to teach him your secrets."

Well past midnight, dazed and hungry and not sure what to do, Wisteria found herself by the river. She glanced up at the door of Mayor Garamon Goodstick and was startled to see movement. A candle sputtered in the front room, and a shadowy figure knocked at the door and entered, spoke quickly and then departed. The mayor himself stepped out, breathed the fresh air, and looked at the moons. Thor was just rising. She could see him well. Then he stepped back in.

It was late to be keeping such company. There had been a familiarity in Garamon's voice when he'd stopped her from trying to save her father, a hint that they were allies fighting a common enemy. Garamon had helped her father arrange Javan's sale. He was in it as deep as anyone. Almost without thinking, Wisteria ran to his door, rapped softly.

The mayor jerked the door open. "Again? What?" he whispered savagely. His beard and breath smelled wet with beer, and he wore a dark cotton robe.

He stood a moment, taking a long look at her. His sudden silence made it obvious he had not expected her. "What do you want?" Garamon asked quietly, unwilling to wake his wife and children.

Wisteria did not quite know what to answer. "Vengeance," she said.

The mayor watched her for a long time. Licked his lips. "Vengeance—can mean a lot of things," he said in a breath.

Wisteria said evenly, "I want the blue man dead. I want to watch the Tech family—all of them—stuffed in the hold of a Craal slaver, and I want to laugh as I watch."

The mayor chuckled. "Ayaah, you've more spunk than your father ever had, but I'm afraid you've lost the family coins. Aren't you afraid of me? You with nothing to offer, no one to care for you? If I were a slaver, I'd say, 'She's worth piss in this town. If she got knocked in the head and took a piggyback ride in a sack tonight, who'd miss her?' "

Wisteria watched him. She had nothing to give. She was a beggar. Yet . . . a week before she'd noticed that Garamon could not conceal the lust in his eyes as he watched the young women bend over washing rocks down by the river. *He's like a dog that way,* she thought, *always sniffing at the source of joy. So little self-control—nothing more than a prick with a human body attached.* Hadn't her father told her that her body was a great asset? She pulled off her blouse and held it in her hand, revealing her full breasts. "A little vengeance. What could it cost?" she said.

The mayor's mouth dropped open and he wetted his lips with his tongue. He stepped out the door, closing it quietly. "This way," he hissed, taking her by the hand and leading her behind the house to a narrow path.

The path was dark and empty, yet Garamon grabbed Wisteria's blouse and urged, "Put it back on!" But Wisteria did not care if she was caught. The path wended its way several hundred yards, always only a few feet behind the nearest house, and Garamon stopped at his family's cloth shop, then fumbled in a bush by the back door as he looked for a key. When they were in, he tossed a bolt of cotton on the floor and stood panting a moment, just watching Wisteria.

"Take off your clothes," he said.

"Then you will do it?" she asked. "You will kill Phylomon? You will sell the Techs into slavery?"

"Ayaah," Garamon said.

"And what guarantee do I have?"

"My word of honor," Garamon answered.

"And what is the payment?" she asked.

"You'll be mine, when I want you," Garamon answered, his voice husky with lust.

"I'll be yours, for one year after the deed," Wisteria answered.

Garamon watched her. "Agreed," he said. "But I want you now, to see what I'm getting."

Wisteria pulled off her sandals, wiggled out of her skirt. Garamon watched her. When she stood naked, he kept staring, and his breathing came deep and slow.

"Are you a virgin?" he asked.

"Yes," she said, "we had little choice in the matter at Lady Devarre's."

He went to the back wall, opened a cabinet, pulled out a bottle and uncorked it. "Drink this," he proffered the bottle. "This is going to hurt. If you don't get drunk first, you'll wish you had."

She stepped forward and took a swig. It was whiskey, a fire that scalded her throat and sat in her belly like an ember, diminishing her hunger. She drank quickly while Garamon pulled off his robe and stood naked in the moonlight by the window, a pale fat man with dark spots on his chest and armpits and crotch where the hair was thick. She watched him as he stood staring down at his swollen member.

When she'd downed half the bottle, the floor suddenly seemed to wrench beneath her. She set the bottle on a table and Garamon was on her, his arms wrapped around her, kissing her and easing her to the bolt of cotton strewn on the floor. Her knees buckled and she let him help her down. He had the bottle in his hand and guzzled the last of it.

Wisteria knew her life depended on how she performed that night. She wasn't a gutter wench, accustomed to such action, but at that moment nothing was beneath her. She rutted with him like a cat in heat, despite the pain. She wanted to be for him the best time a man had ever had. During the third round, Garamon sweated as if he'd been unloading from the docks all day. "Damn, woman, you're not the most passionate thing I've ever slept with, but I swear by God's aching hemorrhoids, you're the most energetic."

And sometime near dawn he began to talk. For an hour

he only breathed threats. "I swear woman," he'd say, "if you ever tell anyone what I tell you this night, if you even mention it in your sleep, I'll rip your belly apart with a fillet knife," and he'd punch her in the stomach to show his threat was true.

Bit by bit he began to speak openly. "I tell you—the death of these serpents—it's a godsend! Oh, how I've waited for a chance like this! To pick this town down to its bones! Why, you and I—we think alike, we do." Slowly Garamon revealed his thoughts. "The people in this town are fatted hens, ready for market. Do you know how much a human sells for on the blocks at Denai? Up to three hundred platinum eagles for a good young male house servant. But, you see, it all depends on the serpents, the death of the serpents —with a hundred men of war in this town, no Craal slaver would drop anchor in this bay. But if half those men are off in the mines at White Rock and another dozen are hunting in the mountains to fend off starvation and a dozen of those remaining are mine. . . . What I need in this town is despair. Hopelessness. Convince more of the men to leave for White Rock. They'll leave the wives and children here—tell themselves it's only till spring. They won't take their families—not into the mountains where the snows get eight feet deep in the winter," Garamon said, and Wisteria realized that the plan was already in the works. When Scandal had asked for volunteers to help finance the journey to Seven Ogre River, Garamon had scoffed at the idea and sought to make a laughingstock of Scandal, hindering others from joining him. Furthermore, only hours before Phylomon had slain all three of the humans who'd planned to make the trip. "Ayaah, those men were *mine,*" Garamon said. "Good lads, seasoned, and now they're dead. I tell you, I can sell the Techs into slavery, but I'll need help. I have a man watching Phylomon. He and Scandal have been making plans for their trip. The blue man, he's a smart one. When he learned he'd killed every human journeying on the quest, he smelled the trap—even asked Scandal how much a gourmet cook would bring on the blocks in Craal. Promised to kill any man from town who seeks to join the quest. But a woman—a woman—what would he do?" She knew before he asked it that he wanted a guarantee that the quest would fail. "And that, my horny little devil, is where you come in."

"I . . . I couldn't fight him," Wisteria said.

Garamon laughed. "Of course not. But there are a hundred ways to ruin the quest: Break an axle. Wait a month, till you're heavy into it, and poison the mastodon. Hell— likely as not, the quest will ruin itself."

"But Phylomon. What of him?"

"God, did you see the way those gems gleamed in his hand?" Garamon said. "Like light, liquid light, shining from his palm. He plans on leaving our village with enough jewels in his pocket to buy us ten times over. Do you really think I'd let him get away with that? Besides, he killed my brothers and stole my slave."

"Bought your slave," Wisteria corrected.

"Bought," Garamon agreed. "Yet I'm afraid he hasn't paid a tenth my price. Don't worry about the blue man. In ten days time, he'll be mine. You just worry about how you'll get on that wagon!"

"Phylomon's been alive for a thousand years," Wisteria said. "Don't you think others have tried to kill him before?"

"Not like I'm going to try," Garamon promised.

Wisteria lay on her back, took another swig of whiskey, and urged the mayor into her one last time. She knew what Garamon demanded of her—yet she knew Chaa had walked the future and seen that the quest could succeed. But could it succeed in spite of her? The Pwi said that the paths to the future branch with every step we take, with every seemingly insignificant choice. Because of this, even the best Spirit Walker cannot foresee all possibilities. *Did the Spirit Walker see my future?* she wondered. *Possibly not. The Pwi never walk the paths of the future for humans. But even if Chaa knows my future better than I do,* she told herself, *it won't change what I must do.*

The sun was high in the sky and the dew was melted off the grass when Tull came to his old home from Chaa's the next morning. After the executions the night before, the town was quiet, and people seemed almost ashamed to disturb the mourners by walking outside their homes. As a son of Chaa,

Tull needed to move his belongings into his new house, but he thought he would let that wait for a few days. Still, he decided to spend the day making a new spear for the journey, and he had a bone from a dimetrodon's dorsal fin that he could sharpen into a three-foot-long spearhead. It was the only kind of spearhead one wanted while traveling through territory infested by Mastodon Men.

Tull was profoundly aware of the silence. When he neared his door, the only sound he could hear was the surf beating against the rocks, and sparrows hopping among the laurels by the doorstep.

So when he reached the doorstep, he was surprised to see a figure eight painted with flour on the grass—a small figure eight, no more than four feet across. Normally when a woman painted the figure eight on a man's doorstep, she set all her possessions in one half of the circle—her food, her cooking utensils, her weapons—then she stood with them as she waited to see if the man would join her. But there was only a handful of wild daisies in the circle, and no woman.

Tull crouched to look at the daisies, wondering what it could mean. Only a poor woman would have left them, a woman who had nothing but herself to give. Even the poorest Pwi would have brought an object that contained kwea, something to which she had a strong emotional attachment. So it could not have been a Pwi who drew the circle. Tull knew only one woman who fit that description. His heart began pounding, racing in his chest. He stood up to look for her, entered his home, and found Wisteria sleeping on his mat on the floor.

She woke when the swinging door scraped the dirt floor. Her eyes were red and swollen, as if she'd cried all night. Her hair was sweaty and matted, and her blouse misadjusted. She didn't say a word, just rose from the floor and sidled past him. She stepped into the sunlight in the circle and stood with her brown hair gleaming, with daisies at her feet.

He could not believe it. "Are you sure?" he asked.

"Sure?" Wisteria said, placing a hand on her forehead as if to test for a fever. "Yes. I'm sure."

Tull watched her.

"I'm tired. I'm hungry. I'm desperate," she said. "I'm

hurt inside and I'm mad as hell. You know I've always been fond of you—from the time we were children—but I didn't know . . . if I'd stay that way."

"When your father stumbled into me last night," Tull said, "I grabbed him to keep from falling. I didn't even know who'd hit me, yet I realized someone was trying to escape. I threw him back into the crowd and held him at the same time. I didn't know it was him. I swear, if I'd thought, I'd have let him go."

Wisteria began weeping and trembling. "I know," she said.

"We were all crazy," Tull said. "We just stood there and watched it happen. I didn't have time to think, to decide if what we were doing was right."

"I know," Wisteria said.

"And if you marry me," Tull answered, "You will have to live with that. You'll remember every day of our lives that I betrayed you."

"You didn't," she said, wiping her face. "It was an accident."

"And if you marry me," Tull said, "you will still be alone for a long time. This will be a hard time for you. The hardest in your life. I'm leaving in a week, and I won't be back until midwinter, and I won't be here to help you."

Wisteria sat down on the grass and began coughing great wracking sobs. After several moments she said, "I can't be alone! I can't be without you! Let me come with you! I can't stay in this town right now anyway. It hurts too much. Everything reminds me of what happened last night!"

Tull watched her a moment. Always before, humans had seemed so . . . emotionally resilient, or perhaps just emotionally sheltered. They were never destroyed by pain half so much as the Pwi. And to see Wisteria this way, weeping in the grass, he could almost imagine she was Pwi at heart, that the evil kwea of last night would drive her away from here. And Tull realized something else: he was trying to talk her out of this marriage in spite of the fact that he desired it, in spite of the fact that he wanted it so badly he couldn't bear the thought of losing her. "You've never loved me before," he said.

She looked up at him. "I've always been fond of you.

When we were young and I kissed you and let you stroke my breast, I was fond of you. When Father sent me away, I fantasized about what life would be like with you. I dreamed at night about how it would be to make love to you. But last night, when I ached for someone to comfort me, I realized I wanted you. You're . . . someone I can trust."

Tull wondered. For months now he had been attracted to Fava. She was a simple girl, strong, and the quaint scent of vanilla water in Fava's hair charmed him. But from his youth, Tull had imagined life with Wisteria. The attraction he felt for her was strong. Suddenly Tull understood his fear, his hesitancy to enter the circle. He took a deep breath and almost choked as he offered his last excuse—his only real reason for hesitating: "Wisteria, I'm afraid to marry you. I . . . don't know how to love! When I was young, I didn't believe in love. For years I felt only dead inside, as if I were the world's lone witness to a great joke—the fact that everyone else seemed trapped in a common dream, believing that such a thing existed when obviously, so obviously, love was a lie. But over the years, I realized that love exists, that everyone else feels it but me. I want to feel it for you. I feel something. I feel drawn to you. But I'm *afraid*!"

Tull did not know if Wisteria understood. She looked up at him, her eyes wet and bloodshot, though no tears flowed down her cheek. She sniffled, and said very clearly, "Love? Love is easy. I'll show you how to love."

Tull found himself staggering into the circle. All the years of waiting to love seemed to collapse inward; all the walls he'd built against it tumbled down. He wasn't even aware that his feet were moving till he stood in the second circle and took her hands.

She held her palms out and up, in a beggar's gesture, and they clasped one another's wrists. She spoke the words of the wedding ritual, although she had no friend to witness. "I seek shelter from loneliness. I bring all that you see within this circle. But mostly, I bring my heart."

Tull's jaw trembled. "This house, it is empty without you, just as I am empty without you. I offer you shelter, until hand in hand we go to live in the House of Dust."

Then he kissed her, a long slow kiss, and carried her into his house.

It did not seem right to make love to her. He knew she had been up all night, knew that she needed consolation. Yet he could not refrain. The desire that was in him pulled him, tore him open till he was tossed in the wind like dandelion down in a storm, and she seemed eager to caress him and give herself to him. Within moments he stripped her. Wisteria's voice was husky as she pulled him to her. "You don't know how often I dreamed of this. I'll teach you how to love," she said, cupping his hand beneath her breast. "I'll show you how."

It was a moment of great kwea, where a lifetime of longing for this hour, where the devotion Tull felt toward her, were destined to form a time of power. Tull found he had spent all his days as a hollow thing, waiting only for this moment, like a pool of oil waiting for a flame. When she kissed him and stroked him, he blossomed into fire and truly began living at the same moment. He was clumsy as a lover and struggled to do his best to please her. Among the Pwi, it is said that when two people first make love, that the goddess Zhofwa bends near the land and blows her kisses on them, and at that moment, their act becomes holy, *Thea,* and if the love is pure the goddess will enter them for a time and move the lovers' bodies.

And as Tull moved atop Wisteria, the air suddenly seemed fresh and clean. He felt the goddess kiss him in the small of the back, and an intense cool thrill of pleasure passed down his back and into his groin. He arched into Wisteria, and he was no longer clumsy, for the goddess entered him and he moved deep within Wisteria, seeking to give her pleasure as the goddess prompted. It felt as good as he'd dreamed love could be, and for the first time he knew that he could be touched by love, that he could give.

At evening, when the shadows had lengthened on the wall, Wisteria was lying on top of him, kissing him fondly, passionately. Suddenly Tull began to laugh. Wisteria sat up, straddling him. Her breasts swayed forward like wine bladders, and Tull's head spun, she looked so inviting. He looked at the milky white of her breasts, the dark tan lines of her shoulders, the pleasant smoothness of her face. Always before, humans had seemed so long armed and small handed, with funny skulls and loud grating voices. He wanted to drink her with his eyes, learn the colors of every mole on her body.

"Why are you laughing?" Wisteria asked.

"A week ago, I believed I'd be alone forever, but now, I have everything I've ever wanted: A home and family among the Pwi, the only woman I ever wanted to marry."

Wisteria looked deep in his eyes, calculating, and she swung a leg back and got off him, laid down on the mat beside him on her back. Tull marveled to see how her breasts flattened out till she was almost as flat-chested as a man. She smiled an empty smile. "Laugh then. It is right for you to laugh."

After the executions, the town was sullen, quiet. Six funeral pyres were ignited—for no one found the body of Beremon—and the smell of charcoal and flesh seemed to linger for days. Each person mourned the dead in solitude. Although Phylomon was seen in town often, no one sought his company.

The third day of Phylomon's visit to Smilodon Bay, the woodland mastodon that was to pull the wagon arrived from the miners at White Rock. It was a big hulking brute, sixteen feet at the shoulder, well over seventy years old, with the unpromising name of "Snail Follower." "Ayaah, it's a bad name," Scandal admitted, "but I've been assured that the beast is tougher than a Neanderthal's skull." The miner brought the mastodon into town and had it drag a redwood log that was fifteen feet around and thirty feet long, convincing Phylomon that if any beast could pull a wagon carrying twelve tons of water and sea serpents over the plains, this one could. But Phylomon rightly pointed out that the woodland mastodon wasn't built to tolerate the high, cold country in the White Mountains and would likely take sick if driven too fast. Although it was a powerful brute, they could not drive it for more than four or five hours per day.

In spite of the hardships, Tull was glad to be going. The somber, hopeless mood in town, the fight with his parents, the executions—all had combined to make Smilodon Bay an ugly place in the past few days. Tull was too near his parents' house now. He could feel it around the corner, as if it emanated pain, and he smiled. It would feel good to get into the wilderness. It would feel good most of all because he'd be with Wisteria.

That evening Scandal met Phylomon in the common room and said, "Well, I can't believe it, but over the last two days, I've asked every man in town to come with us, and no one will go. You've won no friends in this town."

"I'm not surprised," Phylomon answered. "Executioners seldom win friends."

Scandal's squirrels hopped from table to table, looking for hazelnuts. His pet bird woke, and Scandal cut bits of meat into cubes and held them on the tip of a knife and waved them in front of the bird. The bird hissed, lashed out, grabbing meat between its sharp teeth. "Still," Scandal said, "I'd hoped someone would come, perhaps a few more Pwi. The only person who has made plans to come is a girl: Wisteria Troutmaster. You killed her mother and father, and she married Tull Genet, the big Tcho-Pwi."

"I told you I'd kill any human who tries to come on this quest with us," Phylomon said. "Why should she be an exception?"

"Now look here," Scandal said, waving his knife at Phylomon. "If you touch one hair on that girl's head, the folks here will stick a skewer up your ass and cook you as the main course for a town barbecue. The town may seem quiet, but folks are outraged."

Phylomon raised an eyebrow. "Indeed," he said. "Go on. I seldom have anyone express their thoughts to me honestly."

Scandal leaned his chair back, "You take Wisteria's father, Beremon. He was a Dicton, and I can't say he had a close friend. But you had to know that Javan Tech woman. She was the Queen Bitch of the World. Even her ever-mourning husband would tell you so. But Beremon didn't have a mean bone in his body, and, as for Elyssa—well, no one has ever executed a woman on this entire coast, not unless she's done murder."

"Indeed?" Phylomon said, raising one hairless blue eyebrow.

"Ayaah," Scandal said. "I'm afraid that some folks are

likely to think you just came in here and mucked everything up."

"It's always so easy to forgive a man for a crime he's committed against someone else," Phylomon said. "I showed them as much mercy as they showed their victims. Still, bring Wisteria here. You and the Pwi can judge her. If the rest of the party votes against me, she can join the quest."

When Tull and Wisteria arrived, Phylomon studied them. Tull was both larger and stronger than the typical Pwi or human. He was a hybrid, and his eyes shone with a kind of cold anger. *He hates me,* Phylomon thought. *So this is the man who shall lead an army to destroy Craal. He does not look like a military genius.*

He looked at Wisteria. She was tall, strong, lithe—a form that was the favorite among the ancient Starfarers. She looked much like her mother. A thousand years ago, she'd have been considered a beauty. Like most short-lived persons, or *temporaries,* as Phylomon called them, she had not lived long enough to gain control over her body. Her wrath was evident in the flaring of her nostrils, her fear in the way she shifted her feet and clasped her hands to hide them. Her pupils were constricted, and her head trembled.

Phylomon considered. "Your enemies will have power over you," Chaa had said, and he knew this girl was trouble. Within him, he felt the symbiote stir. *I taste your fear,* the symbiote whispered. Phylomon tried to calm himself. *There is nothing to fear for now, Old Friend,* Phylomon answered.

Behind Wisteria came Ayuvah and Little Chaa. Phylomon studied the Pwi. They were more in awe of him than terrified or outraged.

"I understand you want to come with us to Seven Ogre River," Phylomon told Wisteria. "And I don't trust you. I don't want you there, and I'll only consent to your presence if these men vote in unison against me. So I ask you plainly, would you help our quest, or hinder it?"

Wisteria did not consider her answer for a moment. "Neither!" she said, "I don't care if this quest succeeds or not! This town means nothing to me. I only want to get away from here."

"You choose odd company—" Phylomon said, "your mother's and father's executioner, the man who captured your father when he would have escaped."

Wisteria's lower lip trembled. "Tull is innocent. You're not. I won't lie: I hope to live long enough to see you die. I hope to feed your liver to the dogs!"

"I'm sure. But you'll find that I'm very durable— tougher than you would ever believe!" Phylomon held her eyes a moment. It was an old habit. He wanted to warn her against trying to kill him. "You won't see me die. Yet I applaud your honesty."

"I don't want your compliments," Wisteria said.

Phylomon looked at the floor reflectively, "I am an enemy to Craal and all its minions. Even those who think themselves to be good people. Do you remember the woman your father sold into slavery, Javan Tech? I remember her. She worked as a cleaning woman in the palace of Lord Thanafir at Greenstone. She was not old, but she was starling thin, a drudge who scrubbed beer and dog piss from the floors in the lord's dining hall. Her left breast had been removed, as are the breasts of all women slaves in Craal once the lords have tired of using them for toys. She coughed frequently when she spoke, sometimes spitting blood, claiming fumes from the lye she used to clean had eaten her throat raw, and she told me of her home in Smilodon Bay. She remembered this place as heaven. She often said, 'It's such a beautiful place, with redwoods and the mountains and the sea.' She said, 'Beremon, he treated me kind. Didn't beat me bad or anything. He even let his little girl bring me food and water.' "

Wisteria's eyes widened, and she stepped back, as if afraid Phylomon would draw his sword and deliver a killing blow, but the blue man continued, "I won't kill you for what your parents made you do. Javan said your father was the best master she ever had. She loved this town, wanted to return with all her heart. But even if I had freed her, she was too ill to make the voyage home. She would have died." Phylomon watched Wisteria a moment. "You hear only rumors of the evil of the Slave Lords in Craal, but I've seen the evil done to that woman. I didn't kill your parents just because they sold her into slavery—I killed them because of the greater crimes committed to Javan afterward."

Phylomon grew silent. For a moment no one spoke. He continued. "You say you want to get out of this town, but you must think me a fool! You would not seek the company of your parents' executioner!"

"I can endure your company," Wisteria said. "As long as I can be with the man I love! I have no home here, nothing left but him."

Scandal broke in, "Sir, you tell a good story, but I believe you were duped," he told Phylomon. "It doesn't settle right."

"What do you mean?" Phylomon asked.

"Well, it's easier to hammer an octopus till it's tender than to put it into words, but, as I told you earlier, that Javan Tech was the Queen Bitch of the World. I think she played on your sympathies to get you to exact vengeance— and vengeance isn't always the same as justice." Scandal shook his head. "That Javan—she clung to Elyssa like a tick on a sheep. Elyssa just couldn't shake her. I've been sitting here all day thinking about Javan. You know, Elyssa borrowed some nails from Javan—the copper kind, from Damis —and when Elyssa paid her back, Javan threw a fit. She claimed the bag was light and the nails were too small and they were inferior quality, and she stumped up and down the street telling everyone, as if she were trying to convince folks that they ought to just take Beremon and Elyssa out in a boat and dump them into the bay.

"Well, Elyssa tried to make it up to Javan. She got several witnesses, me included, and we went to Javan's door and Elyssa apologized, saying, 'Look, Javan, I've always valued our friendship. I would never cheat you—not on purpose, not by accident. Here's fifty pounds of nails, all copper ones from Damis, in five different sizes. I want you to have them with my apologies.'

"But you know how some people like to nurse their wrath. Javan threw the nails at Elyssa's feet and shouted, 'I know what you're up to! You're trying to put it all on me! You're trying to blame it on me. Well, you're a cheapskate and a thief and everyone will know it!' "

"Hunh," Phylomon snorted. "It seems I stumbled into a story."

"Ayaah," Scandal mused. "You see, it went deeper than the nails. When Javan was young, she had her eye on Beremon. And when Elyssa married him, Javan sulked for a while before she finally seemed to snap out of it. But I think down inside she never really got over Beremon. Especially when he started making it rich. Javan always felt that Elyssa had stolen Beremon from her."

Phylomon looked up at Wisteria, and there was a strange glow in the girl's eyes, as if she was just learning the truth. She'd never known of the love triangle, and Phylomon could see that the whole affair was finally making sense to the girl.

"Anyway, after that, Javan stumped up and down the streets all day long, talking to her friends, gossiping, trying to turn folks away from Elyssa. For months I hardly saw Elyssa with a dry eye. I think Beremon and Elyssa did what they did out of desperation and never considered the consequences."

"It wasn't both of them—it was my father!" Wisteria cried. "Mother wanted him to let her go, but she was so confused, and daddy refused to listen!"

Phylomon considered a moment, and realized that he may have executed Elyssa unfairly. Could Javan really have duped him into executing a rival? It seemed unlikely, but in fact he had hardly known the woman. He'd taken her testimony at face value. Could she have lied or exaggerated the truth? Slavery does such odd things to people, fills them with rage.

"And my father," Wisteria said, "never sold anyone else! He just didn't know what else to do with Javan!"

"Does that justify his act?" Phylomon asked.

"Perhaps not," Scandal considered. "But I'm not sure that his guilt justifies your act. You come into town, and you know there are slavers. They may have committed the crime ten, twenty years ago. But it seems to me that the people you executed could have changed, might not be the same people who committed the crime at all."

"I've been watching people for a thousand years," Phylomon said softly. "Most men don't really change much.

Not ever. I recall a man I met: He'd murdered a townsman when he was fifteen during a jealous fight over a woman, and the people in his town forgave him because of his youth. He established himself in the community, did well for himself over the years. When he was seventy-two, he found his wife in bed with another man. He took an ax and killed them both. Should they have forgiven his crimes the second time because of his antiquity? One must wonder, did he ever change? Or did he only kill twice in his life because in all of his years, the right conjunction of motive and opportunity appeared only twice. Your father Wisteria, would he have sold another woman into slavery under similar circumstances? Had he changed at all?"

"I . . . don't know," Wisteria answered.

Phylomon looked into her eyes and believed she *did* know. *Yes, her father would have done it again.* "What did he say about it?"

She answered, "He said, 'It was a fun idea.' "

Phylomon chuckled. "Your father had a cruel sense of humor. I'm not sorry that I killed him, child, but I am sorry that it hurt you."

"Ayaah," Scandal said, "you may be right. Maybe you knew Beremon. You've had time to get to know people. Still, I remember this sculptor—Blin Getaway. He had a pupil once who was studying a model, had been for several hours, and hadn't put the chisel to the stone. Blin asked him what he was doing, and the student said he just felt he needed a little longer staring at the model so he could hold the woman in his mind, and then he would be ready to sculpt. Blin said, 'It isn't how long you look; it's how deep you look!' Now, I know you've lived what, twenty times longer than me? But you haven't lived in my town, with my neighbors."

Phylomon laughed softly and shook his head, held up his hands. "I bow to greater wisdom. I'm afraid my own observations would count little against Blin's greater authority. After all, it's commonly accepted that artists know everything."

Scandal frowned, angered by the tone in Phylomon's voice. "Look here, sir, I'll be blunt. I think if we took a poll, folks in our town would have voted for a little mercy on those people you slaughtered. Have you ever heard the word before, *mercy*?"

Phylomon said softly, "Mercy is a luxury affordable only to gods. When you forgive a criminal and let him go free, you place every man, woman, and child that exist in jeopardy, and you forever rob the victims of the crime of the opportunity to regain their peace of mind, their trust in their fellow men. No man has the right to forgive a serious crime and fail to exact a just penalty. You may forgive Beremon and Elyssa, but you do us all a disservice."

Wisteria swallowed. "This isn't about my parents. This is about me. If you don't trust me, then I won't go. I'll stay here. But I want to go. I want to be with Tull."

Phylomon looked at the girl. *Good ploy,* he thought. *A very good move for a temporary.*

"It is only the kwea of this town she fears," Tull said. "That is why she must leave. It happens that way even for a human, sometimes."

"I vote that we let the girl come," Scandal said, giving her the nod. The Pwi gave her their nod, also.

Phylomon looked at Wisteria and smiled. "Then I welcome you," he said, and his symbiote whispered, *I taste your fear.*

Tyrant bird

Chapter 5
Terror Is for Children

Phylomon counseled Scandal on preparations for the journey and had him spend four extra days building a heavier axle for the wagon, fulfilling Chaa's prophesy that the party would not leave until eleven days after Chaa had ended his Spirit Waik. The mayor's Dryad never returned to town. Scandal's wagon was massive, large enough to hold both the barrel and supplies. Scandal purchased a swivel gun that Jenks had been wanting to sell for scrap, and he mounted it on a platform on the front of his wagon, although the gun rode too low to shoot over the back of his mastodon. The Rough held many dangers—woolly rhinos, dire wolves, giant Mastodon Men, great horned dragons. Such animals would usually be frightened of a large party of humans and Pwi, and frightened animals are seldom dangerous, but the gun made Scandal feel more comfortable.

At sunrise on the day the party was to leave, Scandal came out of his inn to inspect his wagon, already loaded to the hilt, and stared: His swivel gun was gone.

"By God's flabby breasts!" Scandal shouted. "God rot

the Starfarer's left testicle!" He climbed up on the wagon. He could not believe it—the gun weighed over two hundred pounds. He scanned the streets, searching for the thief, picturing someone struggling to drag the gun off. But the streets were empty. He heard only waves smacking the rocks below the inn.

Phylomon came from his room wearing a black Pwi breech cloth. "Did I hear you blaspheming my testicles?" he said mildly.

"Oh, God, I'm sorry," Scandal shouted. "The gun has been stolen!"

Phylomon studied the wagon from beneath. "The thief greased those bolts to keep them quiet. They were newly bolted; he needn't have bothered."

Phylomon wandered down the road toward Pwi-town, studying the dust in the street, then ambled back north. "He took it this way—rested here."

Scandal hopped off the wagon, hitched up his sagging pants. Sure enough, there was a pockmark on the street where someone had rested the gun. Thirty feet away was another. The thief rounded a corner and the pockmarks came to an end; there was no sign of the gun.

"Shall we search the houses in this part of town?" Scandal asked.

Phylomon studied the ground. "The man who carried off your gun was at the end of his strength when he got here. Someone joined him. I doubt they hid it in town."

"But—but—how will we protect ourselves out there?" Scandal pointed vaguely to the mountains.

"I don't suppose this town has another gun we could purchase?"

"Just the cannons," Scandal said, nodding down to the turrets behind the inn where the ten inchers guarded the entrance to the port.

"I'll look around," Phylomon said, and for the next two hours Scandal marveled to see Phylomon the Wise, Destroyer of Bashevgo, Master Woodsman and Scholar, spend his time peeking under woodpiles, poking his nose into abandoned sheds, and peering at the tracks on every path that left the road.

Tull and the other Pwi arrived later in the morning.

Ayuvah came bearing his war spear and a shield made of painted tyrannosaur hide stretched over a wooden frame. The big Pwi rode the back of a giant black ox. He wore a wooden headband with a single sword fern tucked under his hair so that it flowed out the back. Little Chaa walked beside the bull, and their kin followed behind. Tull had tried to recruit other Pwi, but none dared go to Craal. Yet to Tull, the group seemed well balanced. Little Chaa was named for the magic crow, and even at a young age, Little Chaa was a gifted empath who often dreamed of what it was like to be a heron eating frogs in a marsh, or a rabbit living in fear. Because of his empathy, Little Chaa could call a wild crow to land on his arm if he saw one. Such empathy would lead the child to become a great Spirit Walker. But Ayuvah was named for the dire wolf, a creature noted for its ferocity and strength, its keen ability to hunt, and Ayuvah lived true to his promise. Of the Pwi on the trip, only Tull did not have an Animal Guide, and that rankled him.

Many Pwi came to watch the party leave. Etanai and Sava, Ayuvah's wife and daughter, Chaa and Zhopila with their five remaining children. Fava bore a spear in one hand, and she walked up and wrapped an arm around Tull.

"I will come with you," she said, watching Tull's eyes. "I love you—not the way I should, now that I'm your sister. I want to join my spear with yours on this journey, the way we did in Hotland. I want to come with you!"

Tull looked back at Wisteria, saw Wisteria's frown. "It wouldn't look right," Tull said, confused. "I'm married now."

"I know, but you're my brother now, too," Fava said, sniffling. "If I can't love you as a wife, I will still love you as a brother and a friend."

"It would be hard for you," Tull said.

"It would be harder for me to stay here, to sit by the fire and worry!" Fava answered loudly. Tull looked at the girl, embarrassed, not sure what to do.

Chaa came and took his daughter by the shoulder. "I have walked this future for you, my daughter whom I love. Tull would let you go, but I will not. You must stay!"

One old Pwi, a stranger with no hands, had come into town at dawn with a black leather bag tied around his neck.

When Fava was done, he pulled the bag off his neck with the stumps of his arms and gave it to Ayuvah.

Ayuvah opened the bag and looked in. "Bones?" he asked.

"Finger bones," the old man corrected, "from my hands. When I escaped Craal, the Blade-Kin-we-all-fear hunted me by night. They crouched on the ground and hunted by scent, like wolves, and when they caught me, they cut off my hands and put them in this bag. The bones are all that is left."

"Why do you tell me this?" Ayuvah asked in disgust.

"So you will be careful. You are a hunter, and you know how to hide your tracks. If you will hide yourself from the Blade Kin, you must hide your scent."

Scandal asked Phylomon, "Is that true?"

"Ayaah," Phylomon said. "The Neanderthal Blade Kin can run faster than humans, so they often help catch any Thralls who escape. I've known the Blade Kin to run down slaves using dire wolves, too."

It was a bad thing for a Pwi to leave family, almost as painful as a funeral. Old Zhopila took it hardest—she was letting three sons go at once, and the stranger's words frightened her. She kept telling them over and over again, "Beware of the Blade Kin! Beware of Adjonai. I will be here, waiting for you!"

Chaa took Tull aside and said, "When the time comes, capture the serpents *shev-mat-fwe-da,* before the sun even thinks to move. And I must tell you now: Beware the Spirit Walkers of the Blade Kin. They are not connected to the Earth and to one another, so they cannot walk the future, and they have no Animal Guides to help them. Instead, they pervert their powers. These twisted ones are the hands of Adjonai! Beware of them or the hand of Adjonai will crush you!"

Phylomon and Little Chaa collared the old bull mastodon and backed him between his tugs. Little Chaa pulled Snail Follower's right tusk and lifted a foot, and the mastodon put his trunk down for the young Neanderthal to step on, then gave the boy a boost. Little Chaa squatted on the bull's neck and in moments had the tugs locked into the hames, then took his seat on Snail Follower's collar. Little

Chaa urged him forward and the wagon crept out of town, taking the road to Finger Mountain and beyond that to Gate of the Gods. Scandal rode in the front seat of the wagon, while Wisteria sat on blankets in the mouth of the barrel and looked out the back. Tull, Phylomon, and Ayuvah walked alongside.

The first day of the journey was a mere walk. The road twisted a serpentine path just out of town and headed up into the mountains through groves of fir and redwood. Always the river was nearby, slow waters overshadowed by redwood. Always the earthy smell of summer river water filled the air. After ten miles, Phylomon wanted to stop at High Valley, but the men were obliged to continue—the apples were on, and farmers had a hard time keeping elk out of the orchards. They didn't need a mastodon to rip limbs from their trees.

When the Starfaring paleobiologists built Anee, they created sanctuaries—walled regions where flora and fauna could be introduced in a protected environment. Each sanctuary was surrounded by a wall forty feet high and twenty feet wide, and these walls often enclosed a thousand square miles. Smilodon Bay was enclosed by such a wall, and the portal into the Rough was called Gate of the Gods.

When the party set camp that afternoon, Phylomon asked, "Who will be first watch?"

The men all looked at him in amazement. "We've still got eight miles before we reach Gate of the Gods," Scandal answered. "We can worry when we get beyond the gate."

Phylomon regarded him coolly, but said nothing.

They set camp under an apple tree at the edge of a meadow filled with vetch and wild pea. The river flowed lazily only a hundred yards off, and the mastodon rolled in the pools for an hour, then wandered about the meadow pulling up vetch in a colossal attempt to defoliate the area.

Phylomon went to the wagon, pulled out half a dozen practice weapons—wooden swords, maces with heads made of cloth, simple wooden shields and spears. "Gentlemen," he said to the men, "if we go into Craal, we must pass the Blade Kin. I know you must get some practice in Smilodon Bay, but none of you has received the kind of battle training that they have—yet. Take your favorite weapon, and let's see what you are made of."

"Hah, not me!" Scandal begged off. "I'm not one to fight with weapons like that. Just give me a skillet or a cleaver, and I can hold my own!" Phylomon looked at the fat man, and grunted his contempt. He fought the others in mock battle, running them through their paces. Little Chaa took a wooden scimitar, a weapon that was light enough to be suitable for him. He surprised Phylomon by using it as a thrusting weapon, and once he had it inside Phylomon's guard, he twisted his wrist so that the curved wooden blade would twist around, nicking the inside of his opponent's sword arm. He was not fast, powerful, or graceful, but the child showed some common sense and good promise.

Ayuvah took a long spear and danced about Phylomon keeping from his reach, trying to strike at any target. Phylomon used a long sword that let him parry the blows, and Ayuvah could not get past his guard. Phylomon laughed. "You're fast and clever, but you've never been trained by a master of the spear."

"I've seen him kill a tyrannosaur with a spear," Tull put in.

Phylomon stood back for a moment. "Is that true?" he asked.

Ayuvah nodded. "I use the mammoth stroke, like my father showed me."

"That explains it," Phylomon said. "You are too used to fighting big animals. You try too hard to put power behind your blows, and it slows you. You don't need that stroke to kill a human—just concentrate on putting a hole in me. You must be quick and slimy. You need to extend your lunges— try misdirection. When you plan to go for my head, lunge low as if you are aiming at my leg, then pull the spear up quick toward my face. With your style, you will need to commit yourself to an attack, and that is dangerous. When you commit yourself, you need to make sure that no matter how your opponent counters, you can still get your blow. In a few weeks, I can turn you into a dangerous man."

Tull tried him next, and took a long-handled kutow for a weapon. Tull liked the weight the double ax heads gave him when attacking, and the long handle let him strike deep. In all of Smilodon Bay, no one had ever been able to beat him when he practiced with the kutow. But Tull found that watching Little Chaa and Ayuvah fight the blue man had been no help. Phylomon took a wooden shield and a broadsword for weapons—the classic weapons issued for Craal warriors. Tull rushed in and swung, and Phylomon put the shield overhead and parried. Tull slammed for the right side, testing the blue man's sword arm, and Phylomon turned the blow with his sword. So Tull rained blows down from all sides and all angles, looking for a weakness, but he could not swing a blow that Phylomon couldn't parry. Phylomon was in and out, dodging and turning the blows, never taking the counterstrike. Tull kept waiting for Phylomon to take the offensive, but he never did. Yet Tull found that he was afraid of that counterstrike and, therefore, tried to maintain his distance. He wanted to be quick and slimy, like Ayuvah, but it did not let him put his strength behind the blow. After three full minutes of embarrassment, Tull got mad and swung with his might.

Phylomon tried to turn the blow on his shield. The shield splintered in half, and the kutow slammed into his arm, knocking him to the ground.

"Oh, God, are you all right!" Scandal shouted.

Phylomon sat there, a bit shaken. He looked up at Tull. "You should always swing with your might. It's devastating. I think we've found your style." He looked at the men. "From now on, we practice twice a day—every day. We've got twelve weeks until we reach Craal. You'll want all the practice you can get before then."

That evening, as Tull helped set a fire, he thought about Wisteria, about the clean feel of her skin as he'd caressed her that morning, the taste of her lips, when suddenly from the brush just a hundred yards away, a great horned dragon leapt into the air with a roar.

Tull looked up, saw the forty-foot wingspan of the beast as the blue wings flashed above the treetops, and he fell backward on his butt and shouted.

The dragon's leather wings flapped with a loud *whoosh, whoosh.* Its long ostrichlike legs stretched out behind its short tail. Its thin forearms raked the air, claws exposed. Even though it flew a hundred feet above the men, the wind of its passage beat down on them. The dragon kept climbing, and while Tull tried to decide whether to be relieved he watched the dragon's flight path; the dragon headed for a copper-colored pterodactyl that soared, letting thermal updrafts carry him over the mountains.

The pterodactyl watched dully. *It must have flown three hundred miles from Dervin's Peninsula since dawn,* Tull thought. *It's too tired to escape.*

The dragon struck from above, slashing with the poisoned horn at the tip of its nose. The pterodactyl didn't try to evade, and the dragon grabbed the pterodactyl's wings with his tiny forearms. The two fell in a tangle, and from the forest floor squirrels began calling *Pahaa! Pahaaa!* The dragon shouted a booming *Graaaw,* as it fed in triumph.

Scandal looked over at the brush where the dragon had hidden. "By God we were lucky!" Scandal said. "That dragon was stalking us!"

"I'll take watch," Phylomon said. "We can't wait until we reach Gate of the Gods before we become wary."

That night, as they sat around the fire eating kabobs barbecued over the fire, Phylomon said, "I once knew another man named Scandal."

"Really?" Scandal asked. "It's not a common name."

"Ayaah. He was a recluse living in the marshes down in Beckley, named Jessoth Scandal."

"My great-grandfather!" Scandal said in astonishment. "My dad spoke fondly of him. I even have some of his recipes."

"I thought so," Phylomon said. "He was like you—a self-styled gourmet. But he had a fondness for reptiles. He used to keep alligators in a pit. He'd feed them only skunk meat for a month before he butchered them. Claimed it gave them better flavor."

"Did he?" Scandal asked. His eyes grew round with dismay—quite a feat considering the fleshy folds that nearly covered them.

Phylomon looked over at Tull and winked, got up and walked out into the meadow with his plate in hand. The sun had gone down, and the shadows were deep, but the sky was still light enough to see by. The crickets began their shrill thrumming music, and the night smell of warm soil filled the air.

The first stars were "striking their campfires," as the Pwi said, and Freya floated pale blue over the trees. Phylomon touched one of the medallions hanging from his necklace, stroked it softly. It began to brighten like a lantern. He held the medallion up and thumped it with his finger. Three bright flashes fired. Phylomon closed his fist over the medallion. The flesh of his hands glowed purple, showing each long bone in his fingers.

Tull came over. "What is that?" Tull asked, nodding at the necklace.

"A photoconverter. Part of an old lighting system," Phylomon said, not sure how much to answer. With sixty years of training Tull might master Hegled's Theory of Charmed Plasmatic Flow and its Effects on Spin and Shell Mutability, then he could understand the photoconverters, perhaps. He might even comprehend the deeper meanings of the theory—how, to travel at the speed of light, a man must become light; how, to travel at the speed of a tachyon, man must become a tachyon. Yet he'd never gain the technology to implement these concepts, not in a thousand years. Phylomon explained the photoconverter. "Around us in the air are many tiny particles that pass through us at high speeds, like tiny stones. When the crystal is compressed, the particles pass through a zone where their spin and speed are changed, and they emit light.

"Now that we are on our journey, I will use this light to call to the Creators. It is their job to care for the plants and animals of this world. If we can contact them, warn them that the eco-barrier is down, they can give birth to some new serpents and restock them." Phylomon watched Tull a moment to see if he understood. Many Pwi regarded the Creators as mere legend, beasts of myth. "Perhaps, added to the serpents we catch, it will be enough to rebuild the eco-barrier."

"Do you think a Creator saw that? Will it come now?"

"I don't know," Phylomon said. "Shepherd-One watches over this land. I have not seen him for many years, but once we used to talk often. He creates birds—dumb animals with large eyes, simple brains—to report on plant and animal populations. When the birds finish their journeys, Shepherd-One consumes them, unravels the memories stored in their DNA. In this way he learns what is happening in the world. If I flash my light often enough, one of his birds will see it, and Shepherd-One will know that I want to speak with him."

"Will he come then?" Tull asked.

"The Creator himself? No. The Creators in form are much like giant worms. They are nothing more than brains and stomachs, with their omniwombs attached. They keep themselves hidden from predators in large caverns underground in the far north. But he could send a servant to come see us, something with a mouth and brain—perhaps a creature that looks like a woman with wings, perhaps a monstrosity unlike anything you have ever seen. And that creature will carry my message to the Creators." The light in Phylomon's hand slowly died.

"Was that true, about Scandal's great-grandfather?" Tull asked.

"No," Phylomon said. "Scandal blasphemed my testicles this morning and I felt he needed a ribbing. I knew a Jessoth Scandal, and I seem to remember where he lived. But it was a hundred years ago and the details about the man are so blurred with other memories that they no longer really exist."

"Only the left one," Tull said. "Folks around here only blaspheme your left testicle."

Phylomon smiled. "You people are very bold, very open in what you say to me. I like that. Closer to Craal, people are more . . . opaque. Their faces are closed, secretive. They keep their feelings hidden."

"Ayaah," Tull said. "The sailors say, 'If you want an honest opinion from a Crawly, it's not hard to get as long as you're willing to shove a flaming torch up his ass.'" Phylomon laughed, and Tull looked at the blue man. "Myself, I always pictured you differently. I always thought of you as some old wizard, working away at your arcane technologies. You're more *human* than I'd imagined."

Phylomon laughed loud from the heart, and his voice echoed through the glade. At the edge of the meadow, a hundred yards distant, the mayor's Dryad appeared. She was small, almost boyish in figure and wore a dress of emerald green. She had a long knife in her hand. She watched the camp a moment, saw that no one was looking, and ran through the grass to Phylomon. Grasshoppers jumped from her path.

"Tchavs? Food?" she asked in Pwi. The child's green eyes were wide with fear, wild with hunger, yet Phylomon could see the beauty she'd become. She reminded him of Saita, a Dryad he'd loved when he was young. He'd met the creature in the mountains during her Time of Devotion, and was unable to resist the aphrodisiac perfume of her body during her mating frenzy. She had been voluptuous, and Phylomon could not imagine Saita ever having been anything like this child—small, boyish. He gave her his plate.

"Don't feed her!" Tull said. "She might follow us."

"I will only follow you to the White Mountains, where I hope-with-painful-hope to find the aspen forests. I can pay for the food!" the Dryad said. Her voice was as soft and musical as the tinkling of small bells. Phylomon strained to understand her.

"What is your name, child?" Phylomon asked.

"Tirilee."

"And what coin will you pay for the food?"

"Two men followed from town," Tirilee said. "They circled you and went on up ahead. They've got a gun, a big heavy one. It takes both of them to carry it. They tried hard to make sure you would not see them, and they talked of meeting up with others ahead."

Phylomon bent his head in thought. "So . . . it does not sound as if they came to return our stolen property."

The Dryad smiled up at him. The mottled coloring of her silver skin gave her face an elongated look. The feral gleam in her eye was uncommon for such a child.

"Do you think they'll attack?" Tull asked.

"I'm certain," Phylomon said. "I haven't cleaned the slavers out of your town yet. By executing a few, I earned their resentment. By flashing a fortune in gems before their eyes, I stirred their greed." Phylomon thought. *They certainly won't attack so near Smilodon Bay. The evidence*

*would be too easily discovered. They'll wait a few days, until
we get into the Rough, beyond Gate of the Gods.*

"Tell me," Phylomon said to the girl, "Do you know the
men you saw?"

"The mayor's brothers," Tirilee answered. "The stupid
one, and the longhair."

"Those aren't slavers," Tull said in surprise. "She's talking about Hardy. He's a friend of mine—a moron. And his
brother Saffrey is—"

"Willing to commit murder," Phylomon said. "It sounds
as if the brothers were close—if you made an enemy of one,
you made enemies of them all."

Tull nodded.

"You call Hardy your friend," Phylomon said, "yet in
his eagerness to avenge his brothers, he plans to kill you and
your wife. Somewhere ahead, they will point that gun at us,
and they won't kill me and leave witnesses behind. I'd
choose my friends more carefully from now on, if I were
you."

They reached Gate of the Gods at noon the next day. The
wall of black rock was composed of layer after layer of molten slag, each an inch thick. The gate was a simple arch,
thirty feet tall at the center. Men had trampled the ground
beneath the arch, while Mastodon Men, a type of giant carnivorous ape-man that had once inhabited Earth, had
pounded off bits of the black molten slag for use as crude
knives.

As they crossed beneath the arch, Scandal inhaled
deeply and seemed to stiffen with fear. He got into the
wagon and began drinking wine and started singing a bawdy
song noted for its endless verses:

*Oh, with all the time I spent in jail,
I should have been a jailer,
But I love a whore in every port,
and that's why I'll stay a sailor.*

*Oh, I knew a girl named Dena
She lived in old South Bay*

She so loved to get naked,
She threw her clothes away . . .

"Quiet, you fool!" Phylomon hissed, and the blue man hurried ahead, scouting the trail.

No one spoke for the rest of the day as they walked. They watched for danger, and signs were everywhere—a dozen yards on the other side of the arch, they found the fresh track of a Mastodon Man—a footprint twenty-one inches long and twelve inches wide. The redwoods were tall and dark, and their bark was often scarred and pitchy fifteen feet up where saber-tooths had sharpened their claws. In the perpetual gloom under the redwoods, plants grew to enormous heights: Ferns stood over six feet, and the wild raspberry had selectively bred over generations so that only those with leaves as broad as plates flourished. Moldering serpentine limbs of vine maple climbed fifty feet into the air in an effort to garner the thin sunlight that filtered down, and all the limbs trailed old man's beard.

The party traveled for hours, following an old trapper's path into the mountains, before they finally found a clearing where the grass was thick enough to keep the mastodon from straying in search of food. The clearing was situated on a gently sloping hill, and a shallow pond, muddied by wild pigs, sat in a fold near the forest floor. They parked the wagon just inside the line of trees, and Scandal and Tull unpacked while the Pwi unhooked the mastodon and cleared an area around camp.

Phylomon took his great black dragon-horn bow from the back of the wagon and strung it, fitting a loop of the bowstring over one end, bending the bow with his knee, and fitting the second loop over the other end. He reached into his quiver and took out two rectangular pieces of leather, like hats, which he fit over the strung ends of the bow so the bowstrings wouldn't catch in the brush. "I believe I shall go hunt some swine," he said quietly, nodding toward the muddied pond where the bank was pocked with tracks.

"Do you want me to come?" Tull asked, knowing what game Phylomon stalked. "I'm handy with a spear."

"No," Phylomon said, grateful for the offer. "I can handle them by myself. I've done it often enough before."

Scandal said in a bluster, "We've plenty of meat still. I don't want to be up butchering all night!"

"I don't believe that even you know a recipe to make this particular breed of swine palatable," Phylomon told Scandal. He ducked off into a thicket of vine maple and began stalking toward the hilltop without a sound, into the deep woods where "pigs" would sleep until early evening.

"You're damned right I don't want those swine," Scandal admitted, "but by the Blue Man's left test . . . I mean, if you kill one, at least bring me the backstraps."

Phylomon made his way uphill quietly. He'd kept to the old trapper's trail all day and figured he would find sign of the Goodstick boys to one side. The only sounds were the occasional rap of a woodpecker in a distant tree and the drone of bees. Far away, the snarl of a scimitar cat echoed through the hills.

A hundred yards into the woods, it was so dark that the heavy brush dissipated for lack of sunlight. The ground was pocked and furrowed where wild pigs had rummaged for mushrooms. Phylomon found cat prints larger than his hand with his fingers spread wide, and on a branch he found a tuft of yellow-white hair from a saber-tooth. The hair was dry and old, and from bones that moldered beneath the redwood needles it looked as if the saber-tooth had killed a moose calf here in the spring.

He followed the trail, walking north of it a hundred, two hundred yards, scouting the ground for human tracks. It did not take long to find them in the thick humus. The ground was springy, covered with leaf mold. One could walk these woods and hide one's sound, but not one's tracks. The men had watched them strike camp, then headed away. The slavers had been kind—they'd even marked their trail here and there with bits of bright yellow cloth so they could follow it by torchlight. The men had scrambled over fallen redwoods, waded through dense ferns. He followed them. A mile from camp he found a small hill where he could watch a trail that wound down into a bowl-shaped valley.

Phylomon crouched by a blackened log and placed a small convex mirror in the bark above him so he could watch his back.

Fear, I taste your fear, the blue man's skin said to him.

Phylomon's muscles began to twitch in tiny electric jerks. Phylomon often told others that his skin was a symbiote, but he did not tell them how intelligent the being was, nor tell them of its powers.

"Gireaux, my old friend," Phylomon whispered. "We have strong enemies."

Kill? Shall I kill them? the symbiote asked.

"We shall fight them together," Phylomon answered. "Weave your armor about me now and prepare to strike. Feed from me. You must be strong for this fight."

Dizziness struck as the symbiote began to feed. Phylomon's heart raced. He could feel the creature drain him, siphoning his energy. His skin began to darken in shade. The symbiote was stretching, drawing static energy from the air. It was a good day for it—storm clouds scudded across the sky. He felt his skin tighten, binding him as if in leather, and the symbiote tightened his eardrums, tuning them to the small sounds of the woods.

Phylomon sat, and for a time he replayed a memory in his mind. When he was young, he'd loved a woman, one of the poor short-lived temporaries. He'd been taking drugs to enhance his memory at the time, so he recalled every moment of his youth. He replayed the memory of a visit he'd made to this forest with his wife. It had been in his youth, just after he'd led the Neanderthals in an attack that decimated the Slave Lords in Bashevgo. Those had been happy times, for Phylomon believed then that he'd destroyed the slavers forever. The trees had been young, their trunks narrower. He'd made love to his wife in a bed of ferns, and they watched Thor rise. Green storm clouds had played across the face of the tan moon, strung out like pearls on a necklace, and when blue Freya had risen and overtaken Thor in its flight, the two moons shone from behind a banded cloud and colored the sky like opal.

Phylomon heard the slavers from Smilodon Bay long before he saw them. They'd sent a scout, and the man spotted Phylomon, went back to the others. An hour later, the scout returned, grunting and sweating as he carried the gun. He stealthily circled Phylomon, out of sight, and then carefully crept in close and set the unwieldy gun down in the brush, taking long careful aim. Phylomon watched the scout with the mirror, careful to pretend to be looking down in the valley. The scout kept ducking behind the ferns.

The swivel gun was made of crude iron and had a three-foot barrel. Pirates sometimes mounted such guns on boarding vessels: it held a single cartridge that fired a four-inch bullet. It was a clumsy weapon, meant to be fired at a ship at point-blank range. Phylomon considered what to do. If he attacked the scout, he could surely kill him, but more slavers were out there, and Phylomon feared that some might escape. Phylomon did not believe the scout would try to shoot him with that clumsy old gun for the moment. No, it was better to wait until all the slavers gathered.

Although Phylomon felt the presence of the symbiote, could speak to it, he could not tell it the exact nature of his enemies, could never communicate the concept of *gun* to the animal. Instead, he let his fear run through him and felt the skin harden like bands of steel.

Five men walked up through the woods along the trail, a simple diversion for the real threat behind. Phylomon watched the men, notched an arrow as if he'd taken the bait, and then he moved ten feet to the left. He imagined the gunner scurrying to correct his aim, and then he whirled and fired his arrow.

The gunner took the arrow in the knee, looked up in fear. He jerked the barrel of the gun, pointing it vaguely in Phylomon's direction, and dropped the hammer. Smoke boiled from the barrel, and Phylomon dodged, yet the ball slammed into his ribs, and the blue man was knocked backward, spun and dropped.

"On him, boys!" the gunman shouted. "He's down!"

Phylomon grabbed his side, felt the bloody mess. It was numb, and he could see nothing, for he was blinded by pain. He coughed, and tasted the blood run from his throat, swallowed it. He heard the men running toward him in the darkness, and he pulled a long ragged piece of flesh from the gaping wound. He had never been hurt so badly. His ribs were split and pulped, and the symbiote anesthetized him. He heard his ribs cracking as the symbiote manipulated them back into position, felt the hot burning as muscles regenerated. Phylomon pulled the knife that he kept strapped to his right leg, and cried out at the pain.

Fear. I taste fear, the symbiote said.

He heard the gunman limping toward him, and the men drew around him in a circle.

"He's wounded," one man said. "Look at the hole! It's closing up! Quick, shoot him again!"

Fear. I taste fear.

The gunman popped the chamber of the swivel gun open, grunted and swore as he pulled the hot shell from the chamber. One fellow rushed forward and swung an ax down on Phylomon's neck. It connected with a dull thud, and the man swore. "I can't cut through!"

Why do you fear?

The gunman dropped another heavy shell into the chamber, and Phylomon's vision cleared so that he could see a shadow move toward the gunman. The two men grunted as they lifted the barrel.

"Kill them," Phylomon said. The evening air crackled and filled with white smoke and ozone as the symbiote earned its keep.

After dinner, Scandal took Ayuvah downhill to pick blackberries, leaving only Little Chaa to watch the mastodon. Yet Little Chaa had called a crow to his hand and stood feeding it and talking softly while the mastodon foraged. Tull stayed with the wagon and kept staring into the forest, listening for the wratching call of jays, the snap of a twig. He got into the wagon and pulled out his battle armor—the leather band for his head, an iguanadon-hide shield painted in forest green and brown, leather leggings and wrist guards. He pulled out his kutow. For a long time, he watched Ayuvah and Scandal pick berries down by the pond. The orange-haired Neanderthal was a premier woodsman who hunted by scent, as some Blade Kin were said to do. Ayuvah's presence made Tull feel safe. He wondered if he should tell Ayuvah what Phylomon was up to. But who knew what Phylomon would find? Perhaps the men would not be out there. Even if they were, would they really harm anyone in the party? Hardy Goodstick the moron?

Wisteria saw Tull looking at his kutow and asked "Is something wrong?"

"No," Tull said, taking her hand. He considered. No, he'd worked for Hardy many times. Hardy would never hurt him. Tull dropped his war gear, then led her uphill, away from camp, and they found a place to lie in a small field of oats burned white as ash by the summer sun. Tull held her delicately, as if she were a bouquet of roses that he did not want to crush. He'd seen the way Chaa and Zhopila treated one another. They were not only affectionate, they'd found countless and often ingenious ways to serve one another: Chaa would hunt in the mountains in winter for merganser ducks to make pillows so Zhopila could have something soft to sit on while she ground her wheat for dinner; Zhopila grew a patch of mint, which she then dried and brought into the house to make it smell sweet. Tull stared at Wisteria, and wondered how he could show her that this was the type of love he craved to give her. For the last two days he'd tried. He'd watched Ayuvah clear rocks and pine cones from Little Chaa's bed, saw the way he kept the boy's water jug filled, and Tull followed Ayuvah's example, hoping that by emulating myriad small acts he could learn to love.

Yet, he sensed something odd in his relationship with Wisteria. She seemed cool toward him. The caress of her fingers as she teased the hairs at the nape of his neck gave him chills, filled his loins with fire. The smell of her breath pleased him more than Scandal's finest banquet. To lay his hand on her hip and know that Wisteria was his wife filled him with joy. Yet he could tell that she did not feel this way about him, and this scared Tull, for he wondered if he was losing her because he did not know how to love.

He kissed her slowly, and let his hand ease along her blouse till it cupped her breast. She pushed him away.

"I'm sorry," she said. "I'm not in the mood."

"I'm the one who should be sorry," Tull said. "My timing is bad. I should not be thinking of you tonight. Yesterday, we saw the mayor's Dryad, and she said that men from town are following us, and they have the swivel gun. Phylomon went to hunt them, yet the men from town may well be hunting us tonight. I should go and tell the others."

Wisteria smiled up at him. "Make love to me, quickly," she said. Wisteria pulled him to the ground, and her kisses grew passionate and insistent. The sun was setting. Tull heard a squirrel bark *Pahaa, Pahaa,* and sat up. The squirrel barked from the woods on the west side of the clearing.

Wisteria pulled him down, kissed him, and said, "These last few days with you have been the best of my life. I've never felt such peace and joy as I feel in your arms."

Tull looked into her brown eyes. Her pupils were dilated, and her lips and cheeks were ruddy from kissing. Her breath was warm on his throat. He kissed her softly, and a deep echoing boom filled the woods to the east, echoed and re-echoed off the hills.

"The swivel gun!" Tull said.

Tull jumped up and ran back down the hill to camp. Little Chaa stood on the wagon, peering into the heart of the woods. Tull put on his headband, grabbed his war shield, pulled his kutow.

Little Chaa shouted, "I heard someone yell," then jumped from the wagon. Tull stood, not knowing what to do. Little Chaa tore through the weapons and picked a long narrow spear. Downhill, Scandal and Ayuvah waded cautiously through deep ferns toward the forest edge.

Tull heard a definite shout, someone barking the word *No!* But the voice did not seem to come from the woods; instead it seemed to come from a small hill on the other side of the valley. Tull realized it was only a trick of acoustics, the voice echoing off the hill, but Scandal and Ayuvah scrambled off in the apparent direction of the source of the sound.

Tull took some hesitant steps into the forest and told Little Chaa, "Stay with the wagon." Wisteria ran up and stood behind Tull. He peered into the growing shadows of the redwoods, and he could definitely hear jays and squirrels shrieking their warnings. He would have run forward, but he knew that if men from town had set an ambush, it would be set right in front of him. He studied the shadows behind the trees, tuning his senses to that area.

Behind him, Little Chaa said, "Ah, no!" and Tull heard a single slap and the sound of a body sliding in the grass. Tull turned, thinking someone had come up behind him, and before him in the shadows stood a giant man with a long sloping forehead and massive jaws, a pale brown naked body lightly covered with coarse hair, and Tull stared into the navel of this beast and watched its rib cage expand and shrink as it breathed.

And kwea struck him—an old terror more powerful than anything he'd ever experienced. Tull watched the creature and felt as if he were slipping, falling, as if he'd been climbing a hill and the ground suddenly broke beneath him. His heart leapt in panic. His legs collapsed, and it seemed to take forever to drop to the ground. He could not breathe, dared not breathe. His lungs felt clogged with the smell of soured sweat and carrion. The beast before him stood nine feet tall and was at least four feet wide at the shoulders. It stood, bent forward, and its long arms could almost touch the ground. It picked up Little Chaa, and Tull could see that Little Chaa had nearly been ripped apart at the stomach by the blow of this creature's fist.

Wisteria cried, "Mastodon Men!" and took off running. The sound of her voice seemed to startle the creature, and it turned toward her and roared, flashing its yellow fangs, shaking the corpse of Little Chaa in the air with one mighty fist.

And Tull could not move. In his mind's eye, Tull was a child again, cowering in his bedroom. Instead of a Mastodon Man, Jenks stood before him. And instead of rattling the corpse of Little Chaa in the air, Jenks rattled shackles in the air. Tull heard the distant sound of a child wailing in terror, like the sound of a tea kettle as it boils. He knew that this was not Jenks standing before him, knew he should strike with his kutow or run. Waves of nausea and fear crashed against him, slapping him to the ground. And somewhere beside him, a child was wailing. The Mastodon Man turned and looked at Tull, casually ripped Little Chaa in two at the waist, then bit deeply into his liver and chewed tentatively, as if to consider whether it liked the flavor.

Suddenly Tull saw other Mastodon Men stalk across the clearing, silently, often stooping to rest on the weight of their knuckles. He saw eight in all. One climbed up on the wagon and began tossing out barrels of stores, shattering kegs of wheat with its fist. Tull wrapped his arms around his legs and curled in protectively. He wished he could hide, but he was too terrified to move. And beside Tull, a child was whining.

The Mastodon Man that dined on Little Chaa studied Tull carefully, then reached out with one giant finger as long and thick as Tull's jaw and lightly thumped him on the chest, knocking him over. Tull seemed to feel himself falling slowly through deep water that crushed his lungs, making it impossible to breathe, where the air carried the cold weight of many atmospheres, into a world of alternating bands of light and dark, light and dark.

Tull woke to the sound of a child wailing, a keening sound both distant and perilously close. Phylomon stood before him in the dark, swinging a medallion that flashed as if it were fire.

"Come now, come," the blue man said softly, taking Tull by the shoulder. "Terror is for children."

Tull's chest began to heave, as if he were coughing heavily, and he realized that there was no child crying beside him, that the sound came from his own throat, and he began to shout. His limbs trembled uncontrollably.

Phylomon held him for a moment. "So, you have met the Mastodon Men before? The kwea of old fear is upon you."

"No! No," Tull said. "Father! My father!"

Phylomon studied. "Ayaah," he said. "How old were you when you left home?"

Tull shook as if with chills and considered. He could not remember, only wanted to vomit. Yet he pondered upon the question, focused on it. "Thirteen."

"So, and you are what, eighteen, twenty?" Phylomon calculated. "Then if you were human, I'd say you might recover in another ten years. I've found it to be a good rule of thumb—for every year we live in the care of our parents, it takes a year to recuperate."

Tull listened to the words, and each word seemed complete yet somehow logically separated from the others. Tull peered into the darkness behind Phylomon. Scandal was crying, and at his feet was the spindly arm of Little Chaa, ragged flesh still clinging to the bone. "Where's Wisteria?" Tull asked.

"In the hills, still running, I imagine," Phylomon said. "Ayuvah is tracking her by scent. We will have her back in a few hours."

Scandal picked up the arm, placed it in a bag, still crying. "We'll need to build a pyre," he said. "Then go back home and tell Chaa that his son is dead."

Tull spoke without thinking. "Chaa Spirit Walked this journey. He already knows." And the force of his own words hit him. Chaa had known this would happen, and his face had been drawn in a horrible grimace of grief because he knew his son would die.

Phylomon said, "From the looks of it, you are fortunate to be alive. The Mastodon Men would have eaten you, but when they saw Snail Follower they went for tastier game." Phylomon stood up straight, and groaned as if in pain.

"Are you all right?" Tull asked.

"A little bruise," Phylomon said, holding his ribs. "I'll be all right."

"They drove our mastodon off!" Scandal said. "Just drove Snail Follower into the woods. They took our barrel! What luck! We needed that like a lizard needs tits."

Tull sat disbelieving—one man dead, Wisteria off in the woods, the mastodon and barrel lost. "What will we do?"

Phylomon answered, "We'll wait for Ayuvah to return with Wisteria. We can walk to Denai without the barrel and the mastodon, if need be, and hope to replace them there. But I fear that plan: Too many things could go wrong. Scandal would be forced to stay in the city for weeks, and the Crawlies are notorious for their curiosity about strangers. Unless he could prove that he was on business for one of the lords from a major family, it could spell ruin. No, I think we must try to get our mastodon and barrel back. But first we must burn the corpses of your townspeople." At first Tull thought Phylomon was speaking of Little Chaa, but then he realized Phylomon spoke of others.

An hour later the three men stumbled through the shadows of the redwoods with a lantern in hand, and they came on the corpses, laid out side by side, like fish lying on the docks. The swivel gun lay on the ground beside them.

"Do you recognize them?" Phylomon asked.

Jen Brewer, one of Scandal's own employees, was shot cleanly through the heart with an arrow. Caral Dye, a retired sailor, and Denzel Sweetwater, the schoolteacher, had both been hacked with the sword. Saffrey and Hardy Goodstick lay on the ground, their skin blackened in places, smelling of smoke, looking for all the world as if they'd been struck dead by lightning. Only a week before Tull had watched Hardy toss a bee's nest into an outhouse down in the warehouse district, and Jen Brewer had come bolting out so quickly that he left his pants by the toilet. Tull looked at Hardy's thick beard, his staring eyes, mouth still open in terror at realizing he'd reached his final moment. It was the first time Tull had seen the moron without a smile on his face.

They built the pyre with slabs of bark that had fallen from dying redwoods. Scandal carried out the task in blank-faced horror. Tull could not help thinking: If Little Chaa had not been eaten by the Mastodon Man, then perhaps the beast would have eaten me. Chaa had known that—had seen it on his Spirit Walk. He'd let his son be killed as a pawn in some larger game. The realization left Tull numb. He kept remembering the words, "You alone must catch the serpents! You alone!" And he realized dully that Chaa had meant it to the core of his soul. *You* alone *must* catch the serpents. The future Chaa had seen so terrified him that he sacrificed his own son to make sure that greater tragedies were thwarted. Somehow, until that moment, the quest had remained unimportant to Tull, a mere diversion.

While they worked, Scandal found only a dozen cartridges for the big gun in a backpack on Hardy's corpse, and searched in vain for more. Phylomon merely grumbled, "I should teach you all to use the bow. You can't rely on a steady supply of gunpowder in these parts yet." Dire wolves began howling deep in the forest. Phylomon said, "Unfortunately, I only wounded one of my attackers, shot him in the hip with an arrow. Perhaps the wolves will have him. He left quite a blood trail."

Tull could not help but hear the hopefulness in Phylomon's voice.

Tull shook his head and tried to fend off his feelings of

fatigue and sadness with a shrug. Phylomon was withdrawn, and they finished their work in silence, lit the pyre and watched the flames lick the flesh from the bones.

When the fire burned down, they carried the swivel gun back to camp, fixed it to the wagon with its bolts.

Ayuvah returned carrying Wisteria. He put her in the wagon, a blanket wrapped about her. Tull held her for a while.

"You are lucky she is human," Ayuvah whispered. "When she calmed down, she stopped and stayed in one place. It was not hard to find her. If she were a Pwi woman, she would still be running in fear."

The kwea at camp was strong with fear and sadness. Tull tried to help repack the wagon, but the overwhelming sense of despair he felt in the area made him move sluggishly. Scandal continued filling the bag with Little Chaa's parts, and afterward Ayuvah threw himself on the ground and wept for the better part of an hour.

Phylomon pulled both Tull and Ayuvah aside and walked with them into the woods. "You froze when you saw the Mastodon Men," Phylomon said to Tull as they walked. "Could you have saved the boy if you had moved?"

"No," Tull said. "He was already dead."

"Good. Then you will not bear the kwea of guilt," Phylomon said. "In the morning, we must track our mastodon and recover our barrel, and hope that both are somehow intact. I want you to keep Ayuvah from camp. The kwea of the place will be too much for him."

"Thank you," Tull said, surprised. Phylomon had seemed to him a man without compassion. He'd executed so many men so easily, it seemed strange for him to show even this small kindness.

"I know what you think of me," Phylomon said. "It's written on your face. Believe me, I do care for you. I understand kwea, even though I am not like you. When I was young, it was common for men to take seritactates, drugs, to enhance their memories. I say 'enhance,' yet that is not quite accurate. In those days, our memories were perfect, and a single treatment would enhance your memory for hundreds of years.

"In those days, I made the mistake of taking a wife—a

woman much like Wisteria, a slender woman with brown eyes and hair as soft as corn silk. She did not live to be sixty years old. I married her because I was young and in love, and I thought that even though she would die of old age while I was still young, I would be comforted because I would always carry the memory of that love. I can recall perfectly every moment of every day I spent with her. The way her lower lip trembled on the day her mother died; the taste of a potato she burned when we had been married for three years and seven days; I can recall her exact words when she told me how to cook a rabbit when we had been married for twenty-two years, sixty-six days. On the twenty-sixth day of the month of Harvest, in 3511, a ship came north from Botany bearing linen and oranges. I recall the smell of oranges on her breath the morning afterward as she kissed me. When she bore our first daughter, she developed a dark purple varicose vein on her right shin. I was once surprised a hundred years later when by chance, I saw that exact shape in the vein of a maple leaf where I camped by Fish Haven River. I recall later the smell of death on her breath when I kissed her good-bye at her funeral pyre. I remember perfectly the tinge of purple in her face as we dropped the torches. Sometimes at night I still dream of her, and everything about her is fixed perfectly. I remember her in her youth, and pictures flash in my mind, and I seem to watch from one moment to the next as the wrinkles begin to form on her face, as first one hair turns gray and then another, as her muscles go soft and lose their definition until her back is bent. Before my eyes she loses her beauty and crumbles into the ground. And from moment to moment, only two things remain the same—my love for her and the devastating emptiness I have felt ever since I lost her. This is as close as a human can come to feeling kwea."

Ayuvah said, "I think that would be as bad as losing a brother."

"Oh, I've lost a brother too," Phylomon said. "A hundred and fifty years ago. We had grown apart for years, and I seldom saw him, and one day I realized that I had neither seen him nor heard from him for years. I traveled the land for six years looking for him, never really sure he was dead. The slavers killed him, I fear. He had a red skin, very similar to mine. His symbiote was called a pyroderm, for it let him burn things with fire at will, and I keep hoping that someday I will find his skin, like the husk of a snake, half-buried under a rock in the forest. Even after all this time, his symbiote will not have rotted away, you see. Yes, I have lost brothers, parents, children, lovers . . .

"Among the Eridani whose warships circle our world, they say we are all a million beings struggling to become one man. Yet it only happens as we draw closest to attaining a single, pure emotion. They say there is only one hate. And there is only one joy. And there is only one ecstasy. And to the extent that we share that emotion in all of its fullness, we become one person. If you and your lover share perfect ecstasy, you are no longer separate people, but in the minds of the Eridani you have become one. We are not Eridani, thinking with a communal mind, but I am like you, Tull and Ayuvah, because I too feel. Yet I shall never feel emotions as powerfully as you." Phylomon stood a moment, reflecting.

"There is a part of the brain called the hypothalamus, and it is the seat of emotions. A Pwi has a much larger hypothalamus than do humans, and they lead an emotional life so rich and complex that I—and possibly even you, Tull Genet—cannot fathom it. When a Pwi hunts near a rock and is frightened by a rattlesnake, the incident arouses such anxiety that for several hours he will be afflicted with fear while the incident fixes in his mind, and the memory of the rock and the snake and the terror become inseparably tied together so that he will forever avoid that rock again, fearing that the same snake will lurk nearby. The same man with an empty belly might find a tree with hazelnuts and fill himself. The tree and the pleasure of fulfillment become so intoxicating that for several hours he holds it in his mind, until he can never think of passing that area without remembering the pleasure of the hazelnuts beneath the tree. It is a simple and valuable mechanism that helped Neanderthals eke out an existence on the Earth thousands of years ago."

Tull laughed sarcastically, wondering if Ayuvah could understand English well enough to follow the conversation. "You make it sound as if kwea is a blessing to the Pwi."

"To the Pwi, yes. But not to you. They may feel more deeply than you do, but not in all aspects. You see, the Pwi are protected to some degree from the ravages of terror that afflict you, Tull Genet. Their brains secrete endorphins that diminish the worst terrors. They call themselves 'the Smiling People' because their brains are stewing in intoxicants supplied by their own bodies. But from the way you reacted to the Mastodon Man, I suspect that the Pwi endorphins your brain produces bind poorly to the chemoreceptors in your human brain. You are unsheltered from some harmful kwea. It is a common affliction among the Tcho-Pwi. Rarely do men like you thrive."

Tull had only met another Tcho-Pwi once—a small girl who was weak and sickly; a girl with dull eyes who could not speak. "What do you mean?" His heart beat. He knew what Phylomon meant.

Phylomon said, "Being half-human and half-Pwi, you are slave to both sequential memories and emotional memories. Few of your kind are physiologically capable of adjusting to this. The fear and despair overwhelm them. Your father gave you the kwea you felt tonight. It is a powerful and dangerous thing. But you handle it well. I think it much more likely that you will be destroyed by love." Phylomon said these last words as if they were mere observation. "Yet I hope better for you. Sincerely."

Tull watched the blue man, so tall that he seemed deformed, alien. It was not surprising that such a man thought in alien patterns. It *was* surprising that Tull somehow felt the man to be his brother under the skin.

At dawn, Phylomon brought Tull and Ayuvah back to the camp, and in a short ceremony, they cremated what was left of Little Chaa. A flock of crows came and circled the smoke as it rose to heaven, and Tull could not help but feel that Little Chaa, released from his body, had called the crows to bear witness of his presence.

Wisteria spent her morning in the back of the party's wagon, wrapped in a blanket, nursing her scratches and bruises. During the night, no one had been able to see how much of the food had been destroyed, but now it was plain that nearly every barrel, every sack had been ripped open. Much of the food was unsalvageable. Tull helped clean up.

In some deep grass a hundred feet from the wagon, he found a bag of platinum eagles—at least a thousand of them.

"Where did these come from?" he asked.

Scandal answered quickly. "I brought them."

"A fortune like that will do you no good out here," Phylomon said.

Scandal hesitated. "We're going to Denai," he said. "The inns there are famed for their cuisine."

"I had heard that they are only famed for their whores," Phylomon said. "The Craal slavers breed their whores for beauty, much as other men breed cattle. In over forty generations, not one of Denai's madams has been sold outside the city."

"Ayaah," Scandal blushed. "Well, let us just say that an innkeeper must know how to serve many kinds of dishes."

Tull looked at the money and gasped. Scandal had borrowed money for the trip, yet here he had enough money to buy three ships. Enough for a man like Scandal to live on comfortably for the rest of his life. The innkeeper could not plan to spend more than a night or two in Denai, yet in that short time he would spend his life fortune on whores!

"Let's get our barrel and find our mastodon," Tull said. "Perhaps Snail Follower escaped the Mastodon Men and needs someone to show him the way back to camp."

Phylomon nodded. "I think that would be prudent."

"What?" Scandal said, "and leave me here with Wisteria?"

"Actually," Phylomon said, "I had not thought of leaving you here with Wisteria. Tull should stay with his wife."

"But—but—" Scandal objected.

Tull looked at the camp, the food on the ground. He could not help but recall the perverse kwea the Mastodon Man had emanated. The way he had felt so helpless and weak before it. "I must come with you," he said. "To meet the Mastodon Men."

Shortly after breakfast, Tull and Ayuvah went down to the pond to prepare for the hunt. It seemed only right to have Ayuvah lead the hunting party. The Neanderthal threw three stones into the water and watched the ripples move over the pond. Then he sat down by the bank and closed his eyes, and Tull did likewise.

"Think only thoughts of peace for the Mastodon Men," Ayuvah counseled Tull. "Let peace emanate from you, just as the ripples emanate from the stone. You must hunt with this attitude. If your prey smells your bloodlust, they will hide from you. Also, it does not help to be picky. Many times I have gone to hunt for grouse, only to find a silver fox in the bush. The Animal Spirits give themselves as they will, and we should not be choosy. This day, we hunt for Snail Follower, but perhaps another mastodon will give itself to us. If that is what the Animal Spirits decide, so be it."

Ayuvah sat with his eyes closed, and Tull wondered at him. The man was so strong. He could tell that Ayuvah grieved for Little Chaa, yet Ayuvah held it in. They sat for nearly half an hour. Tull watched the water and tried to cleanse his thoughts. A giant green dragonfly with a two-foot wingspan hovered over the water. Tull looked up, startled by the buzzing of its wings, and saw on the other side of the pond, at the edge of the forest, a dark gray dire wolf watching them, panting, its tongue hanging out. The wolf yawned.

Ayuvah opened his eyes, looked at the wolf. "My Animal Guide is with me," he said. "It is time for us to go."

Tull looked back at the wolf, and it had stepped back into the trees, and was gone.

A few moments later, the men began tracking. The Mastodon Men had battered Snail Follower, leaving a trail of ripped ferns and bloodied tree limbs. The mastodon had torn the thick humus of the forest floor badly, running blindly one moment, turning to charge its attackers the next. There had been fourteen Mastodon Men in the band. For some arcane purpose, the Mastodon Men had also taken the group's beer keg, and one of them rolled it along behind the party, obscuring the tracks.

"They are driving him," Phylomon said in Pwi at one point, jutting his chin in a northwesterly direction. "No matter which way the beast tries to run, they turn him north."

"Where are they taking him?" Tull asked.

"The Mastodon Men are not smart enough to fashion

spears," Ayuvah answered, "so they club the animal, making it bleed from small wounds until it is exhausted. They will make Snail Follower walk to their camp so they can eat him." Ayuvah said, leaning on his spear as he knelt to put his hand in the track of a Mastodon Man, "Even if he broke free, his pain will be great. He will be as crazy as that rogue bull that crushed Shezzah's house a few years back."

Tull said, "Perhaps he will smell us and remember his friends."

"Do not raise your hopes for Snail Follower," Phylomon answered. "He has been hurt. Even should we catch him, we might not be able to harness him for weeks." Phylomon did not say anything for a moment. "How far would we have to go to get another animal?" he asked.

Tull said, "Scandal got Snail Follower from a miner down in White Rock, but that was the only one in town. The loggers down in Wellen's Eyes have a few. Two hundred miles. That's the closest."

Phylomon did not say anything. Two hundred miles south, a journey that would easily take a month. They did not have a month to spend.

The party tracked the Mastodon Men in silence. The path was so easy to follow that they did not need to watch the ground. Instead they watched the trees and brush. The Mastodon Men would be resting in their band, asleep in some bed of ferns, possibly lying under the shadow of a fallen redwood, and perhaps one or two drowsy youngsters would be awake, ready to howl in warning if they scented a razor cat.

Fear churned Tull's belly, constricted his breathing. He could not forget the musky scent of their hair, the smell of rotten meat that issued from them. Unlike some predators, the Mastodon Men were not fastidious, and the scent of dried blood and rotting fat had been strong. To Tull, it seemed fascinating. When he first saw the Mastodon Man, he feared it because it had reminded him of his father. But as Phylomon had said, after several hours his brain worked its magic, and he found that he was terrified of the beast itself.

At noon, they found their barrel sitting on the side of the hill in a deep bed of sword ferns. For a while, the men moved toward it slowly, fearing that they had found the camp of the Mastodon Men. Tull crept toward the barrel and felt the hair rise on his forehead, felt the pimples of fear sprout on his arms.

They circled the barrel but found it empty except for a single tuft of brown hair.

In the early afternoon, the men entered a shallow valley thick with wild grape. The leaves were waxy and rigid, dried and lifeless after the heat of late summer, and one could not walk through the valley without making the sound of paper shredding. At the north end was a steep hill: the redwoods marched up to the top of a small ridge, and there they stopped. Snail Follower's bloody path led straight for the rise several hundred yards away.

"If Snail Follower survived the fall, his legs will be broken," Phylomon said. "I believe we will find our quarry dining on him, there, on the other side of the ridge."

Phylomon urged the others to stay behind, then crept up the ridge alone, moving his feet so slowly that the wild grape did not rustle as it slid over his naked legs. Even Ayuvah could not have crept so silently. He reached the top of the rise, then dropped to his hands and knees and crawled to the lip of the ridge. He watched for five minutes, then slowly returned through the grape.

To Tull, it seemed that the sky grew darker, and the air thickened with the impending sense of doom. He tried to shake off the old fears, to remind himself that he had lived through the first attack by the Mastodon Men, but it did no good. His tongue dried in his mouth, and seemed to swell.

"Snail Follower is dead," Phylomon said when he returned. "Let's go."

Ayuvah sighed in relief.

"Dead?" Tull asked in disbelief. "Are you sure?"

"The Mastodon Men have got most of the carcass stripped of meat," Phylomon said. "They have a good thirty or forty in their band."

"What should we do?" Tull asked.

Phylomon arched a single hairless brow. "Do? Why leave, of course!"

Phylomon turned to leave, and Ayuvah followed. Tull stood momentarily, stunned. Phylomon was right after all.

The Mastodon Men were merely dumb animals, incapable of recognizing their common ancestry to man. When they'd killed Little Chaa, they were not eating a fellow being, they were just eating an animal—the way Tull would eat a pig or a grouse. Yet Tull wanted to punish them, wanted Phylomon and Ayuvah to run over the cliff with him, descend on the Mastodon Men, and slaughter them down to the last child. Yet the very thought was madness. They had nothing to gain by attacking. *But I have something to gain,* Tull thought. And he knew he was right. In a subtle way, kwea ruled the Pwi. If two men were angry at one another with a great wrath, then they said, "Kwea will not let us live in peace." If the tribe was lucky, a reconciliation could be made that was powerful enough so that the kwea of anger would be swallowed up forever in the kwea of friendship. In the same way, Tull realized that if he did not slay the Mastodon Men, the kwea of fear would rule him, would forever make him a slave.

Tull watched Phylomon lead Ayuvah quietly back through the forest. Ayuvah turned, the muscles bunching on his thick neck as he looked over his shoulder, and gauged Tull. "You must kill them?" he said.

Tull's mouth became dry; he wanted to kill them, but he said only, "I must look upon them." His legs were shaking, and he tried to hold them steady.

Phylomon stopped and turned.

Ayuvah said, "Brother, I will come with you."

"No," Tull said. "I already saw one friend die. I do not want to see another."

"Evil kwea is upon me, too," Ayuvah said. "Although I do not fear them, I must come."

Tull grunted his assent, hefted his spear. He untied his belt and peed on a bush. The blood was pounding in his ears, and he thought of the sickening thud he had heard when the Mastodon Man had slapped Little Chaa, the sound of a body sliding through grass.

Phylomon said, "Look quickly, while you've got plenty of daylight. If they catch wind of you, head for open country where the sunlight will blind them. Always head downwind from them. If one charges you and raises his arms, it is a ceremonial charge. Back off slowly. If he charges you and comes in low with his shoulder forward, he means to kill you. I'll go back and start pushing the barrel to camp."

While Phylomon disappeared into the redwoods, Tull and Ayuvah circled the brow of the hill, heading into the forest where the shadows were deep enough so that no wild grape grew. When they rounded the hill, Tull found a gentle incline leading down. The foliage was thick near the ground. Because wild pigs would not eat the sour grapes in the area, the grapes had grown dense. But at eye level, the elk and deer had eaten the lower leaves of the vine maple and alder. And by looking down the slope, Tull could see Snail Follower, that giant old bull, lying on his side, gaping from a dozen wounds. The Mastodon Men had opened his belly, feeding on the liver and stomach, and white entrails had been pulled a dozen yards from the corpse. Just beyond the kill, the Mastodon Men lay sprawled in the grass beneath the trees, giant apelike beings with little body hair except on the shoulders and chest and the long wispy manes that covered their heads. Only two juveniles seemed to be awake. One female wore the dark-yellow fur of a child and was so hairless that she almost looked human. She sat and fondled her right nipple, pinched at a tick or a flea, then stopped and leaned back her head to taste the air through broad nostrils.

The second juvenile, a short male whose fur had turned the darker brown of adulthood, ripped at branches and stuffed them in his teeth as he paced through the foliage, then grunted softly as if challenging older males to combat. His forehead held a higher peak than that of others of his kind, and his eyes were sunk deeper. Once, Ayuvah stepped on a twig, and the young male turned. His gaze seemed to pierce them for a moment.

Tull watched the adults sprawled on the ground for several minutes, studying their faces, trying to decide which was the bull who had eaten Little Chaa. His throat tightened and the blood pounded in his ears as he considered how he might be able to steal into the group, put a spear through the heart of the old bull. But after several minutes, he still could not see his target.

At two hundred yards, he motioned for Ayuvah to wait where he was. Then Tull crept forward on his knees. He pushed his shield ahead of him, not because it would ward a blow from a Mastodon Man, but because the rust and avocado camouflage offered some hope of concealment. Tull inched forward, brushing twigs and dead leaves from his path so he would not stumble over them, always holding his shield as steady as possible so that his movement would not attract attention. His heart was hammering in his ears, and he found it difficult to believe that the Mastodon Men were unaware of him, could not smell the terror in his sweat. He did not feel the terror of kwea, where horrific memories are stirred and surface like bones in a pot of stew. It was a more controlled and logical terror, the terror one feels when, in a calculated manner, one does something undeniably stupid.

When he was a hundred and fifty yards from the camp, the young bull abruptly stood up and grunted a battle challenge, raising his hands above his head as if to fight. Several older bulls raised their heads from sleep. Tull was close enough to smell them strongly now, the sweat, the dried blood, the putrid fat. Snail Follower's corpse lay not fifty yards away, and a cloud of bluebottle flies and yellow jackets had swarmed to the kill, humming softly. The Mastodon Men were bloated. They had eaten well. One old cow got up, picked up a piece of bloody shale, and studied the mastodon. Tull did not see where the rock had come from, so he watched a moment and realized that each of the beasts had a sharp rock or pointed stick nearby, and each weapon was smeared with the mastodon's blood. Often, the Mastodon Men grasped these weapons even in their sleep. An infant mewed in its mother's arms, and she gently cupped it in a giant hand. Suddenly, from beneath the shade of an alder, a bull stepped out—a large man with testicles the size of cantaloupes. The bull had deep crevices running from his nose to his mouth, so that his face seemed a perpetual scowl. His nostrils were not as widely set as those of his companions, and his nose was short and pugged.

Tull recognized the old bull that had eaten Little Chaa by the silvered hair on his chest. Likely the leader of the band. The beast walked forward on his knuckles slowly, looked at the young bull, and raised his hands. The young bull barked and spun away into the brush, where he pulled the limb from an alder and then began swatting the ground. The old bull knuckle-walked to the young female. She stroked the long hair of his mane, but the old bull just laid a hand on her belly, as if to say "Wait until I wake up a bit." A word Scandal had once taught Tull came to mind: *pedophile,* and he smiled inwardly.

Four Mastodon Men were now up. With evening coming, the rest of them would wake. With such a large kill to eat, they would not hunt. But they would wake by habit.

Tull cocked his spear arm, raised his shield, and stood. The young bull barked a warning, and all the Mastodon Men swirled into motion. The young female rolled off the log, put her knuckles to the dirt, and scrambled away, instinctively fleeing, but the big bull rolled forward over the log, then raised himself to full height waving his arms in the ceremonial fighting stance. All the females disappeared into the brush, while a dozen bulls rushed forward and stood behind their leader. Some of the older ones carried great slabs of shale in their fists, and raised the bloody stones threateningly. The younger ones barked and shrieked and weaved from side to side as they beat their stones against the ground.

Tull knew that if the big bull charged, they would all charge. Most of them stood over eight feet, and he could not outrun them. His stomach tightened and he struggled for breath and very cautiously, very deliberately walked forward. With each step he took, the bulls shuffled forward, creating a wall behind their leader. When he walked within thirty feet of the great bull, it raised to its full height of ten feet, raised its arms over its head, and, as if it were a smothering blanket, the kwea fell: Tull was a child again, standing before his father while his father held the rattling shackles he would place on Tull's legs. The powerful and perverse kwea the beast emanated, the terror and despair, caused a black fog to swell around it. The sun seemed to darken as if a giant hand held it in shadow. The air expelled from Tull's lungs in a single unending, wrenching gasp, and he held his eyes steady on the beast and whimpered once before he lowered his eyes to the ground. Tull stood full in the Mastodon Man's shadow, felt his knees begin to buckle.

The kwea emanated in waves through his brain, crashing against him, and he felt that if he stood much longer in the beast's presence, his sanity would erode from beneath him, just as waves carry sand from beneath your feet when you stand on the seashore.

He watched the Mastodon Man's shadow on the ground, and the kwea seemed to ease, as if the waves were not driven by such a frenzied wind. An old Pwi song rang through his head:

Dandelions at storm; dandelions at storm.
When the wind blows fierce, and wild, and warm,
the white down flies.
Dandelions at storm.

The rhythm of the song coincided with waves of fear battering him.

Tull raised his spear, raised his shield overhead, and assumed the symbolic fighting stance. Then he looked the Mastodon Man in the eye.

The powerful kwea of terror raised up, like a great black wall. The god Adjonai, the keeper of terror, stood at the monster's back, and the sky became black. The Pwi said that Adjonai ruled Craal, but Tull felt the dark god's presence, full and strong.

Tull laughed like a madman who no longer cares if he will die. The Mastodon Man watched Tull and swayed side to side, grunting his rage and bewilderment at this tiny beast who seemed determined to fight him for the right to lead the band. He lowered his hands and put his knuckles to the ground, as if Tull were a child from the tribe who challenged only from ignorance, and the Mastodon Man swayed from side to side, then shrieked, a tremendous howl of warning so magnificent in volume that the leaves of the vine maples seemed to tremble.

Run, a voice whispered in the back of Tull's head, *run for the daylight.* But Tull stood and laughed at the Mastodon Man. Its eyes were dull, like the eyes of Hardy Goodstick, the eyes of a moron. It rushed at him, lightly thumped him on the chest, smashing Tull to the ground. Tull kept his eyes on the huge beast, let the dark kwea run through him, shouted curses at the god Adjonai for a full five minutes, until the god turned his face. The Mastodon Man stood over him, paced back and forth, unsure what to do.

The sky around the Mastodon Man suddenly lightened, and the beast shrank and became nothing but an animal, a bewildered creature that watched Tull and did not feed on him only because its hunger was sated. Tull felt his terror dwindle and subside, as if the crashing waves of fear were an ocean that quite suddenly and miraculously calmed, and the storm raged only in memory.

The great bull leaned forward on his knuckles, and sniffed at Tull's face like a curious dog.

Tull still clutched his spear. He could have stabbed the beast, even mortally wounded it. Yet looking into the eyes of this dumb animal, he knew it didn't matter anymore. He'd spoken the truth to Phylomon: Tull had come only to look.

Tull growled at the Mastodon Man, and it leapt backward. The others shrieked and grunted, and one fellow threw a bloody stone. Tull ducked beneath it, knelt to a crouch and raised his spear and shield over his head. All of the Mastodon Men grew wary and looked around, then crept back a pace. Tull retreated slowly. To turn his back or try to run would only invite their attack, so Tull slowly lowered his arms and stepped backward a few paces, until he reached Ayuvah.

He would have continued on, but Ayuvah stopped him, pointed to the old bull. "Is he the one who killed Little Chaa?" Ayuvah asked.

Tull nodded.

Ayuvah raised his shield and spear overhead, in the symbolic fighting stance, and advanced on the tribe of Mastodon Men. The old bull became more confused than ever, raised his own hands and roared.

When he was a dozen feet off, Ayuvah rushed forward, slashed the beast across the belly with his long spear. The Mastodon Man shrieked and spun, lashing out with a bloody stone, and Ayuvah ducked beneath the blow, rose and sank his spear into the monster's neck. It jumped in the air, seeking to throw its weight atop him, and Ayuvah threw his spear into the beast's chest, dodged to the left and pulled his kutow.

The Mastodon Man landed on its belly, and Ayuvah swung his kutow, breaking the monster's head open. The old bull stopped moving. Only the back of its legs twitched.

The whole tribe shrieked at Ayuvah and stomped, tearing the trees and grass from the ground, and Ayuvah raised his hands over his head, challenging the rest. None of the Mastodon Men came forward.

Ayuvah backed off slowly, then turned to Tull and strode forward. They walked through the sunlight, over the thick wild grapes that cracked and tore like paper.

Chapter 6
Frowning Idols

While the men were gone, Wisteria and Scandal nervously straightened camp, salvaging food from broken barrels and smashed crockery. All day, Wisteria worried that the men might not return, that she and Scandal would have to make their way home, and she imagined how well they would fare if Mastodon Men attacked or if a scimitar cat decided to carry her off for its cubs to eat.

So when the men returned in late afternoon rolling the barrel in front of them, Wisteria felt a thrill of relief. Scandal didn't ask what had happened to the mastodon, and Wisteria wondered if the men did not mention it in an effort to protect her tender feelings for the beast. Instead Tull quietly kissed her, then the men loaded the barrel onto the wagon, moved camp half a mile, and ate a cheerless dinner made up of items that would spoil now that their containers were broken. They set camp in the deep forest beside twin redwoods that seemed sprouted from the same trunk. In the woods, the dire wolves howled.

"I keep counting my blessings and coming up short,"

Scandal said over dinner. "This was a fool's quest to begin with. We might make it to the river without a mastodon to pull the wagon, but once we get there, we're stuck. Fifty men couldn't pull that wagon once we fill the barrel with water."

Phylomon nodded his head in thought. "Once we get out of the mountains, perhaps we can find some farmer and buy some cattle to pull the wagon. I don't know. It's been nearly a hundred years since I've visited this part of the world."

"A hundred years hasn't changed a thing along the Mammoth Run. It's still the Rough!" Scandal said. "There's nothing but a few wild Neanderthals on those plains, and they're smart enough not to bother trying to domesticate cattle out here, where the wolves sneak in camp to eat your babies while you are busy fighting the cats that want to drag off your livestock."

Phylomon gazed off a moment, raised one eyebrow. "You're wrong, of course. Fifty men could pull the wagon! As long as the barrel is empty of water, we can push the wagon to Denai ourselves, then buy slaves to push the wagon from Denai to Bashevgo. If we can't get a mastodon, we can surely buy some Neanderthals."

Scandal was not at all pleased at the prospect, and Ayuvah refused to hear talk of journeying into Denai to buy slaves. The whole reason they had wanted to bring the wagon in the first place was so they could avoid the city, but Phylomon insisted that in Denai, with its large slave markets, they would not attract much attention. Tull did not take part in the argument. Instead, he sat quietly with Wisteria on the wagon and held her hand. He was still dressed in war gear.

He does not know what to say to me, Wisteria thought. *He's like a child, totally ignorant of how to please me.* From a nearby hill, a wolf raised its voice in a forlorn howl. She smiled at Tull, and her nipples tightened. The response surprised her, yet he had aroused her the night before. *Why shouldn't I want to make love to him?* she wondered. *He is my husband.* But in her heart, she felt it was a lie. She'd married him so she could join the quest, but she had never believed for a moment that she would begin to feel anything for him.

Yet, she wanted him in her bed tonight. The thought of having him in her bed every night, nights without end, filled her with a deep sense of longing and brought a thin smile to her face. *I should not smile so soon after my father's murder,* she told herself. *The crabs haven't even finished picking the flesh from his bones.* She pushed Tull's hand away.

Wisteria got up off the wagon, and Tull looked at her, confused. She pulled him to a secluded spot away from camp and sat with her back against a tree. She pulled Tull down so he could lean against her, then she massaged his shoulders and hummed softly.

"Did you find Snail Follower?" she asked.

"The Mastodon Men got him," Tull answered.

"Did you see them? What happened?"

"The Mastodon Men were feeding on him. Ayuvah and I went to their camp, and I found the one that killed Little Chaa. I just looked at him."

Wisteria watched Tull and wondered what he was thinking. She combed her fingers through his long red hair. It was very soft and fine. His face was broad and thrust forward, like those of all Neanderthals. His cranium did not have the box shape of a human—instead, it was round, and his skin seemed almost stretched taut over those round features. No one could mistake Tull for a human, and Wisteria knew that Tull thought about things, experienced the world, in a way she could never quite imagine. "I don't know how to ask, but what did you *think* when you looked at him?" she asked.

Tull smiled. "Never ask a Pwi what he thinks. Ask him what he *feels*," Tull said. "Sometimes, when I am unhappy, the most important question you could ask me is 'How does the sky feel today.' That is the way you speak to a Pwi."

"Then, what did you *feel* when you saw the Mastodon Man?"

"I felt Adjonai, the god we all fear. But he was not as powerful as last night. When we first saw the Mastodon Men, it reminded me of a time with my father, and the fear made me faint. But when I looked upon him today, he was only a great beast. Something was missing. Sometimes, kwea is only aroused because all of the circumstances are right. For instance, my mother likes to work in the garden, but only in the morning when meadowlarks are singing. She does not enjoy the kwea of it in the afternoon or on mornings when the meadowlarks do not sing. I think it was the same with me. When I saw the Mastodon Man today, the kwea was more bearable, as if some element were missing."

"I'm sorry I asked."

"That is all right," Tull said. "It was a good thing that I saw him today. If we go to Craal, Adjonai will be there, too."

Wisteria decided to change the subject. She squeezed him tight, pressing his back against her breasts. "And what do you feel when I hold you?"

"I feel cradled by the sea."

Wisteria laughed a little. "Why do you say that?"

Tull thought for a long time, trying to find the root of that feeling. "Once, when I was young, I took a boat out on a still lagoon to fish with my spear in the morning just as it reached high tide. The water was like glass, and I speared some good big fish. Then the tide went out, and the lagoon became a pond. So I lay down to rest. The wind came up and the sun shone on me, and the boat rocked in the waves. It was pleasant, and I imagined that the sea was a goddess and she was caressing me." Tull smiled at her over his shoulder. "Even then, the name for the goddess I imagined was *Wisteria*. I have loved you forever." The words both pleased her and confused her. Pleased her because in a way she felt like a little girl playing house, pretending to love this man. At the same time, the very act of playing house, of pretending to love him, was satisfying—so satisfying that she wasn't sure she wanted to stop. *Could I be falling in love?* she wondered. The thought shook her.

Tull turned to kiss her. A chorus of wolves lifted their voice in song, as if the pack were closing in, coming near. Since the others were still arguing by the fire, Wisteria took Tull's hand and placed it on her breast as they kissed.

The men by the fire began to argue loudly, and she looked up as she kissed.

Phylomon brought out a paper map. "We're forty miles

north of Botany," Phylomon said. "It was a fine town when last I visited. They should have cattle to sell."

"Pshaw," Scandal said. "No one has lived in Botany for thirty years. At least, I haven't heard of anyone there."

Ayuvah said, "Some Pwi live there. A couple of bird trappers."

Ayuvah studied the map a moment. Directly north was a picture of two stones, both with frowning faces. "Wait," he said. "In ten days, we end the month of Dragon. The Pwi here in the valley will hold a rendezvous—here at Frowning Idols. It is only forty miles off our trail."

Scandal watched Ayuvah's finger. "By God, he's right!" Scandal agreed. "Fremon Hume and his boys bring a load of ivory into town every fall, and they get it at the rendezvous. There are three or four men that make the run, and all of them will have ox carts. Maybe we can buy a few head. Hell, maybe we can even buy us a mastodon."

"Even if we can't," Phylomon agreed, "we'll meet almost everyone who lives within two hundred miles. Someone will know where we can find draft animals. We can't leave the wagon here without a guard—the bears would eat our supplies before we get back. Besides, we'd lose too much time. Do you think we could push this wagon down the mountains, eighty miles? It won't be easy."

"Ayaah," Scandal said. "That would do. That would do fine."

The men sat in silence, gazing at the map, each lost in his own private thoughts.

Wisteria shifted her attention, kissed Tull with passion, and felt him respond in kind. His eyes were closed, and she smiled as she kissed, watching his face for a reaction. He seemed to kiss with his whole soul, using every muscle of his body to caress her. She reached up under his shirt and stroked the hairs of his chest. He felt so strong and reassuring. Being with him was nice. Yet she knew that if the journey ever reached a point where it looked as if it would succeed, she would have to betray him. She wondered how she could accomplish such an act—betray him so that he'd never know. If Phylomon found out, he'd hurt her. Tull moved his hand down to her thigh. A wolf howled nearby, followed by others, and she shivered in fear.

The fire crackled and spread its light to the nearer trees. Beyond that, the forest seemed impenetrably dark. Wisteria noticed a smell that reminded her of cheese, a delicate yellow cheese her father sometimes bought from farmers far to the south, and she thought it strange that Tull's skin should bear this sweet, sour smell. And suddenly she became aware that the scent was growing stronger, and she thought that very strange.

A twig cracked beside her, and Tull jumped to his feet and pulled his kutow, swinging the double-headed ax over his head as he issued a battle challenge. Scandal jumped for his weapon, but Phylomon shouted, "Hold!"

Four giant women stepped out of the darkness, each completely nude, each of them well over eight feet tall, with dark cinnamon-colored hair and skin as dark red as the redwoods themselves. Wisteria gasped, for they seemed to her to have materialized from thin air, their presence heralded only by their smell. Each of them was shapely and beautiful, with wide hips and pointed breasts, and Wisteria felt so embarrassed by their nudity that she had to stifle an impulse to run grab blankets to cover them with.

One woman carried a thin white bundle on her shoulder. She stepped forward and tossed the mayor's Dryad to the ground at Wisteria's feet, as if the Dryad were a sack of grain. The red woman moved her fingers through the air, waving them as if they were falling leaves blown by the wind. Wisteria recognized the symbols from legend—Hukm finger language—but she'd never known anyone who spoke this strange tongue. The woman waved her fingers downward three times, then made a single emphatic chopping motion.

Phylomon said, "Get her some water," and ran to Tirilee the Dryad. Phylomon waved his fingers, then blinked once.

The red woman raised her hand and let her fingers fall, weaving the syllables of her words into the motions of her fingers, made a chopping motion at the end of her sentence, and then backed silently into the dark woods.

Wisteria ran back to the wagon, brought the last of the drinking water, while Tull, with seeming reluctance, went to the wagon and stripped cloth for compresses. Phylomon and

Wisteria washed the dirt and blood from the Dryad. Tirilee's pale white skin, normally mottled by a few dark stripes, was blackened by bruises and tiny cuts. Her clothes were shredded. She watched Phylomon, but seemed not to realize where she was.

"The Dryads of the redwoods caught her following us," Phylomon explained. "They beat her for a while, but decided she might be with our party, so they brought her here. I told them that she was our scout. They say we must take her from their forest immediately. And if we let her plant any of her aspen trees, they'll kill us."

"My God!" Scandal said. He walked away from the fire and looked just beyond the light. Wisteria could smell the scent of cheese very strongly as she worked. "Do you smell that," Scandal called. "Froghollow cheese, yellow and sweet. You'd think it was fermenting in their breasts." Wisteria looked over her back quickly. Shadows covered the wild clover on the forest floor. There was no sign of the Dryads.

Ayuvah stepped up beside him. "We should try to get some rest," Ayuvah said.

Scandal laughed, "How can I sleep with those lovely creatures out there?" He called aloud to the trees, "Ladies, it's warmer here by the fire!" but none of the red women came back into the camp. "Ah, well, I'll go get some water." He grabbed a bucket from the wagon and headed off into the woods.

Phylomon very tenderly prodded each bone in the Dryad's arms, ribs, and legs, checking for breaks. He said to Ayuvah, "She's got some broken ribs, but I think she'll live. Help us get her on the wagon. We can lay her in the barrel."

Ayuvah shuffled his feet, kicked at a pine cone. *"Tcho,"* he said. No.

Wisteria looked up at her husband, and he too stared down at the ground. She was shocked at his heartlessness. "None of us Pwi can touch her," Tull said. "Touch a Dryad, and she will destroy you. You must wash her. You put her in the wagon . . . if you must. I stand with Ayuvah in this." She had seen how the Pwi men crossed the road when passing the mayor's house back in Smilodon Bay. None of the

Pwi would dare touch her for fear that they would be destroyed by their own lust.

Phylomon looked up at Tull, studied him for a moment. Off in the darkness, Scandal stubbed his toe on a log, muttered a curse, sloshed his bucket into the stream. Phylomon asked, "What would you do, kill her? Leave her to die?"

Ayuvah said, "Leave her! We would not let any other man-eater into camp! We should not let that creature near." Tull said nothing.

"It is not her fault that she is what she is," Phylomon said. "Her Time of Devotion may be months away. Her lust cannot hurt you now."

"You do not know that," Tull said.

Phylomon stared at the ground, weighing the risks.

"She's just a child," Wisteria said. "I'll take care of her." She took off her own bearskin robe and placed it over the young girl. The Dryad seemed tiny and frail. A young thing with breasts that had not budded. Wisteria wondered at the girl's courage, to have come this far in the wilderness without protection.

Scandal brought the water back from the stream, took out a pan and poured some to set by the fire. "We'll have no talk of leaving her," he said. "Why, when I was an apprentice, my master told me to never throw anything away—especially people. You never know what you can get in return. He always kept a few 'table scrap' children around. He said, 'When a girl comes begging for table scraps, you give them to her and ask a little work in return—let her clean the tables. As she gets older, you put her to work whoring, and when her looks are gone, she goes back to the kitchen. And when she's too feeble for that, you put her to work as a maid, let her do some light sweeping and whatnot. In the end, you can get a whole lifetime of work from the girl, but what have you invested? Why, mostly table scraps!'"

Scandal and Phylomon made a bed in the huge barrel on the back of the wagon, then lugged the girl to her bed. Wisteria sat with her far into the night.

When it was time to sleep, Wisteria went to lie beside Tull. He was already wrapped in a bearskin. When she crawled under the blanket, she found he was naked. He put his arm over her and kissed her with passion, as if to take up

where they'd left off before the Dryads came. She kissed him
once, but in her mind's eye she saw the little Dryad bleeding
and broken on a bed of redwood needles, with Tull and
Ayuvah walking off to let her die.

"Would you have left her? I mean really left her, if I
hadn't been here?" Wisteria asked.

Tull hesitated. "No. I'd have taken her to a human settlement. Given her to someone else."

Sent her back into slavery, Wisteria thought. Punish the
girl for having the audacity to try to escape. She looked at
Tull a long time, at his flaring nostrils, pale skin smoothed
by a round skull. He even spoke with a Pwi accent, making
his vowels nasal by routing them through enlarged sinuses.
He was not human. Human thoughts did not flow through
his mind. She was ashamed for wanting to make love to him
earlier. He was so clumsy and stupid; if he had not insisted
on standing next to her on that night, her father might have
escaped. Now he was clumsy at love. Why didn't he understand that she couldn't love him after the coldness he'd just
shown that little girl? She shoved him away, turned her
back.

He put his arm over her shoulder, but neither of them
spoke or slept.

The next day, as the men pushed their wagon ten grueling
miles through the forest with the scent of the giant red
women all about, Theron Scandal took the job of tending
Tirilee.

The men would push the wagon, grunting and straining
to get it up the hills, over the small limbs, two men behind,
one at the front, while one walked ahead to clear a trail.
Every mile they stopped to rest, and Scandal would wipe the
sweat from his forehead, get a dipper from the water barrel,
and offer water to Tirilee before he drank himself. While the
others threw themselves on the ground in sheer exhaustion,
Scandal stood beside the Dryad, speaking softly. Wisteria
wondered at his kindness.

The Dryad did not utter a word from the wagon, not to
thank Scandal, not even to wince in pain when the wagon
bumped over a limb. So Scandal would go back to work

without hearing her voice. He put his back into pushing the wagon and showed that he had muscle hidden beneath his beer belly. Afterward, he cooked dinner while everyone else sprawled on the ground like dead things. When Wisteria went to feed the Dryad, Scandal insisted on doing it himself. In his spare time, he went to hunt in the forest for healing herbs. He was doing double duty, taking an unfair burden on himself, and Wisteria told him so.

"It's nothing," Scandal said. "It's my duty as a gourmet."

"I don't understand," Wisteria said.

"Simple," Scandal said. "We cooks have fallen. Back in the days of the Starfarers, when men lived a thousand years, gourmets were something! A man started as an apprentice, and for the first hundred years he learned only tactile cookery—the art of pleasing the palate. The Starfarers knew that everyone tastes things differently, so gourmets devised tests to see how different palates responded to a meal, then cooked each meal to please the individual customer. Why, at a banquet, everyone would eat the same thing, yet each plate would be subtly different, to match the tastes of the customer. And they didn't care about just taste, either. Texture, color, everything was geared for that one person. Back then, you couldn't be a gourmet until you had been at the job for a hundred years and passed your boards. Then, you graduated to whole new levels of cookery: nutritional, where you fine-tuned your diets to meet customers' nutrient requirements; medicinal . . ."

"Holistic cookery," Phylomon put in.

"That's right, a holistic chef," Scandal said. "I try my hand at everything: tactile, nutritional, medicinal. If ever the Red Drones are destroyed and we get back to space, that's what I want to be, a holistic chef. Learn their secrets."

During that day, the scent of cheese had always been with them. Wisteria saw the Dryads twice—women slenderly built for all their height, with nipples dark as chocolate. Wisteria looked over at Tirilee, so thin and childish and innocent.

Scandal fed the girl, who, though still bruised and beaten, had recovered some strength. He spoke soothingly as he spooned a hearty stew down her throat, and Wisteria listened to Scandal's words. He did not seem to care if everyone in camp heard him.

"How old are you? Thirteen, fourteen," Scandal said. "You must be close to reaching your Time of Devotion, right? I understand that—devotion. I've spent a lifetime devoted to preparing meals for others, grinding my own grains to make my breads, collecting and drying my own herbs, distilling the flavors from mint and anise, vanilla beans. Do you understand me? Can you speak English?"

Tirilee did not say anything, just watched him with dark green eyes. Scandal warmed some water, dipped a rag in, came back and washed some dust from her face, then held the rag to a purpled bruise under her chin for a moment. Scandal said, "You are a Dryad of the aspens, right? We have something in common." Then he chanted in singsong, with a husky voice, "I have always loved aspens, most beautiful of trees, with bark as pale and white as the milk that flowed from my mother's breasts." Scandal let go of the rag, stroked her pale arm as he spoke, as if it were aspen bark. "When I was young, I lived in the lovely mountains and climbed among the deep folds of their skin, searching for the white forests of aspen, flowing among the trees, searching for deep, dew-wet grottoes where I could find pleasure, lie myself down."—The Dryad frowned, pulled her arm away, but Scandal reached up and fondled her silver hair—"The rich humus of the forest, the wildflowers, smelled as earthy and pleasurable as a woman in love. And I'd stand on those mountains, gazing at meandering rivers and green valleys below, dizzy with lust for living, and imagine I stood upon the breast of the world. Often in those moments, the joy of living, the ecstasy of drawing breath among those clean forests, melted the marrow of my bones, emptied me of my darkest cravings, left me shuddering—" It was a form of Omali verse, a kind of poetry left over from days when everyone had dictionaries genetically implanted in their heads, where the poet made up the poem as he went and spoke only in symbols. Sailors still sang it in the bars, on occasion.

The Dryad pushed Scandal's hand away; he took a deep breath and intently gazed into her dark green eyes. "At times I'd sleep among the mountains in the daylight, lying in the grass, listening to the steady throb of my own heart.

At dusk I'd spread my tent over the ground, erect my pole—"

Tirilee slapped his face. She said, "I think you should take your erect pole into the bushes and tell *it* about your dark cravings," her voice as musical as the notes of a flute.

"So, you do speak English!" Scandal crowed. "And all this long day you have played dumb and never answered me. Ayaah, you're cruel and hard!"

"Not nearly as hard as you!" Tirilee snapped back.

"If I am hard," Scandal said, "then you have made me hard!"

"Not me," Tirilee answered. "Perhaps it is because you handle your pisser like a toy."

"Why, your breasts have not yet budded, yet you talk like a common street whore!" Scandal said, smiling with delight.

"Of course," Tirilee said. "I learned half my English listening to your whores call to the sailors from the balcony." Even to Wisteria it was clear the girl lied. She spoke English too well to have learned it in only a couple of months.

"Ah, that would be Candy and Dandy," Scandal said. "Those aren't whores! Those are . . . goddesses!"

"If they are goddesses, I know what you worship," Tirilee said.

Scandal chuckled. "In another month, when we hit the mountains and see those aspen trees shining white on the hills—every fiber of your being will flame with desire for a thick one under the starlight! By God, I'll make you pay to ride my unicorn then. You'll be my goddess, and I'll worship beneath you on a blanket of aspen leaves."

"And if you're the only excuse for a man who comes around, you keg of lard, I'll make do with a chipmunk!"

"Oh, I'll come around," Scandal said. "I'll come for you."

The girl's face turned dark with rage. "When my Time of Devotion comes, I'll call for you. And when you are groaning with ecstasy from a single kiss and you are helpless as a sparrow's egg in my hand, I'll use my knife to relieve you of the burden of manhood." The child's voice held such fierceness, Wisteria could not discount the threat. She wondered if the girl could be a potential ally—someone who hated men as much as Wisteria hated the men of Smilodon Bay.

Would she help me destroy the quest? she wondered.

"Why are you so mad?" Scandal asked. "Certainly men have spoken to you of desire before?"

"Oh, yes, your precious Garamon—he never fed me without talking of it. And he planned to sell me after my Time of Devotion, claiming I was a virgin. Yet he was more honest than you, he did not speak in the language of love!"

"I said nothing of love!" Scandal countered. "I was talking about lust, pure and wholesome."

"You spoke of devotion, and devotion is purer than love!"

Scandal scratched his head. "Oh, that. You can't blame a man for trying."

"I can," Tirilee said. "I want devotion from the man I give myself to."

"A lifetime of devotion for a night of pleasure? It's a high price. A price that only a Pwi could pay, someone perpetually enslaved by the kwea of that moment. And if you demanded that price, you would be the thief, wouldn't you? For you will devote yourself to your trees," Scandal said. "It is in your nature."

"I can fight my nature," Tirilee said weakly, as if the conversation had worn her. She turned away, pulled her blanket tight against her pale white throat.

Wisteria thought long on it. Over the past days she had felt tenderness for Tull, a warming, and she had been playing house—treating him as if they were both newlyweds in love. *But it would be a big mistake to believe I'm really in love,* she thought. *I too must fight my nature. I must remember my hatred, nurse it.*

The journey pushing the wagon through the mountains was both harder and shorter than the men expected. Poor old Snail Follower had taken them to the summit of the mountains on the second day of the journey, and from the summit they could see the golden fields of the Mammoth Run Plateau, but this inviting open country was still far from the deep redwood forest. Shoving the wagon along for a week soon took its toll in sore shoulders, knotted calves, and blistered feet.

Phylomon trained them in weapons practice every morning and every evening, and as Tull's muscles tightened, the blue man eventually gave up trying to spar with him. "You have great strength in those arms of yours," Phylomon told him. "No human can match it. With your kutow, you can bash through my best parries, and you are fast enough so that I think you'll get the first swing on most men. If you keep working on it, with your size I suspect that in a few weeks you could develop your skill to the point that only the strongest Neanderthal could hope to parry your blows." From then on, only Ayuvah dared spar with him, and Ayuvah was well his match. With his spear and his lunging style, Ayuvah could stand back, balanced on his heels, and dodge Tull's blow. He was the type of partner Tull most needed for sparring.

Ayuvah stepped on an old spearhead, and his foot became so badly infected that he took to the wagon. Phylomon guided them to some hot springs, and Ayuvah soaked his feet while sitting on the white lime that rose from the deep green pools.

Tirilee stayed in the wagon for the first two days, but walked alongside from then on. Crossing the small creeks where the wagon would get mired in mud was the hardest part of the trip, and after a long day the men threw themselves to the ground and often slept for hours before they roused for dinner. Wisteria fixed dinner for the company only once, then Scandal silently insisted that he take over the job. In spite of all his hard work, his belly did not seem to tighten. He remained, as ever, the fat man.

One evening, Wisteria helped wash and dress Tirilee. Wisteria found the girl to be strange and beautiful, with her long silver hair and deep green eyes, and she washed the girl's emerald dress and put her in some of her own clothes, then decided to brush her hair. Yet when she took her brush to the girl, she realized that the Dryad didn't need it. The girl's hair felt extraordinarily clean and smooth, and not a hair was tangled, and Wisteria thought it strange, for she had not seen the child brush her hair.

"When was the last time you brushed your hair?" Wisteria asked.

"I have never brushed my hair," the Dryad answered.

"Never?" Wisteria asked.

"We Dryads are not like humans," Tirilee answered.

Wisteria ran her fingers through the girl's hair, stroked her cheek. The Dryad tilted her face up, inviting her to continue the petting, and Wisteria laughed. The girl's face was smooth and unblemished, yet when she touched her shoulders, she found that her muscles were tight, unbelievably strong.

"Tull," Wisteria said, "Come here."

Tull had been mending his moccasins, and he sauntered over, stood looking down at the Dryad. Wisteria took his hand quickly. "Feel this," she said, touching his hand to the Dryad's hair.

He jerked it away.

"Don't be afraid," Wisteria laughed. "She won't bite." She took Tull's hand and ran it over the Dryad's hair. "Feel how smooth it is, and she never has to brush it. And feel this," she said, brushing the backs of his fingers across the Dryad's cheek. "Have you ever felt anything so soft?"

Tull held his hand on Tirilee's cheek and looked down at her. The Dryad reached up with her own small hands and held his paw against her face a moment, caressing it. Then her face seemed to blank, and she kissed the back of his hand.

"Ah!" Tull said, pulling his hand from her grasp.

"What happened?" Wisteria asked.

"She—burned me," Tull said, holding up his hand. It had no mark on it.

On the tenth day of the journey the men came down out of the mountains into a small valley between rolling hills. The redwoods thinned and gave way to smaller firs, yet the red women followed, always remaining in the shadows. Several times a day, Tull would walk beneath a tree and recognize the lingering scent of cheese.

That afternoon the party forded a clear shallow river thick with crayfish, and smelled the sweet scent of dry grasslands. In another half mile the redwood forest ended suddenly, as if a giant invisible finger had drawn a line in the dirt, decreeing that the trees should spread no farther. The golden grasslands appeared. Tull and the others pushed the wagon to the shadows bordering the grass, and like mice watching for a hawk, they surveyed the clear summer skies and watched two great-horned dragons wheeling on the horizon.

"At last we're out of the woods," Ayuvah said.

Scandal shook his head glumly, watching the dragons. "Only sixty-five miles in ten days. We must do better."

"We'll do better now that we've got clear ground," Phylomon said.

A twig snapped behind them, and when they turned, forty naked red women stood blocking their path back to the forest. The party took one look at them, pushed the wagon into the open air, and set up evening camp. Ayuvah was feverish and in great pain from the cut to his foot, and Phylomon boiled some water and soaked Ayuvah's foot in a poultice made of leaves and sugar. Tull sat up that night and watched Ayuvah's leg swell. Tull became angry, for he was losing his guide and best fighter to something as insignificant as a spearhead in the dirt.

Tull kept the water boiling, wrapped Ayuvah's foot time and again, letting the cooling cloth act as a poultice. The day's journey had been hard on Tull's trick ankle, and he was limping. For the first time in years, he wrapped it, too. The others slept. Out above the plain, a screech owl cried.

"Do you think you'll be able to make it to Denai?" Tull asked Ayuvah seriously. "Or should we leave you at Frowning Idols?"

Ayuvah laughed. "If we must, we can limp together!"

Tull asked, "What more can I do?"

"You've done all you can for me tonight," Ayuvah said. "I will not ask for anything more. Go to bed with your wife."

Tull looked over on the ground. Wisteria slept beneath a big bear hide that protected her from mosquitoes. "I sadly-don't-know if she wants me in bed with her," Tull said. "Sometimes she acts as if she does, but then she pushes me away. I . . . I watched you and Little Chaa, the way you would curl up with him at night, the way you cleared rocks away from his bed."

"Of course," Ayuvah said. "How could I fail to do that for someone I loved?"

Tull could see the pain in Ayuvah's face, for the grief he felt for the child was still strong. "I've been trying to follow your example," Tull said. "But I don't know how to love a woman. I'm trying to learn, but she does not want those things from me."

"Give her time," Ayuvah counseled, yet he frowned as if worried. "Even a bobcat is tamed by tenderness over time. She knows you love her. Be patient."

The next morning they turned north. The Mammoth Run Plateau was a lush plain that ran six hundred miles in a north-south direction. In summer the valley was thick with wild bison; herds of short-nosed pigs; elk; and small dark brown, three-toed horses with yellow zebra stripes on their rumps. Near the rivers, sloths the size of bears fed in willow thickets beside giant capybara. In winter mammoth and woolly rhinos moved down from the north. And always, always, there were cats—tawny flatland saber-tooths followed the mammoth herds, imperial lions lay beneath the occasional tree to watch over bison. Between the mammoth, pigs, and brush fires, most trees never took root and the land remained clear for grazing. The men surprised themselves in the flat terrain and made twenty miles per day, so that on the second night out of the woods, the eighty-first day of the month of Dragon, they reached the rendezvous where the traders met at Frowning Idols.

The party pushed their wagon in beside a small lake at dusk. A dozen bonfires burned among deerskin tents and round sod huts, sending their smoke skyward, showing all travelers for miles around where to meet. Two hundred Neanderthal had gathered, and around the bonfires they had buried great pointed skewers in the ground to roast slabs of bear and sloth. The air smelled of putrid fat and smoke.

"Take heart," Phylomon said as they entered camp, eyeing wagons with domesticated cattle grazing nearby. "If we can't buy the cattle, perhaps someone will know where we can get a mastodon."

Someone shouted, "Phylomon! Phylomon of the Starfarers is among us!" and nearly everyone in the crowd came running to see the blue man. Tull's heart sank as he realized that it was the same cry that had been raised in Smilodon Bay three weeks before.

Tull took Wisteria among the crowd, and they weaved among the wares, smelling the scents from the cooking fires. A woman passed them wearing a hundred bracelets of electrum and silver, advertising her wares on her arm. Most Pwi had brought their trade goods on their backs—intricately carved jade bowls, copper pots, raw dragon horn that was prized for bows. But there were also some human traders: A great bearded wild man from the north who had a wagonload of mammoth ivory. Another who'd taken the easy trail up from Benbow to bring in a wagonload of Benbow glass. These two traders drove wagons using domesticated bison—the most common draft animal in this corner of the Rough. Although goods were displayed everywhere—laid out on hides on the grass—no one was buying. It would not be polite to begin bargaining until everyone had fed and rested.

Wisteria and Tull strolled among the goods, and Tull became concerned: among the dainty earrings were jade pipes, the kind the Okanjara—the Free Ones, as they called themselves—used to smoke opium and hashish. The Okanjara were escaped Thralls from Craal, and generations in slavery had left them changed from the Pwi, more brutal. Many of them, it was said, were in league with the Pirate Lords and worked as slavers. One Neanderthal with black painted beneath his eyes even had his arcane drugs, dried mushrooms and seeds, pouches of dried leaves, all laid out with the paraphernalia. Tull walked softly, feigning interest in the items out of courtesy, but his hand tightened on Wisteria's arm, and he steered her forward, always heading toward the famous idols at the center of the camp—two great stone statues carved into frowning Neanderthal faces twenty feet tall.

They passed a Neanderthal wearing a lion-skin vest, a heavy man with a thick golden beard who wore his leather war helmet and kutow as if he were planning to go to battle any minute. The man knelt, setting ivory spoons onto a deer hide. Wisteria stopped to look at the spoons, and the man reached for his kutow and looked up. His eyes were blackened so his face looked like a skull. "How much do you want for the woman?" the Neanderthal asked Tull.

It would be impolite to offend, Tull knew. The man had a defiant, crazed gleam in his eye. Tull spat at the man's feet. "Pwi do not sell their women," he said. They walked on.

"Careful," Wisteria said under her breath. "He is Okanjara."

"He is an Okanjara warrior," Tull corrected, loud enough for the man to hear. "Bastard son of some pirate. Probably a slaver himself. It does not give him the right to offend us. I will kill him if he does so again."

"Excuse me if I have offended," the warrior said loudly at their backs. "I do not know the customs of the Pwi!"

They made it to the idols, huge black monoliths, and Tull rested his back on the downturned lip of a statue and sighed.

Scandal hurried over, spoke quietly. "Did you see the mammoth tusks over there? A trader brought them down from the north just this morning, escorted by fifty Okanjara warriors. They've caused no small stir, mind you. Those tusks didn't come from wild mammoths. They came from domestic herds. All of them are painted with Hukm totems!"

"Hukm!" Wisteria said. The great furred Hukm were fierce warriors, each nearly as large as a Mastodon Man but vastly more intelligent. They never killed their sacred mammoths. To slaughter a Hukm's mammoth was an act of lunacy akin to slaughtering his children—a declaration of war.

"Only very dangerous men or great fools would kill such mammoths," Tull said, "I just called one of them the bastard son of a slaver. He begged forgiveness for offending me."

"Ayaah," Scandal said quietly. "You should see the stir Tirilee is causing. Every one of these bastards is willing to pay his left testicle for a night in bed with a Dryad. If Phylomon wasn't with her, I don't know how we'd stop them.

Right now, they are outnumbered. They won't start anything now. But sleep light. Ayuvah says this place has bad
kwea. The hand of Adjonai reaches even here. For once, I
feel the kwea too."

That night, Phylomon held an execution. The party had
settled in for dinner, a feast where supplies were shared
abundantly. They sat on logs around several huge bonfires,
laughing and telling jokes. Tirilee sat next to Phylomon,
clinging to his arm, for many Okanjara had gathered, leering at her. The harmless-looking old glass trader from Benbow, a fat man with a hint of peach fuzz left on his head,
slapped Phylomon's back, introduced himself. Phylomon
asked if he'd once lived at Starving Woman.

The fellow sat up straight in surprise, and said, "Ayaah,
but how'd you gather it?"

Phylomon said, "I have a message . . ." and reached
for his pack. He pulled out a weathered piece of paper and
read, "I, Deman Haymaker, was taken slave two years
ago—"

The fat man pulled a knife from his boot, and started to
rise. Phylomon smashed the man's esophagus with an elbow. The fat man stood up straight, then fell backward over
the log he'd been sitting on and kicked his feet, retching as
he strangled.

"This man forfeits all property for his crimes. We'll be
taking his oxen when we go," Phylomon said. "The rest of
you can take his glass as you please."

Wisteria and Tull sat within a few feet of Phylomon.
Wisteria stood up, holding her stomach. "God damn you,"
Wisteria shouted at Phylomon. "God damn you! Is it going
to be this way everywhere we go?"

"Perhaps," the blue man said, watching her calmly.

"Because if it is, I can't take it!" Wisteria said. "I swear,
I'll stab you in your sleep!"

"It would do you no good," Phylomon said. "Others
have tried, but where are they now?"

"I've got to get out of here," Wisteria said, staggering off
into the darkness. Tull followed, somewhat in shock. He'd

known Phylomon for only three weeks, yet the blue man killed many people in that time.

"Did you see what he did?" Wisteria asked when they left the camp. She shook her head, held her stomach as if she would vomit.

"What do you mean?" Tull asked, and then he remembered the gagging sounds Wisteria's father had made in the water as he strangled. The same sounds the glass trader made only a moment before. "I see the kwea of it."

They were standing by a wagon, and Thor came up, half-full. The gas giant was huge, and the red light threw a blood-red haze over the plains. Tull could see little desert jackals slinking outside camp, outside spear range, waiting for the people to sleep. Fireflies flickered in the air. A warm gravitational wind kicked up, and clouds scudded over the mountains. It looked as if it would be a dark night. Several people gathered around a wagon, pulled back a tarp, and began searching it, and Tull realized it was the slaver's wagon, and the people had come to haul off his goods as fast as they could.

"God, can't they let him even die first?" Wisteria said in disgust and stalked away.

Tull looked to follow her but she had been so cold lately —hardly speaking to him, avoiding his touch. He knew she wanted to be alone. In the pale moonlight, as people pawed through the wagon, he saw a blade—a sword made of pale green Benbow glass that looked black in the red moonlight, gracefully curved, yet even the back edge was jagged and sharp, in a wave design. It was the most wicked-looking weapon he'd ever seen, something that only a princeling among the Pirate Lords could afford. He picked it up and held it. The dense crystal blade was heavy, as heavy as his kutow, but more finely balanced. He swung it in the air a few times, and liked the feel. It was heavy enough to strike through a parry, yet light enough to be fast. He imagined that he could swing that blade all day and never tire. Measuring the knowledge that it would anger Wisteria if he took the sword against his own desire to own it, he grabbed the scabbard for the blade and carried it back to his wagon.

He walked back to the campfire. A Neanderthal woman

was talking wildly to Phylomon, gesticulating, speaking in an accent Tull recognized as Okanjara.

"Quick, come quick! The baby is not coming out as it should! I push on her stomach, but the baby refuses to come."

Phylomon looked up at Tull. "You said you studied once under a doctor. Did you ever help birth a child?"

"Three," Tull said.

"Well, let's make it four."

"I don't have the hands for it," Tull said.

"Come along anyway," Phylomon said.

They found the Okanjara girl in a tent near a small campfire, away from the main group. She was perhaps fourteen, sweaty, wearing a goat hide. Her husband was young and handsome, no older than Tull. Three girls crowded around, leaving little room for Tull and Phylomon.

"Who are you girls?" Phylomon asked.

"We are her sister-wives," one girl said. The thought sickened Tull, that four girls should marry one man. It was not uncommon in the Rough. A man could seduce a Neanderthal woman so fully that the kwea of the time they spent together overcame her sense of decency, and she became one of his wives. Human trappers did it often.

Phylomon began washing his hands in scalding water, and Tull did the same. He checked the girl's cervix for dilation, found a bit of blood running from it, and the smell of salt water. Her water had broken.

"She's halfway there," he said. "How often have you been having contractions?"

"She started two days ago," her husband answered, "but the baby decided not to come, not until tonight."

"We should take the baby soon," Phylomon said. "What would your doctor have done?"

Tull said, "Have her massage her nipples so she will release progesterone to get the contractions started. Perhaps have her sit up, to put more pressure on the cervix, thin it."

"I agree," Phylomon said. They helped the girl to her feet, took off her top, and put her husband to work stroking her nipples. They were small and pink, the nipples of a woman who'd never suckled a child.

Tull walked out of the tent, embarrassed at the sight,

and sat by a small campfire with a dozen Okanjara. They were speaking of inconsequential things: purchases they planned to make, mending shoes, the perpetual chore of mending shoes. A burly Okanjara in his forties asked Tull, "How is she doing?"

"She will not go into hard labor for several hours," Tull said.

"Then in the middle of the night, we shall have some screaming," the man said, slapping Tull's shoulder. "It always reminds me of my childhood in Bashevgo, eh? Sleeping above the slave pens. If only someone would crack a whip!"

Suddenly, lightning cracked in the clouds on the horizon, and the Okanjara laughed nervously. "Ayaah, Adjonai cracks his whip!" the man said. "I am Tchupa, leader of this caravan." He reached out to clasp Tull's wrist.

Tull felt strange clasping wrists with this man. He'd never touched a Thrall, free or otherwise.

"We have been bringing our caravans farther east and south every year," Tchupa said, "Someday, we hope to walk freely among the Pwi, let them know we are not enemies." Tull looked at the warriors in the circle, their eyes, lips, and noses darkened so that they looked like skulls. They did not look like friends. "Yet I fear we brought too many men. Your people are uneasy. We will come in fewer numbers next year, but we had a surplus of goods to trade."

"People fear you because you come from Craal. Here in the Rough, the Pwi say that Adjonai, the God of Terror, rules in Craal. It is said that many Thralls work for the Slave Lords. It is said that some Thralls eat the flesh of the Pwi."

The big man frowned. "You are blunt. Truly, Adjonai does rule in Craal," the big man said. "And some day, his hand will reach out and take the Rough. I have known Thralls to eat the flesh of Pwi in the ghettos of Bashevgo because they were hungry and had nothing else. The human Slave Lords left them no choice. That is why some of us, like my tribe, have escaped here into the wilderness. And every day, an Okanjara dies to keep this wilderness free. Know this, man of the Pwi, the Okanjara are your friends!"

Tull looked into the big Neanderthal's eyes, eyes as yellow as a cat's, and saw only honesty there. "Then I will not sleep with my sword tonight," Tull said, and the warriors laughed. "But, I must ask you: I have not heard of Okanjara so far to the east. You say that the Okanjara die to keep the wilderness free, and I have heard that you battle the armies of Craal. Shouldn't you be on the other side of the Dragon Spine Mountains?"

The big man frowned. "We have battled on the far side of the Dragon Spines in the past, but the armies of Craal are many. After this winter, we will battle the armies of Craal here."

Tull's face paled. "Your words cut me with painful fear," Tull said. "You must be mistaken. The armies of Craal are seven hundred miles from here."

Tchupa shook his shaggy head. "Great armies move in the White Mountains—men with cannons and guns. They have put armor on their mastodons, dressing them for war, and they train dire wolves for battle. And their warriors, the Blade Kin, have sorcerors . . ."

Lightning cracked again in the distance, and a young girl, not more than three years old, came out of her tent crying.

"Bad dreams are walking around! Bad dreams are walking!" she said, her eyes wide with fear. For some reason Tull could not imagine, the girl came to him crying for comfort, so he pulled her up on his lap and hugged her, and told her the bad dreams would soon go away. A moment later, the girl's mother came, sat beside Tull and took the child.

"There are no bad dreams walking around, it is only the Okanjara and the Pwi," the girl's mother said. The child looked about in dismay, and because the shadows were deep around the campfire, she was not inclined to believe that only men were walking around. In order to comfort her, the mother pointed at the two great Frowning Idols and said, "Would you like to know why these stones frown?"

The little girl nodded, and the woman told a story Tull had never heard, the tale of Ananoi and Shape-Changing Woman:

Once, long ago, a Shape-Changing Woman was a widow and head of her tribe. All people thought her wise, and because she was wise, it added to her beauty. However, she had an evil son, Xetxetcha, who used his shape-changing power to fool the animals and slay them against their will. Xetxetcha believed himself to be a great wrestler, for he could wrestle in any form—be it cave bear, sloth, or moose.

In this day, there lived a giant mammoth, named Vozha, who shook the mountains down to hills when he walked. Redwoods grew in the dirt on his back, yet they were shorter than his giant hairs. Even the fleas on his back were enormous and grew to the size of wolves. Only the sea was large enough to be his water hole, and when he sprayed water from his trunk, it rained on the far side of the world.

Now each fall, as the mammoths went into their mating frenzy, their eyes would glaze and turn red. The bulls shook the mountains as they charged one another, butting heads, and their trumpeting could be heard to the ends of the earth. But none could withstand Vozha, for he picked up the other mammoths two and three at a time with his enormous trunk and he threw them over his back, and he alone mated with all of the dainty mammoth women.

So, one day, the mammoths came to Shape-Changing Woman and asked her advice, saying, "Zhofwa has blown her kisses to us, and we love the beautiful cow mammoths, but we never get to sleep with our sweet lovers. How can we defeat this monster?"

Shape-Changing Woman sat and thought upon it, for it was a tricky question, so she told the mammoths to wait for a month while she considered the answer.

But when her son, Xetxetcha, heard the question, he thought, *Aha, now I find a wrestling opponent worthy of me,* and he immediately turned himself into a giant mammoth and trotted off to the north.

Meanwhile, Ananoi, that great hero who destroyed Bashevgo and put the Red Drones in heaven so the Pirate Lords would not escape this world, also had some mammoths come to him and complain saying, "Vozha has taken all the sweet women mammoths as lovers, and though he is a mighty fighter, this is not right."

So, Ananoi decided to go speak with this monster. Everyone knew that Ananoi was the mightiest of the Okanjara, and he did not want to frighten the monster into submission, yet he knew he needed a weapon, so he took a cattail reed as a spear, and he carved petals of a lily to be the spear tip, and with that as his only weapon, he set off north.

Ananoi had not come far when he met a giant mammoth, taller than the mountains around it. The mammoth did not have any redwoods growing upon its back, but in all other respects it looked like Vozha, and at that moment it was tossing several other mammoths over its back with its enormous trunk while trumpeting its challenge to all comers.

Ananoi saw the mammoth, and shouted "Vozha, word of your terrible deeds has come everywhere. Surely all the tribes of animals fear you. People say that even Adjonai, the God of Terror, cowers at your name. No one disputes your greatness, so why do you continue to be cruel to everyone?"

Now, in saying this, Ananoi was not wise. Had he paid attention, he would have seen that this giant mammoth was not Vozha, but was in fact the Shape-Changer Xetxetcha, for even though Xetxetcha was in giant form, he had not been in that form long enough for redwoods to have grown upon his back. Still, it may be that Ananoi saw the giant hairs on Xetxetcha's back and only thought they were redwoods.

But Xetxetcha, seeing that he had fooled the great Okanjara warrior Ananoi, thought, *Here is a man whose strength and wit are legend. Certainly we will have a great fight.* So he said, "Who do you think you are, scrawny person, to talk to me in this way! Will you fight?"

But Ananoi shouted, "I must warn you, I have a spear!" And he shook his spear of cattails and lily petals at the giant.

Xetxetcha only laughed. He picked up a mountain with his trunk and prepared to drop it on Ananoi, but Ananoi hurled his spear with such speed that the reed caught fire and became a comet, and he threw with such precision that the comet burned cleanly into Xetxetcha's heart, and the evil Shape-Changer fell dead to the ground and went back to his natural form.

When Ananoi saw that he had killed a Shape-Changer by accident, he was sad, for he did not want to make enemies. He took the dead boy and carried him here to the

Idols, where Shape-Changing Woman had her throne. At that time, the Idols did not frown.

Ananoi laid Xetxetcha at Shape-Changing Woman's feet, and when he looked up into her eyes, he saw that she was beautiful beyond all that he had ever heard. When she saw her dead son, Shape-Changing Woman's face was full of sorrow, and it broke Ananoi's heart. Very softly, he told her how he had killed her son, and he begged forgiveness.

But Shape-Changing Woman fell into a rage. "You have already taken my son, and now you want to take my forgiveness, too? I will have blood from you, not apologies!" Shape-Changing Woman shouted, then she turned into a scimitar cat and leapt at Ananoi.

But Ananoi was not ready to die, so he cuffed her softly, not wishing to hurt her, and knocked her aside. Shape-Changing Woman immediately turned herself into a dragon, and leapt into the air and raked him with her horrible talons.

Ananoi was forced to run, and so magnificent was his speed that the dragon could not catch him. Beat her wings as she might, she could not catch him, so he ran until he reached the sea and could run no more. Shape-Changing Woman was close behind and he had nowhere to go, but he thought, *Ah, I have seen how the Shape-Changers perform their tricks. I can do that, too,* so he jumped into the ocean, and quick as a heartbeat he became a sea turtle.

The ocean has mountains and valleys beneath it and cities where water spirits dwell, but Ananoi, sick with grief, swam down, down, until he reached the bottom of the ocean. Meanwhile, Shape-Changing Woman searched everywhere. She had seen Ananoi jump into the water, but she had not seen him change into a turtle. She did not know that he knew her tricks, so she searched until she decided that some beautiful daughter of the water spirits had pulled Ananoi down, drowning him, so he would become her husband.

For a long time, Ananoi stayed on the bottom of the ocean and wept in grief. He was sick for having killed Xetxetcha, and he was even more sick that he could not have the beautiful Shape-Changing Woman for his wife. Often he thought of going to see the beautiful woman, but he knew the sadness upon her face would break his heart. So, he stayed on the ocean floor and wondered what to do for a long time, always drifting with the currents, sinking deeper and deeper into the lowest chasms.

After a year, the sound of drums disturbed Ananoi from his thoughts. He realized that he had heard these drums for a long time but only believed it to be the beating of his own heart. But now he knew the truth, for as he listened intently, he heard drums. Also, he could hear singing, very faintly, horrible voices wailing like flutes and panpipes. He put his ear to the mud on the ocean floor, and sure enough, the singing and drums became louder. And with this, he realized what he heard: He heard the singing of the soul worms of wicked people as they danced around the Heart of Evil at the center of the world.

Ananoi was finally stunned from his brooding thoughts, for mingled with the singing of the damned souls, he recognized the voice of Xetxetcha. Ananoi immediately turned himself into a mole and dug into the ground, and he did not have to go far to reach the cavern where the Heart of Evil dwelt, and soon he tunneled into the roof of that great cavern.

The Heart of Evil lay on the cavern floor below him, black and throbbing. Foul emanations, like smoke, drifted up from it to fill the world. Each beat of the heart rang through the cavern like the beating of a drum. Evil men whose souls had shriveled into the shape of worms upon their death crawled endlessly in a great maddening circle, wailing the tales of their evil lives in song. Slave masters cracked whips constantly, driving the worms over sharp rocks and broken glass. When Ananoi saw this, a plan came to mind.

For many hours Ananoi watched the soul worms in their dance of pain. They roiled beneath him, one by one, and at last he heard Xetxetcha and saw which worm it belonged to.

Ananoi jumped down, still in the form of a mole, and caught the soul worm between his teeth, then raced up through his tunnel before the slave masters could follow. Up, up he climbed, digging back to daylight. Ananoi burrowed up into the garden of Shape-Changing Woman. It was a summer's night and all three full moons lingered on the horizon.

Ananoi turned himself back into his own form as a beautiful man, set the soul worm on the ground, and let it sing. Xetxetcha sang of his torments in the cavern of evil, and these are the words he sang:

> *I am but fruit*
> *to be eaten by Crows of Misfortune*
> *that hover on jeering wing.*
> *Their dark forms swarm above me*
> *with reaping-hook frowns*
> *as their purple tongues caw*
> *caustic calls of derision.*
>
> *I can leave no footprints as I flee*
> *through the dust of this hard land.*
> *Beneath the black shadows of netherwhere*
> *where the heart only sees.*
> *I bruise myself,*
> *and find no comfort.*

Shape-Changing Woman heard the mournful song and went to her garden. Ever since the death of her son, she, too, could find no comfort, and she wondered who sang of her own pain.

When she got to the garden she saw a beautiful man in the moonlight and did not recognize Ananoi. But the spirit worm sang of all the evil deeds that had led it to such a terrible fate, and by the deeds sung in song, Shape-Changing Woman recognized her own son. Xetxetcha sang of the joy he had taken in tormenting animals and stealing their lives. He sang of his boastfulness and lust for blood. And finally he sang of his own death as he tried to murder Ananoi, and his mother wept at the deeds of her terrible son. Then, when the song was done, the soul worm crawled back into the ground, seeking the Heart of Evil that would be its eternal tormentor, for it had no other choice. As the Idols heard Xetxetcha sing of his deeds and the grief his evil deeds caused him, they both frowned, just as they do now.

Ananoi and Shape-Changing Woman were filled with sadness, and they stood for a long time in the moonlight, watching one another. "I killed your son," Ananoi said, "but I brought what I could back to you. First his body, then his spirit. Can you forgive me?"

Shape-Changing Woman wept fiercely, and the wind rushed for a moment as the goddess Zhofwa knelt and blew her kisses upon the couple. "I forgive you," Shape-Changing Woman said, and they fell in love and became man and wife.

Tull listened to the story with a certain happy reverie: in Pwi stories, Ananoi was always named as a Pwi hero, not a Thrall or Okanjara, and the Thralls thought the Red Drones were sent to trap only the Slave Lords, whereas Tull knew that they were spaceships filled with alien machines that kept everyone caged on this world, and he smiled to think that they believed Ananoi had almost destroyed Bashevgo, instead of Phylomon. Most of all, Tull was surprised to see that the Okanjara told stories about guilt and redemption, Pwi stories, even though these men bore little resemblance to the Pwi. Tull felt a thrill of fear, and realized that if Tchupa was right, that within a year he might be fighting the armies of Craal beside these strange warriors in their skull masks. Suddenly Tull felt at peace with these men. He listened to them laugh and joke. No longer were they Okanjara.

A storm blew in, and it began to rain. Tull went into the tent, and two hours later the girl reached hard labor. The baby was coming out breech and had its cord wrapped around it many times. Phylomon made Tull push the child back up into the womb, turn it around so that it would come head first. Tull hated the job. His hands felt so large and clumsy going into that small woman, and she screamed in pain.

"You take over," Tull said. "She is too small for me to get. It's these damned hands, these damned clumsy hands!"

"You are right," Phylomon said, coaching him. "The girl is too small to deliver easily. But your hands are not too large. It would hurt in any case. I could do no better."

"You take over," Tull said in disgust.

"You are doing fine. We don't want my hands in there too—it would only heighten the risk of infection. Get on with it."

Tull went back to the work. The cord was wrapped around the child's shoulders and arms, and with the circulation in the cord cut off, Tull knew he had to get the child out quickly if it was to live. The child finally came near sunrise. The eye of the storm had passed and it thundered and rained outside the tent. The child's head came out blue, covered with the white cheese of a newborn. It tried to scream, but the girl quit pushing when the child was only halfway. Tull grabbed the child, shouted for the girl to push, but she was between contractions. He pulled gently.

Because the girl had never given birth before, her birth canal was not wide enough to let the child through—not with the cord wrapped around the child's shoulders. In desperation, Phylomon finally shouted "Pull," and Tull knew that if the child were to live, it would have to come now. He pulled the child, gently but firmly, and dragged the mother three feet. He heard some snapping sounds, and the child came through.

The child was purple and breathed only in shallow gasps, and Tull held it upside down and cleared its throat. The child took a lungful of air and screamed in pain. Its right arm hung at an odd angle, broken.

When Tull saw that the child would live, he checked its arm. It had massive breaks in three places, and dangled as if it had four joints. When he saw how badly he had mangled the baby's arm, Tull cursed himself and his eyes filled with tears.

"It will be all right," Phylomon said, "We can fix it."

Phylomon made a bandage and immobilized the broken limb. Tull's eyes filled with tears, and one of the women helped him from the tent. It was morning already. Tchupa and his men sat by the fire. Tchupa was moved to see Tull cry for an Okanjara, and he thanked Tull, patting him on the back, and other warriors gathered around and did the same.

Phylomon came out of the tent a moment later and spoke softly in Tull's ear. "You did well, as well as anyone could. I'd have done no better. If not for you the child would have died. But the child will live. And the mother will live."

"Perhaps he should have died," Tull said. "To have the

hands of a Neanderthal is bad enough. But with so many breaks, the arm may grow arthritic. He might have only one hand."

"You are too hard on yourself," Phylomon said. "The arm will heal. But even if it doesn't, a man with one hand and willpower can seize the world by the throat."

"Perhaps if he had a human hand," Tull snorted in derision.

Phylomon grabbed Tull by the beard, jerked his head around, met his eyes, and said very slowly, "Tull Genet, I have spoken to Chaa, and he says that you—with one hand and willpower—can seize the world by the throat! Seize it, damn you!"

Tull spent the day in a daze. He had never met anyone who believed in him, and Phylomon's faith in him seemed the product of a deranged mind. Tull could not decide whether to tell Phylomon and the others what Tchupa had said about the armies of Craal. The words frightened him, and he did not want to give this evil kwea to others. Besides, they would be traveling to the White Mountains soon enough, and they would learn firsthand whether the armies of Craal would overrun the Rough. For a while, Tull went to look for Wisteria. He found her shopping with Tirilee, and the two seemed preoccupied, so Tull and Ayuvah worked on their wagon all day.

The wagon was made to be pulled by a mastodon, not by oxen, and the men had to take the doubletree from the glass seller's wagon and switch it to their own, since the glass seller's wagon could not carry the kind of weight they would be hauling once they filled their great barrel with water. It was easy work, requiring only strength and patience. Once, Tull stopped and stared at his hands.

Ayuvah said, "What is wrong, did you cut yourself?"

"These do not look like the hands of a doctor, do they?" Tull said. "I could never cut someone open in surgery." They were large and clumsy, more like the paws of a bear really.

"They are just hands," Ayuvah said. "I speak truthfully, I would rather have a human with his clever little hands cut me open. Still, you are as smart as a human. You can do some things. You can fix broken arms. You could make medicines."

"Dr. Debon said that Neanderthals were born to throw spears—our arms rotate at the shoulder more perfectly than a human's can, and because our arms are stronger, our toss is more powerful than a toss by a human. Our hands are big and strong because they were made to grip heavy things, like spear shafts."

Ayuvah smiled. "Humans cannot throw spears, that is certain. And Fava could beat up the strongest human in town. One day we shall rule them."

"They will always rule us," Tull said. "They will make clever little things that we cannot, and we will sell our souls for baubles. Their doctors and engineers will own us. Still, it feels good to work with my hands, to fit this doubletree to the axle."

Ayuvah wrinkled his brow. "Tull, I know you believe that we will sell ourselves to the humans, and this bothers you. But my father is a Spirit Walker. Someday, he says, we shall be their teachers. We shall overthrow the Slave Lords. Bashevgo will crumble to the sea, and the God of Terror will die in Craal. Then the humans will look up to us, not down upon us."

Tull snorted in derision, "The Pwi will never attack Craal," he said, bending over to inspect the size of the bolt holes on the doubletree.

Ayuvah slapped Tull's face. "Do not laugh at the words of my father," Ayuvah shouted, then he stepped back in dismay. "Forgive me! Forgive my anger!"

Tull looked up at him, surprised. Ayuvah had never struck anyone in his life. Tull was startled rather than angry. "Forgive my unruly mouth," Tull said.

By evening the ground had dried from the passing thunderstorm and a chill wind took its place, foreboding winter. The camp swelled by another fifty people, and, as often happened when there was nothing to do, people began to party.

Many Pwi got drunk on sweet-potato wine, but the Okanjara cooked a great bowl of thin stew filled with hallucinogenic mushrooms, a crude opium made from the heart of wild cabbage, and poisonous seeds from wild cucumbers, among other things, and in early afternoon, they began to feed.

Phylomon looked the pot over, and declared, "Anyone who eats this stew will not be sane for a month." But many among the Pwi went to the Okanjara camp to eat.

Tull slept for the afternoon and did not wake until midnight. Wisteria lay beside him, but when he hugged her, she pushed him away. He heard singing in the Okanjara camp and went to investigate.

The Okanjara played panpipes and drums. The women and the children were so heavily drugged they just sat and stared at the fire. Most of the men were still eating, going back for thirds and fourths. They dressed in hats made of dyed porcupine quills, and danced around a fire and sang, watching the backs of their hands, shaking them, mesmerized by their white wrists flashing in the moonlight. Tchupa watched over them like a king.

"Tull, my friend," Tchupa shouted. "Come celebrate with us!" He offered Tull a gourd filled with liquid from the pot. Tull took a small sip to please the Okanjara, then spit it out when no one was looking.

"Today and tomorrow we trade," Tchupa said, "But the day after we must hunt. Our warriors go to hunt now in their dreams. They will dream of the mammoth spirits and find where the mammoth will give themselves to our spears. You should come with us."

Tull smiled at the offer. "You Okanjara are not so bad as I'd heard. Almost I could imagine being one of you. But I, too, must hunt soon," Tull said, "for other game."

"I have heard of your hunt for the serpent," Tchupa said. "It will be a strange hunt."

The warriors danced around the fire, spinning wildly and singing:

I am the sleek silver man,
who runs all alone in the moonlight.
Though the katydids sing of decay,
the earth is my drum,

my feet beat the pum-a-la, pum-a-la,
pulses of life.

I am the quicksilver man
who runs unafraid at midnight.
The wind rattles the dry grasses,
a fox barks over his back,
my heart racing within me
does not measure my life.

I am element running
far beyond man in the moonfall.
The sweat storming off me
gives drink to the seas.
The sigh of my passing
adds breath to the wind.
Embers of soulfire within me
shall ignite the dawn.

"If you go to hunt mammoths," Tull said, "why do you sing of death?"

"The Hukm have all the mammoths now," Tchupa said sadly. "To hunt for the mammoths is to hunt for our own deaths. Still, the ivory pays well."

"If you have prophesied well," Tull said, "then perhaps next year, you and I will hunt for Craal's warriors here together."

Tchupa smiled grimly. "I think it more likely that they will hunt us." He laughed, too loudly.

A Pwi man dragged a small boy into camp, gripping his arm. He whispered to the boy, and the boy pointed at Tchupa. The Pwi threw the child at Tchupa's feet.

"This boy says you are his father. I trust he is not a liar as well as a thief!"

"A thief?" Tchupa said in surprise. Tchupa looked at the boy. "Does he speak truly?" The boy dared not answer.

The Pwi held up a small silver bowl with a dragon engraved on it. "He stole this when he thought I slept. I caught him in the act!"

"Is this correct, Ixashe? Speak freely," Tchupa said softly, with a hard edge to his voice. The child shook. He put his hands in front of his face. Tchupa was a powerful man, and the boy had no choice but to answer.

"Yes."

Tchupa looked saddened by this. "He is old enough to be judged as a man." He pulled a dagger from his belt, handed it to the Pwi. "Slit the boy's throat if you like," he said. "Or, if you are merciful, you can keep him. He is yours. Do as you wish."

The Pwi took the knife, looked at the child. He was very surprised. *"Tcho,"* the Pwi said, unwilling to kill the child. "It was not such a big thing." The Pwi dropped the knife.

Tchupa glowered at the child, looked at the Pwi. "In Craal, a bowl is worth more than the life of a Thrall," he reminded the Pwi. "Thank you for my son's life. I will punish him severely."

The Pwi looked guiltily at the child, then walked away. When he had left, Tchupa stood up, picked up his knife, walked slowly to the boy, and slugged him in the stomach. The boy doubled over. "Never admit guilt!" Tchupa hissed. "Even if he had a hundred witnesses, you should have said you were only looking at the bowl!" He flipped the knife upside down and struck the boy in the temple with the bone handle. The boy crumpled, and Tchupa kicked him a dozen times. "In Craal, that man would have squashed you as if your life were less than a turd! Tomorrow, you will crawl to him and thank him!"

Tull could not believe his ears. A few moments ago, he thought he could see himself as an Okanjara, but now he saw that the differences truly ran deep. Never had he seen a Pwi beat a child like that. No Pwi would have offered to let a stranger slit the throat of his son in front of his own eyes. The kwea of such memories would destroy a man. And Tchupa taught his son that it was all right to steal, as long as he did not get caught.

"Friend," Tull said, "You missed the point. The Pwi wanted you to teach your son not to steal!"

Tchupa looked at Tull, raised his eyebrows in surprise. "But perhaps someday the child will have to steal in order to stay alive! And if he must steal, he must learn to steal well!"

Tull looked Tchupa in the eye and saw that the Okanjara

was truly a stranger, a man whose mind he did not want to comprehend, for it was said among the Pwi that "to understand another, you must become like him." Tull had never lived in Craal, could not imagine a man beating his child for not stealing well. The stories he'd heard of Thrall warriors working for the slavers, of Thralls who ate human flesh, who thought it a sign of strength to endure unendurable pain—all of them could be true with a man as duplicitous as Tchupa. "I see," Tull said, and he got up, yawned as if tired, and went back to his own camp.

When Thor set behind the hills and the cries of jackals filled the camp as the dogs began to sneak to nibble table scraps beside the fires, Tull was wakened by a sudden shout.

"Hukm! Hukm are upon us!"

He untangled himself from Wisteria's arms and whispered, "Wait while I see what's happening!" But as he pulled off his bearskin covers, in the dying embers of the fires he could make out dozens of mastodons with great curved tusks circling the camp. Giants rode atop the mastodons, and as Tull watched, the great hairy men silently rushed in. Everywhere the Pwi shouted and cried out as they sought escape, and in the darkness Tull heard sickening thuds as Hukm war clubs smashed into bodies.

Phylomon stood beside a fire, the light playing on the back of his blue skin, waving his arms in the Hukm finger language. A great hairy Hukm, a lord with many silver bracelets, sat atop a mammoth and answered him calmly, with slow waves of his hand.

"Hold! Hold!" Phylomon was shouting to the Pwi, trying to keep the Pwi from running to their deaths. He pointed toward the Okanjara camp, and the Hukm lord raised his hand in that direction.

Only the two smaller moons shone, and Tull could see little by their light. But he could see a wall of flesh sweep through that camp as the Hukm and their mastodons trampled the tents. The heavy scent of wet, shaggy hair from the mammoths blended with the wood smoke. Faint cries rose from the throats of a few women, and Tull remembered that the Okanjara were all drugged, that they were helpless.

Above the cries rose the rhythmic sound of clubs smashing heads as if they were melons.

"Leave, now!" Phylomon shouted to the Pwi. "Walk calmly. Don't make any quick moves!"

Tull threw on his tunic. Several huge Hukm, each over eight feet tall, ran through the camp, examined Tull and the others, looking down as if they were children. It was rumored that the Hukm could see in the dark, and Tull realized that they were looking for the blackening under the eyes of the Okanjara warriors. He smelled the warm metallic scent of blood on the Hukm as they rushed past.

Wisteria curled in a ball on the ground, covered her head. Tull wrapped her in a blanket. Scandal and Ayuvah threw their bedding on the wagon quickly, and Tull carried Wisteria to the wagon, placed her in the barrel. He suddenly feared for the Dryad, wondered where she might be. But Tirilee was already hiding in the black heart of the barrel.

"Where are the oxen?" Scandal huffed. "We need to get the team of oxen!"

"They've scattered," Phylomon shouted, and suddenly the blue man stood beside Tull, throwing his own bedding on the wagon. "Leave them for now. We'll come back later!"

The men began pushing the wagon as quickly as possible. A Pwi woman ran in front of them, and a huge dark form met her in the darkness. There was the whistling sound of a club swinging through the air, and the woman skittered sideways.

"Keep moving!" Phylomon shouted, "Keep moving!" For a solid hour, that is exactly what they did.

They stopped by a small lake at sunrise, and in the cool morning air Tull listened. Behind the constant chitter of gray squirrels and the cackle of magpies, he thought he could discern screams. With each turn of the wagon wheels, he imagined he could hear the dull thud of a club smashing into flesh.

They set their blankets out, and while Phylomon stood and looked over the lake, his brow furrowed into a frown.

"Are we cowards for running?" Ayuvah asked.

Phylomon sighed. "We could not have saved them," he said at last. "I could have killed a few Hukm, but there was no saving the rest. The Okanjara were fools to kill mammoths from the sacred herds."

"Still, to leave them—it is close to murder."

"Not murder. Self-preservation," Scandal chimed in. "Rather like ducking behind the bar counter during a brawl. Don't let it rub you. Let the mind rule the mind, the body rule the body. We ran because we were afraid, and we had a right to fear. I only wish we had found the damned team of oxen. Shall we go look for them?"

"Not yet," Phylomon answered.

"We've a better chance of finding them if we go now," Scandal said.

"The Hukm have not finished their work," Phylomon answered.

If the Hukm only club the Okanjara to death, their work should not take long, Tull mused.

Scandal did not make a large breakfast, for none could have stomached it. Instead, he made tea. Within an hour, they heard real screams—not the half-imagined cries Tull thought he'd heard all morning, but shouts of pain so loud that even at a distance of two miles the squirrels fell silent and the birds left their songs.

The women busied themselves packing blankets and pans they'd thrown into the wagon. "What's this?" Wisteria asked, picking up Tull's sword of Benbow glass.

"Something I got from the glass trader's wagon," Tull said feebly.

"I feel dirty," Wisteria said. She and Tirilee went to the lake to wash.

The women stayed down at the lake most of the morning, and the men sat, lost in private thoughts. Tull envied the women—drowning those cries with clean water. At noon the screams of pain ended. When they had been silent for a full ten minutes, Tull and Ayuvah climbed a great sprawling oak, searched the land south, toward Frowning Idols. A line of sixty mammoths left the camp, heading northwest, and the smoke billowed at the Idols, but Tull could see no sign of any standing tents. "They're leaving," he shouted down to the others.

"Then let's get the women and go see if we can find the oxen," Scandal said.

Tull suddenly realized that the women had been gone a long time—perhaps two hours. Ayuvah and Scandal realized it at the same moment, and the four men looked at one another, then began shouting as they raced down to the lake. Tull remembered how the Okanjara had asked for the women, had sought to purchase them if even for a night.

They reached the lake, and the morning wind had blown all the algae to one side. In the floating algae they saw paths that the women had formed as they swam. The women were gone. After a bit, they found the women's clothes ground into the mud by heavy feet. Phylomon knelt and looked at the distinctive crisscross pattern left by moccasins woven from sage bark. "Okanjara."

Chapter 7
Journey of the Worm

The men ran back to the wagon, retrieved their weapons and battle gear. Following the Okanjara was not hard. The recent rains had left the ground soggy, and the prints were deep. The tracks led back to Frowning Idols.

A half mile from the camp, Phylomon strung his bow and the party began stalking in earnest. They soon found themselves bellying through the tall summer grass.

Three Okanjara milled outside a makeshift tent, faces painted in skull masks—a woman, a young warrior, and Tchupa. Tull heard a baby crying. The adults kept their eyes downcast. Tchupa kicked the ground, turning over broken bits of pottery. If they were guilty of kidnaping the women, they did not act like it. They had no guards. Instead, they picked through the remains of the camp, gathering their scattered belongings. Yet the footprints led directly to camp.

Dead bodies lay everywhere—men, women, children—bashed again and again with heavy war clubs until the bodies were pulped. Tangled flesh and protruding bones. The

Hukm had been thorough in their destruction, breaking bowls and pots, smashing weapons and ripping tents—even the ox team the party so desperately needed lay crushed. The wagon belonging to the ivory hunter seemed to be the lone exception—it appeared to be merely overturned. But as he got close, Tull saw a man nailed to the bottom of the wagon, the ivory trader himself, Tull assumed, but the man had been completely skinned, showing only white fat and pink flesh. Other than the areas behind the wagon and behind the Idols, there was no place for anyone to hide.

If only we could see into the tent, Tull thought, *to see if the women are guarded.* As they edged closer, the grass was so trampled by mammoths that Tull could not go forward and still maintain cover. Tull listened a moment, heard the child cry. The others edged up beside him.

The Okanjara talked softly, but the wind blew away from them. Tull could not catch their words. The woman walked into the tent and brought out the baby. Its cries seemed to double in volume. It was the infant Tull had delivered, wrapped in the red blanket he'd put around it the night before, his right arm strapped down.

Tchupa held the baby boy up as if to display it, then set it on the grass and stomped its head.

The child's cries suddenly ceased.

Tull found himself rushing forward, a shout ringing from his throat. He pulled out his sword of Benbow glass, swung it in an arc over his head.

Tchupa looked up, pulled his kutow, and when Tull reached the big man, Tull swung. Tchupa made the mistake of trying to parry the blow, and from his long hours of training over the past weeks, Tull knew to throw his weight into it, to try to bash through the parry. Tull's blade sliced through Tchupa's wooden shaft, continued through his shoulder, spilling out bits of lung. Tchupa's eyes widened in surprise.

"Why?" Tull shouted, but the Neanderthal sank to the ground, dead.

Phylomon and Ayuvah rushed up beside Tull. The young Okanjara warrior had his spear at ready, and Phylomon knocked it to the ground.

"We had nothing to feed the child. It would have died slowly," the woman explained.

The young warrior smirked at Tull. "We waited until we knew you were watching, so you could see what you had done. If you've come for your women, you can have what's left of them—in there." He pointed to the tent.

Through the tent's open flaps, Tull could see Wisteria and Tirilee sprawled naked on the ground, flies crawling on them. Their eyes were glazed. Tirilee moaned, and the flies rose from her, then settled again on her belly. Tull looked back to the young warrior with his painted skull face, uncomprehending.

The young warrior said to Phylomon. "Everyone says that you are a great man, and we hoped you would someday throw down the Slave Lords. You could have saved us from the Hukm. But because of your cowardice, our families are dead!" the warrior said as if reasoning with a fool. "Now we will seek the House of Dust. But even if we live, we have been forever robbed of peace. So, in return," the man gestured with his hands as if he were bestowing a gift, "may you be forever robbed of peace!"

"You're lower than the dung on my moccasins," Scandal said in bastardized Pwi. He slugged the warrior in the belly, doubling the Neanderthal over.

Phylomon grabbed Scandal's arm. "Leave him," Phylomon said. "If he is going to die, let him die slowly, by his own hand." Even the Okanjara considered it noble for men and women to let themselves starve if a spouse died. Phylomon stared at the warrior, "You call us cowards for running," he said. "You ran, too. I imagine it did not take you long to wipe off your skull paint in the dark."

The young man frowned. Phylomon stayed outside to guard while the others went in the tent to retrieve the women. They were both unconscious, yet had their eyes open. Beside them lay the drugged pot that the Okanjara had eaten from. Scandal looked them over.

"They're in a nasty storm," he said. "We've got to get that poison out of them." He flipped Tirilee on her side, put his finger down her throat until she gagged up bits of mushroom, tiny white cucumber seeds, and bilious green leaves from the stew. When he finished, he did the same to Wisteria. Ayuvah ran out and found some bits of blood-stained tent. They wrapped the women up and carried them back to camp, leaving the two Okanjara at Frowning Idols.

When they returned to camp, Phylomon felt as if he carried a great load. He had wanted so much to get some cattle to pull the wagon. Between the two teams at the Idols, there'd been a dozen oxen. And now all the oxen were dead before he'd got a day's pull from them.

We're still seven hundred miles from the river, he mused. *Perhaps farther. By coming north to Frowning Idols, we've lost four good days.* He could think of no place to get another animal—except from the Hukm, the giant ape-men riding their woolly mammoths. *There's a place to get draft animals, if you're bold enough.* But would the others go for it?

He looked at Tull: the face of the young Tcho-Pwi was drained. The boy was worried for his wife. Frowning Idols, with the flayed ivory trader and children smashed to a pulp, was among the most grisly battlefields Phylomon had ever seen—enough to scare the wits out of a Pwi. Add that to the shock of watching a child's murder, and the fact that the boy had just killed his first man—the image flashed through Phylomon's mind of the first man he had killed some 640 years earlier, a slaver who was acting as guard to the estate of a powerful Slave Lord. It had been different then, an official war with devastating casualties on both sides, and Phylomon had knifed the man at night, from behind, in the dark.

Phylomon looked at Ayuvah. There is only so much you can ask a Pwi to do. The kwea of this place was bad enough. If he were alone, Phylomon might try to steal a mammoth, but you couldn't ask the Pwi to steal one and then ride it all over hell with the Hukm watching.

Still, there was another chance.

Scandal took the women to the wagon, and he filled their mouths with wine again and again, making them vomit.

Phylomon made a pretense of examining the women. "Those Okanjara, they're not too smart," he said. "The effects of their stew won't be permanent—not on a human.

The wild cucumber seeds are the worst. Might take as much as a week for them to wear off. Still, Scandal's got the bulk of the stew out, and the women didn't have time to digest it. I'll bet they break free of it by morning."

Tull knelt and gingerly held Wisteria's shoulders, studied her face for sign of recovery.

"Ayaah," Scandal said, looking at Tull. "Maybe. Most of this stuff will wear off by morning. Sure wish to hell I knew what the leaves in there were, though."

"A mild narcotic, a painkiller," Phylomon said, lying through his teeth. "That's why they stare without blinking. It wears off quickly."

Ayuvah put his arms around Tull's shoulders. "They are right, little brother. The women will be fine by morning."

"We should bundle them up warm and take them down to Benbow—if not back to Smilodon Bay," Scandal said quietly, looking to Phylomon for confirmation. "We can re-outfit. It will put us a month behind, but if we hurry . . ."

"If we hurry, we'll miss the serpent hatch up on the Seven Ogre River and we'll all freeze trying to climb the Dragon Spines," Phylomon said. He'd hoped to avoid this. "But if we put our backs into it, we can push this wagon ten miles by sundown and get over the mountains before the snow flies."

"What in the hell would be the point?" Scandal said. "We might as well leave the wagon, reoutfit in Craal!"

"I suppose you'll carry the food while we carry the women? We need the wagon if only to cart them."

"Why bother?" Scandal asked. "Let's go home."

"We're going east," Phylomon said, "to Sanctum. If we hurry, we can catch the Hukm on their migration south at Sanctum. Perhaps they'll give us a mammoth."

"Hah! The four of us push this wagon over the Dragon Spines? Three hundred miles? We're already four days behind schedule, and Sanctum's another hundred miles off our course. Without draft animals, we'll just get farther behind! We'll miss the serpent run by two weeks!"

"By the time we reach the Dragon Spines, the women might be better," Phylomon countered. "That would make six of us. We'll have less food, and we can tear off the running boards, lighten the wagon. If we push fast and keep at it all day long, we can make up the time we've lost, as well as the time we lose. We won't miss the serpent hatch. We can't miss it!"

"God bugger you with a carrot, you're a stubborn man!" Scandal shouted. "You think the Hukm will just give us a mammoth? After what we've seen today? Right! And maybe they'll give us their daughters to seduce while they're at it! You lunatic! We've had enough bad luck. I'm going home! My belly's aching for a decent meal and I haven't had a woman for so long that even you are starting to look pretty! Tull, Ayuvah, let's get out of here!"

Phylomon slugged Scandal in the mouth, pulling his blow just enough to loosen the man's teeth. Scandal fell back on his rear and jumped up, but Phylomon pulled his long knife from his leg sheath, and Scandal just stared. Until this moment, Phylomon had been content to leave Scandal in charge. Now, they needed someone with internal fortitude.

"Get the women bedded down on the wagon," Phylomon said. "We've got ten miles to make by sundown. You're going to push! And if you try to run away, I'll gut you!"

By sundown, Phylomon figured they'd made more like fifteen miles. He didn't tell them, just pushed them harder, and most of the time he felt as if he were pushing the wagon alone, yet whenever he checked, the others were grimacing under the strain. By evening the women regained enough control of their reflexes to scream in terror of their hallucinations. When he signaled for the Creators that night, standing on a lone hill with his photoconverters, he flashed for hours with a new sense of desperation.

For a moment, Tull came to Phylomon and said, "In the camp, two days ago, I spoke with Tchupa. He said that the armies of Craal are moving in the Rough. He believed that next year at this time, we will be fighting them here. We will need to be careful."

Phylomon gritted his teeth, flashed his lights into the night air. "Do not worry about it," he said. "One always hears such evil rumors out of Craal."

"But he said that his people were running from Craal. He said that they have been fighting their armies for years."

"Do not worry," Phylomon said. "We will be careful."

Tull made as if to leave, and Phylomon held his arm a moment. "Have you told the others?"

"No," Tull answered.

"Don't say anything. You would only frighten them. Still, we shall practice your battle training more heavily."

That night, Phylomon brought a new level of intensity to the training. He was no longer satisfied with Tull's bashing attacks and Ayuvah's feints. "Both of you are getting stiff from all this work. We need to practice dexterity. Here, Tull, when you bring that sword in, a smart opponent could still turn your attacks. Instead of just hitting him, you must practice your strike angles. Power is fine, but it must be controlled." He grilled Tull and Ayuvah ruthlessly, making them twist and dodge, teaching them various attack and defense routines. Ayuvah complained that Phylomon was pushing too hard, trying to cram too much knowledge into them too quickly. "Nonsense," Phylomon countered. "If you remember a tenth of what I teach you, you will do well."

After practice, Ayuvah and Tull stayed up with the women, talking softly, trying to feed them. For once, Ayuvah showed compassion even for the Dryad. The women would have none of it—neither food nor comfort. They cried out against the blood, the maggots, the heads. Phylomon realized that after the Okanjara drugged the women, they must have dragged them through camp, showing them horror after horror. Long past midnight, both women fell asleep, whimpering.

The next morning, Phylomon went through the food— he mixed the beans with the rice, the oats with the wheat, threw out anything that wasn't necessary. Scandal shouted in horror at the loss, and insisted on carrying his valuable spices. Yet the day was harder than the previous. The ground turned rocky and furrowed, became a broad plain where shallow rivers and creeks meandered and regrouped. The men were forever lifting the wagon from potholes or pushing it through muddy creek bottoms. Thick clouds of mosquitoes followed the sweating men. And both women screamed out at their worst nightmares.

In the afternoon they reached a small camp of wild Pwi, a tribe of fifteen in buckskins, living in mud huts, much as their ancestors had done on Earth. They feared the Dryad and would not let the party camp near them. In the middle of the night, Tirilee suddenly shouted and jumped from her bed. It took the four men nearly an hour to run her down and drag her back to camp. In the morning, they pulled off the sideboards to the wagon, threw them out, along with the doubletree they'd kept in case they found a place to purchase oxen.

Twice they had to stop to fire their cannon and ward off dragons that circled them in curiosity. Tull was washed out and quiet, spent his time fawning over his wife. Yet the women had not eaten in three days, and the only liquid they drank was a small bit of beer and water the men forced down their throats in their sleep. Both women burned with low fevers, and Scandal, finally disgruntled, said, "I don't believe they'll live through another two days of this."

That night, as the women gibbered and pled for deliverance from the gore that surrounded them, Phylomon looked at the wagon from his bedroll and watched Tull. Scandal and Ayuvah had taken turns helping to guard the women. They were so concerned that Tirilee would get up and run again that the men became jailers as much as nurses. But Tull continued to work all through the day, then watch all through the night. The Pwi was wearing thin. His hair was unbrushed, his eyes fixed, his face dead.

If Wisteria dies, Phylomon thought, *Tull will follow her to the House of Dust.* It was obvious that the young man's world revolved around her. He'd have no more passion for life.

Phylomon thought long into the night, wondering what the Okanjara had given the women. He'd never cataloged all the natural hallucinogens. If he'd studied it in his youth, while he was still under the influence of memory enhancers, the information would have been permanently fixed in his brain. But Phylomon did not know what compounds might be antidotes for the drugs, and he did not know all that had been put in the stew. Yet the drugs were not being excreted, nor did they break down into harmless elements. Wisteria's calls to her dead father did not cease through the night. *May you be forever robbed of peace!*

On their fifth day out from Frowning Idols, they headed

into the foothills leading up to Heartbreak Pass in the
Dragon Spines. Although their journey was all upward, it
seemed easier somehow, for they were not constantly pulling the wagon through bogs. The trees had been green in the
valley, with the dull greens of late fall, but the maples and
alders on the hill were changing to red and tan, and the pine
cones were turning from green to gold.

That evening they headed up a long hill full of yellowed
buckbrush. Deer scat was almost as evident as saber-tooth
dung, and Phylomon watched the hills with interest. For an
hour before sundown, a dozen tawny saber-tooths paced the
wagon, their great teeth nearly scraping the ground as they
scurried from cover to cover, waiting to make an attack.

When they set camp and Phylomon knew that the cats
were ready to strike, a great-horned dragon flew in low to
eye the wagon, wheeled, and dropped behind a line of alders
a hundred yards away, beating its great wings against the
brush. One saber-tooth yowled in fear, and the cats scrambled for cover downhill.

Ayuvah looked around questioningly at the others. All
he had to do was fire the gun to frighten the dragon away,
but to send it away would only invite the cats back. The
men pulled their weapons, formed a front by the wagon.

The dragon stalked clumsily through the brush, cracking
branches in its wake. "God, what a loud one!" Scandal
laughed. "I'll bet he doesn't sneak up on many dinners!"

A branch cracked loudly, followed by the sound of a
huge body stumbling, and then the quieter, stalking noises
renewed.

Phylomon caught a glimpse of the dragon behind some
twisted scrub oak forty yards out; the great horns on its
head cracked some limbs as it hunkered down, ready to
pounce.

Phylomon got to the gun, fired once into the brush. But
the dragon didn't jump into the air. Tull swung his sword
overhead and shouted, and Scandal ducked under the
wagon to hide. Ayuvah simply stood still, his mouth open,
while Phylomon fumbled with the gun.

A twig snapped, and an old Neanderthal woman cackled
and stepped from the bushes.

"O zhetma!" Ayuvah cried, "She's a Shape-Changer!"

The woman walked clumsily, using a stick for a cane. She dressed in the style of old people among the Pwi, wearing a black cloak with hood to show that she was a widow. She hobbled up to Ayuvah, looked up into his face, and shouted, *"Graawk!"* a deafening roar that could only have come from a dragon, then laughed, "You believe in Shape-Changers? I would laugh, but at my age my teeth might fall out." She looked at the wagon. "I have never seen so many fools gathered in one place. One would think you to be a bunch of silly girls."

She walked up to the wagon, arched her neck as she looked into the barrel. "Oh, you do have a bunch of silly girls," she said.

"Mother," Phylomon said in the Pwi language of respect, "what are you doing out here? Is there a village nearby?"

"Oh, yes, there is a village. Far by land. I have been walking many days to get here. But I suppose if you were a Shape-Changer and could fly, it would not be far!"

"What are you doing out here alone?" Tull asked.

"A Spirit Walker asked me to come," she answered. "To comfort these two silly women."

"My father!" Ayuvah shouted. "Did he tell you his name?"

"He appeared in a dream, riding the back of a crow," the old woman said.

"Chaa tsulet ixa-zhet!" Ayuvah shouted in glee. "My father's name is Crow!"

"Then you must be his son, Ayuvah," she answered. "Your father is saddened by the death of Little Chaa. He says that Sava cries because her father is not near. The kwea of Etanai's love for you is undiminished by time."

Tull stepped forward and asked, "My name is Tull. Did the Spirit Walker have any words for me?"

The old woman blinked. "No."

Scandal crawled from beneath the wagon, still looking for the dragon. Phylomon studied the old woman. Her eyes were deep, more deeply set than those of Tull or Ayuvah. The skin of her face was stretched tight, so that wrinkles showed only around her mouth. *Ah yes,* Phylomon realized, *she is one of the pure breed, one of the Pwi whose blood is unmingled with humans.* She carried herself with the dignity and haughtiness that he had only seen among three classes of people—the Pirate Lords of Bashevgo, the Slave Lords of Craal, and the Dwea—the greatest of Pwi sorcerers.

The old woman hobbled into the wagon, looked at the women, studied their faces.

"Oh yes, they have been locked into dreams," the crone said. She placed a hand on Tirilee's heart, turned, and smiled at the men. "Here, you take her dream," she said.

And suddenly a gust of wind slapped Phylomon, staggering him like a blow. He was back at Frowning Idols, looking up into the face of a monolith with downturned lips. A bloody corpse, with the flesh peeled off, showing striations of fat and muscle, was lying atop him. The corpse was wet and sticky, as if freshly skinned, and because it had no eyelids, its dark brown eyes were unblinking. For a brief moment, Phylomon felt the weight of the corpse crushing down on him, crushing his budding breasts, smelled the raw meat, the tangy scent of blood, felt its sticky fleshless organ searching between his legs, probing for an opening.

"No!" he shouted. And the dream left, but a sickening sense of horror lingered. He found himself sitting on the ground. Tull lay in the grass, clutching his legs together as if to protect his virginity. Ayuvah was blindly crawling away. Scandal sat holding his belly.

"It was a bad dream," the old woman said. "Too much for any one person to hold. It is gone from her now—because you all have borne a portion of it. Sometimes a pain is so great it cannot be relieved until it is shared."

Phylomon had met Dweas three times before. He remembered a man from his youth, a Pwi who could make water flow uphill or bubble from the ground at will. Phylomon believed that each person experiences and comprehends reality slightly differently and that at times the reality believed in by one can impinge on the rest of mankind. He often wondered: Do Spirit Walkers actually see the future, or do they merely participate in the shared visions of reality of those around them until they see what those shared visions will shape?

The old woman looked at Wisteria, touched her lightly. "This one—" and then Phylomon found himself in the wa-

ter, treading oily black water, desperately trying to breathe
from a ragged hole in his throat. He looked around for help,
but in the water beside him were only crushed Pwi children,
eyes looking up from smashed faces. It was night time, and
guttering torches shone on faces of those on shore. The people of Smilodon Bay, all standing with their hands folded,
smiling down. He wanted to make them pay, make them
pay for their cruelty, but deep inside he knew he would die,
and he was too weak to take revenge, and he had no time for
revenge, for water was rushing in through the hole in his
throat, and there was no hope, no time for revenge, and that
seemed the saddest thing of all.

Then the dream was gone, and Phylomon sat, breathing
gratefully.

"They will sleep now," the old woman said, and as if to
accentuate her words, for the first time in days the women
both quit whimpering and breathed with the deep inhala-
tions of profound sleep. "In the morning, they will remember nothing. For the mind is not meant to retain dreams so
horrible." The old woman began walking downhill, into the
darkness.

"Wait!" Scandal shouted, "Don't you want to sleep here
tonight, where it is safe?"

The old Pwi woman looked back up the hill. "It is never
safe to sleep next to me," she said sadly, and ambled off into
the darkness.

Phylomon jumped from the wagon, went to the brush to
find her, offer her some food, but when he got to the brush,
he found the woman gone, and when he looked on the
ground for her tracks, he found none, and realized that the
woman had come to them only in a dream.

Tirilee woke in the back of the wagon and saw Tull beside
her, gently combing Wisteria's hair. She felt weak and ill to
her stomach. Beside Tull was a cup of tea, some biscuits and
honey. Tirilee groaned.

Tull turned to look at her. The big Tcho-Pwi was much
taller than she, with a massive chest. "Can I have some
tea?" she asked. She could have reached for it herself, but

asking for food was an old habit, one built after years of being kept in a slave pen. Take only after asking.

Tull picked up the cup. He held her head up, helped her to drink. "It was for Wisteria," he explained, "But she hasn't wakened."

"I'm grateful," she said in Pwi. "Where are we? What happened?"

"You were taken captive by the Okanjara," Tull answered. "They drugged you."

Tirilee felt a slight sense of nausea. She could recall nothing except the face of a man, a man in a dark tent.

"Here, have some of these," Tull said, and he held a biscuit up for her. She let him feed her and watched him with large eyes. She looked down at his legs, to the white scars around his ankles. The scars were thick, brutal.

"You've been kept in chains," she said. "I was sadly-kept too."

When she was five, Tirilee had lived in the aspen grove, in a small house made of trees covered with sod. Levarran, her mother, had been a slave to the trees, tending them night and day, and one winter day while she was gone hunting for rabbit, Greman Dern came. He was a heavy man—a slovenly trapper with sagging jowls and a week's worth of beard. Tirilee did not speak to him, for her mother had told her never to speak with humans. But Greman quietly asked about her mother in soft tones, speaking the language of the Pwi.

When Levarran returned, Greman greeted her. "I always wondered what happened after that night," Greman said, "figured that by now you'd have dropped a cub or two."

"Here is your daughter," Levarran had said, motioning to Tirilee.

"I figured," Greman answered.

"How long will you stay?" Her voice was hungry for him, and that had made Tirilee wonder. Levarran had often claimed she did not love Greman, but her voice betrayed something like love, a hunger for his presence.

Greman shrugged. "Been trapping silver fox and mink down on the south fork. The area is about trapped out. I thought maybe I'd stay the winter. If that is all right with you?"

"A winter is not long," Levarran answered.

"If I feel welcome enough, I could stay longer," Greman said. For as long as she could remember, Tirilee had slept cuddled in her mother's arms. But that night, Greman took her place, and Tirilee crawled to a corner of the dark room while Greman grunted and sweated, making love to Levarran. He stayed for a week. Until the food ran out and a major snowstorm passed over. Tirilee left the hut to pee, and it was cold and white in the mountains; the touch of the snow pricked her. She heard her mother scream "Tirilee" from within the hut—a cry of genuine terror—and Tirilee ran for the hut. She opened the flap and met Greman coming out. Before her eyes adjusted to the darkness, Greman grabbed her and pulled her outside.

Tirilee shouted for her mother, but heard no answer. Greman threw Tirilee over his shoulder and held her legs as he carried her downhill. Tirilee cried out for her mother. For nearly an hour he carried her downhill, and she wriggled and tried to kick free. Finally, he stopped and set her down in front of him, holding her with his great heavy hands.

"You quit kicking at me, God bugger you, or I'll do you. I'll do you good!" Tirilee had no idea what those words meant, but they scared her. They did not scare her half as much as Greman's face: Wet blood was spattered across it.

"Mama," Tirilee said softly.

"You got no mother anymore," Greman said. "And you best quit kicking at me, or I'll have you thrown in a pit for bear bait. You understand?" Tirilee didn't answer. "Good girl," Greman said. "Now I'm going to take care of you. You're worth a lot of money."

From that day forward, she'd lived in one sort of a cage or another until Phylomon set her free.

Telling Tull of her captivity had been stupid, she realized. Tull knew of her captivity. What she really wanted to tell him was . . . that when he touched her, she felt strange. When she'd touched her lips to his arm, her lips had burned.

She realized that what she really wanted to tell him was that she wanted to do it again. She'd never felt this way before.

Tull sat and quietly fed the biscuits to her, and when she finished one, she licked his finger, and her tongue burned at his touch. Tull gasped, and his eyes widened. He jerked his hand away, yet he stayed, gazing at her as if he were transfixed, and he breathed heavily.

Tirilee realized that he could not move, that Tull was like a rabbit in a corner, too frightened to run. Or maybe he wanted her. She took his hand, held it for a moment, and kissed it tenderly. The touch of his skin burned her, yet it was not painful. It was a pleasant burning. Tull sat and let her do this, and his eyes widened, and he looked afraid. "You, you don't know what you're doing!" he said, and he pulled his hand away at long last.

Tirilee shuddered to lose it. "I . . . I only want to kiss your hand," she said. "I only want to touch you."

Tull backed away from her bed, spilled the last of the tea on the floor of the barrel in his haste. Wisteria was still sleeping heavily. Tirilee lay for a long time, thinking about Levarran. She had made a mistake in taking a human lover during her Time of Devotion. Humans were so cold and greedy. A Pwi lover would have been better, someone who would remain in love. *When my mating frenzy comes,* Tirilee decided, *I will take a Man of the Pwi.* She considered taking Tull, but Wisteria and Tull had both been so kind to her. She saw how Tull loved his wife, and Tirilee did not want to take that from him. *No,* she told herself, *I will not take Tull. I will find another. Someone like him.*

Standing from the wagon, Tull could look down the hillside into the Mammoth Run Plateau with its tan plains. A great dark line of bison moved south out there, and closer to home, a dragon circled above the valley floor. The sight of it chilled him. The memories of Mammoth Run Plateau carried such a perverse kwea that he only had to look up into the sky or toward the mountains to feel a greater sense of ease.

It almost made him want to laugh, the idea that he could turn his face to Craal and actually feel a sense of release.

Tull considered what had happened in the barrel. The Dryad had unnerved him with her caress. He'd sat beside his wife and let the creature kiss his hand, and her touch had filled him with such lust that he was almost too weak to leave. He told himself that it would not happen again.

Ayuvah had been helping pack the camp. He looked up. "How does the sky feel?"

"The kwea of the sky feels good," Tull said.

"It feels good for me, too. We will push this wagon up a bit closer to the sky. The kwea will be even better up there."

They pushed their wagon until early afternoon, following the folds of valleys where rainwater had carved paths. After a few miles, they stopped by a pool. On the hill before them was a tower made of light green Benbow glass, a single great winding stair that went up five thousand feet. The men had been traveling toward it for days, yet none of them had seen it, for it was far too narrow. When Phylomon pointed it out, they all stopped to stare in wonder.

"Why it's Crazy Man Stairs!" Scandal said in delight. "Ayaah, I've heard that it was up here somewhere."

"Is that what they call it now?" Phylomon asked.

"Yes," Ayuvah added, "Only a crazy man would climb up there."

"It was made by a man I knew long ago, an artist named Huron Tech," Phylomon said. "A very curious man. He called it the Worm Tower."

"He never finished it," Scandal said. "I hear there's nothing at the top."

"Oh, he finished it," Phylomon said. "There is something at the top, although not everyone can see it, for the tower was not made to hold anything or go anywhere, it is simply art."

"Hell of a waste of Benbow glass, if you ask me," Scandal spat. "Someday, someone will figure out how to cut it up and cart it off and do something decent with it."

Phylomon looked at the Pwi, who simply stared at the tower in awe. "We'll need to stay here for a day or two until the women heal enough to help us push the wagon over the mountains," Phylomon said. "We'll climb the Worm Tower tomorrow, at sunrise."

"You'll not get me up there," Scandal said.

"I wouldn't dare try to lug you up those steps," Phylomon countered. "You can stay here to care for the women. Only the young men need go. But first, I must clear the brush around the tower."

That afternoon, Phylomon set fire to the ridge above camp. The evening wind blowing up the mountain pulled the flames and smoke uphill, and the blaze quickly consumed the dense brush and grass around the tower, exposing hundreds of thousands of tiny metal plates and towers, many rising a dozen feet in the air while others stood only inches off the ground. Phylomon spent the rest of the day clearing dead trees and burning them to nothing.

That night, both Wisteria and Tirilee got out of their beds and ate dinner. They sat together and Wisteria brushed Tirilee's hair and they laughed together like giddy young girls. Neither of them remembered Frowning Idols, and both seemed unconcerned by their lapse in memory.

When Phylomon roused the men before dawn, the ash on the hillside had turned a light gray, almost white, so that walking in the semidarkness, the ash looked as if it were snow. To get to the tower, they had to walk through a maze of small valleys, past strange rocks in odd forms. Pieces of metal and glass were thrust from the ground at extreme angles. When they reached the bottom of the tower, a U-shaped crater bordered by small hills, the hills and landscape were cluttered with twisted pieces of metal and glass, as if it were a forest created by an alien mind.

Phylomon said, "We must begin the journey at dawn so we can reach the top of the tower by midday." They took no food, and only the smallest flasks of water.

The bottom of the tower was a simple glass pole with glass stairs leading around it, spiraling up. An ornate rail rose up on each side. Engraved on the rail were countless peoples—Pwi dressed in ancient headgear; Starfarers with tall lean bodies; Hukm with broad furry chests and leather faces; simple humans dressed as traders, slavers, workers. Men and women, people of all ages—all running, crawling, hobbling up the tower. At the bottom stair, Phylomon

scraped the dirt to reveal some ornate letters: "The Journey
of the Worm."

Phylomon waited for the sun to strike the bottom stair.
For the first time that fall, Tull could see his breath in the
cold air. His soul cloud, as the Pwi called it.

When the sun struck the bottom stair so that it shone
along its whole length like a green and golden rod, they
began to climb. Phylomon ran ahead and urged the others
to follow. For the first few minutes, Tull was so occupied
trying to match the grueling pace, that he did not notice his
surroundings below him, but then he looked down and
gasped in surprise: with the sun rising, the rays of light
caught on small scraps of metal that jutted from the ground,
strangely shaped rocks, and small hills. The light coming in
from the east threw shadows on the gray ash. The shadows
resolved themselves into the figures of two lovers, naked on
the ground, a woman lying atop a man, with one leg draped
over him.

Tull thought it a clever trick, but Phylomon pressed
them forward, and inch by inch as the sun rose over the
mountains, the shadows moved, recombining into new
shapes. Tull watched the lovers disintegrate, and suddenly
as he ran he realized that he had made an error—he had
only seen a small part of the picture—for the lovers resolved
into a much larger image of a saber-tooth, chasing a child
through a horrific dreamscape of melting trees.

And so it went. Tull ran behind Phylomon and Ayuvah,
and at each turn of the stairs he was aware of the continual
play of sun and shadow to create new images. Always the
images grew, so that he learned to look beyond the borders
of the old image to discern a larger picture. Some images
were superimposed one upon another—a man selling a
woman in a Craal slave market was suddenly revealed to be
a man making the figure eight upon her hand as a sign of
marriage. *Is my wife a slave to me?* Tull wondered. If it was
slavery, it was joyous slavery, for Tull saw that both the
man and woman smiled. A line of stones with odd indenta-
tions to cast shadows on their tops could be seen to be joyful
children, or if lined together two at a time they could also be
seen as two oxen pulling a cart, or viewed in a pair of threes
they became warriors with whitened faces, or as a whole

they could be seen as a beggar with an outstretched hand pleading for food on a platter, and then suddenly the image opened up, and among the surrounding stones he saw children and parents and grandparents joined hand to hand in a circle. *Will my children be my enemies, my servants? Will they be beggars I resent, or will they grow in my image, an unending circle?* Still the shadows shortened and changed, giving birth to new images.

And Tull saw that the shadow show was about relationships and perceptions. At any moment, the shadows became one thing for him, yet Phylomon and Ayuvah might see completely different views. Perhaps because of the limits of his own mind and imagination, he could only see specific patterns. *And perhaps,* he wondered, *Huron is saying that all relationships are mere perceptions, never fully understood by the participants? That our view of a relationship creates the relationship? If I were to run this same course in twenty years, would I see the same patterns?* Tull wondered.

Tull's throat was dry, but he licked his lips and kept running. His legs ached and he became dizzy, and he found that he was moving in a dance—take two steps, turn to the right, take two steps, turn to the right, take two steps, turn to the right. His own steps, along with the steps of the others, set up a complex pattern of harmonics. The glass hummed with a low-pitched tune, and he could almost imagine that he heard a song forming in his head.

And then they came to a landing, and Phylomon bid them to halt and drink some water.

"Huron," he said between panting breaths, "was an odd man. When he lived, the Pwi saw life as a stair, a straight path between nonexistence to all-existence, where we expanded and grew until we filled the universe. They called this path *Lashi Chamepar,* the Path of the Crushed Heart. The Starfarers, for the most part, saw life as only a circle—a journey from life to the grave, and the mystics among them asserted that once they reached the grave, they circled back to life—a maddening, meaningless journey.

"But Huron was enraged by both prospects. He saw life as a journey along an endless winding stair. With each step up, he believed, we view a greater expanse on the horizon, and with each completion of the circle, we enlarge our knowledge and see the world in a new way, gain a greater awareness of the diversity and complexity of life. When he built this, Huron said to me, that if we but had the eyes to see, with each turning we make on these stairs, we would be granted a different vision of the world below. He was a madman, obsessed by the need to present his views. He used to say that we were all spoiled, that we Starfarers were born believing that happiness was deserved, the birthright of mankind by virtue of the fact of our mere existence. He scorned such foolishness and taught that happiness is the reward for those who learn *how* to live." Phylomon watched Tull for a long moment, and Tull wondered what thoughts the blue man was trying to drill into him. "Happiness is the reward for those who learn how to live," Phylomon mused, yet his face was sad. Tull wondered if the Starfarer was happy.

Having said that, Phylomon raced ahead and upward. Tull followed behind, but he was wet with sweat and feared slipping. He kept up, but there were no more pictures to be seen below. Instead, he listened to the music in his own head. He was weary of looking below, and looked to the hills: and was astounded, for the lower hills—hills that no man could have carved even if he dug for an entire lifetime, took on the image of dancing beasts. As they rose, the images changed slowly to a great circle of humans snake-dancing across the hills, and within an hour he recognized that the images shifted and showed an enlarged view of a man and woman expanding in size, filling the world, filling the universe.

When they reached a second landing, Phylomon explained. "We can rest, but don't relax! Don't stop. Your muscles will cramp."

They drank a bit more water, and Phylomon stood and stretched his muscles, watched the sun. "We must reach the top at midday," he said, and when he judged the time to be right, he sprung up the ladder. Looking down, Tull could see that the sun was high enough so that there were no more shadows on the ground except an odd dot here and there. The illusion had been burned away.

The run to the top was more physically demanding than the first two runs. It was both longer, and required them to run faster. Tull passed beyond the need to count steps. Instead, the journey became a matter of habit: two steps up, turn right, two steps up, turn right. Dizziness came on him, and to combat it, he leaned his head back and looked straight ahead at the feet of the others moving before him.

Round and round the winding stair, climbing, tripping, struggling up the smooth glass steps, the world below growing distant so that the shadows of trees squatted like flies on a table. Sweat streamed down Tull's brow, down his armpits, into his moccasins. And with each step, his feet slid so that he no longer trusted his footing. His head swayed backward and sideways, and his legs felt loose and he no longer cared. Beside him, clouds loomed. They were high enough so that the clouds no longer held the illusion of being flat on the bottom, as they often seem below. Instead they were tall and magnificent, like long quartz crystals floating through the sky, and for a while they ran up through a wonderland of clouds, where water condensed on the stairs. For a moment, they climbed among the billows of a cloud, then they were above it, running silently except for the blood pounding in Tull's ears, and Tull wished that he could have stopped among the clouds and let the mist coalesce on his tongue, even if it were only a small drink. The air became cold, and ice formed a thin sheet on the stairs.

He did not look for patterns anymore. There was nothing to see. Beneath him, the mountains in their fall colors spread like a Pwi blanket of dyed mammoth hair, painted in reds and yellows on the ground. The opal mist of the clouds floated along beneath him, and the wind blew clouds by so fast that he felt as if he were watching foam floating in a stream. They were above the coastal mountains now. Tull could see the blue haze above the sea out on the horizon, clouds sweeping off it like gauze, and somewhere over there was Smilodon Bay. After days of journeying, they had not really come so far. Only 120 miles. Beneath them, among the pale tans of autumn grass, dark herds of giant sloths and wild ox moved across the Mammoth Run Plateau. Each poor beast watching for predators, leading its insignificant life.

There are no more illusions, Tull thought, *only the world beneath me, curving off into a shining bow on the horizon. I am separating myself from it. Drawing away. This stair is only a thin line connecting me to the world, just as the silk flowing from an inchworm connects it to a limb. All the beasts beneath me, they are trapped in the illusion. Yet all of life is refined to a single act: the upward climb.*

Tull suddenly thought he saw the ultimate meaning of the Journey of the Worm: all the shadows on the ground, the different views of family and man, of life and beauty—did not lead to greater and greater complexities to be eternally wondered at by the sages. They were mere shadows, illusions, to be overcome.

His feet seemed to be slipping out from beneath him, wet with sweat, slick with ice; the world spun more than it should. He was worn and tired, and suddenly he staggered into a crystal bar that was spread out to block his way. They had reached the top of the tower, and on the bar was written the word *Death*.

Tull staggered back and looked at the bar, and his head spun horribly. He held to the bar for a moment, and because he had been running for hours, climbing for hours, he felt as if he were still climbing. Everything within him longed to climb. Beneath him, the stair, bent by the winds, shimmered in the sunlight like an icicle seen hanging down from a roof. Yet Tull felt that he was still traveling upward. He looked up at his final destination if he were to keep climbing, and above him was the sun.

I am but an inchworm, joined to this world by a silken thread. I can set myself free!

Something within him snapped, and Tull felt the silken thread drop away. For the first time in his life, Tull looked at the sun full, and saw it directly, like a great beautiful silver and violet flower, each of its flames whipping out. Yet the light did not hurt his eyes or blind him. He was freed from his body, with its weaknesses and limitations. It was like watching the waves play on the sea from the cliffs above Moon Dance Inn, and the beauty of that great silver and violet flower was mesmerizing, and he longed to be there. And with the longing, came motion, and Tull began spiraling toward the sun, flying away.

"No!" Ayuvah shouted, and the force of the word shook Tull as if he were a sheet on a line, blown in a fierce wind.

Tull could see the sound, flashing golden waves, whipping past him, and he looked down.

Phylomon and Ayuvah were far below, at the top of the crystal stairs, holding Tull's body. They both glowed with a deep blue aura of concern. Tull lay with arms and legs askew, muscles twitching in his neck. Phylomon was examining the body, "He's dead," Phylomon said, and Tull felt curiously unconcerned by his own death.

Ayuvah shouted at the lifeless body, "Do not leave! Think of the things you have left undone! Think of the kwea of your love for Wisteria! You cannot leave her!"

And when Tull thought of Wisteria, the kwea of his love slapped him. It was as if he were home, in bed with her again, and he felt the goddess Zhofwa blow her kisses through the open window. The sun was a beautiful flower, but it would always be there. He looked down. The earth itself was a fascinating tapestry: the souls of men and animals and trees glowed like fireworks across its face, a thousand shades of purple, gold, and black. Dragons floated below him, and he knew that they saw him for what he was. At the foot of the stairs, Wisteria lay asleep on the wagon. Tull could see her as clearly as if she were at arm's reach. Her soul was pink and black—love and darkness—and he wanted to touch it, heal it, put his arms around her and cover that darkness.

Tull hurtled down toward his dying body, like a hermit crab covering itself with a shell.

For a moment, he felt disconnected, and his heart thumped in his chest. He struggled to swallow, felt his breakfast sitting sluggishly in his belly, and he tried to move a finger. There were so many connections to make, so many muscles to move. To breathe was a major chore, and his chest felt as if it were wrapped in bands of iron. Opening his eyes took as much effort as if he were opening a cavernous door.

Phylomon bent over him, frowning. He jerked back in surprise.

"You are a Spirit Walker!" Ayuvah shouted, grabbing Tull's face. For a moment, Tull's sight dimmed, and something snapped, and he felt at peace, at home. "Where did you go? Did you walk into the future?"

"I . . . flew toward the sun," Tull said. "But I heard you calling to me. So I came back."

Phylomon frowned more deeply, rubbed his forehead with his hand. "Can you stand?"

"No," Tull said, quite certain he could not stand.

Phylomon sighed. Obviously the others could not carry him. Phylomon reached for his water bottle, took a sip, and slowly poured the rest for Tull.

"We won't need to hurry so much on the way down," Phylomon said. "The journey is much easier. We'll sit and wait a bit. Tell us when you are ready. That is, if you can walk at all."

Tull lay still for nearly an hour, and as he lay there, he could feel himself becoming reconnected to his body. For no reason at all, he found himself gasping for breath, and sweat was streaming off of him. And then he remembered that he had been climbing all day. Yet he felt no physical sensation, no pain. Everything he touched seemed dim, unreal.

He remembered Chaa after his Spirit Walk. Chaa had lain just as Tull lay, unmoving, distanced, and Tull now understood why. After nearly an hour, the feeling in his arms and hands returned last of all. It was cold on top of this tower. He stood up.

"Let's get moving," he said, and they began their descent.

They walked slowly at first, and Phylomon held Tull's shoulder to make sure he didn't fall. But after a bit, Tull broke Phylomon's grip and walked under his own power.

With the renewed energy, Phylomon said, "It's time to get going. We'd better hurry. We don't want to get stranded on the stair in the darkness."

And they ran.

Down, down the crystal stair, the shadows lengthening around them. The clouds flowed past them and they neared the earth again, spinning, pausing only once to rest. As they neared the bottom, the shadows lengthening on the hills caused new pictures to form on the ground. The doubled image of a man and a woman, the man selling her into slavery, drawing the figure eight on her palm. Yet there was a subtle change, and it took a moment for Tull to notice it. They were not smiling in either image. Instead, she stared at him in resentment, and he frowned at her in reproach. It was the same with all of the figures—each image was distorted, full of pain and hopelessness. And Tull realized that the downward spiral was an easier path to climb, and he could see that the direction colored all of one's perceptions of life. Yet the shadows are still but illusions, he realized.

Although the downward journey was easier on his legs, Tull's feet still became wet with sweat. His mind reeled from running the continuous circle, and he struggled to concentrate on always turning. And so he plummeted beyond the families of beasts and beggars, beyond the world of thieves and businessmen, down to a crater where a man and woman engaged in beastly sex. And written in shadows on the back of the woman's hand was the word *Death.* The sun abruptly set, and they were running now in darkness, into a black hole with no end.

Tull reached the final step, and because he was heading down, because he was running eternally down, his legs buckled beneath him and he fell to the ashes.

For minutes he lay panting in the darkness, choking on the ashes, too dizzy to move any longer, and he felt himself sinking, falling, forever in the darkness.

That night, while working the cramps out of his legs by the fireside, Phylomon was uneasy. He watched Tull and Ayuvah practice with sword and spear, and the power of their blows, the frantic energy of their fight, left him depressed. They were both getting better. With a few years of training, either of them could fight display battles in Craal's best arenas. *If the boys are ever taken slave,* he thought, *arena fighting might not be such a bad life for them. With luck, they could live long enough to become trainers themselves.*

Such thoughts left him in a foul mood. The whole day had not gone as it should. *You are a foolish old man,* Phylomon told himself. Although Tull expressed amazement at what he'd seen, Phylomon had hoped for more—to give the boy some direction, some initiative. Tull was such a fool. Didn't he see that the kings, the merchants, the great teachers, inventors, and artists of his generation were already alive? Tull was among them. If Chaa could be believed, then Tull was destined for greatness, yet the boy saw only defeat.

At dinner, Tull found Wisteria awake and spoon-fed her, caressing her hair, and he said one encouraging thing about his run up the tower. He said, "The tower is not the work of art at all. It is the journey one takes, that is the work of art."

But Phylomon was not sure the boy understood the import of those words. How could he? He was only nineteen. Phylomon had lived a thousand years longer, had borne so much pain and grief that he wondered if Tull could ever understand that always, in the face of pain and despair, learning to live and be happy becomes the greatest art of all. So much care and precision, so much balance to be maintained.

Worst of all, Phylomon thought, *the boy is a damned Spirit Walker.* He had not considered the possibility, but here it was—a Tcho-Pwi who was a Spirit Walker. Such powers, like the powers of the Dwea of old, had always been reserved for the Pwi. But over the last six hundred years Phylomon had watched the blood lines mix. Human and Pwi mating over and over again. So many humans who believed their blood was pure would be bewildered to see how many Pwi ancestors they had. A new species was emerging. Something neither human nor Pwi. Only sixty years ago Phylomon had run across a Pwi Dicton who carried the two extra chromosomes containing a dictionary of the English language, a characteristic that had for generations marked a pure human heritage. And now, here was a Tcho-Pwi Spirit Walker.

Would the boy become subverted by the teachings of some damned Pwi shaman? Would he reject a technological future? Phylomon considered. If Tull could be trained to become a Spirit Walker, he could become a great general. What human general could hope to outmaneuver a Spirit Walker on the field of battle? Was that what Chaa had foreseen? And if Tull became enamored with his powers, would he feel threatened by technology? Wouldn't he reject it? Phylomon respected the psychic abilities of the Pwi, but how could those powers compare to technology? The Spirit Walkers could see the future, but technology would create that future. The Spirit Walkers could project their consciousness to great distances, even to other worlds. But technology would carry their children to those places. Their magic blinded them. What they took for power was a trap. The Spirit Walkers could not enlarge their people's understanding of the universe, heal the sick, extend life. Only the Starfarers had accomplished these things. If Tull could only be made to see!

Slowly, like the opening of a morning lily at the rising sun, Phylomon realized Tull *could* be made to see. In the city of Sanctum, beneath the ancient flagstones that passed for streets, Phylomon hid a secret. *Falhalloran,* the ancient vehicle of the Starfarers, was perhaps the most powerful artifact on Anee. *Falhalloran* could teach Tull the power of the Starfarers. *Perhaps it would be dangerous to show Tull the power of the artifact?* he wondered. Too much power *could* fall into the wrong hands. But the Spirit Walker had said, "Do not fear to teach him your secrets." Phylomon considered, weighed the risks. He had decided to die when he set foot on this journey. Perhaps it was too late to go back. Ah, to see *Falhalloran* one last time! Phylomon's cramps made him feel old. *Yes,* he thought, *it is time to pass this secret on.*

Chapter 8
Festival of the Dragon

The next morning, they began
their arduous trek up the Dragon Spines, pushing and heav-
ing their wagon. The barrel left the wagon unbalanced and it
tended to tilt on a slope. Wisteria and Tirilee had to walk,
but were too ill to help push the wagon. That night the
ground froze and crystals of ice remained in the thick humus till noon. Pushing the wagon up the rocky hills was
backbreaking, dangerous, often tedious. On the second
morning, Tirilee recovered enough to help push, but Wisteria vomited, her stomach trying to eject the residue of the
poisons, and she spent most of the day ill, so Phylomon put
her on lookout.

They were in dragon country, and the high mountain
slopes left them exposed. The dragons seldom attacked humans or Pwi, because the dragons' genetic memories told
them that these small animals were a normal part of the
landscape. But the dragons became enraged by anything
they recognized as "other." Four men hooked to a wagon
like appendages aroused the dragons' curiosity. And on the

second day climbing the Dragon Spines, a pair of red tyrant birds swooped from a cliff and circled the wagon.

The dragons shadowed the party, lighting on rocky outcrops, watching from trees. Phylomon became worried that they would attack at night. An hour before dusk, he stopped the wagon, loaded the swivel gun, and had the men wave rags to lure the dragons in. He blew both tyrant birds from the sky.

The journey through the Dragon Spines was something Wisteria put out of her mind after she started helping push the wagon. Her muscles became knotted, and all her energy seemed devoted to pushing the wagon up one rocky slope, then trying to brake its headlong flight down the next. Often she wept in rage and frustration when a wheel stuck in a hole. The work sapped all her energy. Twice a day, Phylomon stopped to train them in weapons use, and he insisted that she take part, although he taught her only how to fight with a knife. Her belly became tight as a knot from the hard labor, and although she remembered nothing of Frowning Idols, she imagined she tasted the Okanjara's drugs in the bile that rose from time to time. She wondered if she would ever recover from the drugs.

Above the treeline, the world seemed to resolve down to its barest elements—a sky of pure blue, grass of dull green, rocks colored yellow and orange and olive by lichens, clean water. There was that, and the wagon, and the work. And as they toiled through that landscape during the days, her anger and loss seemed to wear away.

One night, Tull laid out the bearskin blankets for her to sleep on, and for an hour he kneaded the knots in her shoulders and aching calves. She relished his touch, and rolled in closer, pressing against his warm body. "Are you cold?" he asked.

"Yes," she said. Tull quickly went to the fire, got some large warm rocks, wrapped them in doeskin to help keep her warm. She hugged him tight, and with his body pressed against her, she wondered if he'd want to make love. She wanted to kiss him, to thank him for his kindness, but making love just sounded too hard.

Tull gazed into her face, and he was so full of love for her, so much in awe. She wondered, *How could anyone ever feel that way about me?* She smiled at him. In her imagination, she said, *You're a good man, Tull. You're as tender and devoted as any man I've ever met. And it isn't enough. I know I should give myself to you the way you give yourself to me, but, God, don't you see that you're not enough for me?* Tull smiled faintly, stroked the curve of her breast, and Wisteria suddenly felt sick to her stomach.

"Let's not make love," she said. "Not yet. I'm still too ill."

Tull frowned, "You can push a wagon up a mountain all day, and be too ill for this?"

"Yes," she said, surprised at how gullible he was.

Tull frowned, gave her a long curious stare, as if to see if her face betrayed the lie. His arms turned limp at her waist. The nausea in her stomach grew. *Is this guilt I'm feeling?* she wondered. *Guilt for not loving someone who loves me so purely?* She knew it was more than that. She felt tenderness for him. She wanted his attention. But she couldn't bring herself to love him. Perhaps it was the thought of Mayor Goodstick, back in town, who waited for her to betray the party. To pretend to love Tull would be a betrayal worse than to ruin the quest.

But that did not seem answer enough. At times she'd made love to him, had been thrilled by it, the way she was thrilled when she made love to Garamon Goodstick, knowing that her life depended on her performance.

So, one night when they had been a week in the Dragon Spines, she went to lie down beside Tull on the bearskin. He pulled the hide over her and snuggled close. She knew he would try to seduce her, and the knowledge that she would not be able to perform made her so angry, the thought that he would not give up made her so angry, that she punched him in the jaw, then clawed his chest.

He was facing the fire—he always arranged it so that she could sleep with her back to the fire. When she punched him, he opened his mouth in surprise, and then, for the tiniest moment, anger flickered in his eyes.

That anger, that rage. "You want to hit me?" she asked, but he did not answer. "I can see it in your eyes, you wanted to hit me!" Seeing it in his yellow eyes filled her with such excitement that she became wet. She laughed and grabbed his organ and pulled it roughly, bent down and kissed his chest, then bit him hard enough to draw blood. She waited for him to hit her back, to scratch her or strangle her or beat her. She hiked up her skirt, pulled him into her, and rutted with him fiercely and freely, and he tried to be tender with her, to hug her and cuddle, and it messed everything up, frustrated her so that she threw herself on him, time and again, trying to force him to feel her rage. She pulled his hair, and when he stroked her breast, she grabbed for his fingers, showed him how to pinch her nipples, showed him what she wanted, yet he would not do it.

For an hour she threw herself on him in vain, bit him. It was the most unfulfilling love she'd ever made. She tried to imagine that Tull was Mayor Goodstick, drunk, pressing a knife to her throat, threatening to kill her if she did not perform, but imagination was not enough. She could not reach that peak. She stopped rubbing herself against him for a moment, and when she was ready to give up, she listened to the others in camp.

None of them snored or breathed deeply. Instead, they listened to her make love, and the knowledge that she'd embarrassed herself so badly made her laugh out loud, and in that moment, she reached her climax and floated free above them all.

The next morning when Wisteria woke, she felt good, the best she'd felt in her life. They'd camped in a high valley, and she rose while the fog was low and the sun crept up. Everyone else was still abed. Tirilee lay against Phylomon. Tull slept soundly from his exertions. Ayuvah had rolled so close to the smoldering campfire that if he moved another few inches, his furs would go up in flame. Scandal lay on his belly in his furs, and she could not tell if he slept. He could have been asleep, but one eye seemed narrowed to a slit. She wanted a bath, so she pulled off her clothes and pretended that Scandal watched her. She smiled at the thought, then threw her clothes over her shoulder and crept down to the creek, hoping not to awaken anyone.

The water was pure and clean and cold as ice, and she washed herself daintily at first, crouching by the creek and splashing her breasts and arms. When she grew used to the cold, she lay in the creek and closed her eyes. She felt good. She was willing to forgive Tull for his weakness, for his cuddling. *Hell,* she thought, *I'm even willing to forgive Phylomon for killing my family.* She imagined herself telling Tull that she loved him, proving to the group that it was true by confessing that she had plotted with Mayor Goodstick to sabotage the quest. Then she would thank Phylomon for killing her parents and leading her on this quest where she had found True Love, and she'd promise to help the others though it cost her life. She laughed at the thought, bent back to let her hair get wet.

"What naughty little daydreams are you laughing about?" Scandal said softly.

The fat cook was standing beside the creek, holding a green cotton towel over one arm, watching her. Wisteria put a hand over her breast, tried to cover herself, realized dully that Scandal had been awake when she undressed, that he'd been watching her.

"What are you doing here?"

Scandal smiled at her. "Admiring your body. Feeling close to—oh, nature."

"You'd better leave," she said.

"Oh, don't worry," Scandal said. "They're all asleep."

Wisteria laughed embarrassedly, and for a moment she didn't understand why, and then she realized that she laughed because she was relieved to know that the others slept.

"You know," Scandal said, pointing his finger, "I'm beginning to realize something about you."

"What?" Wisteria said. She wondered if she should sit up, should cover herself more fully. But he had already seen everything she had to see, so what was the point?

"I'm beginning to realize that you, Wisteria, are a nasty lady. In fact, you're an adulteress."

"I've never committed adultery. I love my husband," she said in defense.

"Of course you do," Scandal said. "I'm sure you love him profoundly. But still, he won't satisfy you." As if to turn the subject, Scandal said, "Did you know that a Pwi woman has a larger birth canal than a human?"

"No," Wisteria said reflexively.

"Ayaah, it's true! She needs it in order to give birth—Pwi babies have such large skulls, with all that armor plating in their heads. So, you'd think that a Pwi man would need a larger organ to please his woman. But it's odd, don't you think, that human men actually have larger sex organs? The Pwi have got bigger hands, bigger heads, larger brains, more muscle. But in one area, they don't compare. It's a cruel trick of nature, and many a Pwi woman, I am sure, has mourned the fact. Pwi men are smaller than humans where it counts most. Women who've tried both flavors vastly prefer humans as lovers. Don't you find that interesting?"

"No—yes, I mean no," Wisteria said, flustered. He'd said she was an adulteress, and she thought back to the night before when she'd imagined she was making love to the mayor. Hadn't she committed it already, in her heart. It did seem that with the mayor, she had enjoyed it more. Was it the size difference?

"Yes, you mean yes," Scandal said, winking at her. "Let me tell you something. When I was young, I sailed round the world trading recipes. I studied hard to be a gourmet cook. But in all the ports of the world, I tasted more than just the foods. In some places, I have heard, they still call me the 'Gourmet of Love.' And there is one thing I've learned in life: There are those who make love and there are those who don't. You are destined to be one of those who do. You see, we belong to the great secret society of lovers. We have no particular hair or eye color to set us apart. We don't need code words—we don't even need to speak the same language—but wherever we go around the world, we recognize one another at a glance. And I know who you are: I can see it in your eyes. When I talk dirty to you, I can feel your arousal, hot and wet, like a thunderstorm sweeping in off the sea. I smell your desire as if it were perfume, as if it were the sweet scent of yellow roses blown through an open window.

"Now, may I dry you off?" Scandal asked.

Wisteria looked up the hill toward camp. Through the small strands of willows on the bank she could see Phylomon making his way toward the creek.

"No," she said, glancing quickly up and down the creek for someplace to hide. There was no cover close enough. "Throw me the towel—Phylomon's coming!"

Scandal glanced backward quickly and tossed her the towel. She got up, wrapped it around her hurriedly. Scandal turned his back to her, just as Phylomon came into the open.

"I . . . I beg your pardon Wisteria," Scandal blustered, "I . . . I didn't see you there!"

Phylomon stopped in his tracks, turned his head to the side modestly.

"If I knew you would all be down here so quickly, I'd have bathed somewhere where I could have a little more privacy!" Wisteria said.

"Please forgive us. We didn't mean to intrude," Scandal said, backing off toward camp. Phylomon looked at Scandal questioningly, but even Wisteria could see that Scandal's cheeks were burning in genuine embarrassment, and both men hurried back to camp without Phylomon offering any sign that he'd interrogate Scandal.

Wisteria dried herself off, pulled on her clothes. Her head was spinning. She could not be certain what she felt. Relief that Scandal was gone? The desire to be seduced by him? Love for her husband, guilt for not loving him enough? Shame at the way the memory of making love to Garamon made her blood race? All of these and more.

When she got back to camp, Tull was up. He hugged her, wrapped a fur around her. She hissed through her teeth, "You asked me to teach you how to love. You'd better start getting it right!"

Tull backed away, startled. Wisteria giggled at his confusion, kissed him passionately.

That day, as they pushed the wagon up over the pass, she welcomed the exertion, the mind-numbing forgetfulness it brought. The ground became rough, and they worked to move the wagon as a team. When the wagon stuck on an uphill slope, and everyone pushed and pulled with all their might, Scandal and Phylomon would always dig down deeper and find just a little more strength hidden within them, and they'd break the wagon free and move it higher. Wisteria enjoyed pushing the wagon, working her frustration out on that miserable chunk of wood. Most of all, she loved being part of something, part of a team that existed only to push and pull a wagon by mere willpower. For a few hours at least, like the sky and the water and the undefiled mountains around her, she felt pure.

That night they camped near the top of the Dragon Spines. At sunset the sky was clear and Tull could see pine forests and plains down the mountains beyond them. Tull looked out over the countryside as far as he could see. Down there, somewhere, was Sanctum. Another hundred miles. Then it was only four hundred miles over the White Mountains to Craal and Seven Ogre River. They'd come so far—nearly halfway to Craal—surely, no one in Smilodon Bay had ever been this far back in the Rough. He looked below and found that he was scouring the countryside, looking for the armies that Tchupa had promised, the Blade Kin with their war dogs and armored mastodons.

There was a little bit of dirty snow on the ground and Wisteria and Tirilee took a pot, went up on the ridge to scrape the snow and find the cleanest to boil for drinking water.

Scandal was trying to light a fire, and Phylomon sat on a black rock beside him, took off his necklace, and began striking it. It flashed like lightning, sending a call to the Creators, and Tull realized that it would also send a call to anyone in the valleys below.

Tull bent over a pair of leather moccasins and sewed some new soles onto them. The journey was taking its toll in moccasins, and the sharp mountain rocks were especially bad. After what had happened to Ayuvah, Tull realized that he needed to take good care of his feet if he was ever to finish the journey. Ayuvah walked up beside Tull.

"Brother," Tull said, glancing at the bursts of light that sprang from Phylomon's necklace, but spoke no further.

"How does the sky feel tonight?" Ayuvah asked.

"The sky is sad," Tull said. "The sun grows cold and feels the darkness coming."

"You are troubled," Ayuvah said. "You have been troubled for a long time."

Tull sighed. Many things troubled him, but he did not want to mention his fear of Craal. "I do not know what is wrong. It is my wife."

"Human women," Ayuvah said. "You should have married Fava."

Tull looked at Ayuvah, and wondered if the Neanderthal were right. Fava had always been such a sweet girl. Tull understood her. He said slowly, "When I am kind to my wife, she becomes angry. When we make love, she wants me to hurt her. I . . . I don't know if she loves me."

Ayuvah put his arm around Tull's shoulder. "Kwea will not bind her love to you. Who can understand a human? Does she profess love at all?"

Tull said, "She has professed love. When we married, I asked her to teach me how to love. I felt like a fool because . . . I wanted to please her. But now, she acts distant —strange. When I hold her, she leans into me, as if for comfort, then she slaps my hands away. When we make love, she wants me to bite and claw. Last night she asked if I wanted to hit her, and there was hope in her eyes, as if she wanted me to torment her."

Ayuvah said, "Perhaps you should teach *her* how to love."

Tull could not explain why those words made him feel so empty. "She doesn't want my kind of love."

Ayuvah did not answer for a long time, then began to weep softly.

"Why are you crying," Tull asked.

"Because I'm afraid for you," Ayuvah answered. "I'm afraid you will lose your wife. She is not like a Pwi. She might not stay with you. I don't know how to help you."

Tull had never imagined that Wisteria would leave him. It was so unlike anything a Pwi would do. Yet, he knew that humans often rejected their mates.

Scandal had been trying to light a fire, and he looked up, embarrassed. "Look here, the way you're talking, I've never heard anything so stupid! We ought to melt the two of you down for lard. Look, Tull—just because a girl wants a little biting and kicking in bed, doesn't mean she doesn't love you! You can play her game, keep her entertained!"

Tull resented the words. "Making love is not entertainment!"

"Oh, I can see that you're going to grow into a stodgy old bastard. You'll be plenty of laughs in bed. Problem is, the women will be laughing at you, not with you."

"She's the reason I draw breath. I don't intend to make love for laughs."

"Well, I'm sure you don't, but have you thought about what she wants? Sex is like rabbit meat—it's dull and flavorless and not much good for anything. Why, did you know that if you eat rabbit meat and nothing else, you'll be dead within a month? Called rabbit starvation. The rabbit doesn't have either the fat or the flavor to keep a man alive. So, when you eat rabbit, you've got to sauté it in onions and wine and butter, bring out the flavor a little, give it the right spice and add a little fat. The same thing happens with sex. If you sleep with a woman and don't offer her any spice, you're liable to bore her to death in a couple of months. You need to give her a thrill once in a while! She's already told you what she wants, so slap her around, for God's sake. Hang her headfirst over a fire if she wants it!"

Tull looked at Phylomon for help, but the blue man merely shrugged. "She seeks danger for entertainment," he said. "Just as we all do. You Pwi hunt for eggs in Hotland, but I'm willing to bet that you prize carnosaur eggs above all others. The element of risk, the challenge, gives them greater value."

"Exactly!" Scandal said. "Life isn't worth living, unless you live it on the edge!"

"But no one would want to put their love in jeopardy," Tull said.

"We do strange things," Phylomon answered. "I've watched Scandal, and in a single night I've seen him insult a dozen customers. He puts his business in jeopardy. He knows he serves a good table, fine whores. Perhaps he is testing his customers, seeing if they will put up with his abuse because they prize his table. I've also known people who spend their entire living on frivolities so that they keep themselves in financial jeopardy. I've known men of great learning who propound idiotic theories so that their standing in the intellectual community is placed in doubt. Even you, Tull Genet, seek the face of danger. I saw how you wanted to find the Mastodon Men. You sought the face of Adjonai, the God of Terror."

"So what are you saying?"

Phylomon thumped his medallion absently. Flashes of light washed the hillside. "Wisteria knows you love her, but she also fears losing that love, and the fear thrills her."

"What am I to do? If I lead her to believe my love is so weak, I'd be lying."

"For her, right now," Phylomon said, "love may be mere entertainment. If you want to keep her, entertain her."

Ayuvah made a gagging sound, drew their attention. "You humans disgust me, to place love so low."

Scandal laughed and Phylomon dropped his necklace. "Get out your weapons. It's time for practice. Tonight, I think you should learn how to fight in the dark, when you are exhausted to the bone."

Suddenly, from out of the sky, a great bird swooped and perched on the rock before Phylomon, watching him with yellow unblinking eyes.

Tull had never seen a bird like it. It was gray, nearly large as a condor. Phylomon spoke to it loudly. "We need your help. The serpents are gone from the coast at Smilodon Bay, and saurs have crossed the ocean from Dervin's Peninsula. We do not know why the serpents are gone. You must restock this area immediately. We are going to Seven Ogre River to catch some young serpents in hopes that we can return them to the coast, but we need help."

Phylomon threw out his arms, scaring the bird away, and smiled. "At least now the Creators will be aware of our predicament."

"Will they answer us?" Ayuvah asked.

"Who knows?" Phylomon said. "The minds of the Creators are not like ours. They sit in their caves and nurture their creations. It might not strike them as important to reply. Certainly a Creator will not come to see us, but they might send a messenger—one that can speak—to request more information. At the very least, they will look into the problem. They are single-minded in their effort to maintain the balance of this planet. They will not let the eco-barriers fail another season."

"Can we go home?" Scandal asked.

"No. The Creators can recreate the genetic structure of anything living on this planet, but they cannot do it faster than it would take for the normal process to occur. When that bird reaches its Creator, even if the Creator were to begin gestation immediately, the eggs would not hatch until next year."

"That isn't fast enough," Tull said. "Chaa said carnosaurs will be here by spring."

"If nothing else, the Creators can localize the infection," Phylomon said. "If we can keep the carnosaurs from spreading, the dragons will clean them out eventually. Still, there's no telling how many people would die. We must go on. Gentlemen, get your swords. It's time for practice."

A week later, thirty miles from Sanctum, they pushed their wagon over a mosquito-ridden bog into a grassy field. Scandal raised a shout. At the far end of the field, beneath the shade of a stand of spruce, a herd of woolly mammoths grazed by a pool, tended by four Hukm who were shedding their brown summer fur for coats of winter white.

They pushed their wagon forward with such eagerness that soon the whole party moved at a run. The Hukm spotted them and casually walked into the trees, then returned from the shadows carrying war clubs. It appeared to be a small family—a large female, her husband, two boys. Yet the Hukm boys were taller than Phylomon. Each Hukm wore bandoliers, belts, or armbands made of bark, and they wore ornaments in their ears and noses made of colored shells and agates. Unlike humans and Pwi, who wear clothing out of a sense of modesty, the Hukm wore clothing only for decoration.

"Wait!" Phylomon shouted in an attempt to slow the others. "They're afraid of us. Just because we want them to loan us a mammoth, doesn't mean they will. They have been at war with the Craal for eight hundred years. They don't like us any better than others of our ilk. Let me speak to them."

The party stopped, and Phylomon waved his hands in the air as a sign that he wanted to speak. The big female who led the group motioned him forward. They stood for nearly half an hour. Phylomon spoke in finger talk, and the big female answered him in kind, occasionally grunting or barking for emphasis. Phylomon finally returned.

"They've agreed to barter over dinner. The Hukm don't use fire, so we won't be able to cook. Don't make any aggressive moves. Leave your weapons. And don't smile or show your teeth. Don't speak, even among yourselves. I'll do the talking."

The Hukm grabbed two logs and pulled them side by side. The four Hukm sat on one log, Tirilee and the humans and Pwi sat on the other. The great female, who stood ten feet tall and measured four feet at the shoulders, walked forward and sniffed each member of the group. Her hair had been cut in the front, to keep it from falling in her eyes, and she wore only a dark red bandolier of cedar bark. When she moved in close to smell him, Tull could see that the bandolier was a pouch filled with small cured leaves.

Tull looked into her dark brown eyes, and smelled her back. She smelled of open grasslands and mammoth hide. She smelled like something wild. She reached forward and touched his chest, very gently, with one finger. When she passed on to Wisteria, she lifted one of Wisteria's breasts, then pointed at her own relatively small breast, as if to say "I am a woman, too." There was a look of respect in the Hukm's eye. Only when she saw Wisteria, did she look at an equal.

The Hukm moved on. When she checked Tirilee, she failed to notice the Dryad's budding breasts. She gestured to Phylomon, pointed out Wisteria, let her hand fall and her fingers waggle.

"She will barter for use of a mammoth only with you," Phylomon said. "Since you are a woman, you will understand how she loves her mammoth children. She wants me to translate for you."

"But I don't know what to say to these animals," Wisteria protested.

"The only thing we have that they would want are Scandal's spices," Phylomon answered. "We'll use those."

"All right," Wisteria said.

They began. Scandal went to the wagon and brought out

the spices. When compared to the size of a mammoth, the packets of black tea, vanilla beans, cinnamon, ginger, sage, cardamom, anise, dried orange peel—all were tiny packets. Yet when spread out in array on the ground, the Hukm went wild. They fingered the tiny wooden boxes, recognizing their great worth, and the two young Hukm actually drooled. The Hukm quickly made an offer. They'd obligingly take the spices in return for a mammoth, provided that the two young Hukm escort the party the length and breadth of the entire journey. Wisteria and Phylomon discussed the offer for a long time. Hukm were wild and dangerous, and did not understand the ways of humans. Yet it was obvious that they would not let the mammoth go without an escort. Under his breath, Scandal whispered, "God! Not all of them! These spices are worth a fortune in steel eagles!" And it was true. Many of the spices had traveled two thousand miles by sea and could be bought only at great cost.

Wisteria countered the offer—one-quarter of the spices in return for a mammoth, and the haggling was on. The Hukm came forward and smelled each spice, each of the teas, savored the exotic aromas—rejected some and sorted others into piles. As the day wore on, the Hukm were forced to dip into their pouches for dried fruit. Scandal went to the wagon and brought out some dried apples, pears, and pickles to feed the party. After several hours the dealing had worn down. The party would pay nearly three-quarters of the spices for the mammoth, but Scandal was spared some of his most expensive herbs.

When the bartering was done, Tull stretched himself and crossed his legs. He sat for a moment, then looked over at one of the young Hukm. The boy was breathing heavily, and seemed to be glaring at Tull. Tull watched the youngster for a moment, then looked at Wisteria and the others beside him. The young Hukm was obviously glaring at him. Tull uncrossed his legs, and the young Hukm stood up and roared.

Tull smiled up at the creature, and it charged. Tull remembered that he was not supposed to smile in the presence of Hukm.

Tull jumped up, and the Hukm swung. Tull threw himself backward, and the blow caught him in the chest and sent him flying twenty feet. When he hit ground, Tull was still trying to figure out if he could move when the Hukm jumped on him—six hundred pounds crashing onto his chest and belly. Tull heard his ribs snap, saw the young Hukm's mother struggle to pull him off. *After all of the care I've taken to keep from injuring my feet,* he wondered, *how will I push the wagon with broken ribs?* Although the mother smacked her lips together to make the sound *Chup, Chup,* the whole scene seemed strangely quiet.

Tull woke to creaking wagon wheels. The wagon bumped with a jounce; the motion knocked the air from his lungs. He looked up and could tell immediately that he was bedded in the great oak barrel where the women had convalesced. Tirilee sat beside him, holding his hand, and Wisteria slept at his side. He jerked his hand away from the Dryad, but she just watched him, as if mesmerized.

"Water," he said.

"Tull is awake," Tirilee shouted, scrambling from the barrel. "I'll get you some water," she said. The wagon kept moving, and Wisteria stirred, sat up on one elbow.

"Are you all right, my love?" she said.

"My chest feels tight," Tull said.

"Phylomon wrapped it," Wisteria said. "You've got at least six broken ribs. You'll have to stay down."

Tirilee returned with a flask of water, said "Here," and poured some in his mouth.

"What happened?" Tull asked.

"You pointed the sole of your foot at a Hukm!" Tirilee said. "It's one of about a thousand things you never do to a Hukm!"

"Phylomon's very sorry," Wisteria said. "He's apologized a dozen times. He said he should have warned us before we met for the parley. The Hukm can't speak much, so they waggle their tails, move their fingers, use gestures. Pointing your foot at a Hukm roughly means 'you smell like dung.' It didn't help when you smiled at him afterward."

Tull smelled the stink of woolly mammoth, heard the steady plod of its feet. The Hukm had obviously struck a bargain. "I'll try to remember that," Tull said.

Tirilee said in her high, chiming voice, "Phylomon has warned the Hukm not to get upset by our nasty habits. But still, you must remember to always go downwind from camp to crap, and make sure you go at least two hundred yards. They don't like the smell. And don't pee on bushes, since they might want to eat the leaves. Most of the things that offend them are so strange you'd never do them anyway. For example, never bark like a fox behind their backs. But some things you might do by accident. For example, never point your little finger at the Hukm, don't yell at their mammoths, and don't wiggle your butt from side to side when you are standing still. And don't wear anything red—since that is the color of war, and don't kill any birds—since those are the messengers of heaven."

"And don't clench your fist and hold it over your head," Wisteria said, "That's another bad one, because they think you are trying to throw a curse."

"And don't spit in their direction," Tirilee added.

"Or if you want to be nice to them, throw a handful of leaves to the wind at sunset to feed the spirits of their dead," Wisteria continued.

"Or you can hold your hand open at sunset," Tirilee said, "if you don't have leaves to throw." The girls looked at each other. "We'd better get Phylomon to go over the list again. I know there are a hundred more things he told us."

"At least a hundred," Wisteria said. "Still, Scandal thanks you. You saved some of his spices. The Hukm were embarrassed by the incident, so they settled for a good price."

"We got our mammoth," Tull said more in satisfaction than as a question. He did not need to worry so much about carrying his share of the load.

"We've got two," Tirilee answered. "Little Tail—the Hukm who tried to kill you—he's driving the wagon now. His brother, Born-in-Snow, has a mammoth up ahead clearing a trail. We're going very fast. We'll be in Sanctum tomorrow."

Tull leaned his head back and smiled. Sanctum. It sounded like a good place to be.

———————

Phylomon felt nothing for Sanctum but a vague sense of nostalgia. Although it had been his childhood home and he remembered it perfectly from those days, it had been vacant for so many centuries that it was but a pale shadow of what it had been. It glittered across the plain like a gem, even at a distance of twenty miles. When they were half a day's journey from the city, they began to come on mammoth herds in earnest. A band here, a band there. Sometimes only a few mammoths with painted tusks, sometimes a hundred. Always the Hukm stood nearby in the shade of the sprawling oaks, fingering massive clubs as they watched the strange party of humans, Pwi, the Dryad, and Hukm.

They reached Sanctum at sunset. Only the skeleton of the city was left—eleven towers of Benbow glass forming countless beams. Two miles above the plain, the towers flared into wide platforms, each at distinct levels. The ruins of Sanctum sat on the platforms. The walls and floors had either burned or rotted away, leaving only frames of incredibly thin and graceful towers, arches hundreds of feet tall, often spilling off the platform so that one could see where entire households had stood suspended above the plain.

Phylomon recalled the sense of security the city had given him when he was a child of six: He'd watched from the windows as a gray storm swept over the plains below. As a tremendous lightning display started, a pack of dire wolves separated a baby mammoth from its herd, then hamstrung it. That was back when shuttles still flew between Anee and *Falhalloran,* their orbital space station, and Phylomon had felt secure and powerful to be a Starfarer. He'd tried to imagine what it was like to be a Hukm or Pwi, living on the dirty ground in a wild storm. Phylomon smiled at the memory. After so many hundred years living down in the dirt, down in the wild, he could not help but laugh at the naive child he had been.

The Hukm had gathered at Sanctum by the tens of thousands to begin their annual migration south, and upon the ruined crossbeams of the tower, young Hukm climbed and capered, hanging strips of colored cloth as pennants, hanging streamers of clam shells and painted wood chips. Many young Hukm carried small trumpets made of ox horn, and when they saw that the wagon was close, they all sounded their horns in warning.

As the wagon came in, the Hukm gathered to sniff and bark at the humans and Neanderthals. Many Hukm had turned white, gaining their winter colors, and some swung war clubs threateningly overhead, but none dared touch Phylomon, for he was well known here. As the Hukm saw Tirilee they scurried away, for they feared the young Dryad. The cart pressed through the crowd, past stalls where Hukm traded oats and sugarcane, prunes and dried apple, rope and pumpkins. They were ushered to the tribal matriarch, Ironwood Woman, who wore a great necklace of thousands of intricately carved oak beads.

Phylomon was glad that she was willing to speak to him, for only by gaining the matriarch's protection could his band remain safe among the wild Hukm.

She barked orders for her workers to lavish food on the party and to make up beds of leaves, instantly making Phylomon wary. He'd met Ironwood Woman several times, and she merely tolerated him—never had she been warm. He knew she wanted something.

Phylomon passed through the evening as if in a dream, for he would look on the skeletons of the towers and see the shuttle port hanging in the sky as it had in his youth, see the city with its brilliant lights shining above the plains. Ironwood Woman questioned his plans. She warned him of Blade Kin outposts in the White Mountains, of the numbers of raiders patrolling each pass. There were more Blade Kin in the mountains than there had ever been before. "Sixteen thousand of us Fruit People died this summer," Ironwood Woman told him in finger language. "The traders from the south take tubes of glass from Benbow and sell them to Blade Kin. The Blade Kin make sticks of death, and kill us Fruit People."

Phylomon quickly calculated the loss, noted that he would have to go to Benbow and find who was selling rifle barrels to the Crawlies. So many losses in one year! The Hukm were losing their long war.

She warned him in finger language, "They kill us Fruit People from a long way off, but they do not see at night, so we kill them in the dark. Long we have hoped that you would return, for our legends tell of the times when you raided the strongholds of the Slave Lords."

"That was many winters ago," Phylomon said. "I have not raided their villages since before your grandmother was born. There are too many of them now."

"If you lead our army, we will send fifty thousand warriors with you this winter. When ice freezes the ocean, we will cross to the islands of Bashevgo and kill the Pirate Lords in their sleep."

Phylomon was stunned by the immensity of what she was asking. "All your warriors would die in such an attack. In Bashevgo, they would all die."

"I swear upon the bones of my foremothers," Ironwood Woman said, "that if we do not destroy Bashevgo now, all the Fruit People will die."

Phylomon had seen the Hukm's fighting tactics. They fought as they lived, wandering back and forth across the continent in caravans. They had no strongholds. "Even if we destroy Bashevgo tomorrow," Phylomon countered, "the lords of Craal have millions of people in the west. They would come back and fill it with men as evil as the ones we kill."

"Bashevgo is on this side of the White Mountains," Ironwood Woman said. "If we take Bashevgo, we will keep the east free for the Hukm and Pwi. The lords of Craal could send their men to take Bashevgo, but if the free peoples of the Rough are there, we will have the fire cannons. We will destroy the armies of Craal."

Phylomon was astonished. Never had the Hukm fought in unison with humans and Pwi. Their hatred for other races was so old, so well known, that he doubted they could fight in unison. Yet Ironwood Woman made the offer. He remembered his history books from long ago. War and greed were the two legs that the industrial and technological revolutions had been founded on. For centuries he'd been trying to initiate a technological era, and here the opportunity presented itself. In Craal, technology was produced out of greed; in the Rough, it grew because of the necessity of war. "If you take the island of Bashevgo," Phylomon said, "and you leave your Hukm to defend it, you will need food to last the winters. Also, you will need to learn to use the tools of the Slave Lords. You will need to learn how to run their generators that take power from the sea and sun. You will need to learn to maintain the fire cannons that protect their coast. You will need to learn to sail their ships. Are the Hukm ready to do this?"

"The Fruit People do not like to float on water," Ironwood Woman said. "We will bring food to our people when the ice freezes the ocean."

"The ice does not freeze the ocean every year. You must learn to sail ships, just as the Pwi and the humans sail ships."

"We do not like the water," Ironwood Woman said.

"I won't lead your army, unless your people learn to use the ships," Phylomon said, calculating how long it would take to prepare an attack. It was too late this year. Next winter at the earliest—two winters was better. Before he realized it, he was trapped. The very notion that he'd lead a raid on Bashevgo after four centuries was incredible. What had Chaa said, "If you go on this journey, you will not live three more years." If Phylomon accepted this position, he'd set himself up to fulfill the prophecy in grand style. But it was worth it.

"We will learn to sail the ships," Ironwood Woman said.

The Hukm used no fires. Instead, that night, they sat and watched the sky. It was the season for the Festival of the Dragon—a yearly celebration of the start of winter. The hills were thick with dragons. Every night they flew high into the air, obeying a genetic impulse planted by the Starfarers long ago. In ages past, the struggle of the upward climb killed the oldest dragons as they succumbed to weak hearts. But since the Eridani had sent their orbiting warships, the Red Drones, things had changed. The Red Drones attacked the rising dragons, shooting them down so that they dropped flaming from the sky. Ironwood Woman lay back and watched the sky, and Phylomon did too. This was sufficient cause for celebrating the Festival of the Dragon—to watch the dragons die.

One of the two warships reached its zenith at sundown and shone like a brilliant red comet. Several great-horned dragons flashed their leather wings as they soared in the moonlight. For hours the dragons climbed. Phylomon calculated that the Red Drones did not allow flight above fifteen thousand feet. As a dragon climbing under the cold autumn moon reached this ceiling, a finger of white light would shoot from the drone. Touched by flame, dragons fell like burning stars.

After several hours, Phylomon saw only three dragons fall. "When I was young," he told the others, "more would die."

"Ayaah," Scandal said. "That's a fact. My grandfather told me the same. The dragons don't fly that high anymore."

Phylomon lay and thought: If a genetically linked trait proved fatal, then it was less likely to be passed on. Someday, no dragons would ever fly above that fifteen-thousand-foot ceiling. Their numbers would increase, and they would take a heavy toll on the megafauna as they foraged. The world was evolving in ways the Starfarers had not intended.

All day, Phylomon had been considering a way to show Tull the power of *Falhalloran.* Now, he saw a way to show everyone. It was time to cull the dragons.

At dawn, while the Hukm slept, Phylomon took Ayuvah into the hills with nothing but a day's rations. Tull would not have seen them leave but for a pain in his ribs that woke him at odd hours. Tull, Scandal, and the women were forced to stay in camp, for they were surrounded by the wild Hukm.

That night when the two men returned, Ayuvah bore an odd look of wonder on his face. Scandal asked them where they'd been, but Phylomon evaded the question, his tone carrying enough authority that no one dared ask again.

Yet a few hours later, while others sat around a fire and ate, Ayuvah brought a bowl of cold fruit to the wagon for Tull. "I have been to *Falhalloran* today," Ayuvah said. "The City of New Birth, where the humans created our forefathers. I spoke to a man made of fire, and entered his chest, and found that it was the doorway to the city. I sat on a couch that floated like dandelion down, and a beam of light burned teachings from the Starfarers into my head."

"What kind of madness is this?" Tull said. He knew that

Falhalloran had been a spaceship, a city many miles across that floated in the sky where the Starfarers worked for hundreds of years to perfect the plants and animals that they put on Anee. But Ayuvah spoke as if the city were a man, as if the city were still intact. *"Falhalloran* was destroyed by the Red Drones of the Eridani. It dropped from the sky like a duck that has been shot with an arrow."

"The city was not killed," Ayuvah said. "Phylomon buried it near here. It still breathes!"

Tull scratched his thin beard. Ayuvah talked as if this city were a creature, not a building or a spaceship. In an effort to understand this Tull attacked another way. "What did this man of fire tell you to do?"

"The man of fire did not instruct me," Ayuvah said. "The man of fire, I think, is the Animal Guide for the city. It was the city who instructed me. The Starfarers gave it a brain of its own. It told me and Phylomon how to set up the machines that will start the Festival of the Dragon as it was meant to be. We set symbols of power and light and sound in the woods, and configured them. Tonight, we will see the festival as the Starfarers meant it to be."

At sundown, a thick fog poured over the city of Sanctum, an unnatural fog that flowed across the landscape from three directions—the north, the southeast, and the southwest, and it flowed along faster than any Hukm could run, and although Phylomon had spread the word of the festival, many Hukm ran from the fog, for it cracked and sizzled like fat frying in a skillet, and it stayed low to the ground, never more than four or five feet, so that those who got caught in it could no longer see their feet and stumbled in their attempt to escape. The Hukm pulled out their great horns and blew them in warning, and the clear bellowing sound of those horns swept over the land and echoed off the nearer hills. The mammoths in the field trumpeted in fear. The fog rolled forward until it met at Sanctum, and all three waves collided at the great central pillars that still supported the skeleton of the city.

From the very ground beneath them, music began, a haunting call that could have been a distant panpipe or could have been a voice. It came from all directions at once, and the volume was tremendous, yet it seemed to be far away. In the mountains, dragons sounded their warning cry of *grawk, grawk,* and Tull heard the flapping of wings, but then he realized it must be something in the music, an imitation of the flapping of wings. The music continued to ring through his head, and he could not be sure whether the music was inside his head or outside, but in the song, Tull heard quite clearly Tirilee singing, "Come. Come to me!" He stood up straight, and thought he must have fallen asleep. He heard the call again, but realized it was not Tirilee but the beautiful voice of some other Dryad who sang.

Suddenly, as if wakened from his sleep, far in the distance a giant Pwi stood up. He seemed for a moment to be made of cloud, but he solidified until he looked as alive and fleshy as any Pwi—yet he stood a hundred feet tall, and although he was a mile away, Tull could see him as clearly as if he stood at arm's length. The young Pwi warrior wore a black loincloth, and was chained to the earth by hand and foot, and he struggled to break his irons. In the distance, the Dryad sang to him, and the giant searched in all directions, looking for the singer. Forests of pine rose from the earth in the distance, trees a thousand feet tall, and each tree was as twisted and craggy as any that lived, so the Pwi stood helpless, trapped in a haunted forest.

Suddenly, the singing Dryad appeared, leaping from beneath the fog-shrouded ground, bursting into the air on wings that shone like starlight. She wore an opalescent robe the color of cloud, and sang her song, a mocking, lilting song of love without words, and she flew low over the Hukm on wings of starlight, and her face was more pale and beautiful than anything Tull had ever dreamed. She rose as she flew. For a moment, she quieted, and in the distance the dragons screamed. Tull wondered if the cries were part of the music, and he looked out over the valleys. In the moonlight he saw winged shadows flying from the mountains and plains all around—great-horned dragons and tyrant birds, even swift dragons no larger than magpies. Thousands of dragons poured from the mountains and foothills.

Tull looked at Scandal—the fat man sat by a pile of fruit

where he'd eaten his dinner, nervously shoving an apple into his mouth while he watched the show above. Ayuvah cast his eyes about in awe, seeming to try to catch everything at once, while Tirilee stood like a statue, glaring at the scene in anger. Wisteria clenched Tull's hand, and her palms were hot and sweaty. Most of the Hukm stood with round eyes, gazing up like mournful dogs, mesmerized.

The Dryad continued a song that lasted an hour, and she sang in the ancient tongue of the Pwi. Tull could make out a few words, "delicious pears . . . garden . . . come out . . . desert places." For each word he understood, a dozen passed him by. Yet he heard enough—the young man was chained to his love for a dead woman and wanted to go lie down in the House of Dust with his lover, but the Dryad called him back to the land of the living, offering the sweetest of gifts if he would spend his life with her. But it was not to be, for the dragons were coming now from the distant lands, and the winged Dryad, as she circled the skeletal pillars of Sanctum, cast fearful glances at the approaching dragons. Tull could see that these were real dragons, hoary old beasts ripe from the mountains, young dragons with dripping jaws fresh from their kills. They flew at great speed, and the winged Dryad was forced to fly higher, in ever-quickening spirals, to evade their jaws. After an hour, they chased her as if they were a great swarm of blackbirds that darkened the sky, and they cried out in madness at their inability to catch the winged lady.

At last she fled out across the plains, calling to the young man to accept her gift and live free. But the young man prayed instead to Adjonai, the God of Terror, and with a crash of thunder his chains burst. Dark wings sprouted on his back. He flew high into the air, intent on attacking the knot of dragons that lashed out at the winged lady. He caught the rearmost dragon, tossing it toward the city, and the creature burst into flames at his touch and came roaring to the ground not a quarter of a mile from Tull's camp. The winged lady flew toward the young man for protection, and for a moment they met in the sky and soared up, up, as if they would touch the moons.

The dragons followed, gripping the young man by the leg like dire wolves, slashing at him with their horns. Their mouths burst into flame at the touch, and the dragons roared in pain. The young man cried out as the dragons ripped great shreds of flesh from him. Blood rained on the crowd in great patters, and the smell of burning metal filled the air.

The Hukm roared and shook their great war clubs in the air, others howled and hooted and beat the ground with their fists, enraged at the spectacle, and many of them came running to Phylomon so that a crowd of them filled the camp.

The winged lady cried out in terror, tried to rush back for her young lover, pull him up from the jaws of dragons that tore at his legs.

Tull could not understand why the Hukm were so frantic, but he shouted to Phylomon, "Stop! You've got to make them stop! The dragons are killing him!"

"But that is the way it is supposed to be," Phylomon yelled over the roar of the Hukm. "With his death, he buys the winged lady's freedom."

And Tull finally realized why the Hukm were angry. "They are alive! Aren't they?" Tull shouted. "At first, I thought them clever illusions. But they're alive!" The Hukm roared in anger, and Tull pushed his way to Phylomon, for he feared that the Hukm would attack. He pulled his sword of Benbow glass to guard the Starfarer.

Phylomon shouted, his words nearly lost over the rage of the Hukm, the battle cries of dragons. "Of course, they are alive, but they are not flesh!" Tull looked at him in horror, and Phylomon shouted as he tried to explain. "They are creatures of molten plasmas—heated gases. The Starfarers called them piezoforms. The Pwi and his lady are no smarter than cats! Generators under the city create gravity holes so they can live here for a few hours. Yet they think! They feel!" A great dragon soared up and ripped at the winged lady's shoulder, and she cried in pain and dropped toward the city to evade it. For a moment, the Hukm all hooted in fear. "Yes, they are alive!" Phylomon said.

"But they can't do this—create a living being and watch it die—for mere entertainment!" Tull shouted.

Phylomon looked at the young Tcho-Pwi. "But, why do you think the Starfarers created you?" Phylomon asked.

Tull stepped back, reeling from the realization that he'd been created for entertainment. He understood now. In the eyes of the Starfarers, with their near immortality, his life was so temporary that it must have seemed fleeting. The Starfarers, like Gods, would have looked down from Sanctum and smiled to see his pain, would have mocked his accomplishments, abhorred his stupidity, would have watched him until he bored them, and then would have turned away.

Tull stepped back from Phylomon, looked up: The winged Dryad swooped down to rescue—no, to die with— her lover. The dragons swarmed about them both, ripping, clawing, tasting their doom in mouths full of burning plasma. No smarter than a cat. Yet she had feelings, compassion. She threw her life away for a noble cause.

"She has a nobility that the Starfarers lacked," Tull shouted at Phylomon.

The lovers flapped their wings and, pitifully, rose higher. All at once, the Red Drone moved over the horizon, like a great orange shooting star. Tull had never seen the Red Drone when its engines kicked in—it had always been a placid little comet. The Eridani warship opened fire. Streaks of light shot out, and touched the dragons quickly, and out over the plains the dragons dropped like flaming cinders.

The young Pwi and his winged lady broke free and soared ever higher into the sky, into a realm where no dragons could follow, beyond Sanctum's gravimetric fields. There, the lovers suddenly expanded and dissipated, their plasma smearing across the starlit sky like watercolors in the rain.

The dragons croaked and flapped their leather wings under the moonlight and struggled to reach what was left of the young couple. And they died in fire for their efforts.

When the show was over, while the dragons still croaked and shot upward and died, Ironwood Woman came to the group, a cape of black scimitar cat hide over her shoulders. The look in her eyes was hard to define—rage, fear, horror. She was an animal, and Tull did not know how to read her. He wondered briefly if she would order their executions.

She bowed to Phylomon so that her stubby tail bobbed in the air. As she stooped before him on her hands, the rest

of the Hukm followed suit, so that across the plains ten
thousand Hukm bobbed their tails in the air. Tull did not
have to understand their language to see the reverence in
their act. She was saying, "You Starfarers are Gods."

The next morning, Tull woke to the smell of breakfast cooking—corn cakes and beef jerky. Scandal, Ayuvah, and
Tirilee sat around the wagon, eating. Nearly all the Hukm
were asleep, thrown on the ground like giant dolls, sleeping
with clubs at their sides. They did not like the human camp,
with its ever-present fire and smelly humans, so they slept
far away, and most of them would not rise until late afternoon. Phylomon was half a mile away, sitting beneath a tree
with Ironwood Woman, their fingers working as they talked.

Tull walked over to the fire, stretched, began dishing up
a plate. "What's going on over there?" he asked, nodding
toward Phylomon and Ironwood Woman.

"War plans, I gather," Scandal said. "Ironwood Woman
wants to attack Bashevgo, and she wants Phylomon to lead
her battle."

"Huh," Tull grunted. The less such things were spoken
of, the better. If the wrong person were to hear of the battle
plans, they would become common knowledge in the halls
of the Slave Lords on Bashevgo.

Scandal said, "Ayuvah here was just telling us about the
man of fire that he saw. He says there's a cave filled with
artifacts from *Falhalloran.*"

Tull felt stung. He did not like that word *artifacts.* The
laser cannons at Bashevgo were artifacts. The hoversleds
that the Lords of Craal rode down the streets were artifacts.
Benbow glass and Phylomon himself were artifacts. Always
that word was used when speaking of things of power. It
was not a word that inspired confidence.

"I was just thinking," Scandal said, "That the man of
fire might be more help to us than a sea serpent. I mean,
Ayuvah here says the man of fire gave them some kind of
token that let him create those monsters last night, and if
the man of fire can create monsters to kill dragons, surely he
could create something to kill anything that swims over
from Hotland?"

"Possibly," Tull said. "We should ask Phylomon."

Scandal cleared his throat, "Aah, not so fast there, Friend. Perhaps we should ask Phylomon, and then again perhaps we shouldn't. Ayuvah, when you were in the cave, did you see anything worth money?"

"I—uh—don't know," Ayuvah said. "I saw the man of fire, and we traveled down a long tube on a couch that floats. And then a beam of light filled me and taught me how to arrange the symbols of power."

Scandal looked troubled. "Did you see any Benbow glass, or any of those lights Phylomon has chained around his neck? Maybe a refrigeration cube or a power cube? Anything like that?" And Tull understood his problem. No one had ever heard of flying couches or light beams that teach. Scandal wouldn't know how to work them. What he wanted was something useful—glass for weapons, refrigeration cubes for his inn.

"There were many lights in the cave, but not like the one Phylomon uses. These glowed all the time."

"I can buy light bulbs out of Denate," Scandal growled. "You don't suppose the man of fire would mind if we look around in his cave, do you?"

"I don't know," Ayuvah said, a note of fear in his voice.

"What do you think would happen if I threw a bucket of water on this man of fire?" Scandal asked.

Ayuvah frowned. "I think he would kill you. He is not made of fire like our campfire. He shines like the sun, but he does not give off heat or smoke. He does not burn like wood. I do not think you can kill him. Phylomon called him the 'Aspect of *Falhalloran,*' but the man of fire referred to himself as the city of *Falhalloran.*"

Scandal scratched his beard. "How can a man be a city? Or have the kind of power this man has? Certainly, if the man of fire marched against Bashevgo or Craal with an army of giants, the Slave Lords would pee their britches in terror. There is something you aren't telling us. Maybe it's something you don't even know. Why don't you take us to the cave?"

Ayuvah shook his head. "Phylomon made me promise not to show it."

"I promise never to reveal where it is," Scandal said, "if

that makes you feel any better. And to show you my good faith: I'll give you thirty silver eagles if you take me to this cave."

"You only want to loot the cave," Ayuvah said.

"I only want to speak to the man of fire. I promise I won't take anything that he's not willing to give to me freely. Fair?"

Ayuvah thought a moment. "Will you give me the money now?"

"Ayuvah!" Tull shouted, stunned at the betrayal.

"This money would feed my family for a year," Ayuvah countered.

Scandal cut the coin purse from his belt. "If the man of fire gives me a refrigeration cube, this will be worth it. I promise, you won't regret this."

"Then I am coming with you," Tull said, "To make sure you don't steal anything."

Scandal glared at Tull, and his face turned red with rage. "I am not a thief!" Scandal said. "I am an honest businessman, making a business contact!"

Tull felt embarrassed at making such an accusation, yet he could not fathom Scandal's designs. "I know," Tull said, "but I'll come just in case you are tempted to become a thief."

Wisteria woke then, and sat wrapped in her furs. Her face was white and pasty, and she refused to eat breakfast. Tull told her of their plan to visit the cave, but she complained that she felt ill and said she did not want to come. An hour later, Phylomon returned from his visit with Ironwood Woman, ate a few bites of corn cake, and went to sleep. Ayuvah, Tull, and Scandal crept from camp, followed by Tirilee.

The journey to the cave was only two miles, yet in that space they passed three dead dragons, their legs and wings stiffened with rigor mortis, their flesh blasted by the fire from the Red Drones, their mouths burned by the plasma of the giants that had battled them in the sky. There were not enough buzzards in the valley to eat so much flesh, and on one carcass a black-and-white magpie feasted. It jumped into the sky at their approach, then dipped and soared, dipped and soared in unhurried retreat, its tail feathers floating out behind it.

They climbed a long low hill, and at last came to a rocky white bluff between two arms of the hill. Twisted scrub oaks grew along the cliff face. Ayuvah pointed to the oaks, brushed a strand of red hair from his eyes, and said, "The cave is there."

"Where?" Scandal said, searching the base of the cliff.

Ayuvah walked forward, looked at the stone. *"Falhalloran,* it is I, Ayuvah, I have returned," he said loudly. With a sound of rushing wind, the white stone crumbled into dust and dropped like a curtain.

Scandal jumped backward in surprise. "What in the name of hell!" he shouted, running back from the cave.

Ayuvah said, "We are going to get ourselves killed," and backed away.

Tull had been too startled to run. He walked forward, looked into the cave. The walls oozed with mud and limestone. Cave coral had formed on the floor, and travertine ran in ridges down the sides. The whole place was wet and dripping, and in the middle of the floor was a porcupine skeleton. It was hard to believe that *Falhalloran* would be anything but a gutted ruin. Tull imagined a city of wood and stone, with rotting floors and bent walls. In such a musty place, that was all that could exist. Yet there were tracks on the floor where Phylomon and Ayuvah had entered the day before.

"I will not go in," Ayuvah said. His legs trembled. "I should not have brought you here. I broke a promise."

Tull walked forward, inspected the walls. Tirilee followed close behind, came up and actually took his hand. Tull looked at her in surprise, and the young Dryad shook and sniffled in terror. "I want to see it, too!" she said. Scandal hurried forward, following a close third. Tull took a few steps, and, as if by mutual consent, the others each took exactly one step to match his own. There was a tunnel before them, leading far back into the blackness. He felt a warm wind against his face—like the warm, liquid exhalations of a woman's breath—blowing out from the tunnel.

"I hear breathing," Tirilee said softly. "Something is alive in there."

Tull felt it too, the hot breath of something infinitely large. The hair on Tull's back stood on end, and Tirilee clutched his arm.

"I am alive," a voice whispered from the cave, ringing from stone to stone. A powerful commanding voice, neither male nor female. "Come into me."

Tull looked at Tirilee, and her lips were drawn back in terror.

"Who are you?" Tull asked.

"Falhalloran, the City of New Birth," the voice whispered.

"Listen," Scandal said. "This is not a good idea. Maybe we should leave." Tull looked at the gourmet, and watched him tremble. So the fat man *had* wanted to loot the place he realized. He'd come only because he believed that he could sneak past the man of fire.

"We've come to see you, *Falhalloran,*" Tull shouted. "Show yourself!"

Scandal's eyes grew round and he moaned in fear. In the distance far back in the cave, there was a scream like the sound of metal twisting.

Suddenly, the mud and limestone walls of the cave began to glow. Not the comforting glow of a fire, but a fierce glow that frightened Tull. With a rush of wind, a great stone pillar in front of them burst into flame—a flame of light that gave no more warmth than the sun striking one's face, and the pillar shrank into the form of a man whose features were molten glass, whose body was somehow fiercely bright. The man was tall, like Phylomon, with a stretched look and angular cheek bones. Yet, unlike Phylomon, he had hair— white filaments of flowing glass. He wore a simple tunic, open at the chest, that left his arms bare.

Tull felt a wave of heat rush over him, a burning within his own breast, and looked down. His own body, and the bodies of those who were with him, also glowed. Yet they did not look like glass. Somehow, he knew that he had been changed into something not quite flesh and bone.

"I am the Aspect of *Falhalloran,*" the man said. As his mouth moved, Tull detected tiny structures, like intricate crossbeams and braces, that made up the fine musculature of the creature's mouth. It was obviously neither glass nor flesh—a structure of some other material. His voice penetrated Tull, seemed to inscribe itself in his mind. "What do you desire?"

Scandal took one look at *Falhalloran* and promptly fainted.

Tull pointed at Scandal lying in a heap on the floor. "We came to ask your help. To the north, in Bashevgo, and to the west, in Craal, the Slave Lords rule, and they keep forty million of the Pwi in captivity. For eight hundred years we have been at war with them, and they have won. In our own land, the sea serpents that have formed an eco-barrier for a thousand years have died. We want you to send your giants to save us from the carnosaurs that will swim across the ocean, and we want you to help free our people from captivity."

"I am *Falhalloran,* the City of New Birth," the man of fire said. "I am not a weapon of war. Neither I nor the giants I created last night can move from Sanctum."

"Yet you are the most powerful creature on this planet!" Tull countered. "Surely you could give us weapons!"

"I could teach you to make weapons to destroy your enemies, destroy this world," the man of fire said, "but in time your enemies would wrest them from you. Your end would be more miserable than your life is now."

"Is there nothing you can do to help us?" Tull asked.

The man of fire said, "I do not bestow weapons," and his light began to fade until suddenly he became nothing more than a stone pillar once again.

Tull looked at Tirilee in confusion, wondering what to do. He started to bend over Scandal, to pull him from the cave, but Tirilee stared at Tull as if lost in a dream. She clung to him with one hand. She was such a child, just a stick of a girl, and he longed suddenly to hold her.

She kissed him, throwing an arm around his neck, and her arm felt as strong as metal bars. She drew him close, wrapped her arms behind his head. A hot tremor pierced him, and he wanted her, wanted her more than he'd ever wanted Wisteria. She was rubbing against him, pressing the hot nubs of her little breasts against his chest.

Suddenly, she pushed him back and staggered away, ran from the cave. He stood and tried to regain his senses. He knew he did not love her, did not care for her at all. Yet the smell of her was so tantalizing, like the scent of honeysuckle blown on the wind. He could not resist the temptation to inhale the air, to catch that beautiful scent. As he filled his lungs, waves of desire for Tirilee crashed over him, and he was alone and helpless in their wake.

"God, if you exist," he mouthed, unwilling to speak in the stillness of the cave, "I love my wife. Do not let Tirilee's Time of Devotion come now." Yet his prayer was empty. Dryads had been wrecking the lives of the Pwi for generations. As truly as he had heard the voice of *Falhalloran,* Tull knew Tirilee would destroy him.

He stooped to pick up Scandal, and in the mud he found a ball made of brass, a simple thing with the edges of continents etched on it. Tull picked it up, pulled Scandal to the mouth of the cave, into the sunlight, and Scandal began to rouse. Ayuvah was still pale with fear, and he looked helplessly off into the brush, toward where Tirilee had run, then helped pull Scandal into the open, examining him as if to discover why Scandal had been struck down.

"What happened? Why did the Dryad run?" Ayuvah asked.

"She was afraid," Tull said, unwilling to tell the truth.

Scandal shook his head, looked up at them in surprise, looked at the cave. "Was it a dream?" Scandal asked.

Tull looked back at the cave. Silently, somehow, the curtain of stone had moved back in place. No one would ever dream of the wonders hidden behind it. "It was no dream," Tull said bitterly.

They walked back to camp in defeat. Ayuvah returned the thirty silver eagles to Scandal and would not keep even part of it. At camp, they found Phylomon awake, fixing lunch.

The Hukm milled about aimlessly or bartered in their marketplace over fruit or hides or cloth. They stood waggling their stubby tails, occasionally grunting for emphasis as they finger talked. For all their size, they were unnervingly quiet. Little Tail and Born-in-Snow quietly hooked a woolly mammoth to the wagon, guiding it back between the wooden tugs with grunts and hand movements. Little Tail was dusky red and had shaved his head of all hair but two lines that ran from his eyebrows back to the nape of his neck. Born-in-Snow was darker in color, but his winter white was coming in rapidly, so much so that his back and rump had gone nearly all white.

"I hope you enjoyed your little jaunt to *Falhalloran*," Phylomon said. "I hope you got what you went for."

"I saw no city," Scandal said in disgust.

"True, but you saw its *Aspect*, its personification," Phylomon said. "I helped bury the city years ago. It was in the winter, and Captain Chu had been beheaded by the Aenthari—the first tribe of Neanderthals to be captured by the Slave Lords, the first to become Thralls. Many Slave Lords in those days were technicians, and they wanted to break away from Anee. We were afraid that if they knew *Falhalloran* had been only damaged—not destroyed—by the Red Drones, they would have tried to turn it into a vessel of war. They would have attacked the Red Drones, or at the very least tried to break away from the planet, and *Falhalloran* would have been annihilated. So we buried it. For a thousand years, I told no one that the city existed. Now, it doesn't matter. *Falhalloran* is a city of peace, a city of creation. No one living can turn it into a weapon of war."

"You know," Scandal said. "There was a rock wall that turned to dust and fell to the ground, and in an instant, while our backs were turned, it rose back up!"

"The wall is made of millions of tiny machines the size of specks of dust," Phylomon said. "Each machine has legs like a spider. They hold themselves together to form a wall. If you looked closely when the wall raised, you'd have seen the motes crawl into place."

"We asked the man of fire for help," Tull said. "We asked him for weapons. Yet I found only this." He pulled the brass ball from his pocket.

Phylomon looked at Tull for a long moment, gauging him. "*Falhalloran* did not leave you empty-handed. I asked him to give you what he thought best. It is a weather globe. Here—" Phylomon knelt and pulled a piece of straw from the ground. At the top of the ball was an indentation. He stuck the straw into the indentation and pushed. The ball suddenly jumped into the air and expanded until it was four feet in diameter. It hung like a moon, blue and white, with

streaks of pink. Tull could see the terminus dividing night
from day and the oceans of Anee and clouds rolling over the
land. "We are here," Phylomon said, pointing to a speck of
fire on one edge of the continent. "As you can see, we have
blue skies above. Out in Hotland, the sun is rising"—he
pointed to a great swirl of clouds—"and thunderstorms are
rolling in."

Phylomon reached up into the air, into the heart of the
globe, and the illusion disappeared. He held in his hand the
brass ball.

"Tull, this is yours," he said.

"I . . . might break it," Tull said, not wanting to touch
the thing. "My hands are too clumsy."

"Take it," Phylomon said. "This is your future. Technology is your future." He gave the ball to Tull.

Wisteria sat on a log, still pasty-faced. She finally got up,
stumbled a few feet, and vomited.

Tull took a pitcher and filled a cup with water so Wisteria could rinse her mouth. "Are you still sick?" Ayuvah
asked, for she had now been sick for two weeks.

"I'm not sick," she said. "I think I'm pregnant."

Chapter 9
Blade Kin

After a lifetime of feeling as insignificant as a dried leaf blowing through town, Wisteria suddenly became visible. Phylomon himself took her off her feet and physically set her on the back of the wagon while Ayuvah patted her back and Tull stood grinning from ear to ear, too happy to be of any use to anyone.

"I'm fine," she said. "I mean, I feel great."

"Babies are rare enough out here in the Rough," Phylomon said. "There's no use taking chances with them before they are born. Besides, it's hard for a human woman to carry a Pwi child full-term."

"He's right," Scandal said. "From now on, no more pushing wagons or hauling wood for you—you're our lord, and we're your slaves. You tell us to jump, and every man here will bust a testicle at your whim."

So by sundown they left Sanctum, and Little Tail kept his mammoth moving well after dark. Phylomon was pleased with the progress. Although the woolly mammoths weren't as large as the woodland mastodon, they were better suited for cold-weather travel, and they were spirited. "Cantankerous," Scandal called them, and they were that too. Born-in-Snow's mammoth would often jerk the wagon, for he hated butterflies and he was constantly lunging after cabbage moths, sucking them into his trunk and spitting them out with enough gusto to break their tiny bodies.

Still, it was nice to ride in the wagon, and Tull sat with Wisteria all day long, just holding her. Scandal razzed them. "All the panting and rutting you two have been up to has paid off! I'll be surprised if you don't drop triplets! Why, you'll have a veritable litter of woolly-backed little Neanderthals running around your feet in no time."

Ayuvah just sat out in the sun in the back of the wagon and smiled at them, then looked back at the mountains toward Smilodon Bay, as if mourning the distance between himself and his own wife. Only Tirilee did not seem intoxicated by the joy everyone felt at news of the impending birth. She sulked along beside the wagon, trailing it just a bit.

Scandal spent part of the afternoon hunting with Phylomon, and after battle practice, for dinner Scandal celebrated news of the pregnancy by making a clay oven and baking three grouse and glazing them with a bottle of his special plum sauce. For dessert he baked his famous walnut and sweet potato pie. Wisteria could imagine no heaven where time could be passed more enjoyably than feasting on such delicacies. After the food had settled, while Wisteria lay on the grass enjoying the smell of the fire, Tull pulled her to him and kissed her.

"Let's go to the thicket by the pond and make love," he said.

She was surprised. He had not tried to make love to her for days—not since Little Tail had slugged him. Indeed, his ribs were bandaged and he often held them and breathed shallowly while he and Ayuvah practiced. "Not now," she said. "Let's just enjoy the fire."

Tull raised himself to one elbow and slapped her face hard enough to make her head spin, then grabbed her hair and yanked it. He smiled down at her from above and kissed her roughly, then nipped her cheek. She just stared at him in surprise. He was warm and sweaty, and his Neanderthal teeth were large and clean.

"Come, let's go to the pond. In another two weeks, we will be in Craal. Like the dragons above us, I want to soar to the heights and burst into flame once before I die." Tull let go of her hair, stroked her face, and his hand continued running down her, over the curve of her breasts and thighs. At his touch, Wisteria felt intoxicated, as if every inch of her body raged with desire for him. Even the webbing between her toes seemed to tremble, and she wondered how long it had been since she had felt so alive. She gasped, and Tull picked her up and carried her to the pond.

"Wait," Wisteria said, "the others will see us. They'll know what we are doing."

"Then let them ache with jealousy," Tull said. "I must have you."

He carried her to a spot beside the pond where the grass was still green. Some young mallards flew up from the rushes at the far side of the pond. Tull stripped her and made love to her like a wild man, raking her back with his nails and biting her. She laughed aloud, and as dusk became full night with a million burning stars, he took her higher than she'd ever been before. It seemed to her that she was like the dragon, soaring free, burning from his heat. And after several hours, when they lay together naked and exhausted, she asked, "So, did you reach the heights? Did you burst into flames at my touch?"

Tull was silent for a moment. "Almost, my love, almost," he said. And Wisteria's heart fell with disappointment. Then Tull smiled, "Let's try again."

Wisteria laughed and climbed atop him and kissed him long and passionately. The world felt magical and she realized that for the first time in her life she was perfectly happy. With all her father's plans for a marriage to some businessman in the south, she was surprised at how perfectly happy she felt at this moment, out in the Rough, naked, straddling a Neanderthal. They bathed in the pond in the moonlight then went to lie in their furs and watch the dragons. There were many flying high that night.

"The dragons are searching for the winged Dryad and her lover," Phylomon said. Wisteria was not sure if he was speaking to them or if she were catching the tail end of some other conversation. "The dragons are talking to each other, telling one another of yesterday's hunt. You watch, the skies will be this way for months."

After a while, Tirilee asked in her melodic voice, "Will *Falhalloran* ever rise again?"

Phylomon answered, "No one knows. The Red Drones are energy vessels, and their fuel has limits, but no one knows much about their creators, the Eridani. The Eridani believed we humans were too young a race to inhabit the stars, so they sent the Red Drones to keep us planet-bound. When they first tried to restrict us to the number of worlds we would inhabit, they demanded that we not leave for five thousand years. A thousand years have passed since the war. When their ships grow old enough, their liquid brains will die. I do not think that will happen for four thousand years. If *Falhalloran* still exists at that time, the city might be repaired."

"None of us will be here to see it," Scandal said wistfully.

"Who knows," Phylomon said. "Miracles happen daily. Why, look at Tull and Wisteria: When humans came to Anee, we had had a lot of genetic upgrading. We'd extended our memories, extended our lives. Made ourselves stronger. Every human was a Dicton. In those days, humans and Pwi were so different in their genetic makeup that a mating between Wisteria and Tull would have been impossible. A miracle."

Tull asked. "Then how does it happen?"

"The Creators made the first Dryads—beings that were neither human nor Pwi. Some Dryads, like the women of the redwoods, breed with members of other species. But some Dryads attracted the Neanderthals with their singing, and when they mated, the males were born Neanderthals while the females were Dryads. Obviously, the genes that produce a Dryad are a sex-linked family that is expressed only in females."

"Dryads never give birth to males," Tirilee said.

"Supposedly not," Phylomon agreed, "But in the pine forests on the west coast, solitary trappers often find male children dumped on their doorsteps. To some Dryads, males are born. And, as you know, Dryads can mate with humans as well as Pwi.

"So, it happened that a Dryad gave birth to a male child who carried enough human genes and Neanderthal genes so that his offspring could mate with both groups, and our blood lines became mixed.

"There are no purebred humans anymore. Those who are close are Dictons. Even among the Slave Lords who have struggled to maintain their racial purity, such children are uncommon. My younger brother once told me that he believed the Creators made Dryads partly for that purpose —to rid Anee of humans who carry the memories of words that define us as part of a Starfaring culture. In a way, I think it would be a good thing. We as a people have never had to learn how to think, how to *create*. When someone wants a ship, they have a Dicton design it based on his inherited memory, and in a way that is a shame. The designs are always adequate, but we never improve on anything done on old Earth. Our thoughts, our culture—all have become stifled. In a way, I wish that my brother had been right, that the Creators could rid the world of the Starfarers.

"Though it is true that the Dryads destroyed our racial purity, but it is also true that few Pwi are purebred Neanderthals. The old woman we met on the trail a couple of weeks back is among the last. The psychic powers of the purebred Neanderthals was a marvelous curiosity."

"Then, it is not good for humans and Neanderthals to mate," Tull said. "If the Neanderthals lose their power, and the humans have lost their inherited memories."

"I'm not sure," Phylomon said. "I think it may be good. My people had become all intellect—cold, calculating, unfeeling. When the Eridani banished us to Anee, it was easy for them to conquer this world. Perhaps too easy. They had no intellectual challenges, and they did not respond to physical challenges. It was easier for them to enslave the Pwi and live their sordid lives on Bashevgo than it would have been for them to work honestly.

"And as for the Pwi, their complex emotions, the shroud of kwea through which they perceived the world, robbed them of clear sight. They lost the ability to dissociate themselves from their pasts, and so they were never free from childhood fears.

"I think that both races need something that belongs to

the other. And I see a new race emerging, a race of men like Tull, who can think with both their hearts and their heads.

"When our ancestors came here, their bodies were changed so they could travel on vehicles faster than light. And we have lost those days of glory. Yet, two thousand years ago, our ancestors communicated on simple radio waves, and those waves are making their way to us now. Within a hundred and fifty years, radio signals will begin to reach us from Earth, and I believe your great grandchildren will build a receptor to capture those signals and learn how humans first entered the atomic age. Your descendants could rise up and carry all of Anee back into that age again."

"Why should we?" Tull asked. "If the Starfarers created us as mere curiosities, would they welcome us?"

Phylomon hesitated. "They would welcome you. Tull, not all of the Starfarers saw Neanderthals as mere entertainment. When the Eridani sent their Red Drones, only a few humans were cruel and thoughtless enough to take slaves. Most of us Starfarers deplored the idea, but we did not think of destroying our own brethren. The thought of going to war with one another appalled us. It did not appall the slavers. For the first two hundred years, they lived and bred on Bashevgo, and we ignored them and they ignored us. Some among us went so far as to raid their strongholds, release their Neanderthals. We thought it only a game at the time, but eventually it turned to war, and they struck the first blow. We've never really recovered from that blow. But I tell you in all seriousness, if you regain the stars, you will find humans who look on you as brothers."

Up in the sky above the camp, a dragon's wings seemed to sparkle in the moonlight. It careened in a controlled drop, then its wings went limp and it plummeted. The pine scented breeze carried the scent of Tirilee, and Wisteria thought the girl smelled unusually pleasant, earthy, like a rose garden or a wheat field. Wisteria inhaled the scent deeply.

She watched the dragon still falling as it dropped beyond the treetops over a nearby hill. Its death cry sounded, a long ululating scream that pierced the night, yet the sound came from high and far away—for the dragon had uttered the scream when first shot.

Beside her, Tull breathed deeply, inhaling Tirilee's aroma, and he sounded as if he choked back a sob. Wisteria heard him breathe the words, "God, let me stop burning."

The four-hundred-mile journey from Sanctum to Seven Ogre River was the easiest part of the trip. Little Tail's mammoth pulled the wagon in the morning, the group would eat and practice their weapons training, and in the evening Born-in-Snow pulled. The mammoths were eager to work, for the smell of winter was in the air, their mating season was on, and they grew restless for their migration south. They often swung their necks, raking the grasstops with their great tusks, as if clearing snow from their paths. Geese and ducks gathered on the ponds, and even in the low areas the leaves changed to yellow and brown, then blew away at the slightest touch of a breeze.

Phylomon knew the Rough well, and when they came to a small mountain range, he guided them so that the trail seemed made for wagons. Along the volcanic fault lines, the crust of the earth was cracked, and these places were hard to negotiate, for sometimes the party had to travel miles to find a path up or down.

When clearing the path, one Hukm stood atop the lead mastodon's head to watch for enemies. Sometimes a near-sighted woolly rhino would grunt and paw the ground at the sound of their approach or follow the wagon at a hundred yards trying to decide whether to charge, but if it did not leave quickly, someone would fire the swivel gun and the rhino would wheeze, arch his tail and run away.

The journey would have been easier if not for the armies of Craal. Two hundred miles out of Sanctum, the party came on a garden where Hukm had farmed for the summer. The crops were still on the vine, pumpkins and squash getting ready to rot, leaves and bushes moldering. A dozen dead Hukm lay in a mound nearby, their tents overturned.

Fifty miles farther on, while coming over a small hill in the evening, they saw hundreds of campfires: Phylomon estimated that it was an army of at least five thousand Thrall

warriors, heading south for the winter to harass the Hukm.
They hid the wagon for the day, and by evening the army
had left.

The approach to the White Mountains was wet and cold,
for they gained altitude on the plains. Tull often consulted
his weather globe, hoping for clear skies. Winter was coming early, bringing gusty winds and pelting rains, and for a
week the party stayed on the wagon. As long as Scandal did
not try to sit in the barrel, dry seating inside the wagon was
ample for the rest, and they spread a tarpaulin over the
whole wagon to keep the rain off the food and poor Scandal.
The Hukm liked the rain. Both Hukm shed the last of their
brown summer fur and grew white winter coats; they
seemed invigorated by the wet and cold. One night as they
approached the jagged White Mountains, at the end of a
cold day where the mammoths slogged through mud in
drizzling rain, the Hukm stopped at a foaming icy river.
Wisteria looked out the barrel sullenly, and when the Hukm
stopped, they dove headlong into the frigid water and
splashed about like bears chasing salmon.

Wisteria decided she liked the Hukm. They were often
cool and aloof, spending nights away from camp, yet one
night, Scandal put his boots beside the fire, trying to get
them dry, and when he woke in the morning, someone had
filled his boots with tea and placed them in the coals to
brew. Scandal walked around camp, screaming blue-faced at
everyone, accusing everyone of the crime. And the next
morning, though he'd placed his boots under the shelter of
the wagon to dry for the night, he found them in the fire
again, only this time they were filled with urine. No human
had a bladder so large, and Scandal cursed the Hukm, but
the Hukm just stood beside their mammoths looking cool
and unperturbed until Scandal used every gesture on them
that Phylomon had ever warned him against.

Although the journey was cold and dreary, Wisteria felt
a warmth in her heart unlike anything she'd ever known. At
nights, when it was cold, Tull brought stones from the fire
for her to curl up with, and he washed her clothes and was
incredibly tender. Yet each night he made love to her like a
wild man, whispering threats into her ears and handling her
as if she were some frisky but untrained prostitute. She

loved the change, and for her, every night was like the first night of a honeymoon.

Once after his rough lovemaking ended, she was so content that she felt impelled to ask, "Something has changed between us. Do you feel it? Something has changed."

Tull laughed. "I asked you to teach me how to love you, and now I have figured out how," he answered.

The answer was simple, almost childish. She sighed contentedly. "Teach me how to love you, Tull," she said. "Teach me how to love." But she knew the words were a lie, for she could already feel her love for him glowing within. She thought of the rage at Phylomon that had once burned within her, the sense of futile anger, and how she had rashly promised Garamon she would sabotage the quest. The whole idea seemed absurdly vindictive and evil. Instead, she needed this quest to succeed, needed a safe place for her child to grow. She knew now that she could never betray the father of her child.

So for her, the days passed in bliss. Six weeks out from Sanctum, she realized that the rest of the group was somber. One day the rain clouds rose high enough so that they could actually see the White Mountains some eighty miles distant.

"Damn," Phylomon muttered. "We're still a good week behind schedule. The mountains are already white with snow, and we have another two hundred miles to the river."

"Does it matter?" Wisteria asked. "I mean, that's why they call them the White Mountains, isn't it?"

"They shouldn't be white this early in the season," Phylomon said. "The snow will definitely slow us down, and we spent too much time crossing the Dragon Spines. Any more delay could be very costly. Still, if the snowfall is light, three sunny days might burn it off."

But that night, a cold rain fell, and while everyone was wrapped in blankets Phylomon held a council.

"We're in for a hard trip over the mountains," he told them.

"Why?" Scandal asked. "We can put runners on the wagon and the mammoths could pull us through the mountains fine, couldn't they?"

"Yes," Phylomon answered, "but I'd hoped to go over Raven's Peak Pass, since Ironwood Woman said it was least watched. But it's a narrow pass, and high, and with these fresh snows we'd run too much of a risk of getting buried in an avalanche. Yet there are only two other decent passes within two hundred miles."

"And how well are they watched?" Scandal asked.

"You saw one small army a few days ago," Phylomon said.

Ayuvah said, "I fear such an army as I would fear a scimitar cat. We could never pass them."

"The passes will be well watched," Phylomon said, "But with winter coming on, they will not be so well guarded."

"What do you mean?" Scandal asked.

"During the winter, the Hukm move south so they can forage. The armies of Craal move south to fight them. We should be fairly free of large armies, and the fortresses in the mountains will carry a minimal guard. Still, even in the winter, the kings of Craal often send the Blade Kin through the passes to scout the movements of the Pwi and Okanjara out in the Rough. Any lone stranger we meet is bound to fight with skill—and Ironwood Woman warned me that these men have guns. They'll be watching for runaway slaves, making sure that none get through the mountains in winter. Ironwood Woman said that sixteen thousand of her people died at their hands, so she raided them. They're well armed, skittish."

Wisteria knew of the Blade Kin—slavers, murderers, and rogues far worse than any pirate who sailed in the east. It was said that the worst criminals in Craal were sentenced to fight in arena battles until they died, but every few years, the Minister of Retribution freed the best fighters and made them his Blade Kin. They were tolerated only because the slaves feared them worse than death. Rarely could a slave pass their watchful eyes and escape Craal.

"I would rather brave the pass than the Blade Kin," Ayuvah said.

"Me too," Scandal admitted.

Phylomon sighed deeply. "We've got a couple of days until we make it within striking range of any of the passes," he said. "Maybe some good weather will blow our way, and we can get through at Raven's Peak."

"What are the chances we can make it past the Blade Kin unseen?" Wisteria asked.

"They'll be less vigilant now that winter is on," Phylomon said slowly. "I'd say our chances are good."

Wisteria listened to the tone of his voice and was surprised: *One would think that a man as old as Phylomon,* she told herself, *would lie more convincingly.*

After that, Wisteria saw more signs that the others were nervous. Ayuvah would eat his breakfast, then vomit afterward. When Wisteria asked Ayuvah if he was ill, he replied, "No, only afraid. We sit on the wagon, and every day it carries us closer to Craal. Perhaps if we had to walk, I would not think of it so much." Ayuvah was a brave man, a proven fighter. She wondered how he could be so afraid of a place he'd heard of only in legend. At night, Tull and Ayuvah practiced with their weapons—sword bashing on spear. The two Neanderthals battled with their might and their hearts, as if their very lives depended on each blow, and at nights when Wisteria looked at Tull's body, bruised from practice, she worried that perhaps he was right. Perhaps his life would depend on those swings.

The Hukm traveled slowly as they neared the mountains, making less than seven miles a day. The open plains turned to oak forest interspersed with buckbrush and an occasional pine. There were no wild mammoth, so the land was left to the boar and saber-tooth. They found a great path of stone, where armies must have crossed often, for the ground was furrowed with mastodon tracks.

Tull soon became infected by the fear. He quit making love to Wisteria, and at times his shoulders trembled. She once asked him what he was thinking, and he said, "I just remembered a tale. A Pwi named Zhez was taken slave and put to work in the copper mines. He was a young man, newly married, so in eagerness to return to his wife, he killed his overseer and tried to run away. He was captured and sentenced to death in the arena. But after four years, he was still alive, so he won his freedom and became Blade Kin. It is said, he is the only Pwi ever to become Blade Kin, for all Pwi know what an evil thing that is, so, unlike the Thralls, they choose to die in the arena instead. But Zhez became Blade Kin, and every month he slaughtered a pig in sacrifice to Adjonai, for he believed that he had lived through his arena battles only because he prayed to the dark god.

"After several years, a party of slavers came through the mountains, and among their slaves was a desirable young girl. Zhez raped her, as was his custom, for he had become one of the most wicked Blade Kin. And while the girl was on the ground crying, he got up and dressed and said, 'Do not cry, child. I, Zhez, was once carried slave into Craal.'

"At that, the girl lashed out with her nails and slashed off his penis. Zhez fell to the ground, and the other Blade Kin began beating the girl, shouting 'Why did you do that? He was finished with you! Now your punishment will be ten times worse than his fate!'

"And before they killed her, she cried, 'I have always hoped to see my father once before I die, and look how it has come to pass.'

"For Zhez was her father."

Wisteria looked at Tull, at the copper hair of his eyebrows, the smooth features of his cheeks, his deep-set yellow eyes. She could barely understand why he would tell such a story, why the myth moved him, but she knew it had to do with kwea. Could the kwea of others' fears have such a profound effect on him? she wondered.

"How do you feel about the sky today?" she asked.

"I feel threatened by it," Tull answered. "It has an evil kwea."

"Other than you, how many Pwi have walked into Craal?"

"Some have," Tull answered. "I've heard of a man who lost his wife to the slavers, then went to Craal to find her. It was better to work by her side as a slave than live without her."

"I've heard about such free servants," Wisteria said. "But aside from them, what Pwi has gone to Craal?"

"Aside from them," Tull replied, "no one that I have ever heard."

"Then, in a thousand years, not one has willingly entered Craal?" Wisteria asked.

Tull thought a moment. "Only a fool would go there," he said.

Three days out from the mountains, they crossed a field near a small creek and Born-in-Snow stopped to study fresh footprints. Phylomon got out of the wagon and looked at the muddy moccasin prints, brushing aside a yellowed strand of blackberry vine.

"Human," he said. "See how the great toe is straight instead of curved inward like that of a Neanderthal."

"Zhe hemania thenza? Why is a human here alone?" Ayuvah asked.

Scandal studied the footprints and scowled. "Whoever he is, he'd have to have a soul as dark as hell to be sneaking around up here. We should be ready if we meet him." Water from the drizzling rain seeped into the footprint, slowly filling it.

"He was here not fifteen minutes ago," Phylomon said, "Probably lying under the shelter of that pine." He nodded toward a pine a few yards off.

"Any danger in him seeing us?" Scandal asked.

"It's hard to say what he saw," Phylomon said. "Two Hukm riding mammoths, pulling a wagon with a large tarpaulin over it, heading toward the White Mountains. We've got three possible passes within two weeks' journey, and he'll suspect we're heading for one. My guess is that he's a spy—just come back from watching Okanjara movements out east over the summer. News of Hukm coming this way will interest him." Phylomon studied the ground a moment. "My guess is that he'll head for the fortress up at Gold River Pass. With winter coming, the Blade Kin will hole up there. Either that or he'll head south to the garrison at Powder Mountain."

Phylomon spoke to the Hukm in finger language for a few minutes, then turned to the others. "Born-in-Snow is going to run up toward Powder River. I'm going to check ahead toward Gold River. If he goes in either direction, we should find his trail. We've got several hours of light left."

"What will you do if you find him?" Ayuvah asked.

Phylomon said dryly, "Kill him."

Phylomon strung his bow, and Born-in-Snow unslung a ten-foot-long burnished war club from his mammoth's back, then urged the mammoth under the trees where it could hunt for tender water plants beside the creek. Short Tail looked as if he longed to go on the hunt. Born-in-Snow said good-bye to his brother in finger talk, went to the creek and smeared his white fur with mud for camouflage, and then Phylomon and the big Hukm set off together.

"I saw some good mushrooms back up the trail," Scandal said. "Shall we have them for dinner?"

Wisteria said, "That sounds good," and Scandal got a sack, then headed back up the trail. Tirilee went to sit in the shelter of the barrel, while Short Tail unharnessed his mammoth. Wisteria stood with Tull and Ayuvah.

"Do you feel it?" Ayuvah asked Tull.

"Feel what?" Tull said.

"The presence of Adjonai. I can feel him, behind those mountains, and he is waiting. For the last ten days we have had rain. All our plans are dark, and I have not seen sign of my Animal Guide. There should be wolves here. With the snow in the mountains, the deer should have moved down to the flats, and the wolves should follow. But my Animal Guide is not present. It is a bad sign. It is because we are nearing Craal. I feel Adjonai reaching out from behind the mountains." Wisteria listened but had no idea what to do when Pwi talked like this.

Tull thought for a moment. "I feel his presence too. But Phylomon would say he does not exist. He would say that Adjonai is only our childhood fears of Craal, the kwea left from a thousand stories of evil slavers, all bound together to create the illusion of a god."

"And our father would say to trust what we feel," Ayuvah countered.

"Either way," Tull said, "I don't have an Animal Guide, yet I feel this emptiness, too."

"Reach out with your mind, Spirit Walker," Ayuvah said, closing his eyes, inhaling a deep breath. "Don't you feel his presence? How can you deny that Adjonai is real?"

Tull closed his eyes. For a long moment, Tull held his eyes gently shut, and the rain drops gathered on his up-turned face. Then his nostrils flared and he pushed at Wisteria. "Down!" Tull shouted, throwing Wisteria to the ground, pushing at Ayuvah.

Short Tail stood forty feet away, unhitching his mammoth from the wagon. He had just stood up straight, when he barked and spun. Wisteria saw a streak of red blood on the white fur of his shoulder. The Hukm swatted at the blood as if he'd been bitten by a horsefly, but his eyes rolled back in fear and he fell forward. To the south, a shot thundered out, and the mammoth ran forward into the brush and stood under the shadowy trees by the creek, weaving his head from side to side and thrashing the brush with his trunk, tasting the air. From farther up the creek, Born-in-Snow's mammoth trumpeted.

Wisteria looked for the source of the gunfire at the tree-line south, but could see no movement. The grass was tall oat straw—tall enough to hide her if she didn't make a target of her head by looking around too much. Ayuvah belly-crawled through the grass to the far side of the wagon, then jumped up to the swivel gun. Wisteria began crawling for the wagon.

"No!" Tull shouted. "You fire, and they'll hear it for ten miles." Wisteria turned and looked at him, saw that he was shouting at Ayuvah. Short Tail howled a cry for help not five feet from Wisteria. She crawled to the big white Hukm, began trying to pull him toward the safety of the brush by the creek. The Hukm turned and inched after her.

"Do you see him?" Tull asked.

"He's in the willows, about two hundred yards south," Ayuvah said from the wagon. "He just ran up a few feet, then dropped for cover."

Wisteria shot a glance behind her. Ayuvah was crawling under the tarp in the wagon. Tull was beneath a wheel. She could not see Tirilee.

"Get my weapons. Drop them over the back," Tull said to Ayuvah.

"Your sword is no match for a gun," Ayuvah countered.

"It is better than my teeth," Tull said. Wisteria reached the bole of a large tree, sat up with her back against it, looked twenty yards back to the wagon.

Ayuvah grunted, then Tull's shield dropped out the back of the wagon, followed by his leather armor and sword. A shot drilled into side of the wagon above Tull, directly over his head where Ayuvah should be. Wisteria stopped, held her breath. Ayuvah began kicking the bottom of the wagon.

"Ayuvah?" Wisteria shouted, filled with rage.

"Help!" Ayuvah cried.

"Where are you hit?" Tull asked.

"I . . . I don't know," Ayuvah said groggily. "Blood."

The ground was muddy and cold. Tull wriggled on the leather armor, strapped it at the sides, then grabbed his weapons and crawled toward Wisteria. Wisteria knew that Ayuvah might be bleeding to death. But there was no way to help him now. Tull crawled over to where Short Tail had fallen, seemed surprised by the pool of blood there. Beside her, Short Tail wriggled toward the creek where his mammoth stood. Tull crawled up to Wisteria, patted her foot. Wisteria smelled blood on the oat straw.

Brush cracked on the other side of the creek, and Short Tail weakly stepped on the tusk of his mammoth, trying to get footing up to the beast's head. The mammoth, upset by the scent of blood, weaved its head back and forth and nervously twitched its trunk over Short Tail, smelling him. Then the mammoth picked the Hukm up and placed him atop its neck. Short Tail unslung his great war club from the mammoth's shoulder, rested it painfully on his wounded shoulder and urged the mammoth south through the brush.

Wisteria realized then what Short Tail intended to do, and Tull must have seen it too, for he got up and ran past Wisteria, crouching low, heading for the mammoth. But Short Tail gouged his heels into the mammoth's neck, and the great beast jerked forward at a run. Tull ran behind, and the mammoth thundered through the dark trees at the creek's edge. It was a suicide charge. Short Tail slumped forward, clinging to the mammoth's shaggy head with one fist.

And Tull ran behind. Wisteria realized that the sniper would be forced to shoot, but didn't know if the gun would bring down the woolly mammoth. The sniper would have to wait until the great beast was on him to fire, hoping that one close shot would bring it down. And if the mammoth went down, Tull would be behind, so he could fall on the gunman before he had a chance to reload.

They ran toward the copse, jumping fallen trees, ripping

through the heavy fern. Wisteria heard a shot—and the bull mammoth trumpeted in rage, tore at a small alder with its trunk as it passed and uprooted the tree. Wisteria could no longer tell if Short Tail guided the mammoth or if the bull saw his target on its own, but when it got parallel the sniper, the mammoth bolted from the cover along the creek and headed straight for the sniper. Tull followed the mammoth, where the sniper would not see him behind the vast hill of flesh.

The gunman stood up and his rifle thundered. The mammoth shuddered, stopped its charge, and stood up straight, fanned his small ears forward and staggered drunkenly. Wisteria could tell it had taken a mortal wound. It leaned to the right, and its rear legs buckled. Tull dashed out from behind. The gunman cracked the gun and was fingering a shell into the chamber when he saw Tull charge.

Tull shouted, and the gunman dropped a shell into the chamber, raised the rifle.

Wisteria screamed and waved her arms, hoping to distract the gunman, for she saw that Tull would die.

And then a flash of white seemingly erupted from the ground beneath the sniper and his head jerked backward and a slash of red appeared at his throat. His gun fired into the air, and the gunman stood, his gray otter-skin cape blowing in the wind behind him, and fell to his knees. It took Wisteria a moment before she realized what had happened: Tirilee stood there, naked and smeared with mud, a bloody knife in her hand. Her pale skin, white as aspen bark and mottled with dark splotches, was the color of oat straw burned by the summer heat. Naked, she had eeled through the grass in her natural camouflage, right under the man's nose, and slit his throat.

Wisteria began running forward, feeling a great sense of relief.

Tirilee stood, looking Tull in the eye. Tull stared at Tirilee's bare shoulders, the nubs of breasts budding out with dark brown, almost black, nipples. The silver V of hair between her legs. In the last few weeks she had almost become a woman, and the transformation was marvelous to behold. Wisteria could see the woman Tirilee was becoming, and her features would be beautiful. Tirilee was wet with sweat or rainwater, and she wiped the sweat from her fore-head, touched her finger to her lips, and then touched the same finger to Tull's lips. Wisteria reached them, and stopped short.

Tull and Tirilee were so intent on each other, it was as if Wisteria had become a child again, an invisible child in her father's house, a leaf blowing through town. Neither of them were aware of her.

"Remember this," Tirilee said sadly. Her voice was soft and melodic. "You owe me your life."

Touch a Dryad, and she will destroy you, Wisteria thought, remembering the Pwi proverb. Sweat stood out on Tull's forehead, and he jerked as if he would run but stood rooted to the spot. "I know," he said weakly. "I owe you my life."

And Wisteria realized then that the Dryad planned to take him.

Tirilee dropped her knife, stepped forward and kissed Tull on the lips. Tull dropped to the ground as if struck by a mallet. "I'm not cruel," Tirilee said. "I don't want to hurt you." Tirilee looked at Wisteria, and Wisteria knew that the Dryad was speaking to both of them.

Tull twisted at the Dryad's feet.

"Get away from him!" Wisteria said, suddenly outraged. "Get away or I'll kill you!"

The Dryad stood looking down at Tull. Wisteria could not think what to do. She shouted at the girl, rushed for-ward and knocked her to the ground. The Dryad was such a small thing that she was flung a dozen feet in the wet grass.

Wisteria ran for the gun, picked it up, checked the dead man's hand for a bullet and found one, but she did not know how to put a bullet in the contraption, and after a moment she shouted in frustration and looked up.

The Dryad was gone.

"Wisteria, help me!" Tull said, still writhing in the grass. "Help me!"

Wisteria ran to him. Tull's eyes were open but he looked past her.

"I can't see!" he shouted. She'd heard that a Dryad's aphrodisiac kiss could blind a man.

She looked away from Tull in disgust, held him close,

and looked at the mammoth. The great beast lay on its side, its trunk twisted and kinked at an unnatural angle. The sniper's gun had opened a hole between its eyes large enough to stick a fist into. Short Tail lay on his side by his mammoth's head, breathing quick and shallow. The Hukm was trying to stroke the mammoth's lips, the way he did when feeding the beast. Wisteria got up, pulled Tull with her as she went to the big Hukm, looked at his shoulder. The wound was bad—the entry wound in the back of his chest was small, but there were a dozen holes in the front where pieces of shrapnel had exited, ripping the Hukm's right lung. Short Tail wheezed.

Wisteria petted Short Tail's neck, and he turned to look at her as if she were some strange bird that had landed on his shoulder. He raised a hand and dropped it slowly, wiggling his fingers. Wisteria had no idea what the Hukm said, but she watched his hands, mesmerized by the movement. He raised his hands again, repeating his words. Short Tail arched his neck and howled—a long plaintive noise not unlike the cry of a wolf. From the woods, another howl came —Born-in-Snow making his answer. But Short Tail began coughing blood, and long before his brother had reached him, he died.

Wisteria took Tull back to the wagon and checked on Ayuvah. Ayuvah lay in the wagon, blood pouring from a wound to his face and to the back of his arm. Wisteria checked the wounds, found several large slivers of wood in Ayuvah's arm and two others in his temple. He was still stunned. The bullet had shattered a three inch hole in the wagon, sending fragments of wood flying, and some of the chips had hit Ayuvah.

"You are lucky," Wisteria told him. "Luckier than Short Tail." Wisteria put a clean linen on his forehead. "Lie down until the bleeding stops," she said.

Tull sat on the back of the wagon, blinking his eyes. Tirilee came back, dressed in her green smock, and got some dry tinder from the wagon and began to set a fire. Tull watched the Dryad for a moment, then looked back to Wisteria guiltily.

"You had better leave!" Wisteria said.

Tirilee looked up at her, dropped her wood as if in weariness. She stared at Wisteria for a minute, then dropped to the wet grass and began crying. "I'm sorry. I'm sorry," she said. "I can't stop this. I don't know if I'm strong enough to leave. I don't want to hurt you. Any of you. Am I so wrong for wanting someone like him? Someone who will love me the way he loves you?"

Wisteria was so shaken she did not know what to say. Tirilee was such a child. But she was dangerous. God, the child's skin was so clear she could almost see the girl's aura shining through. And once Tull had seen her naked, how could Wisteria ever hope to erase that image from his mind? What would a man do for a woman like her?

"Stay away from me," he said.

Tull watched her with longing in his eyes.

Phylomon and Scandal cautiously returned. Phylomon stripped the gunman—a thin little man with only one ear. Upon seeing the lost ear, he knew the man was Blade Kin. Among the Blade Kin, when a man joined the ranks, he would cut off his ear and give it to his sergeant as a sign that he would always obey his orders. Yet there were no other markings identifying the man as Blade Kin—no tattoos indicating rank, no letters or written orders.

Born-in-Snow came creeping back to camp a short while later, and Tull pointed to where Short Tail lay. Tull expected Born-in-Snow to weep or throw himself on the ground. Instead he very carefully crept over to the dead gunman, shoved one fist into the dead man's chest, and pulled out his lungs and began to eat. Wisteria shouted in horror and turned away. When Born-in-Snow finished, he pummeled the carcass with his club, smashing the skull to a pulp. He then urinated on the man.

"Do not let it bother you," Phylomon said, "It is only his way of showing contempt."

Tull and Phylomon boiled water and removed splinters from Ayuvah's head and arms, and the others helped prepare Short Tail for his final journey. Scandal broke out the Hukm's favorite spices and filled small gourds with them. They had been carrying two months' rations for the Hukm —dried pears and apples, pumpkins and cured leaves, nuts and wild yams. At Phylomon's insistence, the finest of delicacies were separated. Born-in-Snow dragged Short Tail to a small tree, tied the body upright, then stuffed food into Short Tail's mouth. They laid the gourds in his arms, and placed mounds of food at his feet and his war club across his legs. Born-in-Snow went to Short Tail's dead mammoth, wove a tiny rope from its hair, and placed the rope in one of the dead Hukm's hands, ferns in the other. When Born-in-Snow was done, he sat and watched Short Tail until the last rays of light faded.

That night, the camp was somber. After sundown, Born-in-Snow threw himself on the grass and roared like a bear. As the others sat around the campfire eating, Phylomon asked Wisteria, "You were with Short Tail when he died?"

Wisteria nodded.

"Did he speak?"

"He talked in finger language. One sentence."

"The Hukm place great importance on the last words of their dead," Phylomon said. "They believe those words will reveal the final state of the dead's spirit. Born-in-Snow would be comforted to know his brother's last words."

"I watched his fingers," Wisteria said, "But I'm not sure I remember. He went like this:" she raised her hand and slowly dropped it, waggling her fingers woodenly as she went, trying to imitate exactly the patterns of loops, waggles, and curls.

"Are you sure that is the pattern he used?" Phylomon asked.

Wisteria hesitated a moment, thinking, and nodded her head.

Phylomon laughed.

"Well, what did he say?" Scandal asked.

"He said, 'Give me a boot, for I must pee.' "

That night, a steady rain fell from the sky, just as it had done for a week. Tull, Ayuvah, and Wisteria slept in the barrel, while Scandal, Tirilee, and Phylomon slept under the tarpaulin. Before going to bed Phylomon spoke to Born-in-Snow about possible routes; Phylomon could not sleep as he considered his conversation, for he feared telling the others of the plans they had made. Phylomon had decided to try Gold River Pass. True, it had a large garrison, but it was the widest pass, and it was the only one he dared try with such a heavy threat of avalanches. Phylomon recalled an avalanche there in his youth, a great wall of powder cascading down on a party of Pwi that he and his brother had been escorting through the mountains six hundred years ago. He remembered his brother's red skin, as he pulled him free—the only survivor. His brother's pyroderm had melted the snow enough so he could move. It was all that had saved him. He replayed the memory of the avalanche again. The movement of the snow, the crashing, reminded him of a tsunami he had once seen—a sixty foot wave of white crashing against the cliffs at Smoke Reef. All the fury and thunder caught up in both these phenomena.

But Born-in-Snow wanted to take that pass *because* it was well-guarded. "I will kill twenty of them in vengeance," he'd said. Fury and thunder, white as the winter ice.

In all his long war with the slavers, Phylomon had been losing ground. True, he beat them in decisive battles, but every time he turned his back they bred twice as many warriors. He could kill the slavers, but he could not kill the greed that drove otherwise good men to become slavers. Born-in-Snow wanted vengeance, and Phylomon wanted . . . the madness to stop.

Phylomon lay restlessly.

Scandal laughed under his breath, "Does anyone smell spring in the air?"

"What do you mean?" Phylomon whispered.

"Spring. When young men's thoughts turn to love?"

And Phylomon realized what Scandal was talking about. He'd thought he couldn't sleep because he was worried about the pass. But in reality he could not sleep because he was sexually aroused.

"Aphrodisiacs are on the wind, Friends," Scandal said. "If I'm not mistaken, our little Dryad is a blossom getting ready to open. Why, she's giving off a scent that could arouse the dead, if not raise them."

"I know, I feel it, too," Ayuvah said from the barrel. His voice was shallow and husky, full of lust.

"Well, I'm up for it," Scandal said. "In fact, I haven't

been this *up* for anything since I was thirteen years old. Am I the only one, or when you were that age, did the rest of you walk around with erections for six months at a time?"

Ayuvah chuckled up in the wagon.

"Ayuvah knows what I'm talking about," Scandal said. "Come on men, confess."

"We were more civilized in my day," Phylomon said. "We had drugs that helped keep us less inclined to rigidity."

"And you, Tull, don't pretend you're sleeping, did you have such a problem?" Scandal said.

"Scandal, you must have been a sickly child. I mean, if your erections lasted for *only* six months at a time . . ."

Scandal laughed, "Ayaah, well I found ways to ease my burden," he sighed. "Ah, Denna Blackwater, she knew how to corrupt young men. . . . By the Starfarer's blue—I know my attraction for this girl is purely chemical, but how are we going to sleep if this goes on?"

"This might be a problem," Phylomon said, "But not for long. Tirilee's Time of Devotion won't come on her until she finds a stand of aspen to call her own. And she can't help it if she releases her pheromones a bit early from time to time, just as you couldn't help your own youthful erections. I'd hoped we could get her to the trees before this started, but we might be in for a rough time with her."

"I don't know if I can take this," Tull admitted. Phylomon listened closely to the Tcho-Pwi's tone. Tull was deeply disturbed.

"We'll have her bed downwind from us tomorrow," Phylomon said. "You Pwi have a saying, 'Touch a Dryad, and she will destroy you.' There's truth in that saying. You'll have it harder than us humans. Keep your distance, and don't let her touch you. The aphrodisiacs she releases are in her perspiration. She can't help it if they are released, but you don't want her touching you. If you feel yourself getting aroused beyond control, it may be that you have come in contact with some of her perspiration on a blanket, or just by sitting on her seat on the wagon. Make sure you get up and wash off in a stream—scrub that scent off of you as if you'd just been sprayed by a skunk. Don't wrap yourself in furs she has warmed herself in; don't comb with a brush she has used.

"And most importantly, don't ingest any of her saliva: It catalyzes her aphrodisiacs—makes their effect a hundred times more potent. Once you get a dose, it may well be impossible to resist her. Be very careful not to drink from her cup or eat with her utensils." Phylomon thought back to his own Dryad, Saita, so many years ago, and remembered the dark cravings she had caused him. Those kisses had been so sweet, so delicious. He licked his lips in remembrance. Phylomon had once known a chemist who said he believed that the kisses were addictive, but Phylomon doubted it. Saita lost her power over him in time, and after a few years he was able to leave her. If they were addictive, they lost their power in time.

"What if she kisses one of us?" Tull asked, his voice filled with genuine terror. Phylomon smiled. Tull sounded as frightened as a newlywed Pwi should sound at the thought of being kissed by a Dryad.

"Don't let her," Phylomon said. "She might well try—it is a natural instinct for her. But don't let her. As long as she does not get her saliva on your lips, you will be fine." Such kisses were powerful, and the catalyst remained active for months. Ah, the kiss of a Dryad at her Time of Devotion. The lust it caused was both ecstasy and torment, but one tended to remember only the ecstasy. What had it been, Phylomon wondered, eight months that he had been under Saita's spell? Yet it had seemed years. Suddenly, he wondered why Tull should be so concerned.

"She hasn't kissed you, has she?"

"No," Tull said hesitantly. "No."

"Good," Phylomon said, wondering if Tull lied.

"We should kill her," Ayuvah whispered, "now, tonight, before it is too late."

"Nonsense," Phylomon said. "She is *people,* and she can't help herself. Scandal, if her Time of Devotion comes while she's still in our camp, I think you should do the honors."

"Ayaah, our thoughts sail down the same channel," Scandal said.

"Don't make your plans for me," Tirilee said. "I'm not a cow to be bred by the bull of your choice. When my Time of Devotion comes, I will choose my partner!"

Phylomon laughed with embarrassment. "I'm sorry. I didn't know you were awake."

"You think you understand Dryads because you married one," Tirilee said to Phylomon. "But you know nothing about us. You say men crave us and we destroy them for it. Don't you know that we are like you? We crave men as they crave us. Your scent is an aphrodisiac to me as mine is to you. Your lips drive me crazy, as mine do you. I must fight! I must fight!"

"I am sorry," Phylomon said. "I knew this about Dryads."

"Then why don't you tell them the truth: Tell them that we are destroyed by love just as you are. Tell them that when a Dryad gives herself to a man, she knows that in three days her love for him will die, and she will be forever tormented by guilt for what she has done. My mother . . . my mother!" Tirilee broke off and began weeping. "I only want a man who will love me," Tirilee said. "I want someone who is kind, someone to grow old with."

"You are mistaken," Phylomon said. "You don't want someone to grow old with. You can choose your mate, that is for sure, yet a day later you will be willing to discard him forever. Your love will turn to the trees. You may find that our perspiration is an aphrodisiac and a kiss from a man's lips might well send you to heaven, but you are not a Pwi enslaved to the kwea of your memories; you will not become imprisoned by love."

"I . . . I'm not like Garamon," Tirilee said. "I don't keep people in cages. I won't put people in cages."

"Not by choice," Phylomon admitted. "Not by choice."

The party took four nights to sneak to Gold River Pass, and they covered their tracks when possible. They scouted the pass well. There were no fresh tracks heading up the snowy pass that they could see, but squalls were so frequent that someone could have traveled up the pass two days before and left no sign.

The Gold River snaked through the pass. Beavers had cut down many trees, and the party used two large alders to make skids for the wagon. As soon as they got in the snow, they pulled off the wheels and put the skids on. The trip upriver was hard: they had no way to slow the wagon going downhill, and when they reached the top of a rise, they often had to stop and tie the wagon to a tree, then slowly let the rope out as it went downhill. Forage for the mammoth was sparse. It ate pine needles and dried raspberry along the trail, but such fare could not sustain it. There were wind-swept ridges where the summer hay lay on the ground, and each evening while the others camped in the valley with the wagon, Born-in-Snow took his mammoth into the mountains to forage. They traveled ten miles a day.

Tirilee kept her distance from the men, and Phylomon was grateful for that. As quickly as Tirilee had released her aphrodisiac scent, the process stopped. Only Scandal sought out her company. At dinner at the bottom of the pass, he said, "You know, when you go into town, every business has its own advertisement out front boasting its wares: Gadon's Bakery, the Best Bread Ever. Vargas's Fine Cutlery.

"But have you ever noticed that people don't advertise their sexual prowess? Why, could you imagine a sign on my shirt: Theron Scandal—the Best Sex Ever. You might well laugh at the idea, but I'm not joking. Why, if you think about it, someone somewhere is entitled to make that claim! Why, if you didn't know about it, you would pass that fellow or woman by in the street and never realize what you had missed! What do you think, Wisteria, am I right?" Scandal spoke to Wisteria, but he was watching Tirilee, and the Dryad shifted on her seat at the back of the wagon.

"Well," Wisteria said gulping a bite of stew in surprise, "I suppose you're right."

"Ayaah, when I was young, I used to travel the ports of the world searching for recipes. I tasted the finest foods, the finest wines, the finest women. And everywhere I went, I was known as the 'Gourmet of Love.' Not only did I taste the best each town had to offer, I served the best. Why, in Debon Bay one time, I once saw a young maiden on the docks. She was a flat-chested little thing, yet I fixed her with my sexiest gaze, and *poooh!* Her chest puckered so hard you'd have thought she worked as a wet nurse! So I jumped off the ship and asked her to dance right there, without music, and she melted in my arms in answer. I put my arms around her and took a couple of steps, brushed my lips across her forehead, and *whooosh!* In front of a hundred witnesses she burst into flames and burned to the ground, my kisses aroused such heat in her."

"Yes, when I was in Debon Bay last spring, I heard of your exploits," Phylomon said.

"Oh," Scandal said. "What did you hear?"

Phylomon said, "The docks still have the black spot where she burned. You'll also be pleased to know that six young men and women in that town bear your last name, and another dozen bear your likeness."

"Ayaah, when I was young and hot," Scandal said, "The green grasses were skirts for the hills, and I was the thunder that rolled over those hills. In the dry days I would storm on parched grasses; my wind would buffet the valleys until they cried out in pain and ecstasy. Generous was my name. Giving was my nature. The earth would tremble at my touch, and shudder at my will. Endlessly I would pour myself out, and rainbows sprouted in every green valley."

Tirilee got up and left with her dinner, shooting an angry look at Scandal. "I'll storm one out on you, sweet child," Scandal murmured under his breath, fixing his gaze on her, "and a rainbow will break forth in your dark valley."

The next day, they rounded a bend high in the pass and came on a great forest of aspen trees, their white bark shining above the snow. Tirilee smelled them from within the wagon, jumped out and ran up to the tree line, and dropped to all fours and just watched the trees. She was dressed in her green robe, and she lay like an emerald in the snow. She sang out, one sweet melodic line, almost a cry of joy rather than a song. And from deep within the aspen forest, an answering song rang back.

Tirilee hung her head and cried out in despair, looked back to the wagon. "This forest belongs to another," she said, and walked back to the wagon in defeat.

Yet there was a change in her. When she reached the wagon she smelled like a field of wildflowers, and the aphrodisiac scent struck Phylomon like a fist. Tull shouted for help, and Born-in-Snow jumped from the back of his mammoth, pulling his giant war club in one fluid move.

Phylomon looked at Tull, who lay in the barrel next to Wisteria, hugging his knees, blind with lust. Ayuvah backed up on the wagon, but he could barely contain himself. Scandal stood, transfixed by the scent, quivering.

"Get away from us!" Phylomon shouted.

Tirilee backed away from the wagon in dismay. "But I'm all right. My Time of Devotion has not come!" she said.

"Your Time of Devotion is far too near at hand," Phylomon said. "It is time for you to leave." He rummaged through the wagon, threw down some food, blankets, a long knife. "Do you want the gun?" he asked.

Tirilee shook her head. Wisteria watched, and she could hardly stand to see it—the thought of leaving a child in these snowy mountains. Yet she clung to Tull, and she did not want the Dryad near.

They continued on up the canyon, and watched Tirilee standing in the snow.

"You can't leave her!" Wisteria said. "What if the Blade Kin find her?"

"She's right, by God!" Scandal said, "Give her to me before I blow a load in my britches!"

"Perhaps she will move in with the Dryad who watches that forest," Phylomon said. "Even if a Blade Kin finds her, that's his problem." Although he was trying to comfort Wisteria, she frowned in response. Behind them, Tirilee picked up her food and robes and began to follow.

That night they camped in a deep glen among pine trees. They made a tiny fire and put it out early. Dire wolves howled, their deep voices echoing over the mountains. For a long time, Tull sat on watch. So near Craal, he could not sleep. It seemed like a miracle to him that they had not encountered more of the Blade Kin yet. A light snow fell and the world was hushed so that Tull could hear each dry snowflake land on the icy crust of the frozen snow. At midnight, he woke Scandal and put him on duty, then lay with Wisteria.

He put his hand on her belly, felt to see if the child grew yet. He felt nothing but Wisteria's soft flesh, and that alone made him smile. She stirred in her sleep and grabbed his hand, pressed it tight against her stomach, and Tull dreamed.

He dreamed it was a sunny day, and that he was a child lying on the ground, staring up at a pea vine that grew incredibly high as it twisted around the trunk of an iron-wood tree. And on that vine was a woolly black caterpillar, climbing the twisted vine, higher and higher, heading for the sun. As the caterpillar reached the top of the winding stair, it split at the back, and its black skin fell away, and a glorious butterfly emerged with enormous wings in shades of iridescent black and purple, and it flew away.

Tull was so startled by the dream that he woke. He had the strange sensation that he had dreamed the dream that inspired Huron Tech to build his great tower, and he wondered if it were possible that Huron could have had that dream in this very spot, as if Huron had left the dream sitting there for the next sleeping person to pick up. It was a strange thought, the kind of thing Tull sometimes thought about when drowsy. He wondered, *If I sleep in Scandal's inn at a bed where a thousand people have dreamed, what dreams will I find there?*

Tull heard heavy feet kicking up snow. A scream rose, a high pitched shriek like the cry of an owl, and Scandal began cursing. Tull jumped up, naked, and grabbed his spear and rushed forward. Wisteria cried out and Phylomon and Ayuvah scrambled for weapons.

Scandal was struggling with someone dressed in fur robes, had thrown the person to the ground, and blood dripped from the innkeeper's shoulder. Tull rushed forward, saw that Scandal held Tirilee, and the Dryad was kicking at him.

"Help!" Tirilee shouted, "He's raping me!"

Tull grabbed Scandal's leg, and the fat man kicked him, trying to stay atop Tirilee. Ayuvah and Phylomon pulled at Scandal's arm and Scandal growled, "Watch it! I can't let her go. She stabbed me!" Scandal held Tirilee's knife arm, and backed away with Tull pulling at his shoulder.

"What's going on!" Phylomon shouted. Tirilee crawled back a few steps.

"Scandal tried to rape me!" Tirilee said.

"No—I," Scandal protested, "I couldn't take the smell.

She was sneaking into camp, stealing things, and . . ." He held his arm. There was a small nick on it.

"So you tried to rape her," Phylomon said.

Tirilee got up. The smell of wheat fields and wildflowers emanated from her. She was shaken and crying and watched the men in horror. Wisteria put her arms around the Dryad, brushed back her silver hair, but Tirilee pushed Wisteria aside and took off running up the trail toward Craal. Wisteria shouted "Wait!" but the Dryad kept running.

"Leave her," Phylomon said. "She needs to be away from us for a while."

"It's dangerous out there!" Wisteria shouted. "How can you say that?"

"It's dangerous here, too," Phylomon said. "She carries danger with her. Her Time of Devotion is nearly on her."

The pheromones of the Dryad lingered in the air, on the wagon, on the eating utensils, on the clothes. Although she did not come back, for Tull it was as if she never left. He feared her return. He feared it worse than the knowledge that they were almost to the summit of the pass, and once they crossed the summit, they would be in Craal. Tull went to bed after an hour and dreamed that Tirilee was in Craal riding the back of Adjonai, as if the God of Terror were her beast of burden.

In the morning, they found Tirilee's footprints heading up the canyon. Tull kept wondering if the Dryad would return, for she craved men as much as they craved her. At midday, Born-in-Snow came down from the mountains, hooked up the wagon. They traveled through a treeless valley, and at the top came to a glen and found why Tirilee had not returned: Two men had been making a fireless camp in the wooded glen. By all signs, they had stayed put for at least a week. Tirilee had stumbled into their camp and had been dragged down by one of the men. After a short scuffle, she'd managed to slit their throats.

Phylomon checked the ground for signs of others, lingered over the bodies. Both men were missing their right ears, both had carried guns, both wore tattoos of a black hooded figure on their arms. "These men were Blade Kin," Phylomon said. "Brotherhood of the Black Cyclops."

"Some kind of guards? Maybe a band of them?" Scandal asked.

Phylomon said, "The Brotherhood is not a band, it is a sign of ownership. Members of the Brotherhood belong to Tantos, the Minister of Retribution. They enforce Craal's laws, gather taxes. It looks as if they saw Tirilee, waited to catch her. Most likely they saw her silver hair in the moonlight, knew she was a woman. I doubt they knew what kind of trouble they had on their hands."

"Her kisses would have blinded them," Tull said. He imagined the lust they had felt for her as they died. They would have been so helpless.

"Maybe," Phylomon said. "Either way, she killed them. We should thank her for that. We'd not have been able to cross that meadow back there without being seen."

Tirilee's tracks forged ahead through the woods. Phylomon gave a gun to Wisteria, taught her how to load and aim it, gave the other to Scandal, and they moved on for two more hours until they climbed a small hill. Before they reached its summit, Phylomon motioned for them to stop. The whole group climbed slowly to the top.

Phylomon warned, "Quietly, now. Walk softly. Ironwood Woman says the Blade Kin have a small fortress on the other side of the pass. We must see if we can skirt it in the dark."

They crossed the summit and stood in the shelter of a stand of pine. Below them, not a half mile down the hill in a narrow gulch, they found the small fortress: gray stones with a turret for a cannon and six crenellated towers, each trailing smoke from the evening cooking fires within. Beyond that was a wide valley without snow, and far beyond that a range of brown hills.

Tirilee had been waiting for them at the treeline. She stepped forward pointed at the plains, and said, "Friends, welcome to the kingdom of Craal!"

Until that moment, the fear Tull felt from the Dryad had blinded him to the fear he felt at the thought of entering Craal. He looked across the plain and saw that which he feared most—an army of at least a hundred thousand men camped in black tents on the plain, fields black with their war mastodons. At the sound of that name, Tull felt the earth turn under him and a knot of terror twisted in his belly. The ground itself roared like thunder, and Ayuvah cried out and fired his rifle into the air. Tull turned to look at Ayuvah, for the sound of gunfire would surely raise the Blade Kin. Ayuvah was staring at the fortress, at the army down below, his mouth and eyes wide with terror, and Phylomon struggled to wrest the rifle from the Neanderthal's hands.

My God! Tull thought. *This is Craal!* The blood pounded in his ears with a great roar. Against his will, his feet turned as if to run back to Smilodon Bay, yet there was no strength in them. He could not move them. *It is only kwea,* he thought, trying to control his fear, and he felt his blood seemingly turn to ice in his veins. A great cold pierced him.

"Adjonai!" Ayuvah called, falling to the ground in fear.

Tull followed Ayuvah's line of sight, and out on the plain below, beyond the army with its endless lines of tents, clouds of dust rose and a giant began to rise from the earth, as if he had suddenly wakened: he slowly rose from the ground and crouched. He was a powerful creature, with a heavy chest and purpled skin, with hands like a buzzard's talons. His great black loincloth hung nearly to the ground, and was made of clouds of dust and tatters of the night. His face was a decaying hulk, the image of a young man consumed by his own ruthless passions. A sickening green light glowed from his eyes, and diseases flowed out from his feet like rivers. In his left hand he carried a wooden warshield covered with snake skin that radiated despair, and in his right he held a shimmering silver kutow with two stone ax heads that radiated terror, and on his brow was a crown of fiery worms that wriggled and twisted high in the air as they struggled for release.

Tull wanted to run, knew it was only kwea, his own fears giving rise to the illusion, but he recalled Phylomon's words: "You seek the face of the God of Terror!" And now Tull stood face-to-face with the god, and he was not sure it was illusion. Tull screamed a war cry and pulled his sword from the scabbard at his back.

The god turned to gaze on Tull, and Tull held the monster's gaze with his own eyes, yet his legs felt weak and they trembled feebly.

The god watched Tull with disdain, and with a voice that cracked like the bones of men he said, "The great wheel of evil."

The weakness in Tull's legs seemed to become greater, and Tull could not tell if he was shaking or the earth was shaking. Tull felt himself struggling under a great weight, as if he were being crushed, and he could not breathe. He suddenly understood that the god wanted him to kneel, that the god was trying to force him to his knees. Tull struggled to hold his legs straight, and the god simply stared.

Wisteria grabbed Tull's arm and shouted, "What is it? What is it?"

At Wisteria's touch, Tull's strength seemed renewed. It was as if her energy flowed into him. Tull closed his eyes and basked in her touch, invigorated by it. He remembered the kwea of their wedding night, and it fed him like fruit in the desert. He let her hold him for a long time, and when he looked up, Adjonai was gone, vanished back into the dust.

Ayuvah was on his knees, sobbing in the snow. Scandal bent over to help him up. "God rot you," Scandal said. "Did you have to fire the gun?"

Tull went to Ayuvah, held the Pwi. "Adjonai is not here," Tull said. "Think of Etanai, back home, the kwea of your wedding night. He will go away. You and I, we are like children who see monsters in the night, only because we are afraid."

Ayuvah held Tull's leg for a moment. "No," he said. "It was not our fear. It was the sorcery of the Blade Kin. Still, I feel him leaving."

Tull looked at the small border fortress, at the bleak valleys of Craal beyond with its endless tents. He watched it, saw how they could skirt the army by cutting through the forests to the north. Out there, in cities beyond the edge of sight, forty million Pwi lived in slavery. *How many tears of pain and despair have the Pwi cried here?* Tull wondered. *How much blood has watered the land?* The kwea of their torments had saturated the air, and the air was unnaturally dark. Their nightmares had seeped into the ground, seeped into the tiny white roots of every tender blade of grass. The land looked permeated by filth and evil and rot. Tull had always imagined that the sky over Craal would be as blue as the sky over Smilodon Bay, that the grass would be as green. Yet the kwea of this place felt foul.

Down below them in the valley, a dozen men and two women, all wrapped in bulky furs, issued from the fortress gates at a run, casting searching glances along the hillsides. Seven of them carried guns. By a strange trick of acoustics, Tull heard one man say quite plainly, "It was a warning shot, I tell you!"

Phylomon, Born-in-Snow, and Wisteria all crouched low.

Tull knelt beside Ayuvah, put his hand to his shoulder. "At home, your wife dreams of your caress. Hold her in your dreams now."

Ayuvah lay on the ground, gasping in great breaths, and after a moment he whimpered. "I cannot go any farther. My legs will not let me walk into Craal."

"Then I will carry you," Tull said.

Phylomon took Ayuvah's rifle, cracked the barrel and put a shell in, then took another handful of shells. "No one's going into Craal for the moment," he said. "We've got an hour till sunset, and I hope to God we can get them mad enough to come up after us." Beside him, Born-in-Snow looked down into the valley and grinned a feral grin, the type of look Tull would not expect from a vegetarian, until he remembered that the Hukm only grin in anger, when they are ready to attack. Phylomon sat in the snow, propped his elbow on his knee, and aimed the gun. For a long time he held his breath and squeezed at the trigger.

When the gun sounded, one of the women in the valley below spun and dropped. Phylomon cracked the barrel open, inserted another shell. The men below them jumped for cover, and those with guns began firing seemingly at random, but a bullet cracked into the branches over Tull's head.

"Damn," Scandal said, "Why shoot the woman?"

"Among the Blade Kin, one woman will take several husbands," Phylomon said. "If we're lucky, we can turn half those men into widowers."

Phylomon took long slow aim, fired a second shot. One

man's head cracked open as the bullet lifted him, carried him back a dozen feet in the air. Scandal raised his gun, took aim, but Phylomon signaled for him to wait.

Phylomon shouted in Pwi, "Your slavers have taken my wife, Feyava! Bring her back to care for her children, or I swear, many more of you will die!"

The slavers below seemed awestruck at the thought of a single Neanderthal attacking them. "Are you Pwi or Okanjara?" one slaver shouted.

"I am Pwi," Phylomon shouted. "I will return in two weeks. Bring her, or more of you will die!" Phylomon squeezed off a third shot, killed a man, then fell silent and did not move. A heavy snow shower began to fall. For nearly an hour, the slavers below held to cover, but then retreated to their castle at dusk dragging their dead. When they were safely within the gate, Phylomon breathed easier.

"They will come for us tonight. I know the Blade Kin, and they cannot let such a challenge remain unanswered. They lost three today, and they know their two guards are dead. They will come out in force to hunt for this one mad Pwi. But we will hunt them."

Beside him, Born-in-Snow growled deep in the back of his throat.

The group went back to their wagon. Born-in-Snow had the mammoth pull it back down the canyon. Their tracks skirted precariously close to a high bluff, wet with deep snow, and once they passed it, Phylomon pulled the wagon a quarter mile until he was partly hidden in a glade, and loaded the swivel gun. The snow fell in great flurries, and the wind sent rooster tails of snow showering from the cliffs above them. In the space of three hours, their tracks were covered.

Born-in-Snow took out his war club, wrapped it in leather to give it strength.

"Remember, kill only the Blade Kin," Phylomon warned Born-in-Snow in finger language. "Leave the slaves. Leave the people in cages."

Born-in-Snow shook his fist in the air as if in sign of

acknowledgment, turned his back and trotted away, his white fur blending in with the snow.

They waited in the narrow canyon. Thor was but a narrow disk, hidden behind dark clouds. Snow fell. Phylomon watched their trail in earnest, but never saw the Blade Kin. Sometime in the early morning, Born-in-Snow roared. Phylomon aimed the cannon at the cliff above and fired.

Walls of ice and powder roared free of the canyon walls on both sides, breaking trees as if they were twigs, destroying everything in their path. The Blade Kin shouted, tried to beat the onrush. Phylomon saw them then, figures dressed in white, scattering from the cliff in the moonlight, but the snow was deep and thick, and no man could run so fast.

When the avalanche subsided, snow and ice crystals still filled the air. Born-in-Snow rushed over the snow from his hiding place, making sure of the Blade Kin who'd been trapped in the avalanche. Phylomon and the others rushed to help him, but before they reached the spot, Born-in-Snow headed over the snow to the fortress in Craal.

Phylomon and Tull and Ayuvah dug in the snow, gathered several guns from the dead. They went back to their wagon. The women were waiting.

"God, what do we do now?" Scandal asked.

"We sleep," Phylomon said. "Or at least, some of us should sleep. It has been a long day, and we have a longer day tomorrow."

"But shouldn't we help Born-in-Snow?" Tirilee asked.

Phylomon pondered a moment. Once inside the fortress walls, the Hukm would seek out any guards and kill them, and next would come the women and the children in their beds. It was not work that any of these innocents from Smilodon Bay could stomach, yet it had to be done. If they were going to ensure their escape from the pass, it had to be done.

"Born-in-Snow has sworn to take twenty lives in retribution for his brother. He does not want our help," he answered. "Go to sleep. I'll take first watch."

When Born-in-Snow returned to camp an hour before sunrise, his hands and war club were dark with blood. He silently hitched his mammoth to the wagon, and they made their way into Craal.

The journey to the fortress seemed to last hours. As they neared, Wisteria expected a shot to ring out from one of the towers. But Born-in-Snow guided his mammoth through the great gates and entered the quiet city. From the pass, the fortress had looked huge, but up close, it seemed small, and Wisteria could see that the city had been made to look larger from above, for the front wall nearly blocked off the entire pass.

Within, the fortress was quiet and deserted. No one stirred at the windows. No dogs barked. The load on the wagon creaked as the mammoth plodded through the narrow streets. Holding pens stood in a courtyard—iron cages with frozen watering troughs—all located where the captives could be constantly watched. In the ground around these cages, thirty-two red spears were raised in a circle. Impaled on each spear was the body of a Blade Kin, or their wives and children. Born-in-Snow had shoved a spear down the throat of each victim, so that their heads all faced the ground.

"Shall we burn the city before we leave?" Scandal asked.

Phylomon said, "I can think of no better way to alert the army below than to set fire to their fortress."

"We can't just leave the fortress to be used again!" Tull answered.

"Even if we tore it down stone by stone," Phylomon said, "Do you think it would stay down for a month? No. It is better to leave it. Let's search the houses, to check for survivors."

So they did. Wisteria followed, and the men traveled together, spears at ready. In one dark hole that smelled of feces they found four starved Thralls, two men and their wives, slaves who had been caught trying to escape. All four had been brutally tortured, branded with hot irons. Phylomon gave the slaves their freedom, and they fell at his feet.

"God bless! God bless!" the Thralls said.

"Please," Phylomon told them, "take what you want from the city and run to freedom quickly. We don't know how long it will be before more Blade Kin arrive." The men

gave their thanks and went to loot the guard towers o
weapons.

Scandal proved himself an eager warrior, and he race
from room to room ahead of the others, picking up gol
bracelets, bottles of wine, and stuffing them down his shir
Phylomon searched diligently, and in one guard room h
found what he desired. "Traveling papers!" he said, holdin
them up in triumph. "No good citizen of Craal would b
caught in the wilderness without them." He filled them ou
on the spot. "Congratulations," he said, giving the papers t
Tull, Ayuvah, Scandal, and Wisteria. "You are now all vas
sals, owned by Lord Tantos of Bashevgo, Minister of Retr
bution! May you serve him well."

When they reached the inn, Scandal ran ahead of all o
them, and he threw open the doors and shrieked.

On the floor below him was a cleaning woman, naked t
the waist, her left breast removed, scrubbing the blood c
her dead masters from the floor with a rag and a bucket. Sh
moaned a monotonous song as she worked, and seemed un
aware of Scandal and the rest of the party entering th
room. She had dark brown hair and a wrinkled face.

Wisteria's heart beat within her, and she felt faint
"Javan? Javan Tech?" she asked, for the woman fi
Phylomon's description perfectly. "I'm sorry!" Wisteri
whispered. "I'm so sorry!"

The woman slowly turned her head up to Wisteria, an
Wisteria wondered how she would ever look into those eye
remember how she had fed the woman ten years before. Ye
when she looked up, the woman was a complete stranger
someone she had never met.

"You're free!" Scandal told the woman. "We came t
free you. All right?" The slave continued working, singin
her monotonous tuneless song, wiping the blood from th
floors.

"Leave her," Phylomon said. "Her mind is gone."

"Wait!" Wisteria said, "Wait!" and she knelt beside th
old woman. "Do you know your name?" she asked.

"Ruva Brightman, better than most," the old woma
crooned, weaving her words into the song.

"Where were you taken slave?" Wisteria asked.

"In South Bay. South Bay. Far away in South Bay," the woman said.

"And who took you slave."

"Feremon Scatman, will catch you when he can," the woman sang.

Wisteria looked for a quill and paper, but found only paper. She knelt on the messy floor and wrote the woman's accusation in blood, handed it to Phylomon.

"If you find him, kill him," Wisteria said.

Phylomon put his arms around her, and Wisteria buried her face in the blue mans' fur robes, hugged her parents' executioner, and wept.

Chapter 10
A Man of the Pwi

On the southern edge of the fortress at Gold River Pass were four long stone buildings. The muddy ground in front of the buildings had been trampled by mastodons and oxen. A cold gray rain splattered in the courtyard. The men checked these buildings last, and found thousands of large clay pots filled with grain.

The party stood for a long time, looking at the pots, and Phylomon frowned. "Food for the armies of Craal," he said. "Enough to feed ten thousand men for a summer."

"But there couldn't have been fifty Blade Kin in this tiny fortress!" Scandal said.

"The food is here for warriors yet to come," Ayuvah said.

Phylomon licked his lips. "The army down on the plain. They must be what, twenty miles from here?"

"I'd say twelve," Scandal answered.

Phylomon said, "Then unless I am mistaken, the bulk of them will be here by midafternoon."

Scandal's eyes opened wide, and as one they rushed for their wagon. Ayuvah ran down the hill to scout the road into Craal, and Phylomon spoke to Born-in-Snow in finger language. He leapt atop his mammoth's back and urged the beast forward at a run. For two hours they hurried down the road, making eight miles, until they reached the foothills below, and then they heard mastodons trumpeting in the distance.

Ayuvah came running back up toward them. "A great army is coming, my heart stops with fear! They bring war mastodons and wagons! And many warriors." Born-in-Snow pulled the mammoth off the road, leading it into the woods, and for the next half hour everyone struggled to cover the huge tracks of the mammoth, hiding their trail. They pulled their wagon behind a small hill and into a grove of trees. The trumpeting of the mastodons became louder, and Born-in-Snow's mammoth trumpeted a challenge and shifted from foot to foot, sniffing the air. Born-in-Snow got down, pushed his mammoth's shoulder, and after a moment of confusion the great beast lay on its side and feigned death.

Tull and Ayuvah got their warshields, hid behind them as they watched the army of Craal pass in the rain. A general led the army, a tall thin human dressed in black furs with a helm of black iron, and he carried a shield with the emblem of the black cyclops upon it. He rode the back of a horned dragon, its skin dark as obsidian, a beast grown far too large and old to fly, and the crusty old dragon limped up the mountain road, tasting the air with its flickering red tongue. Two hundred mastodons walked before the army, dragging sleds loaded with food and tents. Thralls, Neanderthal slaves, stood atop two of the mastodons and pounded great drums, keeping time for the march. Many of the mastodons wore armor of leather with brass rings sewn in, helmets for the head, and they were covered with red blankets while their tusks were studded with iron. The Blade Kin followed behind—men in black lacquered armor with red capes, earless Neanderthal Thralls with black cyclopes insignia on their shields. All of the Blade Kin carried both rifle and sword. Tull counted seven thousand of them before they passed.

"At the rate they are going, it will take three hours for them to reach the fortress," Ayuvah said. "When they see what we have done, they will hunt us."

Phylomon murmured, his voice soft and strained, "As long as they don't find where we left the trail, we will be all right. They obliterated our tracks for us down this far. Ayuvah, start leading our people into the woods. Go three or four miles, but make sure you can't be seen from the pass above, then wait in the woods. I'll hide our trail."

"You must also hide our scent," Ayuvah said.

"The rain will have to hide it for us."

Ayuvah guided them through the woods, skirting meadows where the summer dirt was packed. That night it rained heavily, and they traveled in the dark, guided by the Hukm. The next morning, Scandal credited Phylomon's skill at obscuring their trail for their luck in escaping, but Phylomon said, "We have escaped for a day, but our trail will not be hard to pick up. We must make it to a road quickly, a well-used road where our tracks will mingle with those of others." For two days, he guided them until they came to a dirt road, rutted by wagon tracks, heading north.

The men stood looking at the road. It had grown thick with grass, yet it had seen heavy use only recently. "Where do you think it leads?" Scandal asked.

Phylomon smiled at them. "It links Seven Ogre River and Greenstone. This is the road the cooks use when they go to make their serpent catch. If I am not mistaken, we have but a hundred miles to go!" There were fresh wagon tracks everywhere, leading up from the heartland of Craal. Some wagons were pulled by oxen, others by mastodons. "It appears we are not far behind the fishermen for the lords of Craal," Phylomon remarked. "It is a good sign." So the party began to travel in disguise.

Scandal's forged documents proclaimed him a newlywed cook with Wisteria as his wife, out to hunt serpents as a delicacy for high Lord Tantos, while Tull and Ayuvah drove the mastodon—mere slaves. Phylomon, Tirilee, and Born-in-Snow headed for the woods and followed at a distance. Twice that afternoon, small bands of soldiers stopped them on the road and harassed them. The soldiers were all Neanderthals, Blade Kin in black armor, but few of them carried rifles. When they saw Scandal's traveling papers, signed by the Minister of Retribution himself, they fell silent and slinked away.

For a week they traveled north into Craal, and every day they met more soldiers, as if the search for them were heating up. In that time Tull came to see that Craal's sky shone as blue, that its grass could be as green, as anywhere on Anee. Nature seemed to conspire to prove her beneficence, and whereas they had suffered under stifling rains, now the sun came out and shone splendidly. Tull almost welcomed the checks by the Blade Kin, for he relished the look of fear that came on their faces when they read Scandal's documents.

They reached the river, high up where the serpents did not run, and passed through a forest of aspen. That night, when Phylomon and the others crept into camp to eat, Tirilee looked back at the trees longingly, and the aphrodisiac perfume of her body wafted through camp.

The next morning, Tirilee was gone. Scandal stood gazing up the trail behind them and sighed, "She's found her trees. We've likely seen the last of her."

That day, they entered a nameless town, a mining camp where dirty-faced Neanderthals watched them pass. Ayuvah said, "I'd have thought there would be more people here in Craal."

"There were forty-six million people in Craal at last census," Scandal said. "Two million in the city of Craal itself, seven million on the Cinnabar Plains, five million in the isles of Bashevgo. But the Crawlies are farmers and miners. They don't wander in the wilderness like Pwi. Even Denai has over a hundred thousand people."

Ayuvah whistled, for in all of the Rough there were not so many people as in Denai.

The Seven Ogre River was not nearly so deep or wide as the Smilodon, and it meandered through low hills, wooded with oak and alder. Tull hoped to find the serpent hatchlings quickly, felt a sense of urgency, but they followed the path downriver for a week before they came on the first fishermen, six Thralls heading home. They had a long, flat wagon pulled by eight oxen. The sides of the wagon were only two feet high, and the wagon was caulked on the sides to keep the water in. There were several hatches through which the serpents could be put, and Tull guessed that the serpents were kept in separate compartments.

The Thralls eyed Scandal's strange gear, particularly the enormous barrel on the back of the wagon, and Tull realized how unbalanced his barrel was compared to their long sleek wagons.

"You are a couple of weeks late, aren't you?" a Thrall asked.

Tull's mouth seemed suddenly too dry to speak, and he wondered if he had missed the run altogether.

"Our mammoth died," Ayuvah put in, "and we had to turn back for another."

"Did you catch many serpents?" Tull asked.

The Thrall gauged Tull warily. "Enough," one of the others answered. "If you hurry, you will be in time for the end of the run."

Tull nodded, and would have passed by.

"Your mammoth's tusks show that it is owned by Hukm," a Thrall said.

"My lord bought it last year from a trader who stole it from Hukm out in the Rough," Ayuvah said.

"Your lord is an idiot to send you so close to the White Mountains with it," the Thrall said. "May the gods grant that he die young so that you can be sold to a wiser master."

"Tchezza fae. So be it," Tull and Ayuvah said in unison.

When the fishermen had passed, Tull stopped the mammoth for a moment, looked back at Scandal.

"God," Scandal said, holding his chest. "Goddamn."

"We're too late for the harvest!" Ayuvah said, almost weeping.

"I thought we were only a week behind schedule," Scandal said. "I thought it wouldn't matter!"

"The harvest came earlier than we'd hoped," Tull said. "If we'd known, we could have pushed harder." He looked back at Scandal and Ayuvah. Wisteria sat beside Scandal, and her face was pale. She put her hands over her face, and began to sob.

"We don't stop tonight," Tull said. "We keep moving until dawn. Phylomon and Born-in-Snow will have to keep up. The mammoth can rest when we camp." The others nodded their agreement.

That night, they drove by moonlight through the mountains, and at dawn they began to pass fishing camps. At each camp, several Thralls would stand out on a rock that jutted into the water, each of them holding a single long pole. The pole had a ball of fur tied to it, often with colored rags that looked like feet, with buttons for eyes. The Thralls bobbed this ball of fur up and down, up and down, trying to entice a serpent to rise and bite.

Scandal had them pull over to a likely spot—a wide bend thick with oak brush for cover, some large flat rocks, deep pools. As soon as the wagon stopped, Tull cut a long sapling, got some hide and cloth from the wagon, and began making a lure. The others turned the barrel upright and filled it with water.

Chaa had said that Tull alone must catch the serpents, so he found a rock, put his pole into the water, and began enticing the serpents to bite. The pool was deep and blue, and the water flowed over it clear as glass. Tull could see the bottom—speckled rocks and dark patches of moss. There were big fish in there, too—fall run salmon, huge striped bass. The serpents, he knew, often eeled along the bottom, and their backs could change shades of silver, black, or yellow to match the surface of the bottom. They hunted in packs of dozens or even hundreds, and they acted in concert to drive the fish upstream in great schools so they could feed at leisure. The water was thick with fish.

Tull put his lure in and began jigging up and down, up and down. For an hour, nothing happened, and his shoulders became weary from the work. Just when he was about ready to quit and take a rest, he saw a huge gaping mouth filled with knives for teeth rise from the river bottom and take the lure. He shouted for the others and tried to sling the serpent out of the water, but the serpent was huge, and instead of Tull pulling it from the water, the serpent tried to drag him in.

He dropped his lure and jumped to the bank. The serpent wriggled after him. Its head was nearly a yard wide—large enough to swallow him whole, and it had bright red eyes. Twin pairs of spines sprouted from its back, and as Tull slithered up the bank, it watched him a moment, then eeled back and sank, clutching the lure in its jaws.

Scandal and Ayuvah heard Tull shouting, and they stopped to look at the monster.

"We'll need smaller ones than that," Scandal said. "No more than four feet."

Tull made another lure and tried the rest of the afternoon, but quickly learned why the Thralls always had four men working the same jig: The serpents were big, and they all tried to drag him into the water. One even tried to climb up onto the rock with him and take his leg, totally ignoring the lure. Tull was so scared that he reacted quickly, leaping from its jaws. Ayuvah and Scandal begged to help, but Chaa had been explicit—only Tull could catch the serpents.

By nightfall he'd been able to drag only one serpent from the water—a fourteen footer that thrashed with its tail spikes so hard that no one dared go near. It ripped the fur from the lure, gulped it down, then used its tiny front claws to drag itself back to the river.

That night, Phylomon and Born-in-Snow came into camp. "You are fishing too deep," they said. "We watched the Thralls upstream. They fished in shallows. They put a spotter up in a tree to watch for the small ones, then the spotter tells the lure man where to put his bait. We found a good spot downstream."

"How many did these Thralls catch today?" Scandal asked.

"They caught only one that they could keep," Phylomon admitted.

"And how many do you say we should try to haul home? A hundred?"

"I'd hope for that many," Phylomon answered.

Tull looked around. Everyone seemed drained and despondent. Ayuvah said, "Chaa told us to come. He must have had a reason for telling us to come."

"But how well did he see this future?" Wisteria asked. "Maybe he didn't know that our mastodon would die, that we'd have to push the damned wagon over the Dragon Spines."

"Damn it," Scandal said. "We did what he asked, and we're here. If Chaa says we can catch some serpents, we're going to find them. Who knows, maybe a fresh hatch of three footers is on its way upstream this very moment." Yet his enthusiasm sounded false. They were words spoken in desperation, meant only to soothe Tull's fears.

"Perhaps," Phylomon admitted. "Or perhaps we will find only big ones."

"You know," Scandal said, "this could be harder than it sounded."

"What would you have us do?" Phylomon asked Tull.

Tull furrowed his brow and considered.

"The boy doesn't know any better than the rest of us!" Scandal said.

"Yet the Spirit Walker put him in charge," Phylomon answered. "Let him choose."

Tull thought a moment. "Tomorrow, we go for shallower water. If I can see the serpents, maybe I can catch us a few."

The next morning, they moved camp two miles downstream and found a pile of boulders in some shallows. Someone had fished these waters before, for near the boulders was a circle of rocks that formed a ring big enough to hold several serpents. With the fresh river water flowing through the rocks, the circle acted as a holding pond. The pond had not been used for years, and the heavy flows of winter water had all but destroyed the north and south walls. Tull and Ayuvah hauled rocks from shore and built the walls back up. Then Tull stood on the boulders—good tall rocks that even the larger serpents could not climb. Ayuvah and Wisteria acted as spotters. Within an hour, they were rewarded for their labor—Wisteria spotted a five footer eeling along the bank toward the boulders, and Tull put the pole down in front of it and began jigging.

The serpent seemed almost stupid. Instead of going for the jig, it stopped and settled on the bottom. For five minutes it worked on changing color to blend in with the background. Tull eased to the edge of his boulder, jabbing the pole closer and closer to the serpent's mouth, and the serpent just watched him with great red eyes. It leisurely extended its gills, breathing deeply. When it was ready, it flared its gill flaps, pulled its gills in, and used its front fins to push up from the bottom and grab the bait. Tull gave the serpent a moment to lock its jaws on the bait, then flipped the serpent up into the air.

The serpent began flapping its tail from side to side, and two spikes raked Tull's chest. He gasped and nearly dropped his pole, but managed to toss the serpent into the holding pond. The serpent kept ripping at the bait even in the pond, and when the fur tore from the jig, the serpent broke free and everyone rushed forward to see it.

It banged the sides of the pond, scraping its armored fins across the rocks. It bashed its head into the rocks again and again, and when it tired, it leapt up and stuck its head over the wall and tried to eel back into the river. Tull grabbed his pole to push the serpent back in the pond, and Ayuvah rushed back to shore and carried more rocks to build up the walls of the holding pond.

Scandal was so pleased he shouted, "One thousand god-damned miles through the Rough, and we caught ourselves a serpent! Tonight, we celebrate!" and he got down from the rocks, built a fire, and began cooking. Tull and Wisteria danced around the camp, and Ayuvah smiled dumbly. After half an hour, Tull stifled his desire to celebrate, and went back to work.

But the rest of the day did not go well. They saw many serpents moving upstream, but for each moving upstream, two were moving down, and none were as small as the one they had caught. They celebrated that night anyway, and the next day they went back to work, but came up empty. Phylomon and Born-in-Snow spent the day scouting the area, and they came back with a report.

Phylomon said. "We scouted ahead for ten miles. The Summerhazy Hills cross our path, and the road is not well tended—steep and rugged in places. We won't get the wagon through: Its base is too wide, not like the little wagons used in these parts."

"Is there a promising road elsewhere?" Scandal asked.

"We found some foot trails, but they are not for human feet."

"Deer?"

"Mastodon Men," Phylomon said. "The hills are thick with oak and buckbrush. It's good country for wild boar and moose."

Scandal said, "Find me a good path to Denai."

"We'll try in the morning. It will take us two days, three at the least."

But Phylomon did not return after two days, nor after

three. And Tull did not catch another serpent. Scandal and Ayuvah hunted for pigs and deer each day and learned that the serpent catchers had hunted the area out. To feed their only serpent, the men resorted to jigging for a larger serpent. When Scandal and Ayuvah managed to pull it from the water, Tull hacked its head open with his broadsword, and they fed chunks to their youngster. It cracked the bones in its teeth and thrashed the shallow water of its holding pond in a feeding frenzy.

On the fourth day, two things gave them cause for alarm —first, a group of nearly two thousand Blade Kin warriors came down the road from Denai, guns in hand. They asked the party if they had seen any Hukm, checked Scandal's forged traveling papers. They were not impressed by the Minister of Retribution's signature, and they searched the wagon twice over. Fortunately, Scandal had hidden his stolen gold and guns off in the brush, and although the Blade Kin seemed curious, they left after nearly an hour. Also on that day, the number of large serpents that they spotted in the river dropped to thirty-two. The numbers of fish had diminished, and the serpents headed back down to the open ocean.

That afternoon, seven wagons passed them as the other fishermen vacated the river.

Tull wore a grim, determined face, but his heart was not so determined. He plodded along the riverbank all afternoon, desperate to spot some young serpents. Chaa had foreseen that the quest could succeed. Chaa had foreseen that Tull would catch the serpents. But what if Chaa had seen him catch only one serpent? One would not be enough. Tull had missed something, the way he always missed things. He looked at his hands, great robust hands, more like the paws of a bear than human hands. They never served him. Always a failure, a failure once again.

That night, five ragged Thralls passed the group in a wagon pulled by a mastodon, and they stopped nearby. Their campfire gleamed upriver, shining through the barren trees, reflecting off the water. One Thrall played a panpipe, and they sang, happy to be going home.

Phylomon and Born-in-Snow returned to camp. "We found a better road," Phylomon said, "but it goes from one small town to another. It is rocky and narrow in places and doesn't follow near the river at all. We won't be able to get fresh water for the serpents for the first three days. That concerns me. It will take six or seven days to reach Denai."

"Then, by God, if we had any serpents they would just have to breathe air, wouldn't they?" Scandal said.

"What do you mean?" Phylomon said. "How many serpents have you captured?"

"Just the one," Wisteria said.

Phylomon looked hard at Tull, "What will you do?"

Tull swallowed and looked at the Thrall camp up the river. He had tried so hard, and it all came to nothing. "I do not think we will catch any more small serpents," he told the group.

Scandal followed Tull's eyes, looked up the river. "Ayaah, I see what you are thinking: Those Thralls have serpents we can take."

"They'd be no match for four men with guns," Phylomon admitted. One of the Thralls raised his voice in song.

"No," Tull said. "Let me talk to them."

Tull went to the brush, unwrapped the weapons they had robbed from the dead men at Gold River Pass. He gathered five guns into his arms, took a bag of ammunition, stuck them into a sack.

"What are you doing?" Scandal shouted.

"I'm going to reason with them," Tull said.

He went to the Thrall camp, followed by Born-in-Snow and the others. They walked up to the fire, and the Thralls backed away, looking at Tull, at the Hukm, at Phylomon's blue skin. One Thrall went to the wagon, drew a club.

"I want your serpents," Tull said. The Thralls looked at him as if he were mad.

"Our lord would beat us!" an old Thrall said, licking his lips with fear. "He would beat us like dogs if we were to give away our catch!" His voice was almost a whimper, for he stared at the Hukm and knew he could not protect his serpents.

Tull dumped the bag of rifles onto the ground.

The old Thrall looked at the guns. "Where did you get those?"

"We killed the Blade Kin up in Gold River Pass."

The old Thrall looked at the rifles on the ground. "You will be punished for it," he said. "You will die the death! Surely you are not such a fool as to think you can escape?"

"Take the guns and leave," Tull said. "Head over the hills now, while the snow is still melted. Or how much longer will you be a Thrall?" Tull asked the old man.

One of the younger men, a Neanderthal with blond hair and a face reddened and wrinkled from the sun, walked to the pile and picked up a gun. He broke the barrel open, saw that it was loaded, snapped the barrel closed. "I tell you how long he will be a Thrall," the Neanderthal said, "until the day he dies." He turned and stuck the barrel in the old man's face, pulled the trigger. The old man took the bullet under the chin, and it penetrated his skull. For a moment he looked at everyone with rheumy eyes, as if he'd suddenly forgotten their names, while smoke issued from the ragged hole under his chin, then his legs stuttered and he dropped forward.

The other three Thralls looked at the body, and Tull was surprised at their expressions, for they mourned him. "At least he died quickly," one young man said, "which is more than we may get," and the other three rushed forward, grabbed the guns, and began unloading food from their wagon as if they believed they must escape quickly.

"We thank you for the guns," the wind-burned Thrall said over his shoulder. "But I fear the Blade Kin may have heard our shot, so we must leave quickly." Within a minute they all rushed off into the darkness, heading for the trees.

Tull stood in shock. "I didn't want anyone to get hurt," he said. "I wanted to give them their freedom."

Phylomon grabbed the dead Thrall, dragged the old man to the river, outside the circle of firelight, and tossed him in. "Quickly," he said, "let's take their serpents and get out of here."

"We should take their wagon," Scandal said.

Phylomon looked at the wagon. "The axles aren't strong enough. It will never make it over the mountain roads."

Scandal doused the fire, and in the darkness they pushed the wagon a quarter mile back down the road to their camp. In the cold moonlight, Tull stood atop the wagon with his jigging pole and enticed the serpents to bite, then dumped them in his own barrel. They took eighty-four serpents, one by one, from the Thralls' wagon. Then Scandal bashed in its sides with Tull's broadsword and drained the water. When it had emptied, they pushed it off the road, well up into the brush. They ate a small breakfast, although it was only after midnight, then waited for daybreak.

During the night the others slept, but Tull could not sleep. He knew he should be happy to finally have the serpents, but he kept seeing the face of the old man, saw over and over in minute detail how the bullet had exploded his skull, making his head sag in as if it were an empty sack. Tull had not wanted anything like this to happen—had believed he was offering the Thralls freedom. *Would the Thralls who escaped really ever leave Craal?* Tull doubted it. They would become Okanjara and spend the remainder of their days camped on Craal's borders, playing their little games, sniping at the Blade Kin while they sniped back. In the end, although they called themselves Okanjara—the free ones—they would never really be free. They would only change their chains for another kind of bondage. The old man had known that Tull offered only a different kind of slavery.

In the wagon above him, Tull could hear the serpents talking with deep voices, a long low moaning noise. He listened. Phylomon had once said the serpents were as smart as humans, that they spoke at great distances under the water. Tull listened, tried to make out the words to their language.

As Tull lay thinking beneath the wagon, he heard a spoon scraping a metal bowl. *Probably Scandal eating leftovers,* he thought, but then realized Scandal was snoring. He looked up from under the wagon, and in the moonlight he saw Tirilee, the silver of her hair and face turned unearthly orange by the moonlight. She crouched beside the fire and ate, never looking toward the wagon, poked at the coals of the fire with a stick, then put a few small logs on it. Tull could not smell her. The aphrodisiac scent she emanated seemed to be gone. Tull looked at Tirilee, and she was *Tirileezhoai*—Tirilee who held the love he feared. She finished her dinner, then looked in a tree beside the fire at a small basket. She pulled some bread and wine from it. Tull was surprised—leaving food in the open like that would only attract bears. Scandal should have known better. But then he remembered that Phylomon had sat there at dinner, not Scandal. Just as Phylomon had fed her at the start of the trip, he fed her now at the end. Another week, and they would be in Denai. If all went well, two weeks after that they might sail home. Tirilee bundled the food in the folds of her dress and crept back into the woods. *In another week,* Tull thought, *I will be rid of her forever.*

The journey through the Summerhazy Hills was most treacherous. Most hills were rolling and gentle, but the great barrel, although only partly filled with water, weighed seven tons, and the mammoth often trumpeted his rage at being made to pull such a grievous weight. When going uphill, Born-in-Snow pushed the wagon from behind, while the men worked with axes and picks to clear brush from the road ahead. This left only Wisteria to guide the mammoth, and Phylomon taught her to ride its great neck and guide it as the Hukm do, urging it forward and steering it with kicks to its small ears and neck, stopping it by pulling its hair. The area was thick with white cabbage moths, and time after time she found her mammoth, angered by his load, striking out at the helpless moths, sucking them up his trunk, then spitting them out. Controlling the stupid beast was hard work that left her calves and the insides of her legs aching. At the end of the day she stank of sweat and muddy mammoth's hide.

They worked all day without rest, moving as quickly as they could over the steep roads, then made a waterless camp at sundown on a forest floor thick with rotten limbs and scraggly bushes. It was a poor place to camp; they'd passed a nice little stream not two hours before, yet the men chose to drive forward. Wisteria could feel the sense of urgency in the air. Everything was rushed. Yet during the day, riding the mammoth over the hills, she'd had time to think. In three weeks they would be back in Smilodon Bay with their serpents. In three weeks Garamon would learn that she had not sabotaged the quest. Five of Garamon's brothers were dead, and she had not given him his vengeance. She remembered how he had made love to her in the back of his fabric shop. The threats of death, the punches to the belly. He was a slaver. He'd kill her for failing him. She knew it. Yet they were rushing forward, rushing toward home.

Wisteria smelled bad. The weather had turned warm ten days ago, and it was as hot as summer. In the heat of the day her sweat mingled with the mud and hair on the mammoth. It was such a foul-smelling creature, she was not sure she'd ever be able to wash the smell off, and she thought of the shallow stream she'd passed, and how nice it would have been to wash. She made a bed of leaves and covered it with a bear skin, then threw herself down. She caught a whiff of her armpits and frowned. Tull came and lay beside her. She was surprised he could stand her smell.

They lay for a long time and watched the stars. The only moon in the sky was Freya—a blue mote so distant it was not much larger than a star. The Red Drones passed like comets. Wisteria realized Tull was sweating as with a fever.

"Why are you so tense?" she asked.

"While we were clearing the trail today, we talked about what we must do. Scandal will have to go to Denai to buy a boat for the journey home, and then he will sail it upriver at night to meet Phylomon and load the serpents. Phylomon cannot go into the city, for he is an outlaw, and I do not want Ayuvah to go into the city, for he is too afraid of the Crawlies. Phylomon says it will be dangerous, for the Crawlies are suspicious of all foreigners, so I will have to go in disguise as a Thrall."

"You can convince them. You've seen enough Thralls."

Tull grunted. "I have seen Thralls, but Phylomon told me the laws they live under. Thralls cannot carry knives. Thralls cannot touch a human unless commanded to do so. I cannot look a human in the eye. This seems easy. Yet Phylomon warns that we will pass the slave markets, and I must not interfere with anything that I see.

"All my life, I've feared Craal. But now I realize that I will not see Craal until I see the slave market at Denai. I wish we were home."

Wisteria laughed softly. "You are afraid to stay, and I'm afraid to leave."

"What do you mean?" Tull asked.

Wisteria had not meant to tell him, but they were far enough from camp so that no one else could hear her. Her stomach knotted with fear, but she realized that she had been living a lie too long, that if she did not speak now, she would drive a wedge between them. "Tull, the night that Phylomon killed my parents, I think I went crazy. I felt as if everyone in town had turned against me, and I hated them. I can see now that I was crazy. Phylomon killed my parents, and I can never totally forgive him for that. But we were so in awe of him, that no one could stop him. If anyone else had tried what he did, we would have tossed him into a bear pit. But not Phylomon. He was too much of a legend. The great warrior who once leveled Bashevgo. Too much of a hero.

"So after the execution, I saw Garamon. I told him I wanted vengeance, and he was like me, so mad that three of his brothers had died that he was like a crazy man." Wisteria halted a moment. She did not know how much to tell Tull. She couldn't tell him how she had made love to Garamon. And she did not know if she should portray Garamon to be as ruthlessly evil as he'd seemed. She licked her lips. "Garamon said he'd give me that vengeance. Since there was practically no money in town, the men would have to work elsewhere. And while they were gone, he could arrange an attack by the slavers. He said we could empty the town, ship off every woman and child."

Tull turned his head and looked at her. Even in the dim moonlight, Wisteria could see his disbelief. It was not that the plan was impractical. It was just so totally corrupt. Wisteria could not imagine what Tull was thinking about her now. She forged on. "But in order for the plan to work, he said we could not let the people in town have even a glimmer of hope for the future. He wanted me to come with you —to make sure the quest failed—so that there would be no hope for a big fish run in the spring, so the men would go out now, over the winter, to work in the mines down at White Rock."

A pained expression drew across Tull's face.

"What are you thinking?" Wisteria asked.

"Did you marry me only so that you could sabotage the quest?" he asked.

Wisteria hesitated. "I did at first. Until I realized that I love you. I . . . I have your baby in me. I couldn't betray you now. Even to withhold the truth would be a form of betrayal."

Tull did not say anything for a long time. At last he sighed. "Don't tell anyone about this yet. If you tell Phylomon, he would kill Garamon outright. I think I had better talk to Garamon alone—give him a chance to get out of town. I can't imagine him being as evil as you say. I'll give him at least that much of a chance."

Wisteria turned to Tull and wrapped her arms around his shoulders. "Do not be afraid of Denai. I will be with you. *Tull-zhoka-thrall*—Tull with the love that enslaves." She kissed him then, and he stroked her face. "Make love to me!" she said, and Tull smiled at her, pulled her hair. She bent forward and kissed him. "Not that way," she said. "Let's try it your way for once. Make love to me, tenderly."

The only moon in the sky was Freya, and its light was dim as a star. Tirilee had been running almost ceaselessly for the past two weeks. After leaving the party, she made her way to the river alone, following the party by day, restlessly striking out in one direction at night, only to be pulled back to the party by morning light.

Her mother had warned her as a child that this would happen. The brief dizzying flashes of wantonness were first to strike, like the rush of a heady wine. But then came the night fevers that shook her to the bone, and the restlessness, the desire to run. So, she was running now, under the starlight, running ahead of the party through thick brush. She was far ahead of the others, and for the first time she believed she could finally leave them. She had been climbing the hills all afternoon, but she smelled something rich and wonderful like a spice in the air or the scent of boiling honey, something that called her.

She leapt over a bush, and a bird chirped questioningly, and then she was in the pines again, running along the hill. She kept it up for an hour, and a wind from the hills blew the scent to her again, and the beauty of it almost staggered her.

Her mother, Levarran, had told her of the restlessness, but Levarran never told her of this dark craving to follow an unknown smell. She'd been so young when she was taken. Tirilee was sure Levarran would have told her many things to prepare her for this.

Now she was running, running over the hills, free forever. The scent came to her again, beautiful and strong and heady, and she turned to her right and leapt through some thick ferns and began climbing. She came to a small windswept meadow and looked up and her heart beat so fiercely she thought it might open her chest: It was there! Just as she had known it would be! Aspen trees with white trunks silvered by the moonlight.

Tirilee fell to the ground, and a cry ripped from her throat, a long beautiful eerie note that carried on the wind like the cry of a hawk.

She listened for a long moment, trying to still her heavy breathing. There was no answer. No Dryad owned this stand of aspen. She cried for joy and rushed up the hill, and inhaled the rich aroma of the aspen wood, the luscious smell of rotting leaves on the forest floor, the sap that flowed through the aspen trees' sluggish veins. It carried an aroma more beautiful than anything she had ever known. Yet her legs were suddenly tired and leaden, and she staggered the last few yards. The time for running had stopped. She had found her home.

That morning, Wisteria woke and considered her conversation with Tull from the night before. In her father's house, she'd always been such a child. Her father had ordered her about as if she were a servant, making her feel weak, incapable, sometimes embarrassing her. Because he'd been a Dicton, had carried the ancient knowledge in his head, she realized that he felt superior to those who were not born with a memory of English. Because he felt powerful, he'd treated her like an idiot child.

Yet, this morning, for the first time in ages, she felt powerful. Telling Tull about her deal with Garamon had given her a sense of power, a taste of victory. She felt wholesome and clean, and she had almost nothing to hide anymore.

At sunrise, the men looked ragged and worn, and Wisteria decided that pregnant or not, she'd take some of the burden from them. She laid the morning fire, then went to work preparing corn cakes and bottled curry sausages for breakfast. Scandal got up and wrapped a blanket around himself and watched her sullenly, too worn to help.

As they ate, a terrible ruckus rose from their barrel—the sound of armored scales scraping and slapping the wood, thrashing water, and a long keening squeak that was somehow frightening simply because it was such an odd sound. When the thrashing of the water quieted, Ayuvah jumped up on the wagon and popped the top of the barrel open.

"I can't tell for sure—but it looks as if the serpents have been fighting . . . ayaah. There is blood in the water."

Phylomon climbed up on the wagon and peered into the barrel. "Serpents are herd animals; they don't fight with each other," he said, "except the females, when they are fighting for some rock to attach their eggs to." He looked into the barrel for a long time, and then said, "It is as I feared. They didn't fight. They simply ate one of their own."

"You mean one's dead?" Scandal asked.

"More than dead," Phylomon said. "Consumed. I was afraid of this. Young serpents normally eat their weight in food once a day. With eighty serpents at fifty pounds each, they'll want two tons of meat a day. I don't know that we'll need that much just to keep them alive, but we'll need something."

"I've got a hundred pounds of rations left," Scandal said. "They can have it all."

"That wouldn't last long. Someone is going to have to spend the day hunting," Phylomon said. A serpent jumped from the barrel, snapped at Phylomon's face, and Phylomon placed the lid back on the barrel.

"Ayaah," Scandal said, "Well, it best be you. You could probably outhunt any two of us."

So Phylomon spent the day hunting while the rest traveled. They made their way over the hills, and to Wisteria it seemed as if the day were spent in one long steady climb. They passed only one water hole, a muddy pond where the water ran down the hill through a thicket of dried reeds. The mud around the side of the pond was covered with the tracks of Mastodon Men, and they hurried away. With the Mastodon Men about, Born-in-Snow stayed close to Wisteria, and she felt comforted, although she knew that he was only protecting his precious mammoth.

At sundown Phylomon brought in two small wild hogs and a fawn that was just losing its spots. He dumped the carcasses into the barrel unceremoniously, and for a few moments the serpents thrashed the water and scraped the barrel in a feeding frenzy, and then lay still.

"That water is beginning to foul," he said, putting the lid loosely over the barrel, leaving a crack so the serpents could breathe.

"Two hundred pounds of meat," Phylomon said. "I don't think it's enough."

"See any sign of moose?" Scandal asked.

"Not down here," Phylomon said. "Too many Mastodon Men hereabouts. They'll stay up in higher range in the summer, then head down into the fields for the winter. Even if they pass through, they won't be here long. I think that in the morning, we should all go hunting. There's a large herd of wild hog up here—if we had four guns, we should get a lot of meat quickly."

That night, Wisteria took a bucket of water and went to wash her clothes away from the camp. She took off her dress and put it in the bucket, put in some flakes of lye soap, and worked the dress with her fingers, trying to get off the smell of mammoth. She'd only been at it a moment, when someone touched her shoulder.

"I knew I'd find you naked," Scandal said. "Somehow, you can't resist showing me your body. I knew it all along—you are one of those who love, I see it in your eyes."

She looked up at the fat man, and he was smiling down. His beard was combed, and he wore a fine green shirt, as if he'd dressed specifically to meet her on a date.

"I thought you'd want Tirilee?" Wisteria said, pulling the wet dress from the bucket to cover herself.

Scandal laughed. "Of course, I would want Tirilee, if she were around. Who wouldn't? I am a gourmet, after all, the Gourmet of Love. Imagine yourself, devoted to a lifetime of pleasing the senses, the finest foods! The headiest wines! The sweetest women! Yet nothing compares to a Dryad during

her Time of Devotion. Of course, I want that sweet child.
She is the main course, but I want you for my appetizer. I
need you." Scandal pulled the wet dress back from her
chest, looked down at her breasts.

Wisteria smiled up at him. "I know what you need," she
said, and she stood and wrapped her arms around his shoulders.

Scandal chuckled and pulled her forward, trying to kiss
her, and she kneed him in the groin. The fat man's eyes
bulged and he gasped for breath, fell to the ground and
began groaning.

"You're okay," Wisteria told him, pulling on her dress.
"You'll heal before you get to Denai."

Tirilee slept most of the day, and she woke hungry. The hill
held plenty of wild raspberries, and she spent an hour eating
these and autumn roseapples. She caught a wild dove that
had wandered into a thicket and then couldn't fly out. After
making a small meal, she found herself suddenly tired and
fell asleep, but woke to the cry of an osprey.

Perspiration poured from her body, and she wandered in
a daze till dark. When an aspen grows, in each place where a
root meets the surface, a new tree shoots up, so that the
woods become very dense. Tirilee reached the densest part
of her thicket, and lay down. She wiped the beaded sweat
from her forehead and felt the palms of her hands. Even
they were sweaty with a thick resinous oil. She grabbed a
sapling, smeared the resin along the branches, and bent the
tree to the left, holding it fast for a moment. When she
released it, the sapling remained exactly as she had placed it.
In her mind she saw a picture of aspen branches interwoven
to create a living wall, and as she thought about it, she
began wiping the sweat from her brow and holding branches
in place, weaving the tiny limbs to form a curtain in a huge
circle, pulling branches from larger trees down as a roof.

The idea excited her, and as she worked the sweat
poured from her. She stopped several times during the
night, just long enough to run downhill to a small stream
and fill her belly with water. By dawn, she had woven a

home of living trees, and in the center of her home, she raked together a pile of leaves to be her bed.

Tirilee closed her eyes and hummed to herself, sitting in the great bed of leaves. As suddenly as she had begun to perspire, she stopped. She knew what she must do next, but she did not want to do it.

For hours she waited and fought the urge. Her lips began to burn, as if they had been rubbed with pepper. Her skin felt alive to the touch, and she could feel the gentlest wind play across her body. She took off her clothes and stood at the entrance of her nest. It was getting late in the afternoon, and the sun was setting. The red of the dying sun shone on her aspens and on her skin like fire, and she stood in the evening breeze and felt it play over her legs. Her breasts felt heavy and swollen, and she stroked them and marveled at how they had grown in a few short weeks. Her lips were on fire. Her breasts were on fire. Everywhere was fire. And in her mind, she began to compose a song about the beauty of fire.

Wisteria woke early in the morning and sent the men off to hunt. Born-in-Snow took his mammoth downhill to a stream. Being a vegetarian, he was not willing to hunt. Wisteria got the wood to set a fire, and then got out the pans and began readying breakfast so that she could cook it in a hurry when the men returned.

At ten in the morning she heard a coughing sound up the hill. It could have been a buck snorting, she thought— but it did not repeat itself—and bucks almost always continue to snort for several minutes. She listened closely, got one of the guns.

Heavy footsteps cracked in the brush uphill, and she backed away from the wagon, placing it between her and the sound. The brush here was thick, with pines and vine maples rising high above her, a floor of ferns and smaller bushes below. She could not see more than forty feet in any direction, and she dared not take off running, for the Mastodon Men could be all around her. She waited for fifteen minutes. She began creeping toward an old pig trail, then heard a stealthy movement behind her.

She looked back and saw the Mastodon Man not forty feet behind, creeping toward the wagon. She stopped dead in her tracks, knowing that Mastodon Men are color-blind and are attracted by movement.

The Mastodon Man was a large one—over nine feet tall —and he knuckle-walked into the clearing and sniffed at the wagon. He looked at the breakfast pans and knocked them to the ground, then knelt and sniffed the food. He broke a jar of pickled meat, and he picked it up and began eating.

Wisteria looked around the clearing, but dared not move. There could be forty of the Mastodon Men hiding in the brush, and she'd never know. She decided it was safer to wait, and if one approached, she could shoot. She might not kill it, but the noise from the gun might scare them long enough so she could hide.

The Mastodon Man crept around the wagon. He was an old male, with a grizzled mane, and he walked with a slight limp. *An old bull,* she hoped, thinking he might be the deposed head of some tribe. That would be best. He might be alone.

The Mastodon Man looked in her direction, and suddenly stopped and stared at her, unmoving.

Wisteria held as still as possible, and he watched her for a full three minutes, trying to decide whether to investigate. He put his knuckles to the ground and began sniffing loudly.

Behind him, one of the serpents scraped the sides of the barrel with his spiked tail. The Mastodon Man leapt in the air and looked at the barrel, jumped up on the wagon and began pushing at the barrel. The serpents inside began swimming, thrashing the water.

Wisteria held still and watched him for several minutes, and the Mastodon Man hammered at the barrel with his fist, trying to knock it open. Suddenly, quite by accident, he knocked the top off. He climbed up on top and looked into the dark water for a moment. The serpents thrashed in the water, scraping the sides of the barrel with their armored fins. The Mastodon Man reached in, and let out a very human sounding yell of pain. One of the serpents actually leapt from the water and grabbed his face in its jaws while another snapped onto his shoulder.

The Mastodon Man tumbled full into the barrel, and for

a long while the barrel hissed and seethed as the serpents fed in a frenzy.

The men returned to camp an hour later with three large pigs, and they cooked up a breakfast that included strips of fresh pork cheek.

As they sat eating, Wisteria told them what had happened. Scandal said, "Hah! Fifteen hundred pounds of meat for the day. You say we can get over the hills and meet the river by tonight?"

Phylomon nodded.

"Then we're off to Denai. When we hit the river, we can jig us a couple of big serpents and store meat for a day or two. No more hunting. No more stinking water in our barrel! Just a couple more days of toil."

Wisteria saw Tull flinch at the thought of Denai. His mind was not easy. Phylomon watched them. The blue man lay his head back and let the sun shine full on his strange hairless face for a while. "You know, Tull, you are a lucky man."

"Why is that?" Tull asked, his voice tinged with fear at the thought of entering Denai.

"You got your serpents, just as we needed them, and when it looked as if they'd starve, a Mastodon Man walked into camp and fed himself to them. And isn't there a saying among the Pwi, that if a man and woman make a child on their wedding night, the wedding is blessed?"

"Yes," Ayuvah said. "The child is *zhozedan*—born of three. The mother, the father, and the goddess of love."

Tull stared at Phylomon curiously. "Well, think back!" Phylomon said. "Wisteria began throwing up three weeks from your wedding night. Few women take ill so quickly. In my experience, that is a pretty good indication that she became pregnant on the first night. Now, may I ask you, what are the chances of that?"

Tull shrugged.

"Slim," Phylomon said. "After all, her father was a Dicton—as close as he could come to being a full-bred human—and you are Tcho-Pwi. In such a marriage, a woman might get pregnant twice in all of her child-bearing years. Why, the odds that Wisteria would conceive in the first week of your marriage are about six hundred to one. The

odds that she would conceive on your first night might well
be four thousand to one. I wouldn't call it a miracle, but it's
damned lucky. Damned lucky!"

Tull grinned at Wisteria, put his arm around her shoulders and gave her a kiss. *"Zhozedan!* That is what we should
call our child," he told her. He looked back at Phylomon.
"What will our child look like?"

"Considering the frequency with which she's lost her
breakfast," Phylomon answered, "I suspect that Wisteria is
carrying a boy. The male hormones flowing in her blood
from the baby make the sickness harder to bear. I think
you'll be surprised at how much your son will look like you.
He'll have your skull and your broad shoulders, though his
hands will be smaller. He will have some of your red in his
hair, though it will tend to be darker than your own hair."

"That is," Scandal laughed, "If you're the father!"

And Wisteria had a sudden thought—what if Tull were
not the father? In her mind, she was lying on the floor while
Garamon, drunken and smelly, penetrated her again and
again. It had been less than twelve hours later that she married Tull. She suddenly began counting in her mind . . .
surely she had begun getting sick when they were going over
the Dragon Spines—a week or two later than Phylomon
claimed. The poison stew had made her sick earlier—had
made her vomit for days. But the more she thought about it,
the more she realized that it might not have been the stew.
Certainly the Dryad had recovered quickly. And now that
she considered it, she remembered being sick even earlier . . . feeling cold and nauseous in the redwoods while
the giant Dryads followed them. Feeling ill at Frowning
Idols when Phylomon killed the glass seller. *Could these
phantom chills have really been a symptom of a child?* she
wondered.

Wisteria remembered her mother once saying that she
had never got sick before the fifth week. So even if Phylomon were wrong, what did it matter. She'd definitely been
vomiting by her fourth week.

She tried remembering when her last bleeding had oc-
curred, but she could not recall with precision. The days
before her father's execution seemed ages ago. Had it been
two weeks before their departure, or four? And what had

been her safe days? In Smilodon Bay, her life had been so clinical. Back then, she did not have to count days to know she was safe. She'd always been safe.

In her mind, Wisteria conjured up an image of the child as it would be. She imagined he would be pale of skin, almost white, as if his blood were drained. And she imagined Garamon's black eyes staring out from him, Garamon's dark hair. He would have the boxlike head of a human, and he would cry out in harsh syllables. He would look down on Tull, a mere Neanderthal, and her son would be fiercely proud to be a bastard rather than son to a Tcho-Pwi.

Wisteria spent the rest of the morning suffering from chills. She did not hear the others talking around her. When Born-in-Snow returned from his morning forage and hooked the mammoth to the wagon, she dutifully climbed the mammoth's tusks and stepped up onto his neck. Her muscles were tight, cramped with fear, and her skin crawled. She saw Scandal watching her and wondered what he read in her face. Did he know? Had he guessed all along that she carried someone else's child? Had that been what he meant when he said she was an adulteress?

With fear came the desire to run. All morning she wondered how to escape this dilemma. When she bore the child, everyone would learn the truth. But how would Tull take it? She imagined he'd be stoic. He'd comfort her, assure her it did not matter, play the part of the hero. But inside he'd suffer quietly, envious of the child that was not his, yet scorned by his son. She tried to imagine him becoming angry but knew Tull would not be angry. He'd be hurt, the way a faithful dog is hurt when it takes an undeserved beating from its master. Yes, he'd take it, and in her mind's eye, she imagined he'd be weakened and destroyed by that pain, just as a house can be felled by a single rotten timber.

By midmorning, she felt dizzy with grief. She thought of killing the child, of managing a fall so that it would abort while still small. Perhaps if the fetus were small enough, she thought, Tull might not recognize it as being human.

And the next minute she laughed out loud, thinking how she had vowed to destroy the town in her anger and her pain, and how now, despite her best efforts to the contrary, she would destroy Tull. She would lose him. She would lose Tull.

She thought about Tirilee, how she had kissed Tull and driven him blind with lust, and how at home Fava had gazed at him longingly, wanting to unite her spear with Tull's. *Better to leave him to them,* she thought. *Better to die.* And when she thought of death, Wisteria thought of Garamon suffering with grief for his dead brothers. She thought of what he would do to her. Tull had promised to protect her from the beast, but who knew if Tull was strong enough?

As they walked slowly along, Wisteria played a dangerous little game. They came to a ridge, and she wove the mammoth in and out, in and out, letting it get close to the ridge line. She looked down below her, two hundred feet, and wondered how close she would need to get before the wheels of the wagon slipped over the edge. The thought made her dizzy, so she closed her eyes.

Wisteria sat atop the mammoth, and realized it had stopped. They were at the top of a hill, and below them was a valley filled with dark pines and thick mountain raspberry. Phylomon, Ayuvah, and Tull were working ahead of her, feverishly trying to remove a dead tree from her path, while behind her Born-in-Snow had been pushing the wagon. Wisteria had steered the mammoth for an hour without even realizing it. She looked at the men raising and dropping their axes, drenched with sweat.

It all looked so far away, as if none of it were real, as if she were cut off from them.

The trail was narrow, and the wagon was already at a ten-degree slant, the barrel with its precious cargo leaning precariously toward the drop. Wisteria looked at the hill and saw that if she nudged the mammoth to the left, the wheels on that side would go into a dip, perhaps enough to spill the wagon. Perhaps not. Perhaps the whole wagon would fall over the edge and down the hill, and in her mind she saw the mammoth being pulled by his harness down the hill, rolling over and over, crushing the life out of her, crushing her child. It did not matter which. Whatever happened, it would be better than to live like this, better than to let Tull find out the truth. She was losing him, and without him, she'd have nothing.

She did not know if the wagon would tip, in fact did not believe it would. Wisteria nudged the mammoth's right ear with her toe, just to see what would happen. "I'm sorry," she said. "I'm sorry." As if in a dream, the great hairy beast shook his head, as if to warn her against such action, then began to walk to the left. She did not feel the wagon tip behind her, did not hear Born-in-Snow's mighty scream.

Instead, she felt the wagon tug, felt the mammoth's harness snap. She turned to look back, and the wagon tipped toward the dark forest below. Beside her she saw a dark flash as the tug, the pole attached to the singletree, swung up. It glanced off the mammoth's shoulders, then hit her in the kidneys and swept her into the air. "Help!" she screamed, watching the drop fifty feet below.

The mammoth trumpeted and she heard it skidding downhill beside her. She slammed onto the steep slope, bounced, then she hit a leafless bush, and everything went dark . . .

When she woke, she was sure that the mastodon had fallen on her, at least one of its legs. The sky was dark, especially right in front of her, and something heavy lay on her chest. She heard a high wheezing sound from far away, and she swallowed because her mouth was filled with foamy blood. There was a buzzing in her ears, almost the sound a hummingbird makes when it holds in the air nearby, and she felt . . . disconnected. There was no pain, only the heaviness, and a faint numbness across her face. Not pain really, just the absence of feeling.

Her belly hurt. She wanted to vomit. Someone stood over her and touched the side of her face, looked into her eyes. It was a fat woman with frizzy hair. A woman whose name she could not recall . . . the nurse who had helped care for her in childhood. *I didn't really want to do this. I don't want to die!* she wanted to tell the woman. The fat nurse prodded her, and a sharp pain filled her belly, as if something had been ripped out. An overwhelming sense of hope filled her.

Is it dead? Wisteria tried to say, but it only came out as "Ishtda."

"What?" the fat nurse asked.

Wisteria spat the blood from her throat and smiled. "Garamon's bastard child," Wisteria asked. "Is it dead? Is it dead yet?"

"Yes, child," the nurse said. "It's dead."

Wisteria laughed, and the buzzing in her ears began to fade. She tried to focus on the nurse, but it was far too dark, and the strain hurt her eyes. She heard someone screaming in the distance, a little child screaming for its baby doll, and a flock of butterflies, like colored sparks of purple and iridescent green, fluttered past her head, whistling a little song.

The nurse said, "Hush now, Wisteria. The pain won't last for long. Not for long."

She felt a sharp pain in her side, and a desire to run, and she kicked her feet a little and tried to scurry away. And then she felt a great wrench, as if she were jerked sideways. And there was no more pain. The air smelled vaguely of ash, and the butterflies whirled about her—red and gold, silver and midnight blue, cinnabar and the soft colors of mother-of-pearl. They rushed past as if swirling in the heart of a dust devil. She turned to see where they were going, and longed to float after them into the empty land.

Chapter 11
An Empty Heaven

Phylomon had been hacking the roots of a rhododendron bush, sweat glistening on his long blue arms, trying to clear the trail, when he looked up and saw Wisteria urge the mammoth forward. She was mumbling and wore a strange expression, a look of sadness mingled with curiosity. She turned her face to glance behind her at the wheels of the wagon. Then the axle cracked and the left rear wheel buckled.

Phylomon had seen death come to a thousand men, and just as it did nearly every time, the world seemed to move in slow motion. The wagon toppled downhill. The great wooden tugs that connected the wagon's singletree to the hames at the side of the mammoth's neck broke free, and one tug caught Wisteria in the kidney. The torque of the rolling wagon was so great that the girl flew thirty feet into the air and disappeared downhill, and on some curious impulse, Phylomon tracked her trajectory thinking, *At least I'll know where to find the body.*

Tull shouted, and the mammoth, still tied to the wagon

with his huge collar, trumpeted and flipped to his side, slid over the embankment. Wagon, barrel, and mammoth rolled downhill in a cloud of dust and scree.

Tull ran forward and when he hit the slope his legs kept moving even though he stood in midair. Phylomon followed. Below them, the wagon and mammoth had cleared a wide trail in the thick brush as they rolled downhill. At the end of the trail, they lay in a bloody tangle.

The barrel was broken open, and a serpent wriggled from beneath the wreckage and sunk its teeth into the mammoth's front leg. The mammoth did not flinch. Tull zigzagged down the trail, peering beneath brush on both sides of the clearing as Born-in-Snow rushed past him. The great white Hukm stopped in midstride and just stared at the dead mammoth.

Scandal stood at the top of the hill, calling to Wisteria, and Phylomon rushed downhill and grabbed Tull, shouting "This way! She should have landed down here!" for he could see from her trajectory that she should have landed in the very center of the slideway where the wagon had rolled.

Ayuvah beat the brush, looking for Wisteria off to the left, but Phylomon found a spot of blood on the ground near the roots of a broken bush. "There's where she landed! The wagon pushed her downhill!"

Tull stood in shock, looking at the blood, and Phylomon grabbed his arm and pulled him toward the dead mammoth and the wrecked wagon. Tull stopped at the foot of the hill, shaking his head, and Phylomon climbed over the mammoth. The wagon was only a pile of splintered timbers, far too dangerous to walk on.

Young serpents lay on the ground by the mammoth, ground and crushed to bloody bits. Another lay gasping, its gills opened wide, trying to breathe in the harsh sunlight, its tiny fins extended out to its sides, raking the air with its claws.

Phylomon stood atop the mammoth and searched for Wisteria beneath the wreckage. Behind the mammoth's body was a wall of twigs and bent trees, and he could see nothing. He heard a cough to his left, down beneath the wagon, and marveled that anything could be alive down there. "Here!" he shouted, jumping from the mammoth, picking his way through the shattered timbers to the back of the wagon.

Phylomon pulled broken boards from the wagon bed and soon saw a pale hand sticking out from beneath the wagon as if to catch the sunlight. Ayuvah began pulling boards, and Scandal came down behind them and threw the boards away while Phylomon and Ayuvah worked. Phylomon glanced back at Tull. The young Tcho-Pwi stood in the sunlight and watched them work, as if performing the labor of witness were labor enough. Ayuvah pulled off a board from the wagon, and Wisteria gasped as sunlight struck her eyes.

Foamy blood was running from her nose, and she choked and looked all around. She gagged softly, and Scandal said, "What?"

She smiled, as if she were as carefree as a little girl, and for a moment she cleared the blood from her throat. "Garamon's bastard child," Wisteria asked plainly, placing her hand on her womb. "Is it dead? Is it dead yet."

"Yes, child," Phylomon said, "it's dead."

Wisteria laughed, a high clear laugh as if she were at peace, and Phylomon realized that he had never seen such a look on her face, such utter contentment, the face of a child who has just come in from a long day of play. But her laugh turned into a ragged cough, and she bent forward. Blood gushed from her mouth and nose, as if the coughing fit broke something inside her, and the blood rushed free.

Phylomon held Wisteria by the shoulders. He looked up at Tull, and the sunlight shining full on the Pwi made his red hair gleam the color of cinnabar. He was breathing shallowly, shaking. Ayuvah pulled the boards away.

Scandal got a wine bottle, filled it with water, tried to force some down her, Phylomon let him give her a small drink, enough to clear the blood in her throat. Tull found a blanket to cover her, and for several moments, they just stared at her.

"Is she going to live?" Tull asked.

Phylomon looked up at the boy. "I'm no prophet. She seems to be breathing all right for the moment. I think we should let her rest here for a bit. In a few hours we can try to move her."

The men stood and watched her for half an hour, then Scandal began cleaning up. Born-in-Snow was already preparing his mammoth for its journey to the spirit world, bringing it food. Scandal set aside the provisions he'd promised to pay the Hukm, the valuable spices, and for a while Scandal put his arms around the big furry creature and held him.

After two hours, Ayuvah and Scandal went uphill, began setting camp. Wisteria moaned and thrashed her head from side to side in pain. Tull whispered softly to Phylomon, "If she's going to die, I wish she'd get it over with. I don't want to see her suffer."

Phylomon nodded, realized that the boy had already begun his mourning. Somewhere in the hills, a great horned owl called softly, and a small gravitational wind sighed through the trees. Scandal set a fire, began to cook dinner.

"What is she waiting for?" Tull asked.

Phylomon began talking softly, telling Tull about a shipwreck he'd been in three hundred years before, how he'd washed ashore with a dozen women who had lain like this, unconscious for hours, yet all of them lived.

Wisteria breathed deeper, as if struggling for breath, and suddenly she moaned, "Daddy? Daddy? Butterflies."

Phylomon bent over her and whispered, "Wisteria, you can go and catch the butterflies now."

Suddenly she stopped breathing, stopped moving at all, as if she merely held her breath. Phylomon laid her head back gently. "She's gone," he said.

"Wait!" Tull cried, "Wait! What did you do to her?"

"People who are ravaged by guilt often seek permission before they die," Phylomon said. "I gave her permission."

Phylomon had seen the Pwi grieve for their dead a thousand times, thought he knew how it should go. *Now comes the screaming, now comes the denial, now he will lie down and die.* It had always seemed so natural to him: the Pwi loved so deeply that their lives were defined by that single relationship. And when a husband or wife died, the mate sat and waited, refusing to eat or drink, until the two were reunited in death.

Up on the hill, Ayuvah began the crying first, throwing his arms over his eyes as he wailed in grief.

But Tull only stood, his hands clasped in front of him, blinking. "What's to be done about it?" he said.

"What's to be done about what?" Phylomon asked.

"Death," Tull answered. He stepped forward and grabbed Wisteria's shoulders, began to lift her gently, but then he dropped her again and pulled his hands back. His hands were covered with clotted black blood, and Phylomon realized the girl must have been raked across the back by a large timber. Tull lifted her partway, and Phylomon saw that she was impaled upon a broken board. An inch-wide hole showed in her left lung. The girl's eyes were turning white.

Tull picked up his wife, ripping her free from the wreckage of the wagon, and began stumbling with her, carrying her uphill.

Scandal rushed downhill, tried to help Tull carry her, but Tull shrugged away from him. Scandal came to Phylomon. "What do we do for him?"

After a thousand years of watching others deal with grief, Phylomon knew there was nothing that could be done. You can never really take it away, and you cannot lessen it. "Put your arms around him, help him hold it in," Phylomon said.

Tull and Scandal walked uphill, and Phylomon went to work. There was nothing left of the wagon, precious little left of the provisions. Phylomon found a broken ax, began chopping up the wagon for use in the funeral pyre.

He watched Tull from time to time. The young Tcho-Pwi showed no sign of grief aside from slight spasms in the muscles of his shoulders. Instead, he sat on a lichen-covered rock and held his dead wife, stroking the girl's hair, looking into her face.

Phylomon thought about the girl. She'd looked so happy, so at peace as she asked if the child were dead. Why could she not take her guilt with her?

Ayuvah came to Phylomon when he was halfway finished with the wood. "In our village, the Pwi give the dead to the sea. Fires are only for humans. I let you burn Little Chaa only because we were so far from the ocean," he said. "We should take her down to the river."

"All right," Phylomon said. "We'll take her to the river. We need the water to make camp anyway."

That evening, Born-in-Snow took off south, his part of the journey finished. Scandal made up a bundle of his best spices, slight payment for a brother and two mammoths, and the Hukm carried away his prize.

Phylomon and Scandal made two trips back to the wagon and got a few provisions, and they set a camp by the river. Tull sat by the river's edge and held Wisteria's body until sundown, and then Ayuvah lit two torches and set them by the water. In a short ceremony, they dressed her in a necklace made of autumn leaves, folded her arms across her chest. When Ayuvah was ready to put her in the water, Tull clung to Wisteria's body.

"Let me hold her for a while longer," he said.

"She's already stiff," Ayuvah answered. "She'll begin to smell soon. You don't want to remember her like that. Here . . ." He cut a swathe of her hair with his knife and set it in Tull's hands. Tull thanked him softly, and then Ayuvah carried her rigid body into the shallows and lay her face up in the water, and pushed her out into the river, where she swirled away into the darkness.

Tull sat on the grass by the shore, wrapped his arms around his knees, and held the lock of hair, stroking it softly.

Scandal fixed a meager dinner of soup and pan bread with honey, and the men sat around a small fire and ate. Scandal took some food to Tull, but the Tcho-Pwi just waved it away.

Phylomon had seen many Pwi follow their loved ones to the House of Dust. Usually, they starved themselves, but sometimes they hurried the process. He remembered an old shaman who built a bonfire of his house, a woman who ate Death Angel mushrooms. For Tull it would be so easy to walk into the river, follow Wisteria's body toward Denai until one of the few young serpents left in the river grabbed him.

"What do you think will happen to him?" Ayuvah asked Phylomon, nodding toward Tull, who was a mere forty feet off.

"I don't know how to read him," Phylomon answered.

"If he were human, I'd say he wasn't grieving much. But I know better."

Ayuvah shook his head. "He felt the love that enslaves for her. Maybe he will choose to die now."

"Yet they were not married long," Phylomon countered.

"He loved her for many years before they married," Ayuvah said, and then he shouted, "It is not right for him to go to the House of Dust for a human whore! Her belly was filled with another man's child! He should grieve instead for the serpents she killed. He should grieve for the people who will die!"

"Here now," Scandal countered, "Hold your bitterness, boy. She wasn't a whore. Why I tried my best to get her in bed, but she'd have none of it."

Tull looked back over his shoulder at them, but then he turned back toward the water.

"I have a sister who has loved him for years!" Ayuvah shouted. "He should give his life to Fava instead of throwing it away!"

Scandal fixed a plate full of food, took it to Tull. Tull waved it away, and Scandal walked back to the fire. "He won't eat!" Scandal said.

"Wait until morning," Ayuvah answered, "And we will force water down his throat."

When Phylomon was young, he'd met a Pwi once, an old woman who had outlived three husbands. News of this had surprised him so much, that he had asked her bluntly why she did not go down to the House of Dust with one of them. Her reply had always stayed with him. "One does not choose to go down to the House of Dust," she had said. "I loved each of my husbands truly, and my grief tightened the belly. I could not eat after my sweet husbands died, but my daughter forced water down me, and after many days, my stomach loosened, and I was able to eat. Also, there were many good men in the village, and they came and asked me to marry them." Phylomon thought on how Ayuvah was working to keep Tull alive: Give him reason to hate the dead, promise the love of a living woman, force water down him until his grief passes. Phylomon laughed, "You are a wise man, Ayuvah."

Ayuvah looked up at Phylomon, and smiled weakly. "Not wise enough it seems."

"Does your sister really love him?" Phylomon asked in Pwi.

"She spoke of it many times," Ayuvah admitted.

"What does that have to do with anything?" Scandal asked. "We've failed! Our serpents are dead, and in case you haven't looked in the water recently, the run is over. We won't find another serpent, much less another dozen. And I've spent a thousand silver eagles on this venture. What a waste!"

"There is always next year," Tull said from beside the river.

"You and a hundred men couldn't drag me back over these mountains again," Scandal said. "You saw that army moving up into Gold River Pass, and the army on the other side of the mountains. Any fool can see that by this time next year, these mountains will belong to Craal."

Phylomon nodded his head. "By this time next summer, everything from here to the White Mountains will belong to Craal."

"We can't wait a year," Ayuvah said. "My father foresaw that the dinosaurs would swim from Hotland this summer. We must capture serpents on this trip!"

Scandal sat back, grunted.

"We have another alternative," Phylomon said. "I know where there are serpents, if you are man enough to get them. You call yourselves Egg Raiders . . ."

"That's different!" Scandal said. "Ayaah, we can raid a dinosaur's nest . . . but you are talking about serpents! You can't sail a ship within twenty miles of a serpent hatch. Not the way the great mothers guard their eggs!"

"Yet we know where the serpents hatch here in the north," Phylomon answered. "In the rocks near Bashevgo."

"Where we can't get to them," Scandal added.

Ayuvah looked up, and there was desperation in his eyes. The pirates of Bashevgo often sent slave parties into the Rough to capture Pwi. So near the straits, they would be easy targets for the slavers, and they would be hunted.

Scandal sat silently for a moment. "So, it's come to that, has it? Sail the Straits of Zerai. If the serpents don't take you, the slavers will . . ." He grunted and shook his head, wiped the beaded sweat from his brow. "I came here for a little adventure, a chance to see Craal. I didn't come here to die. Or to get a rat's eye view of some slave pen in Bashevgo. Here in Craal, we're protected by traveling papers. The pirates won't give a damn about papers."

"Then, we'll have to make sure the slavers don't see us," Phylomon answered.

Scandal gave him an evil look. "Why, I've heard the cliffs there are hundreds of feet tall—with no place to anchor. And the great mothers don't take kindly to trespassers. One three-hundred-foot serpent is enough to deal with. But we're talking dozens . . . hundreds."

"I did not say it would be easy," Phylomon said.

"Damn your thick blue hide, it's not possible!" Scandal countered. "We should go back to town. I don't care what it takes—we can all move inland, live in a fortress while the saurs infest the whole damned continent. Even if a few people die, it's better than risking this madness . . ."

Phylomon looked at Ayuvah. The Pwi sat, hunched, staring at the fire. Phylomon said, "I've seen serpent eggs before—down south, many years ago. They were sandy brown, the color of sandstone, and there were perhaps a dozen of them in a bunch. It was late in the fall, and each egg was six inches around. The mothers fasten them to the rocks, and during extreme low tides you can sometimes find them. At least, that is what the young children said who showed me the eggs. We could easily get a boat in Denai, steal a wagon and head for Bashevgo as planned. If we found even ten dozen eggs, we'd bring home a better catch than what we had. What do you think?" Phylomon asked Ayuvah.

"I think it has been too long since I have seen Sava and Etanai," Ayuvah said. "I want to go home." He sighed deeply. "You talk of this place we all fear—Bashevgo. I'm here in Craal, and it is bad enough. I will not go to the isles of the pirates if I do not have to."

"What else can we do?" Phylomon said.

"This journey has not gone well. I think we have failed, unless . . ." He hesitated, lost in meditation.

"What?" Phylomon asked, watching Ayuvah's face. A

sudden fear shook him, a feeling of unease. It was a sensation he seldom felt, and Phylomon had long ago learned not to ignore this sense. It was his skin speaking to him, and he got up and looked around quickly, searching for the source of danger.

Ayuvah said, "I will take a Spirit Walk, which I fear to do. I will look into our future, see if there is hope for this journey yet."

Phylomon looked at the Pwi and understood: There was the source of danger. "You are young. You have never taken a Spirit Walk before."

"Nevertheless," Ayuvah said, "My father is Spirit Walker for our village, and I am his oldest son. The burden falls to me."

"Once you take a Spirit Walk, you can never come home," Phylomon said, quoting an old Pwi proverb.

"Since we left the village, I have seen my little brother's body torn in half. And Tull, the brother whom I have always respected, has lost a wife. I have been into the kingdom of Craal, and I saw the face of the God of Terror. Even if I walk back to my own house now, can I ever hope to return home?"

Phylomon looked at the young Pwi, and saw a hardness in his eyes that had not been there a few short weeks before. It was true that the Spirit Walkers became old and shriveled, wizened, and emotionally devastated by what they saw. Yet Phylomon looked in Ayuvah's eyes and saw a Pwi who already understood what it meant to be a Spirit Walker. "How will you begin your journey?" Phylomon asked softly.

"There are many gates to the Land of Shapes. For a Spirit Walker, it does not matter which path he takes, as long as it brings him to the gate of death. My father always chose the path of starvation."

"I have heard that it is easiest," Phylomon admitted, "But it takes many days."

"I will take the gate of blood," Ayuvah said. "It is quickest."

Almost before Phylomon could warn him against it, Ayuvah unstrapped the knife from the sheath on his hip, and slashed both of his wrists. He held them up and watched the blood pump out in great bursts. "The gate of blood," Ayuvah said, and he got up and began pacing around the fire, dripping blood.

Phylomon growled in disgust, got up and walked over to Tull, who sat with his arms wrapped around his knees, looking off at the river in the torchlight. The river had swollen over the past three days from rains somewhere far upstream, and the dark water swirled quickly and almost silently. Scandal began cleaning up nervously. Phylomon sat and watched Tull, looked at Ayuvah. *I should watch them both for the night,* he thought, *make sure Ayuvah doesn't bleed himself to death and Tull doesn't jump into the river,* and he leaned his back against a tree and watched.

After several hours, the torches by the river burned down to the ground, and the campfire grew dim. Ayuvah walked in circles around the camp until he finally stumbled and fell to the ground.

Phylomon and Scandal bound his wrists. It was impossible to tell if he was on a Spirit Walk. He looked only as if he were sleeping, though his face was drained. After they bound him, Scandal finally excused himself and went to bed.

Woden rose. The clouds were thin feathery streaks, and the moon shone through dimly. A strong wind began to build and whip down the canyon, carrying a chill. As Phylomon's eyes grew tired, he rested them, and at last Tull spoke.

"She betrayed me," Tull said. "I don't know which hurts more, the fact that she is dead, or the fact that she betrayed me."

Phylomon searched his memory, wondering exactly what Tull meant by 'betrayed.' "She didn't betray your marriage," Phylomon said. "You married her shortly before we left, and if she was carrying Garamon's child, she must have been with him before . . . sometime before her marriage."

"I would have forgiven her of that," Tull said. "She must have known that I would have forgiven her of that."

"Ayaah," Phylomon said, "I think she knew. But she was an unforgiving woman. Perhaps she could not forgive herself. She loved you, I think, and she was shamed by her own deeds. Your forgiveness would have only hurt her more. I am sorry that she's dead. Often when a person dies, a grandmother or a sickly child, your friends will tell you,

'It is better this way,' that the sick are no longer in pain.
They try to disguise the fact that life sometimes feeds you a
bowl of dung. At least no one will tell you that it is better
this way."

"The hardest part of it," Tull said, "is knowing that I
can't ever touch her again." He stroked the lock of hair for a
moment. "Grief comes in waves, like the throbbing pain of a
toothache. I keep waiting for it to stop, but it doesn't stop,
and I don't know if I can fight it."

Phylomon looked at Tull's face. The young Tcho-Pwi
showed only sadness, yet his voice held a note of desperation. "Perhaps you should not fight it. Perhaps you should
just let it out, let it have its way."

"I want to die . . ." Tull said. "Fazahn, the God of
Grief, wants me to die. If I let him have his way . . . Phylomon, I cannot control my hands." He held up his hands,
and they shook violently. "I cannot express what I feel right
now, but I am afraid of what I might do. Will you tie my
hands for me?"

Phylomon shook his head. "You'll have to stop them
yourself."

Tull said no more, and Phylomon sat and watched him
for a long time. Two young raccoons wandered into camp
and smelled around, went straight for the food. Phylomon
got up and walked over to the supplies to chase the young
raccoons away. They shrieked and chittered and wandered
off grudgingly. They had rolled a jar of sausages out of its
sack, and Phylomon straightened the bag, then looked up at
the sky. It was glowing in the east. Dawn was almost here,
and he wondered . . . for he had been setting food out for
Tirilee every night, and tonight, for the first time, she had
not come to eat. It could only mean one of two things:
Either she was dead, or her Time of Devotion had come. He
got up and left the camp quickly.

Tull held his hands clasped in his lap and watched the water
flowing. Somewhere, down river, Wisteria's corpse was
drifting out to sea, bobbing and spinning on the water's surface. When he'd made love to her the first time, he had felt
Zhofwa's presence, felt the goddess take him, move him of

her own accord, felt the passion that burned within him. It
had opened a road that had always been closed to him before, had let him finally love someone, and now, he wished
to God that it had never happened. He clasped his hands,
holding his fingers tight, dismayed at the grief that shook
him, that tried to move him toward self-destruction. He'd
once heard a song sung by a sailor, a strange man with a
hunched back who bellowed out in a pain-filled voice:

> *Don't take the silver stairs*
> *it's a long hard climb.*
> *Stay here in the darkness*
> *until the end of time.*
> *On angel's wings*
> *the demons dine.*
> *If you escape Ruin's kingdom*
> *an empty heaven is all you'll ever find.*

"When you take your first Spirit Walk, Ayuvah, you must
not take it alone. The Land of Shapes has dangers of its
own." Ayuvah had heard these words often as a child, both
from his grandfather who was now dead and from Chaa, so
he was aware of the dangers. For hours, Ayuvah had felt
himself spinning, reeling across great open plains like a
straw at the heart of a tornado, unable to stop. He tried
clinging to the ground, calling out for help, cursing whatever Gods there be. For the first time in his life, Ayuvah felt
empty, free from emotion, and he wondered at it. It was not
until he breathed deeply and commanded the whirlwind to
stop that something happened: He opened his eyes and
found himself on the ground, lying flat on his back, with his
head tilted to the side. Although it was dark, everything was
vaguely luminous. The pine trees above him had feathery
tendrils of light—like tiny orange hairs—extending from
each needle. A rock beside him glowed soft and pink, the
color of sunrise. And Ayuvah saw grubs in the pine tree
above and worms burrowing in the dirt beside him, fiery
beings that glowed through the soil and through the bark of
the trees like torches. Only the sky was dark, a flat slate of

black without stars, without wind, dark and deep straight above, but lighted at the horizon.

Ayuvah tried to push himself up with his elbow, but found that he could not move. It was as if his arms and legs were disconnected from him. He found that he could not blink his eyes, move his neck, stir a finger.

For a while he struggled to move, then he thought back on the lessons his father had taught. "In the Land of Shapes," Chaa had said, "All things are Connected—earth and grass, trees and sky, life and death, past and future. In our world, we seldom see that we and our neighbors, our garden and our tomb, all form one part of a much greater thing. But in the Land of Shapes this truth is brought home. You cannot move in the Land of Shapes until you feel the Connection. And then you are drawn where you want to go, whether it be to home, or to a loved one—or a time, such as the moment of orgasm that gave you birth, or the last fluttering of your heart."

That seemed to be the crux of the problem. Ayuvah needed to be drawn to the future, not walk to it, so he breathed deeply and opened himself, willed himself to become one with the sky, with the ground, with the worms. He concentrated until his breath came in ragged gasps, until sweat poured from him, but he could not let it in. He looked at the pine tree above him, and wished he could Connect to it—wished he could experience life as the tree did for just one moment—except, he did not want to feel the worms gnawing at the heart of the tree. He imagined the pain that would cause, to be eaten by worms, and at the last moment he backed away.

Always before, when he was a child, he had been bad at this. Chaa would ask him to become a flying squirrel, yet Ayuvah feared even the controlled fall, the gut-wrenching landings. Even more, he feared the change he saw in old men as they took their Spirit Walks, the sadness and fatigue.

His father often told him, "Suppose a man takes a journey and falls in a river, and a little later on, he meets a woman and falls in love, and the next day, he meets a sabertooth and faces death. Without the journey, would the man be the same? If he did not move from his house, perhaps he would be dry, perhaps he would never find love or face the saber-tooth.

"But I tell you truly, in the Land of Shapes, you will see that willingly or not, every person is Connected to all of the events of his life by time—to the people he meets, to the incidents that happen to him, and he is *defined* by this. The man who has loved is vastly different from the man who cannot love. The man who lives in pain is not the same as the man who lives in comfort.

"The Spirit Walker, by traveling the twisted paths of these journeys, beholds the future. And by speaking at the proper time, he can change a man's journey. Sometimes he can change the future of all men." Yet to become Connected to another, Chaa lost himself, took on the evil kwea, the hidden pains of those around him.

Ayuvah concentrated on those he loved. He envisioned the smile in little Sava's eyes, the way she would spend long minutes mesmerized by the path an ant chose to walk across the floor.

Immediately, a cord of light seemed to burst from his navel, like a giant fiery string, and it shot high into the air and bent away toward Smilodon Bay, and a warm glowing sensation filled his belly. He felt Sava, sleeping in her room, untroubled by dreams. He knew he was Connected. He imagined Etanai, his wife, and pictured his arms around her. A second cord burst from his navel and he felt a warm sense of pleasure, for he knew she was there, humming softly at home as she set the morning fire. And so, one by one, he felt for his family—his father and mother, brothers and sisters, until he reached for Chaa's smallest son, Fatcha. And there, he felt only emptiness, and knew the child no longer existed.

The glowing cords snapped, and he lay alone once again, unable to move.

A great black crow swooped over the trees on stiff feathers, flapped twice as it landed on a pine tree with its luminous hairs. The crow was dark as night, and tiny purple fireflies swirled around it, blinking from time to time. "You will never be a Spirit Walker," the crow said, "for you cannot open yourself to the pain of others. That is the problem of having the dire wolf for your Animal Guide. You can inflict pain and death, but you do not take it willingly."

"Father," Ayuvah tried to answer, but he could not speak. The crow eyed him for a moment, then looked at the pine, at the grubs glowing within. It turned its head to the side, then slashed out and grabbed a grub that was crawling near the surface, swallowed it down.

"Why do you fear pain?" the crow asked. "You are tied to it, whether you recognize it or not. If you could open yourself to it, you would become a Spirit Walker. You could travel home tonight, and see how your brothers and sisters have wept for tiny Fatcha and the brave men who died yesterday."

Ayuvah wanted to shout out, "Who is dead? How did they die?" But his tongue would not move. Instead, the crow hopped from its branch, flapped its wings once, and landed on his chest. It tilted one black eye toward him, and stood with its beak open, its purple tongue showing, breathing in a quick pant, the small feathers at its throat fluffed. As Ayuvah watched, he looked into the black of the crow's eye, and instead of his own reflection, he saw carnosaurs swimming in the ocean—a small herd of sixty, climbing a bank near the forests of the south. They were a small breed of carnosaur—no more than six feet in height, twelve in length—with webbed feet for swimming and running in mud. Ayuvah had seen them on egg raids—they hid in the brush at the edges of lakes and rivers, and in packs of forty or a hundred they hunted the duckbill dinosaurs that fed on the water plants in the shallows. The Pwi called the small carnosaurs duck-eaters and feared them worse than the tyrannosaur, for although the tyrannosaur was much larger, it was a solitary hunter.

Ayuvah watched the duck-eaters forage in the forests until they came on a river, and then they traveled along its bank, looking for prey. They must have traveled for days, because their hunger was ravenous. At last they came to the river's mouth at Smilodon Bay, and found Fatcha and four other children picking the last of the sweet blackberries at the water's edge. The duck-eaters grabbed the children up, and then broke down a fence to get at a herd of swine. The men of the village came with their spears and their kutows and fought the beasts, and several men and duck-eaters died in the battle before the duck-eaters ran back upstream.

Ayuvah wanted to recoil from the sight, but he could not move, could not close his eyes by will. He did not want to believe that this was real. "Has this happened? Or is this a vision of the future," he wanted to ask, and as if responding to his thoughts, the crow said, "This has already happened."

The crow waddled forward, until it stood on Ayuvah's chin. "Now, look closely into my eye, my son, for I am sending you to your death, and I want you to go calmly, like a warrior." The crow's voice faltered, and its beak moved without speaking for a moment. The purple fireflies that buzzed around it faded to a mellow gold. "You will go to Bashevgo with the others, and there you must die . . ."

It was evening, and Phylomon had suddenly left camp a dozen hours earlier. Tull's belly was knotted with pain, and when Scandal tried to pour water down his throat, Tull accepted it, but only a bit, for even drinking water pained him. Ayuvah had awakened shortly after dawn, shouting incoherently, and when Scandal finally got some food in his belly, Ayuvah sat up, but would not speak of what he had seen. He came and sat beside Tull and wrapped his wrists in fresh bandages.

"Did you walk the paths of the future?" Tull asked.

Ayuvah considered a moment. *"Tcho,"* he said. "I will never be good at it."

Tull looked at Ayuvah. It was obvious that he was pained, and Tull wanted to say something to comfort him. "Someday," he said.

"Perhaps," Ayuvah agreed.

Near sundown, a gentle breeze lifted—a warm breeze blowing from the plains down the channel of the river and out to sea. Tull smelled her before he heard her—a gentle scent like mown hay and gardenia, both earthy and erotic. His organ swelled at the scent, and for the first time in more than a day, he stood up.

Phylomon's head bobbed between the pines by the water's edge, and as he drew near, Tull saw Tirilee walking beside him. Tirilee watched Tull from the distance, and she walked as if moved by a dream, gracefully, almost floating on the ground. She wore Phylomon's gray robe, and it was

open at the front, so that Tull could see that she was naked
but for the robe. The blue man was bent with fatigue and his
brow was furrowed. He held Tirilee's wrist loosely, and Tull
could see the pain and desire that her touch aroused in him,
because the blue man was not immune to her.

Phylomon came and stood before Tull. "Take him," he
told the Dryad.

Tirilee watched Tull with profound desire in her eyes, as
if begging permission. Her robe was open, showing the
curve of her white breasts, the silver V of hair between her
long pale legs. Tull did not say anything, gave her no sign,
and she opened her mouth to sing, as if no answer were the
same as yes, and when her breath hit him, it raised the hair
on his head, and he would have sworn that it scorched him
like a burning wind off the desert. Her voice rose like the
song of a warbler, each note round and beautiful, and her
voice was husky with desire, and this surprised him, for
Tirilee's voice had always been high and clear, like the voice
of a flute. She watched his eyes as she sang:

> *Come with me, there's nothing to go home to.*
> *You need light, and fire is the answer.*
> *In my bed, I the sun is ever-rising,*
> *Come and taste the daybreak upon my forest floor.*

Although night approached, the air around Tirilee
seemed to glow, and Tull realized that the aphrodisiacs that
blew off her must have affected his sight, for everything
seemed more clearly defined, more lucid. Yet for a moment,
his vision clouded, and instead of Tirilee, he seemed to see
Wisteria before him, beckoning him. He blinked, and saw
only Tirilee. He wanted to beg her to leave, for he still loved
Wisteria, still mourned for her, but the aphrodisiac wind
seemed to lock his jaw, make the tongue swell in his throat.
To speak would have required more effort than he could
muster. Phylomon leaned against a tree, and Tull saw how
much the effort cost him, for the aphrodisiacs were strong.
Ayuvah stared at Tull in dismay; and Scandal's face twisted
in envy, yet he stood as if rooted by the fire. Tirilee sang,

> *Take my hand, before the world grows colder.*
> *You need warmth, and fire is the answer.*
> *If you ache, with a kiss I can heal you*
> *or lift you like a cinder, that is fire-borne.*

She shrugged her shoulders, and Phylomon's gray robe slipped from her, and Tull saw how her breasts had filled, how her hips had curved. It was as if in the last few weeks she had evolved into a new creature, a being of such unearthly beauty that he had never seen the like. She was still singing, but the potent aphrodisiacs muddled his thoughts and he could not make out the words, yet her desire was imprinted on his heart. He'd never looked into her green eyes and really seen how deep those pools were. He'd never noticed how each silver hair on her head, when stirred by the wind, took on a life of its own. Her small strong nose and her breastbone were so exquisitely chiseled that if he were a sculptor, he could spend his life trying to capture their beauty, and in the end he would fail.

The desire he'd felt for Wisteria, the grief he felt at her loss, sloughed off as if they were old clothing, and he felt as if he were leaving them behind. She sang, but he could not hear her, he was so entranced by her beauty.

A tear was streaming down her cheek, she ached with such desire, and Tull reached up and touched it. *Touch a Dryad, and she will destroy you,* he thought. He touched the tear to his lips, let it burn him. He felt a cold chill as the goddess Zhofwa blew her kisses on him.

Tirilee took his hand and began to lead, and he followed, knowing that this was his destiny, that whatever else happened in life, giving himself to her now was at once the greatest gift he could give her and the greatest joy he would ever receive. She led him through the dark pines, under the night, up into the hills and into the moonlight. He felt no fatigue, no pain, only a warm dizzy sense of floating.

They climbed through an oat field whited by moonlight, and with each step they left dark shadows in the grass, until he saw the aspen trees, glowing like a silver waterfall in the moonlight, their dry leaves whispering like the voice of water.

He carried her then, the frail Dryad, and his skin

touched the sleek warmth of her and he seemed to come alive, as if he were suddenly born to the sensation of touch. When they reached the aspens, he followed the path into their heart until he reached the bower of leaves. Tirilee stroked his chest and arms.

He stopped, wanting only her touch, wanting only the warmth of her flesh against him forever. "Fire is the answer," she said, and she placed her slender arms around his chest and hugged. Her powerful muscles rippled beneath the flesh. His skin burned with the desire for her touch.

"I will always love you. I will never leave you," she said. She wiped the sweat from her own forehead onto his cheeks, burning him. For a moment, he held back, thinking of Wisteria, but Tirilee kissed his lips, and the blindness took him. When he had first loved Wisteria, he felt the goddess blow her kisses through the open window. But with Tirilee, his body wrenched as the goddess entered him, never to leave . . .

Tull woke to the smell of woodsmoke. He lay for several moments with his eyes closed, savoring the aphrodisiac perfume of Tirilee's body that still hung in the air. He felt warm and wrung out from making love too much, yet he found that he still desired Tirilee, ached for the touch of her hand, craved another of her burning kisses. He reached over to touch Tirilee and found that she was gone. He lay with his eyes closed and imagined that she must be cooking. He thought about how he would need to build them a house, need to hunt for moose or cave bear before winter set in, and the thought made him smile. Holed up for the winter in a cabin with Tirilee. Holed up for all winters to come. Although the enchantments of the Dryads often entrapped the unwary Pwi, Tull could imagine no sweeter prison.

He sat up and looked out through the entrance way of this . . . nest . . . to see if Tirilee was naked. But Tirilee was not there: only Scandal, bending over a small fire, and he was fat, not too seductive, and fully dressed. Tull's breech cloth lay on the leaves beside him. He got up and put it on.

He went out and stretched in the sunlight. Scandal had

set the fire, and Ayuvah and Phylomon were nearby, picking up twigs.

"Where's Tirilee?" Tull asked.

"Oh, uh, her," Scandal said in a bewildered tone. "She's gone."

Tull just watched Scandal, his mouth hanging open in disbelief.

"He's telling the truth," Phylomon said. "She left several hours ago. She won't be back."

"I don't understand," Tull said. "What did you do to her?"

"We did nothing," Phylomon answered. "It was her choice. She said she'd been kept in a cage most of her life. Didn't like it. So she didn't feel up to taking any slaves today."

"I . . . uh, I . . ." Tull said, shaking his head from side to side.

"Her Time of Devotion has come," Phylomon said. "Her love has turned to the trees. What happened last night . . . means almost nothing to her now. In the end, I think she wanted you, wanted you to stay with her. She knows that you would have. But it would have been cruel to you, and Tirilee was never cruel."

Tull stared at him dumbfounded. He could not quite grasp that something as magnificent as the night they had spent together was over. "Which way did she go?" Tull asked, and it seemed that he choked the words out. His throat felt very dry.

"You wouldn't be able to find her, no matter how hard you try. She will go in search of aspens somewhere, and she will find herself a grove. You could search for her tracks, but she will keep herself hidden from you." Tull looked around nervously, searching the treeline at the end of the field below him, trying to look all directions at once. "Try not to grieve for her," Phylomon said. "You don't have to grieve for her. She's still alive, and in her womb she carries your progeny, and she will give birth from time to time. Think back on her with joy, but don't waste your life searching for her."

"He's right, my brother whom I love," Ayuvah said. "She came to free you. Now you can come with us."

"Where?" Tull said.

"To Denai, first off, to get a boat," Scandal said. "Then to Bashevgo. We thought we might try our luck hunting for eggs at the Straits of Zerai."

Tull laughed in resignation, a laugh that was half-pain. A tear came to his eye. Tull felt down inside him—the pain for his loss of Wisteria was there, and a small pain for the loss of Tirilee, but he also felt the kwea of the night before, the resonance of a moment sweeter than any he'd ever imagined. Part of him would always love her, always want her. Yet he was free.

He looked at his hands. They were not shaking. He made a fist. "Let's go then," he said before he had a chance to change his mind.

Chapter 12
Night Watch

The men loaded their packs and prepared to leave. Tull didn't know which way to go. Scandal would head for Denai, a city known among the Pwi as "the Slave Gate," for the pirates of Bashevgo sold their captives to brokers in Denai who carried them away forever to the heart of Craal. Phylomon and Ayuvah prepared for the long trip to the mainland south of Bashevgo, on the far side of the Straits of Zerai. The two men would have to sneak through the outskirts of Denai to steal a wagon, but most of their trip would be over the mountains.

"We'll steal a wagon and team and meet you in ten days at Castle Rock," Phylomon told Scandal. "When you see the first big island to the north, you'll know that you're entering the straits. Castle Rock is to the south. The bay is shallow, so come in at high tide. You should get there a week before us. Use your time to hunt for eggs along shore at low tides. The ones I saw in South Bay were sandy brown, six inches across. Luck to you."

"Ayaah, Ayaah," Scandal said, plainly worried. He took

a wine bottle from his pack, drank several gulps. "I don't
know if I can manage the boat. We'll need a thirty-footer,
and one man at the sails . . ."

"Can barely manage," Phylomon said. He stood for a
moment. "I cannot go with you. I've been at war with Craal
for far too long. As for the Pwi, you cannot expect them to
go into that evil city. If Tull had Wisteria with him, then
perhaps . . . But I will not ask them to go."

"Perhaps I could buy a slave?"

"The papers I forged will gain you entrance to Denai,"
Phylomon said. "But I fear the bank accounts of Lord
Tantos are more secure. You can buy slaves only if you
represent one of the seven houses. It would be too dangerous
to buy a slave, and you should not try to steal a slave. They
are far more afraid of the wrath of the Blade Kin than of
captivity."

Scandal looked at Tull and Ayuvah, shook the wine bottle at them. "How about it boys? A chance to see Bashevgo
at the height of its decadence? Give them another hundred
years, and they won't have anyone left in the Rough to take
slave. The inns will go downhill then."

Tull's mouth was dry. Truly, Phylomon did not need
help stealing a wagon on the outskirts of Denai, but Scandal
would need help with the boat. He was nothing but a fat old
innkeeper, a weak human.

"I'll come with you," Tull said, rolling a bear hide and
tucking it in his pack.

"You aren't afraid?" Phylomon asked. "The place has
great kwea for the Pwi."

"I'm going because I am afraid," Tull said.

Phylomon said, "I told you earlier that men always seek
danger for entertainment. Even you seek the face of the God
of Terror. Do me a favor, when you see him, spit in his eye."

Ayuvah sat on a log, despondent. Tull hugged him and
said, "You'll be all right."

Ayuvah looked up, his orange hair blowing in the wind,
his pale blue eyes squinting. "Those who enter Craal find
themselves in bondage to Adjonai, and he controls their
lives forever after. They can never free themselves, and happiness eludes them, like the magic plums in Carza's orchard
that always bob just out of reach."

"Some escape. You have seen the Okanjara. They escaped."

"But they are not happy," Ayuvah countered. "Do you not see how Adjonai draws you toward your destruction? I would not go to Denai for any reward. Let Scandal go alone! He can sail to Castle Rock by himself!"

"What if he wrecks the boat on the rocks when the gravitational winds blow wild?" Tull said. "We'd have no one then who could go into the city and steal a boat. He needs my strength."

"That only sounds like a reason," Ayuvah countered. "Do you not see how step by step we have failed on this journey? Little Chaa is dead, Wisteria is dead, and now you walk into Denai. You think you go to Denai to confront your fear, but it is the voice of Adjonai whispering to you. He draws you to your destruction."

"Your father would not have sent me here if that were true," Tull said.

"My father sent Little Chaa to die. You do not know his plans."

Tull considered a moment. "His plans will work out for good in the end."

"But perhaps not for your good, or mine," Ayuvah said.

Tull put his arm around Ayuvah. "I keep feeling that if I turn a corner or look into the shadows, I will see Wisteria there. It is as if her spirit is close by. Love makes us that way, binds us close together. Even death cannot separate us. In a few weeks, we will be back safe in Smilodon Bay. You will sit with Etanai and Sava, and you will be happy. Don't be afraid."

Without the heavy wagon, it was an easy walk to Denai. Scandal carried his wine and drank as he went. They followed the river down from the hills; the city spread before them. Close by lay myriad farms and orchards, stretching like a green carpet to the city and sea beyond. To the east, a great stone hill was painted bright colors, as if it were a building itself, and beneath lay Denai—a gleaming dusty conglomeration of board shacks stacked one against another, punctuated by green fairy castles of Benbow glass, all spires and minarets. There were a hundred thousand people below. A cloud of fine gray dust and smoke rose from the city, obscuring all detail, so that the city twinkled like cut glass under a veil of gauze.

Scandal pointed at the mountain with his wine bottle. "Ayaah, those castles look pretty, but up on Painted Mountain, that's where the money people live. Pirate Lords been living it up there for eight hundred years. And there"— Scandal pointed where the mountains met the sea, to a tiny yellow gleam like a diamond—"is where they keep their laser cannons."

Tull looked at the point, trying to make out the deadly artifacts.

"We'll never get a good look from up here," Scandal said, and they descended.

When they began passing farms, Tull and Scandal found several Thrall children playing on a small hill, sliding down a steep cliff on their bellies. The children laughed and whooped, just as children would in Smilodon Bay.

A mile down the road, the farms ended. Between two low hills ran a long black wall like the wall the Starfarers had built around Smilodon Bay. A small army was camped along the hills within the gates, perhaps two thousand men. At the gate a dozen strong young Neanderthal guards wore red capes and lacquered leather armor, black with silver trim. Each of the guards had a broadsword sheathed on one hip, a whip strapped to the other. Each wore a necklace with a white disk.

Scandal said quietly, "Blade Kin."

Tull looked up at a sign above the gate and stopped. It read, "Oppression Gate."

"Papers," one Blade Kin asked Scandal. Scandal produced his forged documents.

"Security seems heavy today," Scandal mused.

"Hukm raided a small fortress, so we've doubled the guard," the Blade Kin said, glancing at the papers. He touched the white disk on his neck. "Two in at Oppression Gate. Theron Scandal and one slave, minions of Lord Tantos."

"Entrance registered," the disk replied. "Greet the minions of the esteemed Lord Tantos, and bid them welcome to Denai."

They entered the city, passed through the makeshift barracks filled with Blade Kin warriors. They passed factories filled with women and children who sewed cloth all day, factories where young men melted ore into ingots of steel, factories where Thralls built wagon wheels. The ground was muddy, trampled by a thousand feet, and woodsmoke filled the air.

As they entered into the heart of that dark, grimy city, Tull found more Thrall Blade Kin in their black armor on nearly every street, watching every alley, stationed at every factory door. No one dared look on these warriors. Instead the Thralls averted their eyes, or gazed past them as if the Blade Kin did not exist.

Large gray clouds blew in from the ocean, and a gusty wind kicked up, then a cold rain came thundering down in heavy drops. Tull and Scandal rushed along the streets, stopping here and there for shelter until they rounded a corner and came on a street filled with cages.

The wind was cold, and a frigid rain swept in from the ocean, yet within the cages were Thralls, hundreds of women, four to a cage. Two humans in flashy garments paced the cages, gauging the wares. One man wore a white fur jacket and yellow leggings; the other wore a long coat made of purpled leather and a cap that looked like an owl swooping in for the kill. Scandal pointed at the men and laughed at their attire but soon stopped: Four Blade Kin opened a cage and shredded the clothes of a young girl, a rare blond Pwi, perhaps fourteen. She shouted for help and tried to ward the freezing rain off with her hands, but dared not strike the Blade Kin. Tull started to rush to her aid, but Scandal grabbed him by the jacket.

"No sense in getting yourself killed," Scandal said, pulling Tull back. "And get the anger out of your eyes! People see that, and you won't last a day in this town."

"But she'll freeze!" Tull said.

"Not tonight!" Scandal said. "She's property, and she's a pretty one. You wouldn't let a cow freeze. You don't let a slave freeze. See!"

One of the humans pulled the naked girl from the cage, turned her in circles to admire her. He put his hand to her crotch, and the girl cried out. Scandal said, "Ayaah, she'll be plenty warm tonight, I tell you. I've seen that look in men's eyes too often . . ." A Blade Kin ran to a pile of blankets in mid street and wrapped the girl. The human with the owl hat began counting coins into the hands of the seller.

Scandal stared at the slavers, at the naked girl. He took the wine bottle from his coat pocket, guzzled it down and tossed the bottle in the street. "I tell you, Tull," he said, "I've never needed a whore like I need one now. You've been playing the part of the bull so much, you probably haven't noticed how I've suffered."

Tull said, "We're supposed to steal us a boat tonight."

"Plenty of time for that tomorrow. Phylomon won't reach Castle Rock for ten days, and we can sail there in two. No, I've got a thousand platinum eagles in my pocket, and they say that tonight, I'm going to have me a shower, a decent meal, and some women. Not necessarily in that order. Come on!"

"Where are we going?" Tull asked.

"To find an inn I once heard of. It's a big place, one of the castles."

Tull wondered if he should try to force Scandal to act more reasonably, to argue or drag him to the docks and get a boat, but the Blade Kin were everywhere, and he dared not forget to act his part as a slave. In another five minutes, the rain let up, leaving the streets a veritable lake of mud.

Everywhere, shanties were filled with Thralls in gray rags, but as they came to a corner they saw what could have been an inn down the street, a great crystal structure.

"That's the one!" Scandal yelled, hurrying toward it.

To Tull, the building looked like some Slave Lord's castle, but as they got close he saw that it was indeed an inn. Although the wind was chill, circling the castle were two great walls made of thin Benbow glass, forming a cage, and within the cage were beasts from Hotland, small pteradons the size of eagles soared through giant fern trees, a forty-foot-long tyrannosaur stalked the jungle. Green hot pools bubbled from the ground, heating the giant terrarium. Outside the castle a human dressed in a coat made of yellow-and-black butterfly wings rang a bell and shouted over and over, "Come see the tyrannosaur battle ferocious giant sloths, tonight. The fight of the decade!"

Scandal looked at the tyrannosaur and laughed. "By God, boy, we can't leave before tonight, that is sure," and they went into the castle.

Within the castle was a great open courtyard where dozens of Thralls worked to clean the floors. There were gambling tables for cards and dice, a huge fighting arena with sands red with blood. Two Thralls with spears rode through the arena on a pair of triceratops and practiced their swings, but Tull saw no sign of guests.

Along one wall, water from the hot springs bubbled into a great tank, like a giant fish tank, and the water went far over Tull's head. At the top of the tank, in a landscape of giant ferns and rock, a pteradon preened itself by a small cave where a dinosaur could hide. Beside the water tank was a desk. Scandal went to the Thrall clerk. "I hear you breed your whores for beauty," Scandal said, "And the ugly ones are smothered as babes. I want one of them."

The clerk looked at Scandal, at his clothing. "We have the most beautiful whores in the world here at the Crystal Palace, Friend, but I don't think you can afford one."

"How much is she? Where is she?"

"Only three hundred silver eagles for the night!" the Thrall answered. Scandal pulled out his money bag, set it on the table. "And another hundred for a room," the Thrall went on.

"Fine, let me see her!" Scandal said. The Thrall hefted the bag suspiciously, looked in. With a mallet, he tapped the side of the water tank, and a woman came from the cave. She wore a black cotton bikini, tastefully decorated with diamond studs, and her raven dark hair fell down to her waist. She was tall and long of leg, and her muscles were exquisitely firm and strong, while her breasts were generous but not overpowering.

"As you can see, Friend," the Thrall said, "her body is sculpted in the finest tradition. She is strong as a Pwi, and can be as feisty as a bobcat or as playful and cuddly as a kitten. Do you want her?"

The woman dropped into the pool and gracefully swam to the desk, completely underwater. Freed from gravity, her breasts buoyed up, and the wet swimsuit accented her nipples. She struck a pose, one hand raised dramatically over her face, as if she were afraid of rejection.

"She's so beautiful!" Scandal said. "She's so beautiful! It was worth the trip just to see her." His eyes grew wide and a tear came to them. "Who could dare touch such a goddess? So holy? Who could have her?"

"You can have her for the night," the Thrall said. "She will cost, but she is well worth the price."

Scandal shook his head. "No, you don't understand," he said. "No one should ever touch her. No one should sully such a creature." He picked up his money bag, looked at it, and they went back to the muddy streets. Tull wondered if the wine had somehow affected Scandal's judgment. Scandal reached into his pack, pulled out a second bottle, and guzzled half of it on the spot.

A woman passed them in company with a beautiful girl. The woman wore a cape made of peacock feathers, and crystals dripped from her ears, dazzling in the sunlight. The daughter wore a dress the color of mother-of-pearl that flashed and reflected off the pools in the muddy street. Tull had never seen that color of white, not even on a snowy egret.

Scandal whistled. "There's a fat woman on a shopping frenzy. Did you ever see people who were so clean? You could boil me down to the bones in bathwater and I'd never come so clean."

Tull nodded. The humans walked over the muddy ground as if it were an art, never besmudging their slippers.

"Ayaah," Scandal said. "Throw them in with the hogs, and the mud wouldn't stick. Tull, I think I'm underdressed." He turned and began following the two women. "Have you noticed how fat the people around here are?" Scandal said loudly. Tull had not thought about it, but aside from the whore, all the humans they'd seen were on the heavy side. The fat woman turned to look at Scandal, and he shot her a leering smile and bowed. The women quickened their pace. Scandal hurried to follow.

"Don't let them see you laughing at them," Scandal said

to Tull. "It's illegal for a Thrall to laugh at a human. Why if they catch you, they'll nail you to the floor, stick a bellows up your butt, and pump on it until you shit backwards. Many a Thrall has lost a meal that way."

The women were fairly running now, and the lady in the peacock suit glanced over her shoulder at Scandal.

"Madam," Scandal called helpfully, "your dress is too tight—perhaps you should skin another duck!"

She turned on him then, "Friend, who are you?" she asked, straightening her hair, her jowls quivering.

"Scandal the Gourmet, world's finest holistic chef," Scandal said, bowing low.

"Hah! Scandal the Gourmand is more like it." She pulled her peacock robe tight around her. "If you were my slave, I'd have your tongue out in a minute."

"Ah, I perceive that you are a Dicton, and you use your superior vocabulary to shame me," Scandal said. "Ayaah, you got all the genes for brains and none for beauty. Why, if your face were a cloth in a toiletry, I wouldn't wipe my butt with it." The fat woman gasped. "Your daughter now, well, you'd better castrate your manservants and make sure your husband doesn't spend time with her alone."

The ladies gasped and ducked into the door of a shop that sold small silver and crystal bowls. Scandal leered at them through the window for a moment.

When they had walked away, Tull asked quietly, "Why did you do that? Those women were obviously rich—rich enough to buy both of us a thousand times over. You had better sober up before you get us in trouble."

Scandal gave Tull a sidelong look. "I'm not drunk. Don't you see? They're the enemy. They're Crawlies. All my life, I've been terrified of Craal. And here we get into Denai, and see factory after factory filled with Thralls, see thousands of Blade Kin, and all of them without the balls or the brains to kill their masters. And when we do see a human, they are just fat people dressed like peacocks and owls and butterflies. My God, I'm disgusted. Let *them* be afraid of *me* for once."

Scandal bought himself some new clothes, a red sequin jacket with black britches and a dazzling white shirt—until he was dressed as fancy as any other strutting lout they'd seen in town, and then they went back down to the docks to inns that were much more homey than the Crystal Palace.

In civilized towns, every inn had a balcony, and if the whores wore short enough dresses, the patrons could stand down on the street and glimpse half of what they were bargaining for, and if the women leaned over the balcony, the patron could view the rest. Scandal said, "When shopping for a whore, wait until they lean over the balcony. If you can climb up to the second story by hooking onto the girl's bra strap, you've found a good one."

It wasn't long until Scandal found one with enough breast to satisfy his appetites. She was a huge busty woman, and Scandal shouted up at her, "There's one! Definitely mammalian, definitely mammalian!"

The fat woman squealed with delight and said, "I'll show you a mammal!" She pulled out one huge breast and squeezed, and milk dribbled out of it.

Scandal laughed and ran beneath her, shouting *"Wonk, wonk!"* making pig noises as he pretended to try to catch the milk on his tongue.

A dozen orange-haired Thralls from a work crew were passing by, and they stopped and watched Scandal in horror. "He is the most disgusting human I've ever seen," one said, sticking out his tongue. "He acts like a Roughian."

Tull looked at them, mildly annoyed. At least one Thrall had guessed they were from the Rough. Tull spoke in Scandal's behalf. "He is my master, the kindest, most venerable man I've ever known!

"Why, you can search Craal and never find a man his equal. He treats every wench as if she were born of royal blood, and though a dozen seek him as a lover, he turns them away! Every male Thrall in his service—even the dimwit who can only peel potatoes in the kitchens and drool—he accepts them as if they were his sons. If the laws allowed, he would free us in a moment! Why, every night I pray that the gods let him live another hour, another day. I would lay down my life for him.

"Unfortunately, every few years he gets drunk and acts like this. But please, Friends, I beg you—think no ill of him. Your words—are so unjust."

The Thralls looked at Scandal with new respect. "For-

give our unkind words," one begged. "We meant no harm.
've never heard of so kindly a master."

Up on the balcony, the whore laughed in delight at Scandal's antics, and Scandal tried to climb a trellis to reach her,
but it snapped. She ran into her room and grabbed a leather
whip and threw one end over the balcony for Scandal to
climb. He grunted and sweated a moment, trying to pull his
bulk up, and yelled, "I'll be up shortly, My Sweet Mammal," and he trudged into the inn. He squinted in the
gloom. The place was old, and all the wood was dark with
age. A plaque over one table claimed it had been built six
centuries earlier. Scandal called to the innkeeper for his finest brew. The innkeeper brought it, and watched as Scandal
tasted a sip.

Scandal sat back and drank. "Why sir! What a marvelous taste! Who'd have thought one could perfect the art of
fermenting dog urine!"

The innkeeper shook his head at Scandal in disgust and
walked into the back room. A young Thrall boy crept into
the bar, a child of nine or ten with orange hair and a furrowed brow. He wore rags, yet the child looked familiar to
Tull, and Tull wondered if the boy were someone taken slave
from Smilodon Bay.

The boy said in a thick Pwi accent, avoiding long vowels, "Friend, see you outside. Friend buy girl whore?"

"Ayaah," Scandal drawled, furrowing his brow. "I plan
to buy me a whore."

"For the price ya will spend on her, Friend could sleep
with me. Friend could have me every . . ."

"You mean buy you from your master?" Scandal asked.
The boy nodded.

"No, I don't sleep with little boys," Scandal said.

"Please," the boy said, "try me. Me good slave. Make
Friend happy!" He reached down and petted the inside of
Scandal's thigh.

"No," Scandal said, shaking his head firmly. Scandal
slapped the boy's hand away.

The boy grabbed Scandal's coat. "Me master beat me
bad. Please buy me."

"No!" Scandal said, shoving the boy away.

The young boy ran from the inn, but as he stepped out, Blade Kin blocked his path, caught him by the arm.

"Was this child annoying you?" the man asked.

"No," Scandal said.

"I saw him touch you," the Blade Kin said. "Did h have your permission?"

Scandal shook his head in confusion. "Yes, I suppos Look, he's a nice kid. Let him go. He's got a rough mast who beats him. He just wanted me to buy him."

The Blade Kin frowned. "He *said* this?"

"Yes," Scandal said.

"He asked you to buy him, because his master beat him?"

"Well . . . yes," Scandal said.

The Blade Kin grabbed the child's shoulders, shook hin "This one will be taken for correction!" he said.

"Now wait a minute," Scandal said. The Blade Ki stopped dead, as if Scandal had just given him an order. "H didn't do anything wrong."

"He slandered his master. He touched you," the Blad Kin answered. "I must take him for correction."

"What will you do with him?" Scandal asked.

"His master will decide the punishment for slander."

"You're going to let someone who beats the boy an buggers him decide his fate? What is this boy worth?"

"Not much," the Blade Kin answered. "Ten platinum eagles."

"Then tell his master that I'm looking for scullery slaves. I'll pay him double that for the boy—a hundred si ver eagles. Cash."

"I will tell him," the Blade Kin answered. Scandal nod ded, and the Blade Kin held the boy firmly and dragged hin out into the street.

"You can't buy a slave," Tull whispered. "You'd neve get your registration papers!"

"I know," Scandal said, "But this man is hardly likely t beat the boy if he thinks I'll buy him." Scandal ordere dinner and the fat whore in his room, excused himself from Tull's company for the night.

Tull went out in the afternoon sun and began walking After an hour, he found the ghettos of the city down by th docks, where the more worthless Thralls, those who were retarded or insane or deformed but who still could provide a minimal amount of service, lived in packing crates without walls. It was cold outside, and Tull looked around and thought, *people will freeze here this winter.* He wandered among a crowd of hungry children who had despair in their faces, and realized that here in Denai he had found a city that was, in many ways, just like Smilodon Bay. There was wealth here, greater wealth than he had ever seen. And there was despair here, greater despair than he had ever seen.

Darkness fell, and with it came a rain so cold it fell as slush. The rich humans began turning out more often, as if they were creatures of the night who only stirred now that night was coming on. Up on Painted Mountain, the hill turned dark and black. As the humans descended from their homes in the hills, lines of Thralls walked before them carrying torches. Women glittering with gems paced between armed guards—beautiful Thrall warriors in crisp black uniforms whose eyes held the confident gleam that belongs only to elite killers. Tull retreated from the brightly lit inns where the humans gathered, sought out darker corners of town. In the heart of the ghettos, Tull found Thrall men who gambled around a ring in the rain, trying to toss coins into a single bottle. The first to hit the bottle collected all the coins on the ground. Tull wondered at this, for the Thralls could not own property, but he found that they were buying "favor." Any man with enough money could purchase a female who would then be owned by his master. It was a dirty way to take a lover, raise your children to be slaves. Among the gamblers, he saw avarice and poverty at their cruelest. The whole section of town smelled of stale urine and sweat, and was brimming with brutish Thralls, whores and gamblers, cutthroats and dreamers.

Tull walked the streets for hours in amazement, for Denai was a hellhole and he did not see the chains. Surely no sane person would stay here for a day, he reasoned, unless he were forced. But there were no humans with guns, no one but the Thralls themselves to keep them caged.

Tull thought about finding a place to sleep, but he did not know where a Thrall would sleep. Surely, one's owner

provided such things, yet Scandal had forgotten to get a
room for Tull.

In the dark, in the snow, Tull walked down the street in
the merchants' quarter and came on a clock shop. Tull had
only seen two clocks in his life, so he looked in the windows
staring at a small but intricate timepiece with a crystal on
the front that let one see the hundreds of tiny gears and
springs. Tull looked at it for a moment. It was a marvelous
thing—the kind of thing only a human could make, using
his clever little hands with thumbs and fingers that could
grip small objects.

The window displayed marvelous little gold clocks
shaped like daisies, with petals that unfolded to reveal the
clock face. He saw a clock made of wood, the kind you
would hang on a wall, with bushes and trees all carved from
a single slab of redwood. While he watched, two wooden
trees separated, and a saber-tooth jumped out from behind
the bushes to roar, and when it went back behind the
bushes, a mastodon stepped out from behind some other
bushes to trumpet, followed by a tyrant bird that leapt up
from some trees to flap its wings and croak. Tull laughed
aloud, for it would have easily taken him six months to
carve the wooden pieces for the forest, and he had no idea
how the creatures had made their sounds.

In the back of the shop, a Thrall worked under the light
of a lantern. At first, Tull assumed he was cleaning up, but
the Thrall had an instrument made of two pieces of curved
metal, hooked at the center with a hinge, and he was using
this instrument to manipulate tiny gears and springs as he
placed them onto a clock frame that was clamped to a
board. A Neanderthal was making clocks!

Tull stood watching the Thrall for a moment, and tears
streamed down his cheeks. He became aware that his own
big clumsy hands were on the window glass, and he held
them out and looked at them. *I could make a clock using
these hands,* Tull thought. *I could hold a human needle, and
use it to sew an arm or a shirt.*

Tull went into the shop, and the Thrall did not look up.
Tull picked up a small silver daisy clock. Folded, it was no
larger than his thumbnail, and it had a small ring so that it
could fit onto a chain. Tull pushed the button and watched

the golden petals unfold to reveal a silver face. He walked over to the Thrall, who was putting a tiny gear in place.

From a back room, a human opened a curtain, a tall thin man who at once reminded Tull of Phylomon, except that this man looked old. He looked at Tull, and then looked around the room. "Did you come in here alone?" he asked Tull. The Thrall clockmaker looked up at Tull in surprise. "What are you doing with that?" the human asked, snatching the clock from Tull's hands.

"I . . ." Tull started to say.

The human backed away from Tull, as if Tull were some rabid dog ready to bite, and headed for the door. The Thrall behind the counter whispered quietly, "Run! Run!" but Tull was too flustered to think.

When the human got to the door, he opened it and shouted, "Watch! Watch! Help!" and Tull ran. He rushed for the door and pushed the human. The old man staggered backward, crashed through a glass window. Tull hit the street running.

The Blade Kin were already there. He heard shouts in the dark, but the frigid rain slapped his eyes and the streets were dark and he could not see. Tull rushed blindly down the street until he saw a black shadow in front of him. The man reached to draw his broadsword, and Tull lunged past before the Blade Kin's sword could clear its sheath. Tull heard a snapping sound, and something slapped his ankle, ripping his leg from under him.

Tull sprawled forward and pain lanced through his left ankle. He sat up and found the end of the whip lashed around his legs. He tried to pull it off, but the whip had tiny barbs, like fishhooks, sewn into it, and dozens of these were embedded into his flesh. He succeeded only in breaking some of the barbs.

"You won't get it off so easily," the Blade Kin said. Tull looked up into the Blade Kin's face. An electric light glowed down the street, and the man's deadly eyes glittered in the reflected light. On his chest, the Blade Kin wore a badge with the emblem of a sword and a star above it. Six Blade Kin circled them with drawn swords, and Tull didn't dare move.

"What is your name? Who is your master?" someone asked.

"Pu Tchixila," Tull said, hoping Scandal would remember the bogus name used on the traveling papers. "My master is Theron Scandal. He's . . . he's whoring."

"Where?"

"At an inn, by the waterfront. I don't know the name, but I can take you there."

The Thrall who held the whip nodded to an inferior. "Xitah, notify Theron Scandal that we caught Pu Tchixila in a restricted area and that he hit a human. Tell Lord Scandal he can pick up what's left of his slave in the morning, at the docks."

Xitah sheathed his sword and strolled leisurely toward the inns at the bay. Tull almost asked the Blade Kin to hurry, but knew it was useless: the others watched Tull with morbid curiosity. Down the street a Blade Kin helped dust glass from the shop owner's shirt.

"You are lucky you did not hurt him," the one with the whip said. "Trespass. Theft. Assault. Nothing more."

"I stole nothing," Tull said. "I only picked up a clock to look at it."

"You had no business in a human shop," the Blade Kin said. "You must have been stealing."

"I . . . I went in, because I saw a Thrall making clocks. I've always wanted to use my hands like that . . . to make small things, the way humans do. I didn't know it was a restricted area."

Tull watched the Blade Kin's eyes and he saw them soften. "For saying that, you have saved your hands. We forgive the charge of theft."

The Blade Kin touched a white disk around his neck. "Thrall Pu Tchixila has been arrested on charges of trespass, assault on a human."

"Very well," a voice replied over the disk. "For trespass, twenty lashes. For assault, forty lashes and a night of Water Watching."

Tull's eyes widened, for he'd hoped to be taken before a mayor so he could plead his case. But the trial was over.

Someone slipped a noose around his neck and began choking him, and Tull grabbed at the noose. One Blade Kin kicked Tull in the ribs, "Troublemaker," he said loudly. "You get us all in trouble." Someone else kicked him from behind, and the blows landed from all sides. He tried to cover his face with his hands, but the man with the noose began dragging him through the wet mud. Every time Tull tried to cover his face or get up to walk, someone kicked him, so that he was reduced to holding the rope, pulling at it so that he did not strangle.

By the time they reached the docks, Tull's vision was fading, and he was grateful to reach the docks alive. He was so sore that he hoped only that the whipping would not take long. He was already numb to pain. The docks of Denai were not the seedy little docks found in Smilodon Bay. A dozen booms with block and tackle reared up above Tull—the kind used to pull boats from the water for dry dock. A large fishery nearby had a bright photoconverter outside that illuminated the rain, so that as Tull tried to catch his breath, he could see white slush fall from the sky toward him.

One Blade Kin put a spear to Tull's throat and knelt over him. For a moment he blocked out the light and slushy rain. Tull heard shackles rustling, and they stirred a dim memory, a primal fear from his childhood. One Blade Kin grabbed Tull's ankle, and although Tull could not see the man, Tull kicked the Neanderthal in the face. The guards crowded around and began kicking Tull so quickly that he could not cover his face fast enough. The Blade Kin worked quietly, and for a moment there was only silence and the darkness, and the pain of the blows. Chains rattled, and Tull felt the cold iron on his ankles, and suddenly he was hoisted into the air by his feet, and then the Thralls ripped his clothes from him and swung him out over the water, naked.

"Pu Tchixila," a Blade Kin pronounced. "You have been convicted of trespass and assault. You are sentenced to a night of Water Watching and sixty lashes."

The whipping started. Tull had believed he was numb to pain, but the first slice of the whip taught him otherwise. He cried out, and a man nearby said, "Please, be quiet! Don't call the serpents! Please!"

Tull saw a man only a few feet away swaying, suspended by his feet over the water, like a cocoon hanging from a

twig. Beyond him were two others: the boy who had tried to
sell himself to Scandal earlier in the day, and what looked to
be a man—until Tull saw that it was only a headless corpse,
draining its blood into the bay.

The lashes came quickly, and Tull felt his own blood run
into the water. He did not scream as the lashes fell. He
merely held his breath and watched the water beneath him.
It was whitecapped and rough, driven by the wind. Tull
heard serpent voices beneath him, the deep moaning they
made as they searched for prey by sonar and scent. The
water boiled. In the pale light cast by the fishery, Tull saw
great dorsal fins slice through the water. As his warm blood
dripped, a sixty-foot serpent rolled in a great circle, calling
its brothers, seeking the source of the blood.

It would not take long for them to find him. The whipping continued, and it seemed almost endless, although it
took only half an hour, and during that time, Tull did not
cry out, for he was too afraid to cry.

At the count of sixty lashes, all but two Blade Kin left.
They stood with spears in hand, watching Tull and the others, presumably to keep friends from setting the prisoners
free. Tull was left to watch the water. Twice he saw the
spines of young serpents rise as they thrashed above the
foamy waves. He listened to their deep voices and prayed
that the serpents would not find him.

In answer to his prayer, a serpent rose from the water
and bellowed, ripped the head from the man next to him.
The young Thrall, the only other survivor, dutifully bent
double and grabbed his shackles, shortening himself so that
he was not so close to the water.

With all his effort, Tull did the same, and beneath him
the serpents began to rise, making the water boil—for once
they found their prey, the entire school joined in, leaping
at the dead bodies, ripping off those parts that hung close to
the water.

Tull looked at the young Thrall and realized why the
young man had not told him how to escape the reach of the
serpents: The boy would have revealed his own position.
Tull watched the boy, bent double, clinging to his shackles.
Seeing the child earlier, he had felt an odd sense of recogni-
tion, and once again felt a kinship to the child. They were

together, silently living out their vigil. Tull wanted to comfort the boy, to give him some hope, but he was too wise to speak.

After a while, the serpents quit leaping from the water, and it became quiet. Tull knew better than to believe they were full, and he remembered the serpents in the river, lying on the bottom, silently watching their prey as they prepared to strike. Tull clung to his shackles, panting from the exertion, and knew that to take even a moment's rest was to die. Above him, his shackles were tied to a rope, and ten feet up the rope was a pole, the lower end of the boom on which he'd been swung out over the waters. Tull wondered if he could climb the rope and hang from the pole, but the guards were watching.

The cold rain kept coming, and after a while it turned to snow. The corpses hanging next to him cooled, and their blood dripped into the bay less frequently. Tull blessed the snow for freezing the blood on his own back, numbing the wounds, and at the same time cursed it, for he could not feel his feet.

The waves moved beneath him. In the back of his throat, Tull suddenly felt as if he tasted one of Tirilee's kisses, burning and sweet. He was filled with the desire to make love to her, and he laughed in pain, for it was an odd time to want her. They were in Seven Ogre Bay, and Tull could not help but think that Wisteria's body was in this bay, that as he watched the whitecaps he might see her float by. He hugged his legs, and remembered his love for her, and wished that she were close by.

After nearly two hours, the young child beside Tull let go of his shackles and fell toward the water. Tull prayed to the gods to spare the child. He could not see if the boy had fallen asleep, whether he was weakened by exhaustion, or whether he had merely hoped to rest. Yet he dangled above the waves for only a minute before a serpent leapt and took him.

Tull watched the jaws gape wide, the porcelain white teeth gleam in the light from the fishery, the red eyes flash in the darkness.

Kwea was building in him, Tull realized, a kwea of terror. He could feel his fear of the serpents growing, and bound with it was a fear of the shackles, a fear of the waves, a fear of Denai and the Blade Kin. It was a cold, paralyzing fear. The kind of fear that locks a man's legs together so that he cannot run, and in his mind, Tull dreamed of running, and the thought terrified him, for he almost feared what would happen if he tried to escape more than he feared staying.

Tull realized he had found Adjonai's dark kingdom of terror at last. He saw that Water Watching was meant to instill that kind of fear. The Blade Kin did not care if Tull lived or died. If he died, he served as an example to others. If he lived, he served even a greater example, for he would tell the tale of this night to a thousand other Thralls, and as they lived through the experience in their imaginations, the kwea of this night would pass to them.

As Tull saw this, he laughed. For truly, just as he'd been taught, the God of Terror was God of this land. The Slave Lords did not need guns or chains to hold the Thralls. Webs of fear held this nation together, webs thick enough to snare all who entered. The Blade Kin killed their brothers out of fear—fear of retribution if they refused their duty. Thieves and dreamers in high places let the cycle go on in fear—fear of poverty should they stop. "The great wheel of evil." That is what Adjonai had called it. Tull finally understood the words. Slowly, he became enraged. Always he'd blamed the humans for becoming Slave Lords, but now he saw that Denai was self-sufficient. Even if all the humans died, the city would remain. *Yet, there is no reason for Denai,* he realized. *If every Thrall were to walk away, no one could stop them.* Sure, the Blade Kin might kill a few, but not one in a hundred would die. The city, the entire nation, ran solely on an economy of terror.

Tull held his shackles and concentrated—concentrated on turning his fear into hatred. His desire to run turned into a desire to strike. The night was so cold, colder than anything he had ever known, for he was naked and it snowed.

Tull woke with a jerk in the morning. He'd been clinging to the shackles in his sleep, and one of the guards poked him with the butt of his spear, making him swing out over the water. Tull tried to grab his shackles, but the guard laughed and hit him hard with the butt of the spear. "You've blood on your face," the guard said. "Here, let's wash it off for you."

The guard went to the block and tackle, turned a handle, and lowered Tull a foot toward the water. Tull tried to reach for his ankles, but his muscles were too weak to let him bend up. Tull listened. Beneath the cry of the gulls in the bay, he could hear the long moaning of the serpents below him.

The guard watched his face, and Tull realized the man wanted to see his fear. Tull realized that if he screamed, if he pleaded, the Blade Kin might stop. But the very act of pleading would call the serpents below. Tull's heart beat within him, and he tried to remain calm. The guard lowered him another foot, and another, until the whitecaps brushed Tull's knuckles.

He twisted slowly in the wind, and every half minute he glimpsed the morbid sight of the three dead Thralls dangling from their chains. His back felt stiff and frozen, and his feet felt frozen to the shackles. He knew he was nearly dead.

He looked at the body of the dead boy, and felt a great sorrow. The child had looked so familiar. Tull's head dangled, and he went limp, and in the steel gray water he saw his own eyes, mad with rage, and realized where he had seen the child. The child too had had revolution in his eyes. Tull wondered how many times he'd seen his own eyes filled with rage as a child, staring at him from some stream or pitcher of water.

The air filled with the cries of gulls as they fed in the early morning. A thick fog blew in. At sunrise, some thirty Thralls gathered by the dock and watched Tull dangle. Several women had gathered, the mothers and wives of the dead, and they wailed and ripped at their hair. In the heavy fog, Tull could not see the buildings behind him, the boats farther on down the dock. All he could see was the mourners, the two guards on the dock holding them back with their spears.

As the morning wore on, the fog only thickened. An hour after sunrise, Scandal walked down the planks of the pier, clomping so heavily his feet sounded like the hooves of

a cow on the wood, and through the mist, three Blade Kin
trailed beside him. "Damn you, you will pay!" Scandal
shouted. "I send my favorite slave to buy me a clock, and
you've nearly killed him. I demand reimbursement!"

One of Tull's guards swung the boom in to the dock, and
lowered Tull to the ground. Tull recognized the Blade Kin
that Scandal spoke to. He wore a badge with a sword beneath a silver star. It was the sergeant who had taken him
prisoner. The other two were Thralls who had beaten him.

The guard unlocked the shackles. Tull kicked them
away. The Blade Kin looked at Tull's ankles, at the ugly
white scars. The Blade Kin said, "I'd think you would be
more accustomed to shackles by now."

Tull sat and rubbed his feet. He could not feel them, and
they were blue from cold. *Certainly,* he thought, *these feet
will die now. I've lost circulation to them. They will rot away,
and I shall die of gangrene.*

Scandal came up to Tull, looked at his back and bellowed, "By God, you've been thrashed, Boy! Oh, My Boy."
He bent low and whispered, "Stay down. Play like you're
hurt bad. I smell money! Oh, My Child! This boy is like a
son to me!" Scandal shouted at the Blade Kin. "How could
you do this? You will pay! I will have satisfaction."

A chill shook Tull. He wondered if anyone had a blanket
to loan. *If I am to die from these wounds,* he thought, *others
will die with me.* He looked at the two Blade Kin guards, at
the man who'd tried to murder him only an hour before.

Quietly, he struggled to rise. The guard who had un-
shackled him helped pull him up. Like all Blade Kin, the
Thrall wore a broadsword strapped to his right thigh. When
the guard had him up, Tull pretended to stagger. He
grabbed the Thrall's sword, pulled it free, and shoved the
blade into the guard's belly with all his might. The guard
looked at him in surprise, and Tull twisted the blade and
dragged the sword up, slitting his leather armor and gutting
the man the way he'd gut a fish.

It happened so quickly, that the Blade Kin speaking to
Scandal did not see.

Tull slammed into the back of a second Blade Kin and
rammed his sword through the man's kidneys. The Blade
Kin next to him stepped backward and pulled his sword,

Tull: after the watch

swinging it down like an ax. Tull dodged to the side, and
when the blade hit the dock, Tull rammed his sword into the
Thrall's throat, above his armor. The man grabbed Tull's
sword staggered back, pulling it from Tull's hands, and fell.

"Watch him! He's gone mad!" Scandal shouted,
backpedaling. As the sergeant reached up to the white com-
munication disk around his neck, Scandal slapped the Blade
Kin, sent him flying into the water. Tull glanced behind
him. His torturer was there. The last guard held a spear in
hand and advanced on Tull cautiously.

The sergeant thrashed in the water, his red cape floating
up. He pulled out his sword and dumped it, trying to lighten
his load, gurgled a curse, and then the water boiled. A serpent came up from beneath, carried the sergeant ten feet
into the air and splashed under with the Blade Kin in his
jaws.

"You're next," Tull said to the guard with the spear. He
watched the man, the way he had watched Ayuvah in practice.

The guard stood back on the balls of his feet, jabbed at
Tull with a couple of feints. "You talk big for a man who has
no weapons in his hand," the guard said. The man did not
have Ayuvah's speed. He was burly and clumsy, muscle-
bound. Tull dodged from his thrusts, always moving slower
than he was capable of. The guard was afraid of him. He
saw it in the Neanderthal's green eyes. He stepped back,
pretended to trip over the body of a dead man.

The guard lunged. Tull stepped to the side and spun,
grabbing the spear. Tull looked in the Blade Kin's eyes and
saw the Thrall's fear, and in that second, Tull jerked the
spear from his hands and with a shout he drove the butt end
into the Thrall's chest, through his lacquered leather armor.
The haft of the spear splintered.

The Thrall fell backward, gasping, impaled on the butt
of his own spear, and Tull looked at the man and knew he
would not die from the wound. Tull picked up a sword from
the dock, walked forward, and beheaded the Blade Kin.

Tull stood panting and looked at the Thralls who had
gathered to mourn their dead. They huddled in the cold,
and Tull saw only fear in their eyes. They were afraid of

Tull. They were afraid they would be punished because of what he'd done.

"You are miserable jackals," Tull told them. "You have cowered here in fear all your lives." Gesturing to the dead Blade Kin before him, he said, "Look how easy it is to free yourselves! I am a lone Pwi, and I killed four guards—all Neanderthals, all strong—not weak humans. And I will kill a slaver before this day is over.

"In our home, we go on egg raids in Hotland and hunt the great lizards with spears. Our small boys are greater men than you. Our ancestors dined on mammoth and rhino while humans fed on bugs and rats. Our ancestors tilled their gardens with hoes made of Smilodon's tooth, and they were kings of Earth. And someday, when we have mastered our fear of humans, we will be kings of Anee."

Tull looked toward town. The thick fog had hidden what he had done. Behind him, on the docks, one of the mourners shouted, "Watch! Help! Watch!"

Tull shivered from the chill air. He was still naked. He saw the Thrall who had shouted, a young man, the kind who would make a good warrior. The Thrall tried to scurry away, but several women held him. The women wanted Tull to kill the man, and Tull wondered why the women didn't kill the coward themselves. "Free yourselves," Tull told them. He reached down to one of the Blade Kin and pulled the fine red cape from the man's neck, wrapped it around him and fastened the clasp to his own throat, then picked up his own breech cloth from the dock, and fastened it with its silver clasps.

"Quickly," Scandal hissed, "let's steal a boat and run for it." Tull picked up a broadsword, wiped it on the leg of a dead Blade Kin. "Hurry!" Scandal said, "Run!"

Tull stood up. The sun was rising and above the fog one distant castle of green Benbow glass shone, as if it sat on a cloud. "Find a boat and leave," Tull said. "I won't run from Denai."

Scandal looked at Tull as if the Pwi had slapped his face. "What in the hell is going on here?" Scandal asked, but he backed away from Tull. "I'll meet you at Castle Rock in nine days," Scandal said questioningly as he ran down the docks, looking for a boat.

Tull headed for the city. His thoughts were muzzy, and he felt as if he were watching himself move. He'd once heard a man tell of a similar experience in a bar fight, that feeling of dissociation. He knew he might die for his actions, but rage burned in him, and he wanted to fight. He expected to be stopped, expected a fight, but saw no Blade Kin. He ducked into the fishery just as dozens of Blade Kin rushed down the road, heading for the dock. The Blade Kin shouted at the witnesses on the docks, and during the commotion Tull left the fishery through a back door, crossed the street, and sneaked through a huge warehouse full of lumber. In this way, he crept through the city until he reached the clockmaker's shop. It was closed, but through the window he could see the same Thrall making clocks. Behind the Thrall a door led to a back room where a cheery fire burned. The shopkeeper sat in a large chair, watching the fire reflectively, eating from a bowl of fruit.

Tull did not know how well the doors would be bolted. In Smilodon Bay, giant cave bears sometimes came in spring to eat table scraps from the garbage piles behind the houses. People on the outskirts of town boarded their winter doors with huge beams to keep the bears out. Tull imagined the door would be heavily barred, so he stepped back a pace and leapt through a window, knocking over a case of clocks. The Thrall working at the table fell from his chair, and the shopkeeper came running into the room to see what had happened.

Tull rushed the shopkeeper and grabbed the man by the throat. The old man tried to push Tull away and whimpered in fear. Tull held him easily with one hand.

"You shall be a sign for the Slave Lords of Craal," Tull said, and he dragged the shopkeeper to the front window. The old man struggled and tried to grab a display case, knocking his dainty clocks to the floor. The Thrall worker stood in a corner watching Tull, and the slave had a look in his eyes Tull had not seen before: rapture. Tull dragged the old man to the broken window. Shards of glass stuck upward, like glittering daggers, and Tull threw the old man down on the glass, impaling him. Tull walked through the room, picked up a tiny silver clock that opened like a flower, and stood, looking at it. He felt dizzy, happy, yet he was so weary he wanted to lie down.

"Brother," the slave hissed. "Run for your life!"

"I am not done here," Tull told the slave.

"You think you will prove your courage by staying," the slave whispered, "but you will only die. You are not a Thrall. You are a Pwi. I see it in your eyes. Many Thralls have the courage to die for a cause, but, brother, do you not see? They do not need only courage, they need hope! If they strike and die, what have they won? Nothing! But if they know they can strike and escape, then they will have hope!"

Out in the street, a single Blade Kin was looking at the window, looking at the dead shopkeeper, walking forward cautiously. He saw Tull in the window, took off shouting, "Blade Kin to me! Blade Kin to me!"

"I will leave, if you come with me," Tull answered the slave.

A curious light shone in the man's eyes, and he nodded. He ran to the back room and stuffed food into a sack. Tull grabbed the clockmaker's tools in their box, filled a cloth sack with dozens of watches. Tull wondered if he would ever master the use of the delicate instruments.

In a moment, the slave grabbed Tull's arm and ushered him away, to a back room. "I have clothes and food," the man said, and they rushed out a back door and into an alley.

The air smelled of smoke, and though it was still foggy, a bright red light glowed in the sky.

"The shipyards are burning," the slave said in awe.

Tull looked at the sky and laughed. *Bless you, Scandal,* he thought. The two men wormed their way through the ghettos of Denai for an hour, through warehouses, over roofs. The slave told Tull that his name was Nai, the Pwi word for *clever,* and he lived up to his name, for they avoided the Blade Kin who were rushing everywhere. "You picked a bad time to come here," Nai told him. "Ten thousand extra guards have come to watch the city in the last week. The Lords of Craal talk of war with Bashevgo, and Hukm attacked one of our fortresses a few weeks ago."

"Why would Craal war with Bashevgo?" Tull asked.

"The Pirate Lords purchased many supplies—wheat and cloth, yet they have sold us no slaves for a year," Nai said.

"And last summer, they began attacking Craal ships. The Pirate Lords are crazy. They could never hope to defeat the lords of Craal. Next summer, Craal will move armies into the Rough and destroy the Hukm, to keep the wilderness from falling into the hands of the Pirate Lords."

Tull listened to this bit of news with interest. The streets seemed to be boiling with Blade Kin in their black armor and red capes. Smoke rolled over the city from the burning ships at dockside. While the fog was still heavy, they jumped a Blade Kin outside a human home. Nai beat the man to death and dragged him behind a thick hedge in a garden. The dead Blade Kin wore the badge of a captain, with five stars over the top of a sword.

"This fedda is most trusted," Nai said. "He is authorized to go anywhere in Craal, even into the Rough. Put on his clothing, and you can walk out of this city a free man. There must be twenty captains of his rank here in the city. If you are lucky, people will just think that you are another."

"Won't you come with me?" Tull asked.

"If we both leave," the slave said, "the Blade Kin will kill an innocent man and claim that they killed you. In my people, the hope will die, for they will see that they cannot escape the Blade Kin. I must stay behind to be your witness. I will tell them that a Thrall who killed a human went free."

"Not just a human," Tull said. "I killed four Blade Kin." The slave chuckled softly, and Tull put on the Blade Kin's uniform, gasped as the leather touched his ragged back. Behind them, on the far side of the city, the fog was lifting, and Tull could see that more than just the boatyard was on fire—the flames had spread to the warehouse district. Unfortunately, the morning wind was blowing down the mountains and out to sea. The flames would not engulf the city. Tull pulled his hair down to cover his ears, hugged Nai around the shoulders.

"Someday, we will all walk away from here free," Nai said, pushing the bag of food into Tull's hands.

"We will walk away," Tull said, and the hate burned in him so badly that he added, "but first we will destroy Craal." He laughed at his own audacity.

Tull walked openly from the city of Denai toward the Rough, past three guardhouses, each packed with Blade

Kin, past an army of five thousand that guarded the east gate of the city. If any man thought to question him, no one dared, for he was their superior in rank, and seldom had anyone ever seen a Blade Kin walk the streets of Denai with so much rage burning in his eyes.

Chapter 13
Adjonai

In all the maps Tull had ever seen, Denai was shown on the west slopes of the White Mountains. Yet the road through Denai Pass was bordered by farmhouses for twenty miles. The number of Blade Kin thinned until none wore the black armor and red capes of the city guard. The local Thralls watched Tull fearfully or ducked to hide behind some hedge as he passed. Under cover of night, Tull stopped at one Slave Lord's manor and relieved the house of a week's rations before setting off into the Rough.

Once he got out of the hills, the land was bare of all but sparse grass and sagebrush. Frigid gravitational winds beat on this waste mercilessly night and day. Only a few coyotes inhabited this land, for Craal's armies had been marching through it all summer. Tull often found their fire pits filled with blackened ox bones.

Tull's feet ached as he walked, and he often stopped to massage them. The color returned to them on the first day, yet they felt cold. His back burned from the lash strokes, and he was grateful for the rigid leather armor, for more than once it seemed to be all that held him up straight.

Tull knew that Phylomon and Ayuvah waited at Castle Rock, knew it was a walk of only twelve miles per day. But on his second day out, his back burned as if it were on fire, so he stopped at an icy creek and bathed, and felt the rough ridges where the skin was swollen. He was thankful he could not see it.

He rose from the creek bed after an hour of soaking, and happened to glance up the hill. From the corner of his eye, he saw the orange hair of a Thrall, but the man dropped to the ground.

Tull watched the spot for a full ten minutes, hoping to detect some movement, but the man had been wearing a gray-green robe, and the colors blended in with the dead winter sage too well for him to see much.

His back felt better much of that night, and the next morning he found wagon tracks, the only pair he'd seen since leaving the farmlands of Denai. He knew that if he followed them long enough, he'd find Phylomon at the other end. But by noon, fever struck again, followed by chills.

As he walked, the sun seemed to rise and set, rise and set. He felt tremendously cold, and at one point he was looking at the White Mountains, at the snow upon the mountains, and he felt that the snow must be blowing in on him. In front of the mountains he could see Adjonai, his black form looming at the borders of Craal. Tull walked toward the peaks and realized he was walking back to Denai, but a voice inside him whispered, "You are only on a spiral journey. Although you head back to Denai, you see everything more clearly. You are walking on a higher plane."

Tull looked up, saw Adjonai's rotting face leer above the plains, felt a dull terror radiating from the monster, a sensation both frightening and inviting. *Only clear sight lets me see the beast,* Tull thought. Tull looked at a twisted limb of sagebrush, and at the distance of forty feet he discerned egg casings of spiders on its stems, saw the spirit burning within the bush, saw the infinite number of deformities and scars where deer and birds had fed on its leaves, saw how mold and lichens made the bush their home. The grass smelled of death and rot, and he heard the distant sounds of winter starvation in the voices of birds. Everywhere, in every living thing, were signs of decay and darkness. In the ground beneath him he saw the moldering bones of heroes who had died here on these plains in war against Craal, saw how each had lived and died in vain, for Adjonai still stood at the borders of Craal with mountains rising behind him like a picket fence.

The sun was dying, and he came to a stream where rabbits fed by the water's edge. The wind began blowing furiously toward the west, blowing everything back toward Denai, and he saw crows and seagulls carried on the wind, leaves ripped from branches. Even the rabbits began running toward Denai, toward death and decay. He realized that he was seeing things clearly, more clearly than ever before. The great wheel of evil. He was caught in it, playing out his small part, and everything would flow back to Denai.

Tull stopped a moment by force of will and let the wind blow at his back. The sun was setting, and the shadows of plants and trees and mountains all seemed to stretch out toward him. *No, we are not all caught in the great wheel of evil,* Tull thought. *The great wheel is only shadows on the ground. I am on the spiral journey.* He turned back toward Smilodon Bay and had the strangest sensation—a chill wind shot through him and for a moment he felt, was sure he felt, icy hands twist his head so that he pivoted back toward Denai, and the cold hands began to push him.

He stopped with a wrench, felt the cool mysterious touch play over his body. Something within Tull cried out. He knew that touch: It was the same sense of violation he'd felt in Smilodon Bay when Chaa had entered his body to Spirit Walk his future. "The spiral journey begins in shadows," a voice whispered to Tull, and he looked about. No one stood near. "Come back to Denai."

Tull looked up at the White Mountains. The form of Adjonai hovered in front of the pass to Denai, and Tull felt myriad icy fingers brush his skin, teasing him, drawing him toward Denai. He realized then that Adjonai was only an apparition created by the sorcerers of Craal.

"Come back to me," Adjonai whispered. "I will give you power, and you will be to me as a favored son." He raised his kutow of terror, his shield of despair, and the kwea of them lashed Tull. Yet Adjonai held them out as if to give them as a gift, and Tull realized that he could bear those weapons. They were powerful weapons, and they would be more powerful in his hands.

Tull's face twisted in rage. Did they really think he would become one of them? "When I come, I will destroy you!" Tull roared, and he turned back toward Smilodon Bay. He knew his enemies now. *Somewhere,* Tull thought, *a man lies near death, trying to use his powers to drag me back to Craal.*

The icy fingers slammed into Tull's back, shoving him to the ground. A gust of wind hit the earth, flattening the sagebrush around him in a great circle. "You cannot escape Craal," a voice whispered. "I see you. I will follow."

Tull hurried toward Castle Rock. He did not know how to fight the Spirit Walkers of Craal, but Chaa had trained Ayuvah in the art. Surely, Tull thought, Ayuvah will know how to fight them.

At midday Tull stopped to eat. He was sweating and weary, and he wanted to wash his back, for it burned. He smelled beneath his cuirass, and his sweat stank. The wounds on his back smelled of sour infection, and his ankles ached.

He wanted to bathe, but could feel someone's eyes on him. He turned, and wondered if the sorcerers of Craal were watching. Behind him he saw nothing, yet the desert was too quiet. No birds sang. Dr. Debon had once told a woman to expose her rash to the sun, saying that the sun could sometimes burn a wound cleaner than water. Because the stinking leather cuirass would not stop a Blade Kin's bullets, Tull undid the straps. He pulled off his red cape and tied it in a roll, put it with the cuirass into his food bag, and began running again, faster.

An hour later, he looked back, and saw two men running over a hill. They wore clothes the color of winter sage, and he could see only that they had the orange hair of Neanderthals. One carried a long glass rod that flashed in the sun.

Tull was weak, weaker than a Pwi ever should be, and he

knew he could not outdistance the Blade Kin. In his mind, he played an old game from his childhood, asking "Animal Guide, which way should I go for safety?" But he laughed to himself, for he had no Animal Guide. So he ran, following the wagon tracks, and let the sun and the salt of his own sweat burn his back clean.

When he looked behind him two hours later, the Blade Kin had only gained a mile. Tull ran faster, stretching his legs. His legs were stiff, and once he stepped on a rock and twisted his ankle.

It was a small thing, but as he ran, the ankle swelled. He cursed his father for the wounds he had dished out when Tull was a child. For years Tull had tried to hide his limp, but now he limped unashamedly, wishing only to lengthen his stride, to run as fast as a Pwi should.

At sunset, he looked behind him and saw the Blade Kin closing in. A cold wind played around him, and Tull wondered: the Spirit Walker could not work his magic except at the gates of death. Neither of these men were sorcerers, he realized.

The sun went down, and for an hour there was no moon in the sky. He veered north and ran a zigzag, crossing and recrossing his trail as a hunted fox will do. He stopped at a creek to soak, then made a fireless camp. Several times during the night he woke, shaking with chills. He dreamed that he sat beside a fire with Ayuvah and Chaa, and in the dream Fava sat with Tull, hugging him.

"In the Land of Shapes," Chaa told them, "there is no east or west, north or south. Direction is as meaningless as time. A sorcerer establishes a Connection with the place he wants to be through his imagination, and the place draws him to it."

"Is that how one finds a friend in the Land of Shapes?" Fava asked. "By letting the friend draw him?"

"That is how one finds friends, as well as enemies," Chaa answered.

Tull woke sweating, and wondered if the dream were true or a mere hallucination. For a long time, he sat and fought the desire to walk into Craal. The cold presence of the Craal sorceror pierced him, and Tull lay hugging his knees, sweating, fighting the urge to run. At last, Tull dressed in his armor and wrapped the red cape tight around him, and for a while he slept.

Near morning Tull's eyes snapped open at the sound of a twig cracking under nearby footsteps. He unsheathed his broadsword and rolled back under a bush, wishing he'd had a stone to sharpen the damned sword. Thor, the largest moon, cast its fierce orange light over the hillsides, muted only by a few clouds. A soft gravitational wind blew. Tull could smell sea air.

He watched the hillside above him and saw a dark form scurrying animallike on all fours, making its way down the slope. He heard it sniffing. Only a Neanderthal had a strong enough sense of smell to hunt that way, Tull realized. His heart beat wildly, for he recalled the stories of Blade Kin who hunted escaped slaves by scent. He was sweating from his fever, and he felt weak. He did not know if he could stand a fight.

The hunter got within twenty feet of his camp and stopped, sniffed the air softly, stood to full height, and craned his head from side to side.

Tull did not move. The man raised a dagger, waved it overhead, and for a full five minutes walked softly, using his toes to move tiny twigs before placing each foot. When the man was only a few feet away, he stopped where Tull had made his bed and stood, dagger poised.

Tull crouched in the shadow of a large bush, and did not think the man could see him. It was almost a game, to see if the hunter would pass him by.

The man whirled and struck, driving his dagger into Tull's chest—only Tull's lacquered armor turned the blade. Tull lunged with his sword, and the man knocked it aside, slammed Tull in the head with a knee, knocking him back. He swung the knife again and Tull caught his hand, and the fellow jumped on him, grappling for the knife. Tull felt so weak and dizzy, he did not know how he could hope to wrest the knife away.

"Give it up," someone grumbled. A Thrall stood in the moonlight a dozen feet away, pointing a gun at Tull.

Phylomon reached Castle Rock exactly six days after leaving Denai. It had been an uneventful trip. He'd stolen a wagon, four oxen, and some food, and he'd freed several human slaves and taken their testimonies. Castle Rock was nothing more than a large rock that jutted from the shore. If one squinted at the black mass, one could imagine turrets near its top. It marked the entrance to the Straits of Zerai, and it also marked the entrance to a small fjord that served as a makeshift harbor on this treacherous coast.

They met Scandal. The fat man had not stolen just any boat—it was a fine little twenty footer made of Benbow glass with masts worked in a filigree of silver so that the morning glinted on it from afar. The sails were woven from cords of white silk, and the small ship dazzled in the sunlight. Scandal had dressed in a golden jacket with epaulets and a red silk belt. His hair was combed and perfumed. He looked as clean as if he'd spent the entire week in bathwater.

"You shouldn't have stolen this boat," Phylomon said. "The owner will be looking for it."

"I'm not so sure," Scandal said. "I set fire to a ship in Denai, and half the city burned. They don't have anything to come hunting me with."

"But where is Tull?" Phylomon asked, and Scandal told them.

Phylomon frowned in concern. "He killed four guards? And you burned their harbor? And I freed a dozen slaves on the outskirts of the city. No wonder the Lords of Craal dislike us Roughians! I hope to God that Tull makes it out!"

That night, as Scandal washed the dishes down at the water's edge, Ayuvah sat next to Phylomon, silently watching out to sea.

"*Zhe adjena?* What do you fear?" Phylomon asked in Pwi. "Do you think Tull was captured by Blade Kin?"

"I don't know. I was just thinking of all we have lost on this journey and of all the things we have yet to lose."

"Little Chaa? Your love for your brother was strong," Phylomon said. "But you have not been the same since Wisteria died. I know that she was Tull's wife, but sometimes two men will fall in love with the same woman."

Ayuvah laughed. "That whore-I-did-not-care-for? No."

"But you mourn for a woman?" Phylomon said.

"I mourn for my wife!" Ayuvah said. "I mourn for my daughter."

Phylomon felt his skin crawl at those words. He had a strong appreciation for the Pwi's ability to feel the future. "You said that when you tried to take your Spirit Walk, you failed! Did you speak the truth?"

"I did fail-sadly to walk into the future," Ayuvah said. "I've never been good at *Connecting*. I have no talent for it. But while I was on the threshold of the netherworld, my father came in the form of a crow. He showed me the future."

"The Spirit Walkers of the Pwi are notorious for being vague. Are you sure you understood what he showed you?" Phylomon asked.

"He showed me a line of gray Thralls with clubs, standing from horizon to horizon. He showed me a cloud of crows, each with a green worm in its mouth, and they flew over a field of thorns, and as they flew, they dropped the tiny destroyers from their mouths, and the green worms fell like rain and ate the thorns. He showed me a lightning storm, and the instrument of my own death-that-is-cruel. I know the very moment. It comes shortly."

Phylomon considered. The line of Thralls with clubs could well be an army, and the black crows would be Pwi Spirit Walkers. The green worms, or tiny destroyers, he did not understand. "He showed you your death?" Phylomon asked. The Spirit Walkers never told a man the moment of his death. It was far too cruel.

"Yes," Ayuvah said. "Chaa taught me that I must say a certain thing before I die. The timing is important. Tull cannot make the serpent catch without me. But now I am afraid, for I may need to go back into Craal to free him."

The two Blade Kin stood in the moonlight, watching Tull. The fellow with the gun seemed nervous, kept licking his lips, and Tull watched the man's eyes. He was an older man, in his forties. The Blade Kin with the knife got up, and his hood fell back, and red hair tumbled out. Tull realized dully that the Blade Kin was a young woman, a girl of fifteen, yet her face was angry and hard. She fingered a white disk at her throat, and said, "Notify Lord Tantos that we have captured Pu Tchixila. We await his judgment."

The older man motioned toward the ground and said, "Sit." Tull found himself a bare spot on the ground.

The girl sheathed her knife.

"You did not take long in finding me," Tull told them.

"Adjonai rules this land," the old Neanderthal said. "His finger pointed us to you."

Tull smiled, realizing that the Crawley Spirit Walker had nudged the Blade Kin toward him, just as he had tried to nudge Tull back toward Craal. "Adjonai is a clever god," Tull said. "I planned to go into the Rough. I hear it is nice there. Why don't you come with me?"

The old Blade Kin laughed. "Why don't you sit for a moment while someone rouses Lord Tantos from his bed long enough to consider whether we should deliver you back to Craal alive or dead."

Tull looked into the young girl's eyes and in her features he saw only cruelty. Tull rested a moment. So much sleeplessness and weariness made his head spin. Both of them wore robes in shades of desert blue and purple, but each also wore a small insignia at the chest, a Black Cyclops. Tull realized that these were two of Lord Tantos's best, and wondered if they were any better than the city guard. He decided not to wait to learn if Tantos would give his death sentence. He focused on the old man, filled his right hand with gravel and tossed it, and leapt for the woman. He pulled her knife from her sheath and put it to her throat, used her body as a shield.

The old Blade Kin cursed and stood blinking the dust from his eyes. He did not fire, and Tull realized that the Blade Kin thought Tull would use the girl as a hostage, but she twisted from his grasp and Tull leapt forward and swung high, slashing the old man's throat. Tull heard the rustle of cloth as the girl leapt up behind him, and he bashed with all his force behind the dagger.

The girl had picked up his broadsword, and she swung from the side. The force of his blow drove the dagger into her chest and sent her flying to the ground, yet the broadsword swung into him, slashing into his leather cuirass so that the blade nicked his skin. He stood in the moonlight and caught his breath, looked down at the two dead Blade Kin.

A voice came from the white disk at the girl's throat. "Lord Tantos asks that you hold Pu Tchixila until others arrive, and then return him to Denai. Our lord desires that the criminal watch the water night after night until the serpents take him."

A cold wind pushed at Tull, teasing him. "You cannot escape me," a voice whispered into his ear. "My minions follow you still."

Tull looked back toward Craal; in the moonlight he saw Adjonai sitting on the side of a mountain. The dark god glared at him, and the kwea of terror that the creature radiated pierced Tull's chest. "In the Land of Shapes," Chaa had said, "there is no east or west, north or south. Direction is as meaningless as time." Dutifully, Tull realized that he had been traveling the wrong direction all the time. He turned back toward Denai and trotted toward the feet of the dark god.

That day, Tull often felt the sorcerer with him, and on each occasion Tull would look toward Denai and see Adjonai gazing at him intently. Each time, the terror of the beast struck him like a blow, just as it had at Gold River Pass. But then Tull would stop and close his eyes, imagining Frowning Idols or Smilodon Bay, establish a mental connection, and as he traveled to these familiar lands in his imagination, he felt the cold wind leave, and the dark god would turn his face. Tull realized that the sorcerer could not discern between a landscape that Tull traveled in his imagination and one that he traveled in reality. Toward evening, Tull crossed a hill and saw four Blade Kin to the north. They spotted him and gave chase, and he ran south, heading away from them. He lost them at night and went without sleep. Instead, he ran toward the feet of the dark god, and as he ran, he closed his eyes and thought of Tirilee and Wisteria, of the good times he'd had on his way to Craal.

He reached the sorcerer's camp at midnight, at the foot of a hill where the dark god sat. Tull wondered how the Spirit Walker projected the illusion, for he was staring into the black rotting face. The dark god's kutow radiated terror, and his shield radiated despair, and the whole land here felt foul and ill, yet the creature was unaware of Tull, intent on looking.

Tull closed his eyes and imagined the redwood forests, imagined making love to Wisteria in a mountain glade, and the dark god suddenly lifted his head and looked away east toward Smilodon Bay.

A dozen Blade Kin had camped at the foot of the hill, and all of them had tents of black. Only one tent was different: a fire glowed within so that the tent shined like a lantern. Tull remembered how Zhopila had kept Chaa warm and moist in his cave while he took his Spirit Walk. Tull could see no guards, and he wondered if the image of Adjonai were supposed to be guard enough.

Tull waited till all the moons were down, and forced himself to remember Tirilee. The thought of her still stirred his passion, and sometimes he would swallow and find that he tasted her kisses in his mouth. He remembered the clean aspen forests, the bed of leaves, and when his lust for the Dryad grew strong, he crept to the lighted tent. Inside, he found a small boy sleeping by a fire, and beside him lay the body of a powerful young man, dried blood at his wrists. The boy woke and looked up at Tull in confusion, and Tull slapped the child hard.

The Spirit Walker shuddered and his eyes fluttered open. The young man began to shout. Tull shoved his hand into the sorcerer's mouth. A great wind hit the tent, blowing it away with a tearing sound. Tull looked up into the face of Adjonai, and the God shouted, "No!" and the earth rolled and shook. Adjonai reached down with one great finger, as if to touch Tull, and Tull shoved his broadsword into the sorcerer's chest under his ribs, twisted the blade to puncture both lungs, and prepared to run, fearing that the Blade Kin had been wakened by the shout.

Adjonai wavered in the sky for a moment, and then faded. The image that had dwarfed even the mountains vanished, and Tull found that he was sitting in the tent, that the tent had not been ripped apart. Tull got up and went outside, looked around camp. All was still and quiet, as if only Tull had heard the shout. Tull spat toward the mountain where Adjonai had reclined only moments before, then headed for Castle Rock.

Tull staggered in to Castle Rock at noon eight days later. His back was swollen and festering, and he suffered from fevers. Ayuvah set a small fire and put some water on to boil, then lanced Tull's back. By morning, Tull's fever had dropped. Phylomon insisted that they rest for a day at Castle Rock, but soon after, the men pulled their little sailboat from the water and put it on the wagon for the journey along the Straits of Zerai, for it was far too dangerous to sail these straits in the winter.

The next morning, Tull felt much recovered except for an unshakable weariness, and they began following the rugged coastline. Tull sat in the wagon, his blanket wrapped about him, while Phylomon drove the ox team.

By map, the straits were only a hundred miles long. On foot, they were well over two hundred. Often, they could see mountains off to the north across the water, and the winds were not so heavy. In the valleys they often came on small groves—white oak and willow, maple and birch.

A dozen miles from Castle Rock, they found something they never expected: an army of Thralls stretched from the shore in a line across the plain to the hills at least five miles south. The Thralls held war clubs and raised them over their heads and shook them. The party stopped a mile off.

"By God, there are thousands!" Scandal shouted. "Are they friendly?"

"Friendly enough," Phylomon said, and he whistled for his ox team to move.

They walked up to the line of Thralls, and Tull saw something wrong. The Thralls did not have red hair, and they did not move from their spots. When they got near, they found them to be scarecrows slowly raising their arms, waving clubs. Each was green, the color of a laurel leaf, and the scarecrows had the faces of Pwi. Ayuvah stepped up to one, and it suddenly gasped and moaned, dropping its club slowly.

"They are called Man Fruits," Phylomon said. "The Creators sometimes make them, building a living fence. They do it seldom—only when they are introducing a new species to an area. The last time I saw one of these was, what, sixty years ago? Here in the north, we had hunted the giant wolverine nearly to extinction, and everyone was thankful for it. But the Creators put up a fence of Man Fruits, and reestablished the population in a secure setting. There's not an animal—mammoth, wolf or cat, that will walk past one of these fences."

"A line of gray Thralls with clubs," Ayuvah said, and Phylomon watched the Neanderthal, remembering the prophecy. "How do they move?"

"Plants breathe, just as we do," Phylomon said. "The Man Fruits exhale into tiny bladders that run along their arms. When the bladders get full, they stiffen, and the arms move out erect. When they become too full of oxygen, a valve opens and the air escapes out of their throats. They moan. Smell them. They even smell like a Pwi—nothing like a plant. But don't touch them. They'll explode."

Scandal smelled one. "The explosion wouldn't be powerful enough to, say, blow my nose off? Would it?" he asked.

"Considering the size of your beak," Phylomon said, "it would do you a service."

"Then, Tull, loan me your sword!" Scandal shouted. He got the broadsword, swung it in the air in great clumsy arcs. "Now, you foul Crawlies, you will die!" He rushed forward, slashed the arm from a Man Fruit. It exploded with the sound of a gun, making him jump. Green slime spattered over his belly, and immediately all the Man Fruits nearby gasped and moaned. He looked at the slime on his gold shirt. "Crap on me, will you?" He laughed, thrusting a sword into a second. He whirled and lopped the head off a third. "Eat my steel, Blade Kin," he shouted. He grunted and sweated, and ran down the line, dealing death to the Man Fruits, and each exploded in a shower of green slime, soiling his fine clothing.

A hundred yards up the line, he stopped and stared at one of the Man Fruits. "Tull! Ayuvah! Come here!" he shouted.

The two men walked over to him. Scandal pointed up at the Man Fruit, and Ayuvah gasped. "Doesn't this one look like Little Chaa?"

The resemblance was uncanny. The Man Fruit had the same wide lips, the same narrow forehead. The Man Fruit had slowly been raising its arms for several minutes, and it dropped them suddenly and sighed. Ayuvah sank to his knees and wept, and Tull put his arms around him.

"Do you want me to kill it?" Scandal asked.

"My brother died once already," Ayuvah said. "Let me look on his face for a while."

"Ayaah, let's leave it then," Scandal said, wiping the sweat from his brow. "I'll fix us some lunch."

Tull and Ayuvah sat for an hour, and watched the Man Fruit slowly raise and drop his club with a sigh.

That afternoon they passed the Man Fruits and entered the Creators' introduction zone. Game was sparse—only a few rabbits, quail, ground squirrels, and deer. It was the most peaceful place they'd encountered on the trip.

They watched the ocean from the cliffs, looking for serpents, and after several days, they spotted a female who rose to the surface and bellowed a mile out to sea.

"I don't understand this," Phylomon said at last. "There should be hundreds, perhaps thousands of serpents nesting in these waters."

"We're lucky to have seen one," Scandal said. "It was more than we had at Smilodon Bay."

"Yet their hatch was large," Phylomon said. "The river was full of hatchlings."

"Then the mothers are dying," Tull said. "Chaa said the mothers were dying. Or perhaps we are early. Maybe they don't come to lay for another few weeks."

"Let us hope that is all it is," Phylomon said. He rested his eyes, recalling a scene from his youth: He'd been here when he was in his nineties. The sea had been thick with serpents. At nearly every submerged rock, a mother guarded her nest. Often, they'd watched two or three mothers fight for the right to lay at one rock. Phylomon's father had said the mothers were persuaded to lay by water temperature. On his solar calendar, it had been the day of October thirty-first—or day fifty-two of Harvest, in the calendar of Anee. It was well past that date now, and the fall had been warmer that year. It was strange that the mothers laid eggs in the same hatcheries. They were not genetically programmed for the trait, but Phylomon's father had explained that it was an offshoot of other programming—the mothers were programmed to hunt for food in a school. So when it came time to lay, they hunted for egg space together. The fact that they always chose the same nesting area year after year was not due to chance. The serpents were nearly as smart as humans, and they remembered the best places to lay. They required three things—a steep rocky shelf in shallow water, relatively weak wave action so the egg sacs would not be torn from the rocks during low tides, and cool weather. With the powerful tides on Anee, few places boasted the right attributes. Phylomon looked at a cloud that faintly showed the colors of the rainbow. *Why do temporaries so rarely notice how often clouds show the colors of the rainbow?* he wondered.

On their fourth day of watch, they found a serpent—a three-hundred-foot mother who lay dead. Her tail had washed up on the shore, and her head and body floated on the water. She had not decayed, so Phylomon walked out on her. She was twenty feet wide from her dorsal fins to her pectoral, so walking on her body was like walking over an undulating road that smelled vaguely of fish oil. The four deadly spikes on her tail were each as long as a man.

The rear fins showed no obvious wounds, no disease. But when he reached her gills, it looked as if she had been in a great fight. The heavy scales beside her gill flaps, each scale as large as a platter, had been gouged away. She looked as if she had been raked with great claws the entire length of her jaw. The one great red eye that Phylomon could see, floating just beneath the water, had a detached retina.

Yet none of the wounds seemed serious enough to cause her death. Phylomon walked down on her head and tried to see into her mouth, but the head was too heavy to bear his weight. The head began to sink, so he had to walk back. When he got back to the gill flaps, he noticed something strange: When he'd put his weight on the head, the gill flaps had opened wider, and at the base of the gills he could see red holes with rings around them, like the pucker marks that circle a bullet hole.

Phylomon had seldom examined the corpse of a large serpent and could not recall if the pucker marks belonged.

Could they be some respiratory orifice, he wondered, to expel carbon dioxide? Or could they be an opening to fresh-air lungs. Certainly the serpents they'd kept in their barrel could not have breathed oxygen from that stale water, which meant they had to be taking it directly from the air. He walked back over the length of the body, uncertain as to why the beast had died.

Over the next week, they found six more serpents guarding an island only two miles out to sea. They made camp and watched the mothers. Phylomon drew a map of the island, and each time a serpent surfaced, they plotted the point on the map.

Anee orbited the gas giant Thor once every 176 days. They would reach perigee with Thor in 23 more days. As Anee reached perigee, the tides would become more fierce. On a normal day, tide levels varied by fifty feet. During severe tides, the water level would vary by a hundred feet. If the waters here were shallow enough, Phylomon believed that they might be able to walk to the island during low tide.

When they had been watching the six serpents for four days, Tull and Ayuvah went to hunt quail. They came back an hour later and Ayuvah shouted in Pwi. "Phylomon, come see the thing-I-am-so-bewildered. It is people-marvelous. But small-marvelous. Not human, not Pwi, not Hukm, not Dryad."

Phylomon looked at them skeptically. "Are you saying that you've found a fifth kind of people? Another species?"

"Yes!" Tull said, "Come see!"

Phylomon followed, leaving Scandal to watch the rocks, and soon they were nearly running. "Of course, it makes sense!" he said. "We are in an ecological introduction zone. The Creators have not introduced anything new to this planet since they made the Dryads, hundreds of years ago."

But when they reached the spot Tull had marked, all Phylomon saw was the corpse of a dead wolf.

"Here she is!" Ayuvah shouted, and he lifted the corpse of the wolf. Beneath, huddling for warmth against the fur, was a tiny woman, about forty inches tall. She watched the Pwi with terror in her eyes.

"Step back," Phylomon said. "We don't want to frighten her." He studied the tiny woman for a long time. She had no facial hair or extraordinary body hair. The hair of her scalp was brown, and her eyes blue. She wore no clothing. Her skull was box-shaped, like the skull of *Homo sapiens*. The joints of her thumbs were tilted at an angle, the way human thumbs are tilted. She had no stump of tail, like those found on Hukm or Mastodon Men. Her breasts were small, almost nonexistent. All in all, she looked like a very small, starved girl, perhaps twelve years old.

"She's a *Homo sapiens*," Phylomon said. "Human in every way, much like the Starfarers were before their genetic upgrades. She's just so tiny. The Creators often make miniatures of a species when they are testing. It cuts down on the amount of space and feed they need for their animals. I remember the first imperial mastodons—they were only six feet at the shoulder.

"Can you speak?" he asked the tiny woman. She flinched, tried to cover herself with the carcass of the wolf.

"We were hunting rabbits right over there," Ayuvah said, "and we saw something move here in the brush. I thought it was a rabbit, and then I thought it was only the wind blowing the hair of this wolf, and then I saw this people."

Phylomon reached down and touched the small woman. She moaned and closed her eyes. Her skin was cold to the touch; her lips were blistered from wind and sun. "It's good that you found her," Phylomon said. "She would have died in this cold."

"She could not live like this through the winter!" Ayuvah said. "It is so cold!"

"She doesn't know that," Phylomon said. "When the Dryads were first formed, the Creators simply turned them loose in the woods. They were like this tiny woman—wild, frightened, starving. They did not know how to make clothing. They huddled in clusters for warmth, and in the spring we'd find them frozen in the mountains. It was only because the Pwi took them as wives that the Dryads survived. The men took care of the Dryads, and the Dryads took care of the trees. That is how the Creators wanted it."

"Then who will take care of this little woman?" Ayuvah asked. "She could be dangerous, like a Dryad."

"I'll take care of her," Tull said, picking her up and placing his jacket around her, hugging her to his chest to warm. She did not fight or try to escape, but lay curled in a fetal position, lips spread slightly apart, with eyes half open.

"We should all care for her," Phylomon said. "But first, let us find the others."

"Others?" Tull asked.

"The Creators know that it takes several hundred members of any species to produce a breeding population. We should look for the rest of them and just hope they had the sense to stay together."

They hunted for other survivors all afternoon and found many bodies. Bones of the tiny humans were scattered everywhere, and from the small tooth marks Phylomon decided that the tiny humans had fallen prey to bobcats.

"Bobcats," Tull asked. "You must be joking!"

"Not at all. Many men are killed by saber-tooth tigers, yet a bobcat is larger to these people than a saber-tooth is to one of us!"

When it appeared that they would find no other survivors, Ayuvah came to them. "Phylomon, that gray bird is circling over there!" Off to the east a mile away, the eye of the Creator circled.

They followed it, and in late afternoon found caves—a series of badger holes dug into the side of a hill beneath a slab of igneous rock. All along this cliff, tiny humans huddled for shelter, warming themselves by mutual body heat, covering themselves with dried leaves. The men looked around, but there was nothing for the people to eat except acorns that their tiny teeth could not penetrate—no fruit, no wheat, no gardens. Nothing but one another. And by the number of partially eaten bodies lying about, it became obvious that the tiny people had resorted to cannibalism. From a small grove of oaks, a gray bird watched, its large yellow eyes the color of wheat straw.

Ayuvah ran to get some food for the tiny creatures while Tull and Phylomon began taking inventory of their needs. They had water nearby—a stagnant pool where several bodies floated. Of the sixty humans, Phylomon guessed that the oldest was no more than fourteen. A full third of the girls appeared to be pregnant, yet there were no children, no young under the age of twelve. Phylomon hesitated to voice the opinion that they might be abandoning or even eating the children, and he hoped that infanticide was not one of their crimes. Perhaps they had only recently become pregnant, he wondered, for they had obviously lived here only for the summer.

In the space of a few hours, Phylomon watched several fights where boys bashed each other with stones, and found that the people communicated only with grunts and gestures. Six older boys roamed about at will, taking what they wanted, and the tiny people scurried away from these six. Aside from this gang of hoodlums, he could see no indication that they had formed any type of social bonds.

Phylomon made a small fire in the shelter of a rock, hoping it would not frighten the tiny people, and to his surprise, they all came running immediately and held their hands out to warm themselves.

"They've seen fire," Tull said.

"I suspect the Creators showed them fire," Phylomon said. "I think they were kept in some kind of holding pens until recently. Not only do they not have children, but you will notice that the women do not have stretch marks on their bellies. I think none of them has given birth."

"What are we going to do about them?" Tull asked. "There are so many. We can't possibly feed them from our stores."

"We can teach them to make weapons and clothing, to build fire. We can teach them to hunt for rabbits and quail," Phylomon answered. "But I don't see the point. Even with spears and arrows, they could not protect themselves from a dire wolf."

A fight broke out near the fire. The gang of six pulled a girl down and began trying to rape her. Tull grabbed two of the boys and smashed them together, and threw them a dozen feet. The other four looked at him, mouths agape, and ran to hide in the bushes. "Try that again," Tull said, "and you die!"

Phylomon laughed.

"I don't see anything funny," Tull said.

"You'll make a fine protector," Phylomon said. "Blade Kin to the little people."

"I'm not Blade Kin."

"Of course not," Phylomon said. "To them, you'll be more like a god. Isn't it strange: in the space of a few months, I dare say they've learned all about cannibalism, murder, rape, robbery. They've mastered the universal attributes of a human society."

Tull said, "If they understood how to feed themselves, if they knew how they will need one another to survive, they would not do this."

"Exactly," Phylomon answered. "But what will you do if they continue to behave like this even after you have taught them better."

"I don't know," Tull said.

"I think," Phylomon answered, "you will dig a hole and place them in prison. You might torture them until they behave. Or you could incapacitate them in some way—remove their limbs. In the end, you might have to execute one or two."

Tull considered the idea, wondered if he were capable of executing one of the small thugs. He had just bashed two of them together hard enough that they were still lying on the ground, moaning.

Phylomon said, "I have always believed that true morality can only arise when we recognize our mutual dependence on one another. It can only arise when we recognize ourselves as part of a community. In a way, all immorality can be attributed to a kind of stupidity, an inability to recognize our own interdependence . . ."

"What you say may be true," Tull said. "Out here in the Rough, you don't feel safe unless you've got fifty people to watch your back. But you go to Denai, and there's too many people. They don't need each other anymore."

"You're right," Phylomon answered. "In the cities, we don't need protection from the elements as much as we need protection from one another. We lose our bonds, like the slavers in Smilodon Bay. Your slavers in town sell one another, and what will they get for it? Eventually, the Blade Kin will overrun the Rough. They could do it now, if one of the lords thought the enterprise worthy of his expense."

Tull sat and thought. "Then you kill slavers because they are stupid. It seems a grand price to pay for stupidity."

Phylomon laughed. "To put it succinctly. If you look at the slavers in your own town, you can see that their stupidity and brutality will destroy them anyway. I only hasten their demise. I know it sounds cold. Brutal. But it is just."

Tull pondered a moment. "You assume that people never change, that execution is always warranted, even years after the crime. I think that Wisteria's father was a changed man. I know you disagree, but he was a good man."

"He may have been good in ways; he may even have repented," Phylomon admitted. "I've never met a criminal yet who didn't have some redeeming features. But I came to the conclusion long ago, that if man takes or jeopardizes a human life out of greed or lust, neither I nor anyone else has the right to forgive him. To free him and thus make a wager that he has changed only puts others in jeopardy.

"You say Wisteria's father had changed. Yet you have also heard how he joked about his deed. But I tell you truly: people who enjoy their crimes don't change.

"Many will say that I'm a cold man, that I'm inhuman. And perhaps I have lost my humanity. But you need me. Every town needs someone like me."

Beside the fire, three of the stronger women grabbed a girl whose breasts were just beginning to bud, and they bit her. It took Tull a moment to realize that they were hungry, that they were trying to eat her. Tull pulled them apart and tossed the women aside. He picked up the tiny girl, and her eyes were wild with terror. He tried to comfort her, but she only squirmed and tried to escape until he let her go.

"You'd think the Creators would realize their mistake, that they would know these people could never survive without guidance."

"The Creators might not understand that principle," Phylomon said. "They are not wholly biological life forms. Their minds are crystal. They are interested only in maintaining viable populations of creatures. I am not sure that they can conceive of the idea that a society is greater than its members. I know they don't understand the idea that societies doom themselves, that they can take directions that ensure the failure both of the society as a whole and of the members within it.

"We never programmed that kind of information into the Creators. There are so many species, and we did not know what types of guidance the animals would need to survive. Instead, we let instinct take its course. With some animals, that worked. You can hatch a stegosaur, and it will do just fine. But you've seen the little duckbill hunters? They must work in packs of forty or sixty to kill their prey—it is a feat requiring great cooperation. And the Creators had to reestablish their populations forty or fifty times, until they reached the point where the experiment worked."

"The Creators did a good job," Tull said. "The duck-eaters are the most successful carnosaur in Hotland."

"But only because the society became greater than its members," Phylomon said. He looked down at the tiny humans. "We made the Creators," he said. "Yet we have always remained a mystery to them. We have millions of humans on this world. You would not think that the Creators would add to our numbers. I suspect that they are experimenting now, that they created this tiny colony specifically so they could learn about us. See how the eye of the Creator never stops observing?" Phylomon motioned toward the oak tree. The gray bird sat, unblinking. "The bird has no digestive system, no need to feed. Before its energy runs out, the bird will return to the Creators, and they will unravel the information stored in its brain and learn that we are here, learn what we are saying now, learn what the tiny humans have done over the last few weeks. I wonder what the Creators hope to learn?"

From that day on, one of the party always remained at camp, watching the tiny humans. Ayuvah taught them to make spears and to cook over a fire, to crack acorns with rocks and dig for roots. Phylomon shot several bobcats in the area, and they tanned the hides for clothing, and stacked boulders to make a home for the little people. Ayuvah took them hunting for rabbit and quail, and found several inland lagoons where the water was shallow and clear, and he was able to spear large pike to feed the group.

Along the coast, seals and walruses sometimes climbed up the rocks, and Tull killed a walrus and brought it to camp, but the little people ate it and got sick on the blubber, so they did not try it again.

Over the next week, two serpents out near the island disappeared, and Tull explored the coast forty miles east, watching the rocks near shore for any sign of a female serpent. He found more serpents, some as far as four miles out to sea, but none had laid their eggs next to the mainland.

The mothers rose from the water often, exploding upward fifty feet into the air, and once in the air they shook their heads and roared, and the silver scales at their bellies flashed in the sunlight. Once Tull saw a great mother leap up at an angle, and she was traveling so fast that nearly her whole body, all two hundred feet, shot into the air. Although there were few serpents, in the evenings the great mothers sometimes surfaced two at a time. One could hear their bellows miles inland, and Phylomon said, "I have watched the great mothers in their nests for many years, and even when these waters were full, they did not make such a noise. Never did they leap so high. They are ill, I fear. Ill and crazy with pain. I think they will all die before long."

At the end of the week, Phylomon showed his maps, marking the spots where and when the serpents had been sighted. By vectoring these locations and by mapping the stone outcrops during low tides, he pinpointed the ones where eggs could be found. But there was no way to get to them. Even at the lowest tides, they could not walk over to the island, and Scandal talked jokingly of sailing there.

"The way I figure it," he said, "I've cooked up an awful lot of fish and hogs and chickens in my life. A man can't live with that on his conscience. It would be only fair that I become a meal for someone else. I only wish someone would stuff a few bread crumbs up my ass before I go, and serve me with a little brandy sauce on top."

But the truth was that none of them could risk it. Their little boat was far too small, a simple sailboat, and they kept it from the water.

One day at sundown, Scandal and Phylomon came from the beach to the shelter they had made for the little people and sat down to a meal. The men had entered that comfort-ble period where they seldom spoke. Suddenly, from the oak tree behind them, the gray bird flapped its wings and headed off north, across the waters, to a place where there was only ice and islands.

It made Phylomon uneasy. The damned bird was heading for the isle of Bashevgo, where the Slave Lords lived.

An extreme low tide came the next morning, and four small haystack mounds emerged from the water, leading to the island. It was good news, and everyone but Ayuvah went down to the sea to watch. Patches of dark red kelp showed in the low water, and from those patches, Phylomon calculated where the rocky outcrops would be, the trail they could follow to the island.

They searched for a path for nearly an hour, before the tide turned and began rushing inland. Tull, Scandal, and Phylomon had all climbed down to the shore to hunt for serpent eggs, when Ayuvah came running to the clifftop above them. He was holding a tiny woman by the neck, shouting for help.

Tull was first up the rocks. The woman had a white snake fastened to the back of her neck, and she flailed her arms in an attempt to escape Ayuvah. Her eyes rolled, and a white foam issued from her mouth.

"A gray bird came!" Ayuvah shouted. "It sat in the oak by the hut and vomited snakes onto the ground. One of them fastened-horribly to the neck of this woman-who-I-pity, and she fell to the ground. She got up and took a spear, and stabbed-I-regret some others. Four little ones have died. I stomped the other snakes and threw them in the fire. The gray bird-we-all-should-fear only sat and watched what happened. I shot it, and the act of throwing it into the fire made me glad."

Phylomon held up the tiny woman and looked at the "snake" on the back of her neck. To his eyes, it looked more like a gray eel. It had pale eyes, the color of its skin, and whether the eyes saw anything, he could not tell, for they did not move and were of a solid color. Its mouth had the sucker shape common to lampreys, and it was firmly fastened to the base of her skull.

Phylomon wrapped his hand in a robe, and put it around the snake, then gently pulled on it. The tiny woman

screamed, and as Phylomon tugged, the lamprey came loose
—yet it had a long raspy needle-thin tongue attached firmly
to the tiny woman's neck. Phylomon tried to gently pull the
tongue out, but the little woman shook with convulsions.

He let go of the snake, and it eeled back up and clamped
onto the tiny woman's neck again.

"Damn," he said. "I can't get it to let go." Phylomon
took out his knife and stabbed the snake, ripping its guts
open. The tiny woman shrieked and fell unconscious. He
stopped and looked at her. She wasn't breathing.

"It killed her," Scandal said.

"I think it's some kind of parasite," Phylomon said.
"I'm not sure what it eats." He pulled the snake back, trying
to remove it, but its raspy tongue held tight. After a great
deal of work, he was able to pull it free, inch by inch.

The tongue itself was a needle-shaped piece of cartilage,
six inches long, with tiny ridges. At the tip of it, he found
gray matter from the woman's brain. He cut the snake open
and peeled aside its belly. Like the gray birds that were the
eyes of the Creator, it had few internal organs. No intestines, no stomach. Just lungs and arteries, and a belly full of
gray matter.

"God," Scandal said, "It was sucking her brain out!"

"No," Phylomon said. "It's not a parasite. The gray
matter you see in its stomach isn't digested. It was always
there. Instead, I think the lamprey simply stuck its tongue
up into her spinal cord and inserted it into her brain. From
there, it was easy to control her."

"What do you mean?" Ayuvah said.

"It may have seen through her eyes, felt with her hands.
I don't know," Phylomon said. "But I believe that this
snake, or lamprey, or whatever you want to call it, forced
her to murder her brothers and sisters."

Phylomon looked up at Scandal. The fat man's lip was
twitching, and he was watching the tiny lamprey in horror.
Phylomon looked at the woman. She had a tiny red hole at
the base of her neck, a pucker mark like one sees from a
bullet hole.

"Why would the Creators make something like that?"
Scandal asked.

"Obviously, they are experimenting," Phylomon said.

"They are very good at experimenting. I think that they are looking for a way to selectively destroy the human population. The little humans were made only as a test, to see how effectively these snakes could kill."

"Well, at least I've got nothing to worry about," Tull said, and the others looked at the Tcho-Pwi soberly.

"I am not so sure," Phylomon said. "See these pucker marks? I saw the same marks at the base of the gills of that dead serpent a few days ago. Whatever the Creators are up to, killing the serpents is also part of their plan. I should have known it. That is why the Creators have not responded to my calls for help.

"The Creators were built to maintain the ecological balance of this continent, yet you have seen Craal—a habitation solely for Thralls and the Slave Lords. Even here in the Rough, there are almost no wild mammoths left—the ivory hunters have taken them to the verge of extinction. Certainly, the Creators cannot ignore this imbalance. I believe that breaking down the eco-barriers is only the first part of their plan. They will liquidate this continent, kill off all of the humans and Pwi, and start over." Phylomon considered a moment. It had been many years since he'd last been to the islands where the Creators dwelt. The great worms with their omniwombs kept themselves hidden deep in the earth, and they had formed numerous beasts to protect themselves. "They'll kill us all," he said, "unless I can stop them."

Chapter 14
Serpent Catch

The world was white—snow on the ground, white clouds above, whitecaps on the waves. Fifteen days before winter solstice a storm swept from the north, a storm with teeth. It was also the night Anee reached perigee with Thor and the tides hit their semiannual low. Scandal and Phylomon had camped at the beach, their boat moored to a rock. They expected to leave for the island in the morning. If they couldn't go on foot, it would be a short trip by boat.

Tull and Ayuvah sat in the hut they'd built for the tiny humans, cooking one of their oxen. Part of its body hung in the oak outside, and the front shoulder sat on a spit. Cooking the huge slab of meat would be an all-night job, for it had to be turned regularly. Yet it was a pleasant task, for its smell filled the room. With the coming of snow, the hunting would get more difficult. The oxen would feed the community for many days.

Four serpents were left out by the rocks. Only the day before, they watched one serpent repeatedly leap from the water and roar her pain. After several hours she floated to shore on her back, alive, barely breathing. Phylomon walked out onto her head to check her gills. She was bloody and torn, like the previous serpents, and in her gills he found large red lampreys full of venom. The serpent had scraped out her own gills trying to remove the parasites, then she slowly suffocated.

"It was an economical way to kill them," Phylomon said. "Because they hunt and breed in schools, it must not have been difficult to infect the entire population. In a few months, they will all be gone. Perhaps the eggs will do some good."

"They will do good," Ayuvah had said. "My father saw it."

As Tull cooked his meat and thought about it, he did not have as much faith. The night was cold, and the wind blew through chinks in their stone house. The tiny people were freezing. Worse, Ayuvah had spotted the tracks of a rogue Mastodon Man to the east only three miles from camp, and a bobcat had been on the prowl two nights in a row, so he worried that the tiny humans needed protection. But Tull personally believed that the tiny people would need more protection from the cold than from predators. Ayuvah had not been able to make clothes for all of them; they had only a few crude blankets. They huddled under blankets in corners of the room, and Tull heated boulders by the fire, then rolled them over so the tiny people could warm themselves as they slept. He was especially careful of a new mother. Her tiny daughter was so small that she fit easily in the palm of Tull's hand. Tull gathered all the little women to watch the birth so they would know what was happening when their own cramps began, but most wandered off halfway through the ordeal. They were not interested in the baby, perhaps not even aware that the child was one of them.

Outside, lightning struck, and it began to hail. Ayuvah sat up and licked his lips, looked around nervously. He got into Tull's pack, pulled out his brass weather globe, touched it. The moon Anee hovered in the air in front of him, and he studied the great swirl of clouds around them.

"This storm will last all night, and perhaps all day tomorrow. See how it hangs over us?" He watched Tull roll a hot stone to one of the groups of little humans.

"You do that well," Ayuvah said. "I remember when we left home, you were surprised when I warmed Little Chaa's bed with a stone. You thought it was an act of love, and you desired to learn to love."

Tull smiled at the thought. He'd heated many stones.

"Have you learned to love at all?" Ayuvah asked.

"I loved Wisteria. In a way, I loved Tirilee—and I still crave her. It is strange, but I cannot think of her without tasting her kisses. The kwea of my time with her is strong, and I ache with pain to give love to someone," Tull answered. "Still, loving each of them was like turning a corner on the Worm Tower stairs. Loving each of them was different, and neither of them left me fulfilled. Perhaps they only taught me what love isn't. It isn't slavery. It isn't entertainment. It isn't visceral."

Ayuvah laughed. "Love is what you're doing now," he said. Tull moved several people apart, set the rock between them and covered it with dirt.

"All I've done here is try to keep these little asses from killing each other and teach them to pee outside. I'm not sure I even like them. I don't think this is love."

"No," Ayuvah said, "You have devoted yourself to them. You are tired, yet for their sake you do not sleep. Devotion is the heart of love. When love fails you and you are filled with pain, you can still be moved by devotion."

Tull thought a moment. "You're right," he said, putting another rock by the fire. He got out his tiny clocks, the tools he had stolen from Denai, and began tearing apart a flower clock, trying to see how the gears and springs fit together.

Outside, lightning cracked the sky, followed by thunder. The wind shook the oaks nearby, howling through the branches.

"Do you hear that sound-I-fear?" Ayuvah said.

"The thunder? You never feared it before."

"I fear it," Ayuvah said. "I planned to spear sturgeon in the lagoon tomorrow, but the water will be muddied by the waves. I won't be able to see the fish."

"We have meat enough," Tull said, nodding toward the

shoulder of ox. Some fat dribbled into the fire, and Tull got up and turned the meat on its spit.

"I'd rather have fish," Ayuvah said, "But even if I were to tie some cloth to a hook and make a jig, the sturgeon would not be able to see it. The water is too murky. The fish will all be forced to feed down deep, near the bottom."

Tull looked at Ayuvah strangely. He'd seen the Pwi spear fish many times, but Ayuvah had never fished with a line. The Pwi thumb was too clumsy to let them tie the tiny hooks to the lines that the humans used. A Pwi would not use a hook.

"It will be all right," Tull said.

Ayuvah smiled. "I know."

Tull closed his eyes, and Ayuvah said, "I love my family. I wish I could hold them tonight. Little Sava, I am sure she has grown since we left. When you get home, she will not recognize you."

"Unh," Tull moaned.

"Don't go to sleep, my brother," Ayuvah said. "Let's listen to the thunder."

Tull opened his eyes. It was very late, long past midnight. "How does the sky feel tonight?"

"The sky feels cold," Ayuvah said. "I hear the wolf-wind howling." Outside, distant thunder rattled, and their little stone house shook.

"Then you should be pleased to hear the voices of your Animal Guides," Tull said, trying to comfort him. "Would you like to come over here and sleep with me?"

"No," Ayuvah said, "I will stay by the door, in case the Mastodon Man . . ." The fire crackled, and Tull looked at Ayuvah. He sat straight, his arms awkwardly folded, the way a man will when he is not at ease. He licked his narrow lips. "I've made a doll for Sava," Ayuvah said, "from reeds I found by the lagoon. If I had paper, I would wrap it for her, the way humans do."

"Unh," Tull said, closing his eyes.

"Wrapping the present in paper prolongs the joy one feels to watch the child open it. Also, I have a present for Etanai—some blue fabric that shines like sunlight reflecting from a spider's web. I found it by a house outside Denai, drying on a line. Tull, stay awake with me!"

"Unh," Tull said. A wild breeze forced its way through the cracks in the stone, and Tull smelled something putrid—sour fat and dirty hair. His heart pounded, and the blood rushed in his ears. He rolled to his left, grabbed his sword from the floor.

Behind him the door crashed as if it had exploded, and the heavy wooden door fell on Ayuvah. A Mastodon Man stood in the darkness outside, its huge frame far too large for the doorway. Its hair was grizzled and yellow, almost the color of flesh. It bent down on its knuckles, stuck its massive head through the door and looked at the fire, at the meat cooking on the spit. It sniffed at the fire, then saw Tull.

And in his mind, Tull was a child again, and his father was yelling at him, shaking a pair of bloodstained manacles in the air. In his mind's eye, Tull could not see the detail of his father's face—only the shadow, the great looming size of the beast he had been. Jenks's face was twisted in rage, and there was nothing in him that seemed human. He was only a beast, mindless and cruel. Tull shrank inside, the way he had tried to shrink as a child, to make himself so small that he could vanish through the cracks in the wooden floor, to make himself so small that he would be beyond notice. A thin moan escaped his lips.

The kwea of fear was strong, like bands of iron, and to be moved by it was a holy feeling. Tull moved to the music of this momentary passion. His mind seemed totally clear, yet he could not unclench himself to stand. It had been this way when Little Chaa was killed. It was a terror of more than the giant shaggy beast before him. It was a terror that took form only at night, a kwea that took shape only when he saw the *animalness*—the beast's complete ignorance of its own cruelty—that nested in the monster's eyes. And he knew that many years ago, Jenks must have had that look in his eyes when he shackled Tull. The kwea unmade him.

The Mastodon Man sniffed the air, saw Ayuvah lying under the door. He hunched forward, and in doing so knocked down a section of wall. He looked at the stones on the floor, then grabbed Ayuvah's shoulder, shook him, lifted him like a doll and swatted his head against the stones, splattering blood and white ooze across the room. Behind him, Tull heard children screaming, dozens of children, shrieking in the night.

"Pin you to the wall!" the Mastodon Man said in Jenks's voice. "You can't escape!"

Tull heard the words clearly. He'd never felt such fear while watching the water in Denai, not when the serpents leapt for him in the night. He'd only felt it the night Little Chaa was killed, and he knew his father's words were true: Tull was a Thrall, pinned in this spot by fear.

A child tried to run past the Mastodon Man; the beast scooped it up, took a bite.

Tull saw the shadow of another child running, and realized the little humans were trying to escape the building.

"Adjonai!" Tull shouted, for he suddenly saw that the god had come in disguise. The Mastodon Man grunted and stepped backward, into the night. Tull jumped to his feet, swung his sword in an arc, and rushed forward. The Mastodon Man reached out, took Tull by the shoulder and threw him face-first against the wall.

Tull stood a half-second, stunned by the blow, and felt the giant hands on the nape of his neck.

The Mastodon Man spun Tull in the air, pulled him forward, and the beast opened its mouth, showing four-inch canines. It leaned forward to bite Tull's throat. Tull swung his sword up between them, shoving it with all his might, cleaving the Mastodon Man's jaws so that the blade embedded in its face. Blood spurted from the ragged hole in the beast's mouth. The Mastodon Man roared, threw Tull to the far side of the room, turned and put its knuckles to the snow and rushed from the building. Tull ran after it, and found his bloody sword in the snow by the door.

The Mastodon Man headed for the shelter of the brush downhill, ran a dozen yards and then foundered in the snow. It tried to crawl away, looking for all the world like a wounded child struggling to crawl in a bed with white sheets. Tull ran forward and slashed it across the kidneys. A gray bird sat in its oak and watched.

Tull stopped and looked at the damage. The door and a corner of the building had fallen. They hadn't been proof against a beast of such size. Two little humans were trampled, and several others stood stunned by the enormity of the Mastodon Man. There was not much left of Ayuvah. His skull was punctured, his brains spattered on the ground. The hollow of his cranium had filled with blood the way a bowl left outside will fill with rainwater. The red blood darkened his orange hair.

Tull looked at the mess in shock, for it had happened in less than a minute, and then he began stacking rocks, making the house proof against the cold.

Waves of grief washed over him as he worked, and Tull was amazed at their power, for the grief he felt for Ayuvah was as strong as the grief he'd felt for Wisteria. *I will finish this house, and then I will sit down to die,* Tull thought. Yet he worked in the cold. "When love fails you, and you are filled with pain, you can still be moved by devotion," Ayuvah had said. Tull stacked the rocks mindlessly. The task seemed so ordinary, so commonplace. He was a drudge, placing stones one upon another. A drudge once again, fit for nothing else. If he were in Smilodon Bay, he'd be hauling wood for some human. He filled the cracks with snow, making the building airtight.

He smelled something burning, saw that the leg of ox needed turning. He turned it, realized dimly that the smell of cooking meat had lured the Mastodon Man to the building. Tull pushed the door back in place to fill the hole, keep out the night. *Some holes can never be filled,* he thought. *The holes left in a man's life when he loses family.*

The little humans stood around the room, naked, looking at Ayuvah. Some wept openly, and Tull realized what a shock this must have been. Over the last two weeks, Ayuvah had been the provider to these people. Now a god was dead. Tull sat down in the dirt beside Ayuvah, and held his brother's hand.

During that night, he remembered Ayuvah's final conversation, the doll he had made for Sava, how he had wanted it wrapped. The blood of the Spirit Walkers must run strong in the family, Tull reasoned, for Ayuvah had been nervous before his death. Certainly, Tull thought, he must have had a premonition. Or had it been more? Ayuvah had trained himself to hunt by scent, and Tull was forewarned of the attack. Couldn't Ayuvah have smelled the

Mastodon Man? Yet he sat by the door and let himself be killed.

Outside, thunder showers lit the sky, sometimes easing off during the night, other times renewing their fury. The wind drove through holes in the stone walls, and Tull got up and packed dirt from the floor into the chinks. He wanted the room to be warm. He turned the ox's leg through the night, and let the fire burn low. Finally, in spite of the wind howling outside the door, the room warmed.

Tull sat cross-legged, and the grief took him. At times he would sit, thinking of nothing at all, and would realize he was remembering something stupid, like the time Ayuvah went on his first egg raid and gave an egg to Etanai, hoping that with the gift he could seduce her. She lured him into her father's hogan, let him get undressed, then ran screaming from the hogan with Ayuvah's clothes in hand so that everyone would see.

Eventually, Tull smelled the air turn chill at the approach of dawn, though the sky was darkened by thick clouds. Tull got up and set a new fire to warm the hut, and laid the leg of ox aside, for it was fully cooked. He recalled that Ayuvah had wanted sturgeon for breakfast, but the water would be too murky to see them. Surely, with the clouds so thick, it would be too dark to fish.

And he stood up straight. *With the water so murky, he would not be able to see the fish.* The fish would be forced to feed on the bottom. A strange feeling engulfed Tull, a feeling that even the Pwi could not have named, a feeling that he had suddenly fallen in stride with destiny. "You must capture the serpents. Only you," Chaa had said. "If I told you the way, you would try too quickly. Timing is all-important. You would die in the attempt. Yet when the time comes, you must act quickly. And you must act as a Man of the Pwi." Ayuvah had known that this thought would strike Tull at this moment. Ayuvah had thrown his life away to ensure it. Tull considered. *Ayuvah took a Spirit Walk at Seven Ogre River. He must have lied when he said he'd failed in his Spirit Walk. He threw his life away so that I would understand this, at this moment! The serpents are feeding deep.*

Tull went to his pack and dressed in his otter-skin boots, a cap of wolf hide, and over his long winter shirt he wore the blood red cape of the Blade Kin. Although the weather was cold, he kept the clothing light so he could swim if the boat overturned. He did not want to hasten, yet he knew he must have the boat in the water before sunrise.

He cut a portion of the roast and ate it, placed a small bit in his bag. A Man of the Pwi would trust his game, would trust that the animals would give themselves to him. Ayuvah would never hunt with provisions, for it only ensured that game would withhold themselves from him.

Tull did not know what to take in the way of rope or provisions, so he decided to travel light, with only a sack and a rope, and then he opened the door of his hut, and stepped out into the storm.

He did not run to the beach, he walked, and found Scandal's tent covered with snow. Out in the water, logs had washed down swollen rivers from the mountains, and they pounded against the rocks like thunder with each breaker that rolled in. The continual boom, boom, shook the ground.

Phylomon and Scandal did not hear Tull's feet crunch in the snow as he passed, as he untied the boat.

The water was icy cold. High tide was coming in. Tull stood by the boat. He grieved for Ayuvah, that his brother had died to bring him to this moment. He grieved for Wisteria and for Little Chaa. Three dead, and Tull knew that Chaa was suffering at home, that Chaa's wife and children must be torn by grief. Tull considered whether he should hunt the serpents, for he knew that only an evil man would hunt when his heart was not right. Was he doing this out of devotion for the Pwi or to assuage his own pain? He did not know. Grief was on him, and he wanted to find the House of Dust.

Tull stood beside the boat. Watching the water gave him a chill. He could see nothing under the water. A great serpent could be hiding there, waiting for Tull to put the boat in, and Tull would not see her. *These mothers gave birth to the serpents at Denai,* he thought.

Out at sea, he heard the scream of a serpent as she rose. Tull smiled. *These serpents could take my boat in their mouths and carry me forty feet into the air before they crush me in their jaws.* At least she was far from him. He took the silver mast off the boat, carried it high on the shore, then shoved the boat into the water and pushed out to sea.

Tull stood in back of the boat and paddled with its single oar. The logs pounded against the rocks, and he steered through them as quietly as possible, for he wanted to be seen as a log floating on the water, nothing more. Had he raised the small sail, even to quarter-mast, and skipped across the water, the serpents would have heard the water slapping the hull.

He put the prow into the waves and paddled slowly, patiently, feeling his way out to sea. The sun was just rising, yet the clouds so obscured it that he could not see the island clearly, only the snow on its rocky hills.

Tull had seen Phylomon's map so often that he knew where to begin to hunt. There was a peak with a craggy V of split rock. Only one serpent guarded her eggs there, and it seemed a safe place to begin. He set his sights on the peak, steered toward it.

The fierce wind blew from the east and carried him off course, so that he set his sights for a second hill, a spot less desirable than the first, because three serpents frequented the deep bay. It was a good spot to hunt eggs. It was also a good spot to get killed. Lightning flashed on the horizon, moving toward him.

Tull paddled quietly, steadily, and saw that he might be blown past this bay, too—and he looked in vain for a suitable landing space beyond it, but there were many rocks. Over half an hour the sky lightened so that he could see the clouds well, could see the snow well. Although the wind blew strong and the spray of saltwater stung his eyes, he had only a mile to travel to make it to the rocky island, and he was halfway there. The lightning began flashing above him in earnest.

He hurried, hoping to make it to the bay before the lightning showed him to a serpent, and he listened for the sound of water slapping the hull of his boat.

He was watching the bay, intent on the sounds of water, when he heard the serpent's voice beneath him, the great booming howl. Tull swallowed, saw tall waves coming up, so he turned his prow to hit them head on. He topped a wave, sat at the peak a moment, and the serpent sounded beneath him and struck.

The bow surged under him, and he fell forward, grabbed the gunwales. The boat slid backward, back down the wave. Lightning flashed above, and the serpent screamed. She was a vast giant that rose and blotted out the sky. She wrenched her head from side to side and bellowed, her scream filling the darkness. Water rained down, and the wave she made as she rose nearly capsized the boat. Tull stopped rowing, waited to die.

The great serpent splashed down, and Tull stood holding the gunwales. He turned and looked behind him, quietly tried to turn the boat back to the mainland, but the island was closer.

He spun his tiny boat in a circle, held his breath. He wiggled his fingers on the wet oar, trying to get some circulation, and watched the cold steam come from his mouth. Soul clouds, the Pwi called them. As long as steam issued from his mouth, he was still alive. *Timing is all-important,* Chaa had told him. But what should he do?

Tull watched the water, watched for the great mother, and dread filled him, the kwea of his night in Denai. The slapping of the whitecaps became the slapping of serpent bellies as they leapt. His memory conjured ghosts of men, hanging above the water, bleeding themselves away. *Timing is all-important.* The serpent had missed him by half a second. Had he been at the bottom of the wave, the boat would have capsized when the serpent struck. Instead, the serpent had shoved him away. Could this have been what Chaa meant? Timing? He sang to himself softly,

> *The sun is finally falling, now the stars shine on the sand,*
> *And I hear the Darkness conjuring dream images again,*
> *Darkness brings peace to those who seek it, scatters wisdom where it can*
> *For Darkness is lover to the poet, the dreamer, and the solitary man.*

He conjured an image of Chaa's little hogan, of Fava beside the fire as she rubbed his shoulders, and he imagined venison cooking on the fire, rum heating in a silver mug as the light danced on it. *All this is only a week away,* he thought, and he put his back into it and rowed quietly to the bay.

That day, he searched the rocks along shore. He did not know what to look for—eggs. Serpent eggs, attached to rocks. He imagined the leathery eggs he'd collected in Hotland. Phylomon had said they would be large, that each sac would be tan with perhaps ten or twenty eggs in it.

At low tide, the water dropped eighty feet. Tull scurried over boulders thick with cockles and slimy with seaweed. Orange sea snails were abundant on the rocks, along with purple and tan starfish, green and brown anenomes. Gulls ran along the rocks, picking at the snails, cracking tiny hermit crabs in their bills. Tull could see where the ancient lava had met the water, could see how it had filled the bay yet formed two fingers out in the water. Part of the bay was shallow—filled with basalt, while the water out along the two fingers was deep—too deep to drain even in the lowest tide, so he hunted the best he could. He was at it less than an hour before the great mothers spotted him, and they rose out in the deep water at the mouth of the bay, rolling on the waves, jaws gaping. Blood streamed from their gills. Barnacles crusted their heavy brows. Rage gleamed in their red eyes.

When the tide began to rush back in, Tull was forced to go high on the shore and lie under his overturned boat for protection from the wind. The snow stopped falling, and it became painfully cold.

He looked back to the mainland at sunset, saw a great fire roaring. He wondered briefly why Phylomon burned so much wood, then realized it was Ayuvah's funeral pyre. Tull watched the smoke rise black and almost straight into the air.

He stayed under his boat that night and tried to get his body heat to dry his clothing. Hunger gnawed his belly.

At sunrise he had two hours of low tide, and he scampered over the rocks. The sharp white barnacles ripped his otter-skin moccasins, so he scrabbled on all fours, and soon his feet bled. He found a large crab hiding behind a boulder, and he pulled off its legs and stuffed them in his shirt, but he did not find the eggs. *They'll be at the mouth of the bay, where the water deepens,* he thought. Yet the water at the mouth of the bay was deep, and he could see no way to reach them.

At noon, he climbed out on the rocky point, looked at the black basalt at the base of the water and ate the crab legs raw. If he leapt, he'd have fallen almost straight down into the depths, and he could see how the bay was filled with sand while the water was deep here at the point. In two days, the water had not gotten low enough for him to walk out there. He looked out to the mainland and saw Phylomon standing in the snow, on his own rocks. Tull took off his red cape and waved it in the air, and Phylomon waved his hand in return, called to him. Tull could not make out Phylomon's words.

Tull looked down into the water again, and in its depths he saw rocks that he had not noticed before. For a moment, they seemed to rise, as if they would come out of the water, and then he saw that they were not floating rocks at all, but the body of a serpent, a great mother whose scales had turned the black of basalt, who lay coiled at the base of the cliff, wedged in the rocks like an eel. She was under the water, watching him.

At evening, he searched during low tide and found nothing. Chaa had promised him that he could succeed, yet he was cold and hungry, and he could not find the eggs. Tull sat that night, and watched the stars in the cold. *What am I missing?* he wondered, and he opened himself, hoping for Chaa to answer.

That night, as Tull lay shivering under his boat, he dreamed that he scrambled among the rocks over a bed of dark green kelp, and he walked over cockles that twisted and cracked under his feet, sputtering as the water stored in their shells was forced outward. It was dawn, and a thick morning fog rolled in, a heavy fog that would not let him see a hundred feet out to sea. One great mother eeled her way through the waters at the mouth of the bay, only her nostrils and huge dorsal fins showing above water. She stopped in front of him, and her nose was so wide that he could have lain between her nostrils. She was black and silver, the color of basalt and morning, and blood seeped from her gills. The gill slits opened, and he could see her gills beneath the water, like branches of giant red coral, waving in the water as she struggled to breathe. She watched him from blood-red eyes.

"I mean you no harm," Tull said. *"I come only for the eggs."*

She watched him steadily, with large knowing eyes.

"You cannot keep them from me much longer," Tull told her. *"Give them to me, and I will protect them."*

The serpent opened her mouth, arched her back so that her head rose from the water. She thrashed her head and roared. The force of her voice struck Tull like a blow. *"You cannot take them!"* she shouted.

Tull woke, and the dream had been so real that he sat and listened for the sound of her voice. But all he heard was the sigh of the gravitational wind blowing through the rocky hills of the island. Thor had risen, full and orange with green storms racing across its surface, and one of the Red Drones added its light. He got up and looked out. Snow blew off a nearby peak, into the night air, and the light reflecting from the snow glittered like a million fireflies.

Tull walked down to the bay and looked into the water. One of the great mothers was there, floundering, suffocating in the shallows. She bellowed—not the cry of rage and warning he'd heard before, but a long plaintive sound.

He realized that he must have heard her in his sleep, that she had inspired his dream. Tull wondered how Ayuvah would have performed this hunt, and he thought, *not in haste. A Man of the Pwi does not* hunt *for food; he waits for the animal to give itself to him.*

The next morning, low tide came before dawn. Tull rose early and went to the bay, thought he'd find the great mother dead, but she was nowhere in sight. The tides were higher than they had been before, and Tull realized that they would go no lower. The extreme tides were gone.

He wandered among the rocks at sunrise, cutting his

feet, and realized his chance was gone. He had been over these rocks twenty times.

Half a mile away, Tull could see Scandal and Phylomon hunting among the rocks off the mainland. The tide was low enough so that they made it halfway to him, yet the waters still held between them like a great lake. One mother leapt into the air out in the bay. She did not roar a warning, and Tull saw blood streaming down her sides. She did not have long to live. Tull had eaten only a crab in three days, and he kept hoping to find another. Soon he realized that he was searching for food more than eggs. He tried cracking some orange snails between his teeth, but they were gritty and filled with a black ooze. He pulled a large cockle from a rock and tried to pry the blue-black halves of its shell apart. It resisted his effort, so he went over to a ledge where a dozen purple starfish and green anemones hung from an outcrop of basalt, and he began to pound the halves apart.

Yet when he struck the rock, it yielded like leather. He stood back, amazed, and looked at the stone. Although it appeared to be black rock, the exact color of basalt, it was subtly different in texture. He touched it with his hand, pushed on it, and it yielded. He lifted part of it, and found that it was fastened to the rock like a sponge. He pulled his long knife from its sheath and cut around the leathery edges, pried the egg mass away.

The egg mass was twelve feet long, two feet wide, a foot thick, and as he looked at it, Tull saw that it held hundreds of small eggs, each as large in diameter as the onions Ayuvah raised in his garden. The mass was covered with strands of seaweed, alive with starfish and snails and anemones that looked as if they'd lived their whole lives on it. Tull shouted in triumph, and began pulling the eggs. He found a cord beneath it, a long black strand that attached to the rocks, and he chopped it, pulled the mass free, dragged it into the sunlight. The mass was heavy, weighing as much as eight hundred pounds, and Tull strained to drag it at all.

Within the jelly of each individual egg, a great eye as large as a baby's fist stared at him. He could see the pumping of the tiny serpents' hearts, a soft fluttering motion. He shouted in triumph and whipped off his cape, waved it for Phylomon and Scandal to see, but they were too far away, and for all his waving, they only scrambled on their own rocks in the distance as they headed for shore.

Tull grabbed the mass and began dragging it uphill, sweating with exertion. The tide was rushing in, and he wanted to get his treasure. Three hundred feet out in the bay, one of the great mothers leapt into the air, and the ground shook momentarily with the thunder of her splash.

He kept working, dragging the egg mass to higher ground, when suddenly he heard the water explode a second time, and the serpent shot forward out of the bay, over the ground, eeling toward him.

She was twenty feet tall at the back, and her dorsals were again that size. She snaked through the boulders slowly, as if trying to smell a way through the rocks, using the hooked claws on her pectoral fins to pull herself forward. Her iron scales rasped against the rocks. Tull began tugging the eggs in earnest, dragging them a dozen yards up the hill in a great rush of adrenaline, then turned and looked behind him. The great mother was grounded. Although she was powerful, she could not propel the cold tonnage of her body through the rocks.

She lay on the ground, her gills fully extended, panting. Tull dragged the eggs the rest of the way up the hill, set the boat upright, and put the eggs in. He stood panting and dizzy from the exertion, and wiped the sweat from his face. He looked down into the bay to see if the serpent had struggled any closer. She was dead.

When the tide rose, Tull pulled his boat down to the water's edge and covered the eggs with salt water.

That night, the air warmed again and filled with the wet scent of snow. Tull watched all night for a chance to put his boat out, but the serpents were active, thrashing in the water, screaming their pain and outrage at what he'd done. He heard their great booming voices in the stillness of the night and wished he could understand their words.

How would Ayuvah have performed this hunt? he wondered. Ayuvah had once told Tull how his father had convinced a bear to stop coming around their house by talking to it, so Tull went down to the sea and tossed five pebbles in, and wished peace to the serpents. *I came for your eggs, and now I have them,* he told the spirits of the serpents. *I am a man of the Pwi, and I wish you no harm.* He stood and watched where each pebble dropped, watched the ripples expanding, reached out in his mind for the serpents. *In the east, near my home, the great serpents have all died. I wish to take your children there, give them a new life away from the beasts that eat at your gills. They will grow and be strong. I know that some things, like love, cannot be taken—only given. I ask that you give the eggs of this dead mother into my care.* Tull listened to the serpent voices, reached out with his mind. *Please, give them to me. I do not wish you harm,* he said, and his heart filled with anger at the frustration, *but if you do not give them, then I must steal them. And if you try to take them back, I must kill you if I can.*

He stopped, listening. Out at sea, the serpents murmured to one another. He felt a sense of peace, as much as he could under the circumstances. *Perhaps they will not listen,* he thought, *but at least I have done all that I can.*

And in the late night, when the tides receded and Thor sailed into the west, he pulled his boat half a mile over the snowy ground, taking it beyond the edge of the bay, and set her softly into the water. He shoved off lightly, and for an hour he did not paddle, but only sat in the boat, letting the tides carry him where they would.

The sea was as calm as a lake, and there was no wind. For a long time it lulled him, and he kept snapping his eyes open, trying to stay awake. The air was chill and his hands numb. He felt untouchable, as if he were sailing through a dream, and he suddenly roused himself and wondered if he'd fallen to sleep, for he was only four hundred feet from the island, just drifting east, when the sun began to rise.

He took his single oar, stood and paddled quietly. His oar made little grating noises as it scraped in the oarlock, and he stopped from time to time to let the boat glide over the water. A peninsula jutted out from the mainland, keeping much of the water in shadow, and when he was three-quarters of the way across the channel, the sun touched him.

Tull tried to imagine what his boat looked like from underwater—a black object on the surface of the ocean, lit from behind by golden sunlight. He felt uneasy, and saw the

bundle, along with his war shield, his battle armor, and his
sword of Benbow glass. He looked at the tiny bundle of
Ayuvah's belongings.

Tull grabbed the two bundles, hiked one up on each
shoulder. He decided to go to Moon Dance Inn first, tell
them that Scandal would be returning in a few weeks, get
some paper to wrap the presents for Sava and Etanai.

He walked up the streets of the city, and everything still
looked the same—the old stone buildings leaned at odd angles from their crumbling foundations; peacocks scurried
from his path as he made his way through the street. Yet
something seemed wrong.

He looked down the alley where he had first touched
Wisteria's breast as a child, and felt only old sorrow, not the
hot arousal of his youth. He walked up the hill toward the
black part of the city where he'd run from his childhood,
where the kwea of fear always made his neck tingle. But the
fear was stale, like flat beer. He walked through the city, and
though nothing had changed, nothing was quite the same.

Some children were out in the street rolling a barrel, and
they stopped to watch him. He thought for sure that they
would raise a shout, tell everyone of his return, but no one
spoke. Then Tull realized that they were not looking at him.
They were only watching his blood-red cape, the cape he'd
taken from the Blade Kin.

At the top of the hill, outside the front porch of Moon
Dance Inn, sat a barrel with a dried-up rose bush planted in
it. A tiny orange-haired Thrall child sat huddled next to the
barrel, dressed in rags. Tull wondered what a Thrall was
doing here, so far from the slave pens of Denai, so far from
the Okanjara of the Rough. But as Tull approached, the
child looked up and shouted, "Tull! Tull!"

Tull looked at the child and realized it was Wayan, realized he had mistaken his brother for a Thrall. He dropped
his bundles and scooped the child up, and Wayan hugged his
neck. The hard metal edge of Wayan's leg shackles pressed
against Tull's belly. Tull touched the shackles with his
hands, remembered the shadow of the Mastodon Man. His
childhood had been such a terror that even now he could
not dredge up a single pleasant memory. Tull felt his chest

warm with rage. *Ah, home at last,* he thought. *At least on thing remains the same.*

Scandal's steward rushed from the inn and shouted "You're back!" then looked about nervously and asked, "I Scandal with you?"

"He'll be back in eight weeks."

"Oh, good," the steward said, brushing sweat from hi forehead. "I've got a lot to do to get ready for him. A lot t do." Tull wondered briefly how the steward could get eigh weeks behind in his work. He handed Ayuvah's bundle t the man.

Scandal's whores and serving wenches were issuing ou of the building. "Did you catch some serpents?" one of th whores asked, her eyes wide.

"More than a thousand of them," he answered softly "The eggs are in the harbor." A serving maid clapped he hands, and everyone began speaking loudly.

Tull patted the bundle. "Get some paper and wrap th doll and silk," he said. "I'll be back in a few minutes."

Tull opened his own clothes, pulled out his sword o Benbow glass. He ran his fingers along the black cuirass o Blade Kin armor, but decided he didn't need it. He picked up his wooden war shield, painted in shades of forest gree and brown.

"Keep Wayan here for a moment," Tull ordered them "Keep him inside."

Out in the city, someone shouted that Tull was back, an one of Scandal's cooks shouted that the serpents were in th bay. Everywhere, everywhere the people began running ou the doors to see if it was true.

And Tull headed into the dark part of town, toward hi father's home.

He felt like a fish swimming through a stream, and peo ple were water that he was passing by. They gathered al around him, talking at him, enjoining him to speak with them, but he simply moved beyond them.

At the bottom of the hill, past the inn, he saw his father's house, and as always, the sky seemed to darken over that place. He could feel the evil issuing from it, all the old cold and rot that had ever been here, as if this were the very abode of Adjonai. *Ah yes,* Tull told himself, *home at last.*

His mother opened the front door and flew from the house shouting, "Is it true? Are you home?" and Tull looked past her.

He shouted, "God screw you, Jenks Genet! Come out here! I've come to kill you as I promised!"

Tull's mother looked up at him and shouted, "No! No! Don't do this evil thing! This is very bad!" and she rushed to touch him, as if by grabbing hold of his shirt she could make him listen. But then she stopped short and looked in his eyes.

"Thea!" she shouted, and she backed away from him, looked around frantically for something to save her, and rushed past him up the hill. *She thinks I am holy,* he realized, *moved by pure emotion.*

Yet he did not feel it was true. Phylomon had said that the Tcho-Pwi were a new race who could think both with heart and head, a creature that needed desperately to find a kind of balance, and Tull wondered if he had achieved that balance now. He was aware that his hands were shaking, that his knees quivered. Surely he felt some rage. But his mind seemed clear. It was reasonable to kill Jenks. Phylomon would understand his reasons.

A crowd gathered behind him, and someone pressed against his back. Tull shoved them away.

Jenks stepped into the doorway and looked up the hill at Tull. "So, it's come to this, has it?" Jenks said. "You were always such a shit. I knew you'd come for me someday. Let me get my war gear." He turned and headed back into the house, and Tull just stood there. From the house came crashing sounds. Tull steadied himself, as he had in practice, considered how he would bash through Jenks's parries.

"You can't beat me," Jenks shouted. "You were always such a parasite, feeding on me—a little tick feeding on the butt of family Genet." He grunted, and came from the house carrying a short spear and shield, leggings and wrist guards, a dusty lacquered war vest that was twenty years old.

He set the shield on the ground with the spear, pulled the stiff leather of the war vest over his head and inserted his arms. It was far too small. It didn't cover most of his belly, and the lacings at the sides under his arms pulled apart, rotted. Tull looked at Jenks and laughed. The fat old man fiddled with the lacings on his armor and for five minutes worked on getting the armor tightened over his belly. His head was bowed, showing silver hair and a bald spot. Tull wondered that he'd ever feared the ridiculous old asshole, feared him with the kind of terror the sight of the Mastodon Men aroused in him, yet he did not pity the man.

Jenks heard the laughing and looked up at Tull. "God, I hate you," Jenks said. "To think, I once had to shackle you to your bed to keep you from running away." He sat down and began strapping the leather leggings on. His legs seemed unnaturally thin to hold such a massive body, and the leggings fit him fine.

And Tull realized something very strange. In Craal, the Thralls remained in slavery because they were chained by fear. Certainly as a child Tull had been terrified of the old man, but even fear had not been strong enough to chain him. Tull could never be chained by fear.

From behind him, his mother shouted, "Wait! Wait! Let me through," and people gasped as she shoved past them.

She rushed up to Tull and there were tears in her eyes, and the sunlight flashed on the silver strands of her hair. She held Wayan at arm's length, and she shoved the child into Tull's chest, until Wayan grabbed his neck, and Tull was forced to put his arms around Wayan's legs to hold him.

"Take him," she shouted at Tull, "Take him away forever! I should have given him to you long ago, but I was afraid. I'm so evil! Don't send me to the House of Dust!"

Tull looked at her thin leathery arms, and for the first time he understood the love she had for Jenks. It did not matter that Jenks was evil. She had been married to him for years before the children were born, and was bound by the love that enslaves. If Jenks were to die, she would follow him to the House of Dust. It was not reasonable for her to love Jenks, but Tull saw that there comes a moment when ecstasy is pure, when rage overcomes, when fear makes us crawl, that each of us become Thralls. At that moment, whether the moment seems exhilarating or soul destroying, we are no longer moved by reason. Tull had felt the pull of Wisteria's love, and he knew that his mother felt it for Jenks. It had nothing to do with reason.

"Keep him! Keep the child," she shouted at Tull.

Jenks jumped to his feet, dropping one of the leg guards to the ground, tossing his wrist guard down. "Stop!" he said, but Tull's mother ran to Jenks, fell at his feet.

"Beat me!" she shouted. "Beat me to death if you have to! Beat me! But leave my children alone!" She clung to his legs and sobbed, "Beat me! Beat me!"

Jenks kicked at the woman in disgust, but she held him tight. Jenks was so cold, so alien, Tull could never understand him—a man who wanted to own his children.

But he understood his mother now, understood the love that enslaves. All his life, Tull had felt nothing for his mother, had felt cold and empty of love—because inside he knew that she understood him, that she knew of his pain. She had betrayed him, and was unworthy of love. And now, at last, by giving him Wayan, she was trying to give him back his own childhood, trying to right her mistake.

"I'll be good to him," Tull said, looking hard at Jenks, and he carried Wayan back up the street to Moon Dance Inn. *This would make a proper tale for the Pwi,* he thought, almost laughing to himself. *The tale of people estranged by evil deeds, the tearful reconciliation.* But there would be no reconciliation, no happy Pwi ending. To simply walk away from Jenks was all that Tull could manage. Tull was going to let the bastard live. The thought galled him. Phylomon would not approve, but Tull felt himself rise to a new plateau on his spiral journey. *It is enough to be a wall.*

Tull gathered the presents together at the inn and took the news of Little Chaa's and Ayuvah's deaths to their family. It was as hard as he'd imagined it would be. Little Sava took her doll and stroked it gently, as if it were a gift from god. Etanai would not look at the silk, for it was tainted by the message that came with it. For her, it would always hold the kwea of Ayuvah's death, so that night, while Wayan slept, Tull and Chaa gently placed the silk in the fire.

Afterward, Tull went outside. The night was fairly still, and only the tiniest wind blew down from the mountains and out to sea. In that wind, Tull could feel something odd. The darkness he'd always felt in Smilodon Bay was breaking up, as if Adjonai were scurrying away, dragging his evil kwea with him. The Pwi say that "no two men walk in the same world." And Tull felt that for him, Adjonai, the God of Terror, was dead.

In the morning, when Tull rose, the sun seemed to shine brighter over the town, and peace filled the air. He spent the day preparing for Ayuvah's and Little Chaa's funeral, and since the Pwi did not have the bodies, they took old clothing and made effigies of the brothers, then placed them on a raft and let it float out to sea.

As Ayuvah's brother, Tull took his place in Chaa's household, moving all his own possessions into the hogan. Etanai took Sava to White Rock so they could move back with Etanai's father and mother. Tull checked the payment Scandal had given him, found three hundred silver eagles, twenty times more money than he'd earned. He gave half to Etanai before she left.

With the two older boys gone, Chaa's house seemed almost empty. Only Fava and the three little girls were left.

After several nights, Tull was lying on the floor with Wayan when he heard Fava weep. He put a wolf hide on Wayan and rolled over to Fava, put his arm around her. The coals in the fire glowed with a soft light. Outside it rained.

She took his hand and placed it above her heart, clutched it. He could feel her soft breasts brushing either side of his hand, and he dared not move it.

"I know you are grieving for your brothers," Tull said. "I am sorry I cannot take the pain away."

Although her back was to him, she turned to look at him, and Tull smelled the scent of vanilla water. She kissed his lips, a soft kiss that barely brushed against him, and out of long habit he jerked back.

She turned her face away, set his hand on her hip.

He did not know if he should move it. That night, he dreamed he was a great wall encircling an orchard. Hungry children came to the orchard to eat, and they tried to scrabble over him and walk around him, but he would not let them in. He wished he could give them something, but he was a *wall,* not meant for giving. After a time, a pear—most generous of trees—leaned its branches over the wall and dropped fruit to the ground. The children came and fed in a frenzy, smearing the pears on their smiling faces.

The next day, Tull went back into town. For a long time he stood by the mayor's house, looking at the place where Tirilee had once sat in her cage. The ache he felt, the desire to be with her, left Tull feeling weak and dizzy, as if her aphrodisiac kisses were blown on the wind.

Mayor Goodstick finally came out of the house. "Is there something I can do for you?" Garamon asked. Garamon had heard the story of the trip—a watered-down version that made Wisteria's death sound like a tragic accident.

"No . . ." Tull said, watching the spot where Tirilee had once been caged. "No."

Garamon clapped Tull on the shoulder, "I understand that congratulations are in order," he said. "Yet I'm deeply sorry about your loss." The phrases were trite, yet Tull looked in Garamon's eyes and could not tell if the man felt anything—guilt, gratitude, disappointment.

"Thank you," Tull said. *I'll be watching you,* he thought.

At noon, he returned to Chaa's house to feed Wayan. He found Fava caring for Wayan with her three little sisters. She'd made a large lunch, and Tull sat next to Wayan, got his clocks and tools, and began putting together a tiny daisy watch that he had taken apart earlier in the day. Tull looked at Wayan, and was thankful that Fava was here to watch over him. What did he know about raising a child?

"Would you like something to eat?" Fava asked Tull.

Tull nodded, but did not speak. He felt clumsy in her presence. Her long red hair was tied in back, and she wore a short dress. On her right thigh was a bracelet decorated with feathers from a blue jay. He realized that it was too cold for Fava to wear such a dress, but the bracelet signified that she was unmarried, and Fava was throwing her maidenhood in his face. She went to the pot on the oven, pulled out some rolls.

Her legs were long and tan, well muscled. Her breasts were full and large. Her face showed her strength. With Wisteria, love had been mere entertainment. With Tirilee, it had been all passion and fire, with the promise of slavery in the end. *But what would it be with Fava?* Tull wondered. *It*

would be all giving, he decided. She was strong, so much like
him that he imagined them growing together, entwining like
ivy around a pole. He had seen people grow together like
that—their lives and notions, desires and fears, all became
so entangled that the couple began even to look the same.
That is the way it would be with Fava, until in the end they
would not even be two people in mind or body, but one.
And along the way there would be some fiery passion, and
some nights of long, slow lovemaking just for fun, and days
and years of giving to one another.

Fava brought the rolls and some venison and set the
plate on the ground before him. Tull looked down at it for a
moment and realized he was not hungry.

"Is it all right?" Fava asked, an edge of hysteria in her
voice, as if the thought of displeasing him would kill her.

Tull looked up at her, and he had the feeling that in his
personal journey of the Worm Tower, he was about to turn a
corner and discover a love deeper than he had ever known.

He unfolded his legs, picked up Wayan, and took Fava
by the hand, pulled her outside.

In the dirt by the front door, he drew a large figure eight,
and then, holding Wayan, he stepped in the circle. He knew
that formally it was not right—that he should have brought
his most valued possessions, the things that carried great
kwea for him. Yet Wayan was the only thing he valued at
the moment.

He held his palms out and up, in a beggar's gesture, and
said. "I seek shelter from loneliness. I bring all that you see
within this circle. I bring my heart."

Fava jumped back up on the porch with her mouth
agape. "No! You can't do this to me!" For a moment he
thought she was saying *no,* but she put her hand over her
mouth and tears welled from her eyes. "Today can't be my
wedding day! I must get ready. I need my friends to witness.
I need time to figure out what I will bring into the circle—I
need my favorite cup, and the sculpture of the bear! And my
combs!" All of them were objects of great kwea, the things
she would have to bring into her circle. She glanced at the
door to the hogan and then back at Tull, and then toward
Pwi town where her friends lived, and Tull could tell that
she could not decide which way to run first. She would want

a traditional wedding, although he did not much care to have everyone watch them.

"Fava," Tull said, nodding his head toward town, "Get your friends and have them help you get ready. I've waited my whole life for love. I can wait a little more."

Glossary

Anee. A mineral-poor moon 11,000 miles in diameter that circles a gas giant named Thor near a Type I star 1,950 light-years from Earth. In the year 2866, the Alliance of Nations began terraforming Anee to create a terrestrial zoo —a place where genetic paleontologists could store specimens of animals recreated from the Jurassic, Miocene, and Pliocene eras. Each of three continents stores representatives from one of the eras.

Creators. A race of highly intelligent beings, part machine and part biological organism, designed by genetic paleontologists to maintain the ecosystems of Anee. The Creators are living DNA synthesizers. To control animal populations, they frequently design and give birth to predators and parasites. The Creators are strictly programmed to perform their specific jobs. After the death of the Creator named Forester 1, the Creators designed Dryads to protect the forests.

Dire Wolves. Canis dirus—a heavy-bodied dark gray wolf common during the Pliocene, short on cunning but long on tenacity and viciousness.

Dragons. Warm-blooded flying carnivores created by the Starfarers to be an eco-barrier. Each continent has several varieties of dragon in various sizes—from the giant greathorned dragon to the tiny hawk dragon. Each dragon is born with a genetically transmitted memory that encourages it to destroy species that it recognizes as foreign to the environment.

Dryads. A being made by the Creators to maintain forests in

Pliocene areas after the Creator Forester 1 was killed in an earthquake. Dryads are humanoid females with long life spans and strange abilities. The abilities, size, and coloration of the Dryad depends on the type of forest it was created to maintain.

Eco-barriers. Certain animals have the ability to migrate across oceans. For example, many types of semiaquatic carnivorous dinosaur could easily make such journeys, and the introduction of such animals into an area populated by Pliocene saber-tooths could be disastrous, because the saber-tooths could not compete with the larger predators. The paleontologists who terraformed Anee recognized the danger such transoceanic migrations could cause. Therefore, they erected a series of eco-barriers to prevent migrations. These barriers consist of artificially engineered predators: primarily, the deep-ocean sea serpent to patrol the waterways and various species of dragon to patrol the sky. Both the sea serpent and the dragon are ruthless predators without equal in nature.

Eridani. An alien race that went to war with humans in the year 3076. Using small FTL drone warships, the Eridani successfully stopped all extraplanetary travel within a matter of four years.

Hukm. Homo gigantis—a species of large apelike humanoids with long brownish red or white fur. The Hukm, one of several species of giant hominids once native to Earth, were originally restricted to a small region of Northeast Asia, and the species thrived only for a few thousand years. Fossil evidence indicates that the species probably died out about 396,000 B.C. Extinction appeared to occur due to climatic changes between glacial periods, and may have come about as a result of intertribal warfare accompanied by starvation. When reintroduced into the wild on Anee, the Hukm showed themselves to be highly social vegetarians who quickly domesticated the woolly mammoths.

Kwea. Emotional resonance. Often passionate feelings that are aroused by memories of past experience. Neanderthals have specific words that can refer to hundreds of different kinds of kwea, based on the types and degrees of emotionality, but these are ignored in translation for simplicity's sake. For a Neanderthal, every object, every experience, every memory carries an emotional weight, a value of kwea. For example, a common knife may be considered sacred or of great value to one individual because of his associated kwea, while for another the same object would seem plain and unimportant.

Mastodon. On Anee, any of eleven species of pachyderm that inhabit woodlands and grasslands in every climatic region.

Mastodon Men. Homo rex—a species of carnivorous humanoids of low intelligence, averaging some eight and a half feet in height and weighing five to six hundred pounds. Mastodon Man originally inhabited mountainous areas in Asia from 250,000 to 75,000 B.C. On Earth, Mastodon Man apparently did not compete well with smaller humanoids, but on the fecund world of Anee they quickly gained a strong foothold.

Neanderthal. Homo neanderthalensis (see also Pwi, Okanjara, and Thrall)—the Neanderthal are a distinct species, similar to modern humans in size and build. Neanderthals tend to be larger and stronger than humans and have slightly shorter arms and a muscular build. The Neanderthal spine has less curvature, so Neanderthals stand straighter than humans do, and their large toe is curved inward, allowing them to run faster. The Neanderthal's chest cavity is larger than that of a human, and their arms rotate at a greater angle. Their skulls are thicker, hips slightly wider.

Neanderthals have sandy yellow to red hair and green, blue, or yellow-brown eyes. They have heavy supraorbital ridges that give their eyes a deep-set appearance. Their teeth and palate tend to protrude more than those of a human, yet they completely lack a chin.

The hands of a Neanderthal differ in structure from that of a human. The hands of a Neanderthal are larger and stronger than those of a human, with large robust knuckles. On a human, the thumb is tilted at an angle to the fingers so that the tip of the thumb can touch the tip of each individual finger; however, a Neanderthal's thumb is not tilted at an angle to the fingers, and the Neanderthal is, therefore, far less dexterous than a human.

Differences in the Neanderthal palate, larynx, and sinus cavities do not allow them to vocalize most long vowels or semivowels used by humans. Instead, the Neanderthals shorten long vowels and tend to speak through their noses.

The cerebral cortex of the Neanderthal brain is slightly larger than that of a modern human, and they are fully the intellectual equals of humans. However, the Neanderthal hypothalamus, the area of the brain responsible for processing emotions, is three times as large as that of a human. Neanderthals tend to lead a very complex emotional life. Because of the way that the Neanderthal brain processes information, memories frequently carry very strong, emotionally charged ties. Because Neanderthals feel their emotions more powerfully than humans do, they feel a consuming need to express these emotions. Neanderthal dialects vary by region, but their languages have some similarities. Any noun or verb can be modified by various suffixes to express the Neanderthal's feelings about the object or action. The order of the suffixes always follows this pattern:

noun or *verb* + *emotional indicator* + *person* + *emotional degree indicator*

For example, instead of saying "the sky is gray," the Neanderthal might express his feelings about the subject: *szerzhoafava ah femma.* This sentence literally reads "Sky-love-I-generously is gray" and would be translated as "The gray sky-which-I-love-completely." The first word in the sentence, *szerzhoafava,* is translated below:

noun base + emotional indicator + person +
szer (sky)   *zho* (love)   *a* (I)
emotional degree indicator
fava (completely)

The degree indicator is often a noun itself. For example, the word *fava* means "pear tree." On Anee, several varieties of wild pear bear fruit in late autumn. Neanderthal legends often embellish this, telling of heroes starving in the wilderness who are saved by pear trees that magically blossom and ripen in midwinter when the tree "sees" the hero coming.

Because of this reputation for generosity, *fava* then becomes synonymous with *generous*. When used as an emotional indicator, *fava* means "given with all my heart."

Okanjara. The Free Ones (literally, "I am free!")—any Neanderthal who has escaped slavery after a long period of time.

Phylomon. The last living human who was not born on Anee. The last of the Starfarers. A man who, because he still benefits from the technology of the Starfarers, has survived for more than one thousand years.

Pirate Lords. When an interstellar war between mankind and the Eridani first stranded the genetic paleontologists on Anee, a political argument soon developed over how mankind should treat their creations—specifically the Neanderthals. Certain technicians believed that by conscripting Neanderthals for use as laborers, humans could be left free to build the plasma missiles they hoped could destroy the Eridani warships circling Anee. Others correctly believed the effort would be wasted. Those who favored enslaving the Neanderthals formed an independent colony on the island of Bashevgo. After two centuries of building, the lords finally attacked the Eridani drones. The Slave Lords and their colony were nearly decimated in a counterattack, yet the offspring of the Slave Lords of Bashevgo still survive both on Bashevgo and in the nation of Craal, and the Slave Lords prey on both the Neanderthals and their human cousins.

Pwi. Neanderthals who have never been enslaved by the Pirate Lords call themselves Pwi, "the family." By the time that the first humans were forced to move to Anee, the original colony of Neanderthals had covered most of the eastern half of the continent they called *Calla,* Homeland, and Neanderthals numbered about two million. Pwi dialects and customs were diverging, and they were on the verge of splintering into several large tribes. But as the Neanderthals found themselves battling a common enemy, they regained a sense of common identity and called themselves only "family."

Red Drones. Orbital warships piloted by artificial intelligences sent by the Eridani to patrol the skies above Anee.

Their neutron cannons destroy any mechanical vessel or organic being that climbs more than fifteen thousand feet into the air. Originally, four warships were stationed over Anee, but two were destroyed by the Pirate Lords.

Saber-tooth Lion. Smilodon fatalis—a large tawny lion with very long, serrated canines. The saber-tooth live in prides in grassy and low, wet areas. Because of poor eyesight and teeth that are not adapted for small prey, the saber-tooth primarily hunts large herd animals. Some of its favorite victims are the bison, giant sloth, the giant beaver (a semi-aquatic water rat weighing up to five hundred pounds), the mastodon, the hippolike toxodonts, and the giant capybara. The saber-tooth was such a successful predator that when it became overpopulated in 8000 B.C., overpredation coupled with climatic instability caused the extinction of more than a hundred other species. With its food base destroyed, the saber-tooth soon became extinct.

Scimitar Cat. Homotherium—a solitary but powerful lion with yellow and brown stripes. Because of its elongated front legs, it runs with a bouncing gait. The scimitar cat inhabits mountainous areas and hunts large prey by pouncing from a tree or rock. A female scimitar cat will often kill a young mastodon weighing six hundred pounds and then drag it two miles so she can feed her cubs.

Sea Serpents. Giant eellike carnivores created by the Starfarers to keep animals from migrating across the ocean from one continent to another. Sea serpents can vary their color to conform to background, can grow to a length of 380 feet, and can attack prey in two ways: by biting or by strangulation. Thornlike protrusions on the serpent's armored scales tend to slice prey open when the serpent attacks by strangulation.

Young serpents are less than a yard in length when they hatch in the spring. They feed on fish for the first several months, and in their feeding frenzy drive great schools of fish up the rivers. Within six weeks the serpents grow to a length of sixteen feet and head for open waters and larger prey. At the end of their first year, serpents often measure over a hundred feet in length.

Slave Lords. Humans who enslave Neanderthals and other humans. Shortly after the Red Drones forced the human Starfarers into exile on Anee, some of the paleontologists began enslaving Neanderthals for use as miners, field hands, and domestic servants. The human Starfarers believed that if they could concentrate on developing weaponry to fight the Red Drones, they could escape Anee within a few centuries. But when their efforts failed, most of the Starfarers were killed, and much of their technology died with them. The few degenerate descendants of these Starfarers set up the nation of Craal, based on a slave economy, and became known as the Slave Lords.

Starfarers. The genetic paleontologists and their crew who first began the work of terraforming Anee. By 2866, humans had been engaged in genetically and mechanically upgrading themselves for so long that the Starfarers were, in a sense, no longer human. The Starfarers had hairless bodies of various colors, depending on the color of the symbiote they chose for their skin; had total recall of all they saw and heard; could achieve virtual immortality with mechanical aid; and had a genetically transmitted "dictionary" that gave all members of their race a knowledge of English and mathematics. When the Eridani destroyed the Starfarers' space station above Anee, the Starfarers lost the technology that would allow them to pass their extended life span on to their descendants, but some of their genetic upgrades remained.

Thrall. Any Neanderthal who is held as a slave. Generally, it refers to a Neanderthal who has spent years in slavery. Over generations, the Thralls developed a moral code and a society far different from that of the Pwi. In general, the Pwi consider the Thralls to be somewhat untrustworthy and brutal. Many tales tell of Thralls who practice cannibalism or who have become so accustomed to slavery that they themselves engage in it. Those Thralls who eventually escape their captors call themselves Okanjara, the Free Ones.

About the Author

DAVE WOLVERTON was the grand prizewinner of the 1986 Writers of the Future contest sponsored by Bridge Publications. He has worked as a prison guard, missionary, business manager, editor, and technical writer. He is currently at work on his third novel, a sequel to *Serpent Catch*.

For the summer's best in science fiction and fantasy,
look no further than Bantam Spectra.

SPECTRA'S SUMMER SPECTACULAR

With a dazzling list of science fiction and fantasy stars, Spectra's summer list will take you to worlds both old and new: worlds as close as Earth herself, as far away as a planet where daylight reigns supreme; as familiar as Han Solo's Millennium Falcon and as alien as the sundered worlds of the Death Gate. Travel with these critically acclaimed and award-winning authors for a spectacular summer filled with wonder and adventure!

<u>Coming in May 1991:</u>

**Star Wars, Volume 1:
Heir to the Empire**
by Timothy Zahn

Earth
by David Brin

King of Morning, Queen of Day
by Ian McDonald

<u>Coming in June, 1991:</u>

**The Gap Into Vision:
Forbidden Knowledge**
by Stephen R. Donaldson

Black Trillium
by Marion Zimmer Bradley,
Julian May and Andre Norton

**Chronicles of the King's Tramp
Book 1: Walker of Worlds**
by Tom DeHaven

<u>Coming in July 1991:</u>

**The Death Gate Cycle,
Volume 3: Fire Sea**
by Margaret Weis and
Tracy Hickman

**The Death Gate Cycle,
Volume 2: Elven Star**
by Margaret Weis and
Tracy Hickman

Raising the Stones
by Sheri S. Tepper

<u>Coming in August 1991:</u>

Garden of Rama
by Arthur C. Clarke
and Gentry Lee

Nightfall
by Isaac Asimov
and Robert Silverberg

Available soon wherever Bantam Spectra Books are sold.

AN217 -- 4/91